Shadow Hunt

L. J. Kendall

The Leeth Dossier Vol. 3

For my mother, Shirley Kendall: the light and heart of a truly loving family

National Library of Australia Cataloguing-in-Publication entry : (paperback)

Creator: Kendall, L. J., author.

Title: Shadow hunt / by L. J. Kendall.

ISBN: 9781925430103 (paperback)

Series: Kendall, L. J. Leeth dossier ; Vol 3.

Subjects: Magic--Fiction.
 Fantasy fiction.
 Science fiction.

Story length: 145,000 words
Typeface: Georgia 9pt

This book is available as an A or B-format paperback, and in ebook formats.

Original release: Jul 2017.
Release version: 12. Sep 2024. (Fixed 5 tiny typos)

ACKNOWLEDGMENTS

I want to thank my wife, Dr Stella St. Clair-Kendall, for her love and encouragement over the years. Missing you, darling.

An ongoing thanks to Jon Marshall for his insight, support, and help in shaping Leeth over two decades.

Sincere thanks once again to ThEditors.com for Dave's insights and advice. The first book that didn't need splitting in two! (Provided you ignore that it split from the previous two!) Though I didn't follow *all* his advice, so any problems you see will be my fault.

Another special thank you to Mirella de Santana, the artist who designed my cover. See more of her wonderful art at: www.mirellasantana.com.br.

And thanks too to the Online Writing Workshop for Science Fiction, Fantasy and Horror site, sff.onlinewriting-workshop.com, and all the writers who reviewed some of these chapters several years ago, and to my Beta readers, JonM, SandraW, and AndyK.

Thank you, all.

Note: there's a special offer if you're 1st to inform me of errors in the text – see Publishing, 2017 for details.

Novels by L. J. Kendall

The Leeth Dossier:

> *Wild Thing*
> *Harsh Lessons*
> *Shadow Hunt*
> *Violent Causes*

Leeth Ascending:

> *Lost Girl*
> *(Cold Heart*
> *…)*

CONTENTS

PROLOGUE

Locked in his cell in the Institute for Paranormal Dysfunction, Godsson pondered three things.

He pondered his part in the slaying of the Enemy of Mankind, Melisande d'Artelle, fifteen years earlier. A part more significant than his two companions had ever known.

He pondered Sara – *L'ith* – who had helped him end the threat spawned from d'Artelle's death. The girl was changing in ways even he did not understand.

He shook his head. Did her 'guardian' not see that her name itself echoed that of humanity's ancient enemy? Lilith the vampyre, the seductress. Mother of daemons. Whore.

And he pondered the nuclear weapon that he knew lay primed, nearby. Their measure of last resort.

He smiled. A pathetic recourse. Yet thanks to it, no one would expect to find human remains within the blast radius. So when next he left the Barriers of this cell, the Dragon would no longer be certain the guillotine would fall.

But fall it would.

Planning the Dragon's demise would be a pleasant way to pass the time. Perhaps the girl, the latest earthly avatar of his Father's first error, could even aid in that destruction – after his construct's human host had hunted her down and bonded to her. *Correcting* her; inverting the anti-Christ. Yes, L'ith epitomized all that was wrong with humanity. How ironic that it made her the ideal key to correct it.

Yes, when next he was freed, he would be ready. And a Perfected L'ith would make an excellent tool.

PART I

Free

CHAPTER 1

Despite the brutal winds, she liked sleeping on the second floor best because it had so many escape routes. She'd painstakingly hauled tonnes of gravel here, strewing it around the wrecked office building so she could hear people coming in plenty of time. Plus the bigger stones made good ammo for her PowerShot.

She sank back into the freshly scavenged plastic bag she'd stuffed full of styrofoam pieces, and hugged herself. *I'm so lucky!* She peered out from inside her nest of kudzu vines. Propped up by a few hardy shrubs, it made a green igloo that provided two kinds of protection.

Yeah, she had a nice home, now: plenty of food, *three* buckets full of fresh water – with lids! – and a steady income, thanks to her hunters' persistence. But best of all, there was nobody telling her she couldn't do stuff.

She sighed, content. Right now, for the first time in over three weeks, she even had an hour when she didn't *need* to be doing anything. It felt weird to just relax and watch the sun sink to the horizon between the shattered high-rises.

She'd come a long way since escaping and making her way here, into the Hunters Point Dumps. That first wintry night in the urban wasteland, she'd spent excited hours exploring shattered tenements. Feeling like she was the last girl on Earth. In some areas she'd had to pick her way over dark, parched wastelands of jumbled cement. In others she'd had to slash a path through lush vines. It'd felt magical, gazing at the moonlit scene. Weird, though, seeing entire stretches of road cocooned. As if they'd been buried under a green wave that lapped against the sides of buildings, washing up walls to crack concrete bones. Digesting them degree by creeping degree.

It was only with the first chill blush of dawn that she'd paused, shivering. Suddenly tired, hungry, and thirsty, and realizing she hadn't actually found a place to sleep, or hide.

As the cold had settled its claws into her, she'd found Teef's shack-slash-shop. Peering into its dim interior she'd seen haphazard shelving packed with everything from legs of bots, to pans and pots.

She'd stood outside with just her weapon, a hundred creds in her cashstick, and the clothes she'd been wearing. Shivering. Staring at the bucket full of water she could see in the unlit interior, tossing up between buying it with creds she really needed to hoard, or waking the ogre to trade sex for it. Or just bursting in, to kill him and take it.

She'd been *so* thirsty.

And then in the darkness she'd heard the drone above and behind her, hunting her – and all her problems had been solved.

Wriggling deeper into her plastic bag sofa, she smiled, remembering the ogre startling awake at her first rap on the warped door frame. Warily, he'd let her step in, his expression shifting to surprise at what she'd dumped on his counter: a drone, highly prized scav.

She still liked to tell herself it had been one of Nelson's. There'd been a lot of them buzzing around that first week, hunting her. So many that for a while she'd been worried she'd end up being named something awful, like *Drones-layer* or *Drone Girl*. A fate she'd *barely* avoided.

She hugged herself harder, wondering if she dared try and visit Marcie? But they'd be expecting that. They'd be waiting for her. They probably had spy cameras and all sorts of stuff set up watching her house – and the drama school – hoping she'd try to make contact.

And what about Godsson? She frowned. If only she hadn't given her word to Professor Sanders that she'd obey the law. Couldn't she just...? But she remembered how serious he'd been: 'If you ever break Godsson free again, you will go to jail: for a long, long time.' They'd even shaken hands on her promise.

She hunched in on herself. How on Earth was she supposed to make people see poor Godsson shouldn't be locked up anymore, if she *also* couldn't even tell anyone about the Institute? That wasn't fair!

But if she *did* sneak in, she'd also get a chance to visit Faith. And if she went in at night, maybe they could even secretly do a patrol of the Institute together? The idea made her smile – and then, tears swelled, unexpectedly. She shook them away, trying not to imagine hugging Faith again, feeling the purr of her turbines against her chest.

The trouble was, they were probably expecting her to break in *there,* too.

She sighed. It sucked having the Department hunting her. Maybe she should just...?

No.

She wasn't going back to them. Not with Uncle ready to-

The horrid gray confusion swam back in, and she shied away from the thought. She had to crush the urge to scream, her hands clenching in anger that whatever he'd done was *still* affecting her thinking.

Jumping up from her bedding and squeezing through the green curtain of her living doorway, she left her nest and started pacing the cracked and empty floor.

I could try hunting The Breaker again. That'd be fun, *and* doing some good. But he, or it, seemed to have stopped his awful attacks – there'd been no creepy torture-killings since before she'd even got here. *Could he know I'm looking for him, and be hiding?* But that didn't make much sense. Was he waiting for something? But if so, what?

Now that she had spare time, she *could* try again; but honestly, she wasn't quite sure *how* to. Ask people about him?

It'd be nice just to *talk* to someone. Maybe she could visit the Blackberry tribe again? Get more details of that story they'd told, about the guy out in the darkness, screaming death threats and vengeance for 'Marta.' Marta Sanchez, they told her: one of two cops who used to sometimes visit, and actually *help* the people here. But not anymore. Not for a month. Murdered by The Breaker, they'd learned. Possibly, his most recent kill.

She shivered. She'd worked it out: that night had been the night her uncle had betrayed her trust, tricking her into letting him *control* her.

Her fingers itched, death tingling at their tips, and she ground her teeth. With effort, she forced herself to think of something else. *I could Hunt some RedSkulls again.* They were mostly malformed Melt descendants – half-finished ogres and troll-things – living by the law of the jungle. Ugly, vicious rapists and killers, blaming everyone else for the hatred they generated. *This time, I could do it properly.*

Her eyes narrowed, hungry for the challenge. She'd picked this area because it was near their territory, after all. It was one reason so few people dared live here.

She blushed, remembering her initial disastrous 'scouting' expedition the week before. She'd even had to pay a mage to heal her. *Well, not next time!* Next time, she wouldn't underestimate them.

But if she was gonna hunt RedSkulls, she had to figure out how to get the ingredients to make slime. *And if I'm gonna make the 'Skulls think it's some oozing supernatural monster killing them, I should probably work out what to do with the bodies* after *I kill them, to make them extra scared.* Would it be more terrifying if she made it look like something was *eating* the bodies? She grimaced, trying to work out which bits she'd have to remove, and how to get rid of those parts afterwards.

She had to make it look like something unnatural, or they'd start revenge-killing innocent people nearby, figuring someone had decided enough was enough. And she didn't want to make trouble for the people scraping an existence here in the Dumps.

Besides, by keeping it secret, she should make more money at the FistFest. As well as avoid getting named 'Slime Chick' or something. *That'd be worse than Drone Girl.*

The 'Fest was less than a couple of weeks away now. With the winnings from that, she'd be able to buy the gear to let her do all the things she wanted.

Sure, it was great fun being here, but there was some bad stuff, too. Like getting sick. She'd never been sick before. Suddenly coughing, and having her nose run, and aching all over.... Briefly, she'd found herself wishing her uncle was there, to tuck her into a warm bed and rub her nose and forehead, that special way he had on the few occasions she'd sniffled or coughed; with those soothing finger wriggles that sent her to sleep so she felt better in the morning.

But that man had gone. His face, in memory, turned cruel. *Still not strong enough to resist me, Leeth? Or do you really* want *this?*

No. She didn't need her uncle. *No, not my uncle: The Doctor.* Not even if she was dying.

And she *had* thought she was dying. It had been terrifying, coughing up green mucus – she'd stared at it, stunned, not knowing what to think. If she hadn't remembered Crazy Marty getting sick in *Pirates of the Undersea* – filling his cabin with disgustingly-colored used tissues – she would have freaked.

Getting tissues in the Dumps had been expensive. But 'having a cold' without tissues was a special kind of awful.

As was food poisoning. Her mouth turned down. Now *that* was a lesson you only needed to learn once.

And if tissue paper in the Dumps was costly, toilet paper....

She shook her head. Never again.

But she'd wasted enough time, doing nothing more than making a home for herself here. Making herself *safe*. Protecting herself, with a solar panel powering hidden security cams that monitored her den so she'd know if anyone – *the Department* – 'visited' while she was out.

Merely surviving. It was time to start *doing*. Not just wasting time making herself safe, building mage traps and other defenses.

She narrowed her eyes. She'd visit Marcie: maybe, without mentioning Godsson by name, she could see what *she* thought about how to rescue him without breaking any promises.

And they can just try and capture me!

CHAPTER 2

In the end, though, she decided it'd be a good idea to test how hard it'd be to visit the city undetected. Even after three weeks, the Department would be watching. A spider lurking inside digital webs.

Checking her makeup in the sliver of polished metal, she pursed her lips. *Good enough.*

She'd gone for wild non-geometrical interlocking spikes, along with some subtle mis-shading of her cheekbones and chin. *She* couldn't recognize herself now, so hopefully their face recognition algorithms wouldn't, either. Funny to think that some of Nelson's lessons were actually helping her avoid capture.

She wasn't sure whether to be pleased or annoyed by that, remembering his smug lectures and secretive leers.

She shook herself.

Checking her clothes, she had to grimace at how inappropriate they were for the Dumps. Like colors saying she belonged in the city, not here. They'd attract almost as much attention as going naked.

Almost.

That had sure been a mistake. She'd thought maybe clothes wouldn't matter so much here, outside all the laws and regulations of 'proper society.' Instead, it'd been like rubbing herself down with honey and standing on an ant nest.

Anyway. Skirt, blouse, almost-stylish jacket, and even a matching handbag – to hide her PowerShot. She could hardly wander around shopping areas with the obviously deadly matte black slingshot tucked into her waistband. *Nelson probably has it on file, too, along with my face and gait.*

Which reminded her. Folding her legs under her, she selected two small rocks and carefully tied string around each. Scrubbing the worst of the dirt from her now callused soles, she slipped the stones into the pink joggers before sliding them on and getting gingerly to her feet. She shifted her weight, then took a few steps to check how they made her limp. *Yeah. That'll do.* Easier to manage than super high heels that'd have her tottering through the rubble in danger of falling.

Well. Here goes nothing.

As the sun set she headed to the semi-collapsed fire stairs that led down into the sewers: the second thing that helped make her new home perfect.

The sky was her enemy.
But the jumbled tunnels of the collapsed Millennium II Towers were her friends. That titanic domino fall from years past meant she could get from the Dumps to the edge of the city while staying mostly under cover.
Ahead lay the Visitacion Slump. After that she only had to cross the predatory jungle of the McLaren New Forest – fun! – and she'd be in sleepy Excelsior.
Nelson must hate these above-ground tunnels! He'd once boasted to her that in the city he was an all-seeing god. If so, in the Dumps and tunnels he was blind: in those areas, any camera surveillance had to be sent in on wings or segmented legs. All of which were easily caught and hungrily transformed by eager locals, for whom 'waster' was about the worst insult there was.
But it wasn't just a matter of shooting drones from the sky. Her *biggest* weapon in her tiny war with the Department was her hearing. They still didn't seem to know about that. *Which means Uncle must not have told them about it.* She frowned, then realized it would've been for selfish reasons. Obviously.
So keeping her hearing secret had become as important as using it to alert her to the whine of a spy drone. They knew she could hear ultrasonics – but that was only a small part of her super hearing.
It was fun shooting drones from the sky. But not near her nest. She'd even had to resist shooting one that had buzzed by one day, and just hidden instead, grinding her teeth.
She'd shot them down from lots of different locations, so they couldn't single out one area as the place she probably lived. Though she'd had to restrict herself to doing it only in the Dumps itself. She'd discovered that surveillance in the city was so pervasive that taking out drones in her distinctive style was a sure way to attract a lot of heat real fast.
The close calls had been a lesson well learned, if awful. She'd felt betrayed to a whole new level when an *FBI* team had closed in on her; three times in one night. Each time, minutes after she'd taken out a drone on the city's perimeter. And then she'd spied James in the background, watch-

ing on, disguised like some kind of dumb Clark Kent, and she'd retreated.

But that they'd involved the FBI meant she'd probably never be allowed to work with Commander Amanda Stone, now.

Another reason to hate her uncle.

But as if thinking about drones had summoned it, she picked up the distinctive angry buzz of a heavy-duty lifter. Which, given she was currently clambering through the now horizontal elevator shaft of Tower 3, meant the drone was either carrying a serious load – weaponry? – or a tera-hertz imager to see through the meters of earth and con-crete between her and it.

Either way, more than annoying. *I wonder, though?* In the semi-darkness, not changing her pace, she tapped the display of the gadget on her wrist. Teef's young son, Barney, had proudly said it detected *everything*. Sure enough, in the abstract swirls of glowing colors, a spiky red blob she'd never seen before now swelled, growing as she moved forward through the dark shaft.

She hoped that meant it *was* a terahertz one out there: the tech needed to see through walls made teras re-ally expensive – *wonderful* scav!

Unlike that weird cheap-ass drone that'd followed her one night early on, buzzing so loud she thought at first it had to be a decoy. She'd kept waiting for the real trap to spring. It'd been so crappy that Barney had laughed, only giving her five creds for it. 'I didn't know they still made cams with *this* low res,' he'd teased her.

She shook herself. *Concentrate, Leeth!* Continuing along until the drone sounded like it was straight outside, she stopped. Ahead, light from the cracked-open second floor doors illuminated a heavy cable from the elevator. Dust and dirt piled in drifts against its long undulations, a boa constrictor lying in permanent exhaustion on the smooth gray ground.

Outside, the whine changed tone, now keeping pace with her. *Ah ha!* And yeah, the red spiky blob was bigger. Inside the shaft, she closed her eyes, taking a slow breath, then gripped the corroded edge of the lift door and shoved it aside hard, wincing as metal ground on metal. The drone must have seen: it buzzed louder, like it was excited by the show of strength. She pressed her lips tight together, sure now someone from the Department was operating the spy device.

She slipped out through the door, then turned to her left. Stepping along the path she'd earlier cleared of fallen bricks and plaster panels, she headed straight for the unseen drone buzzing away outside the fallen tower. Her jaw clenched at the sound of two more heavy drones zipping hurriedly closer. *I bet* they *have tasers and tranqs and stuff.* She drew her weapon.

From memory, once through the window ahead, there was pretty good footing to the right.

Okay, let's do this! She dived, rolling, out the window.

The small battle lasted almost twenty seconds.

The annoying thing was, because drones had tracking devices buried deep inside, she was now making her way back into the Dumps with three disabled units instead of going into the city like she'd planned. She'd stuffed them into her specially-lined shopping bag. It wasn't perfect, but Barney said the shielding would screw up digital comms really badly. *And here come two more....*

She jerked, lifting her wrist with Barney's technobabble flashing-lights gizmo, again aiming it toward first one, then the other approaching drone to make out like *it* was her drone detector.

She was fuming by the time she made it back to Teef's hut, *six* drones in her bag and her clothes *ruined.* If she hadn't been able to slash the sticky strands of web with her 'claws', she'd have been a helplessly-wriggling cocoon waiting for them to collect her. *Will it be this bad once I actually make it into the city?*

She sighed, thinking about her plans to hunt down The Breaker. Weeks ago, she'd made a map of his known murder sites and hidden it away in her Link, ready for her to investigate. One more thing left behind when she'd escaped the Department.

Like Toby.

At some stage, carving the dolphin shape from the hard wooden block, the small creature had come alive, to her. Patiently waiting to be revealed; not complaining when she made his head a bit lopsided or his tail too thin.

The only thing she'd ever made, really.

No, the map was no great loss. *I'll just make a new one, showing his murders here in the Dumps. It'll give me a chance to talk to people.* But she had to get the Department off her back if she ever wanted to hunt in the city for anything besides dumb-ass drones.

Ahead, heavy male grunts accompanied the humping movement of a shipping container: Teef and several of his friends maneuvering the new annex he'd been telling her about into place. His hut now snaked between three piles of mostly-stripped autos. From inside, Barney's happy humming made her smile.

As she pushed open the rickety door, the young ogre turned from his workbench. He blinked at her through magnifying goggles strapped to his head, his short-cropped blond hair all spiky and askew.

"This is no place for city folk, ma'am," he began, frowning – then his gaze twisted into puzzlement at the globs and ropes of sticky glue draping her clothes, then saw her PowerShot and sniffed the air. His face broke into a large-toothed smile, recognizing her despite her face camo.

"Hey, D.G!" He shook his head, eyeing her ruined clothes. "More drones, right? Don't tell me, they had *web-guns* this time?" His eyes lit up at the thought, then widened comically as she ripped the bulging Faraday bag unstuck from her back, and swung it around to her front. Running over behind the counter, he hopped up onto a box to be nearer her eye level and cleared some space.

"Another big haul, eh? More *juicy* drones, I bet? I don't know how you do it, D.G." Barney spoke well – his teeth hadn't begun their adult growth spurt, and his wizardry with electronics was matched only by his hunger for education. Even though he was only eleven, he was one of the most well-spoken people she'd met here. Not that she'd met many, yet.

They got on fine, after she'd got his promise never to tell anyone that 'D.G' stood for 'Drone Girl.'

She emptied out the signal-blocking bag *he'd* sold her, growling when it stuck to her arm so she had to wrench it free.

"Um, you'll want some acetone, too, yeah?" he asked, then frowned, eyeing her up and down curiously. "How'd you even cut it off? That stuff'll stick to oiled blades!"

But not to magic. "Uh, I had a, sharp stick…"

Barney was shaking his head, though, and now looked *really* interested. He found the drone with the web gun, and set it to one side. They both stared down at the battered, ball-shaped mess. "Chit, what'd ya do, jump up and down on it? Lucky you didn't rupture the chem-tanks!"

"I was cross." She felt her cheeks redden.

"Yeah. I can tell." He eyed the pattern of severed glue-tentacles on her clothes and skin, frowning. "Where were you? And seriously, how'd you get free? Those things are bad biz – and not cheap."

She lifted her eyebrows, and it was Barney's turn to flush.

"*If* the chem-tanks aren't empty!" he shot back.

But their by-play had given her the time to make up a story about going somewhere, 'just happening' to have a laser-cutter in hand. Implying she'd been trying to break in somewhere. She'd had to abandon the cutter when *it* got glued and she'd had to retreat. Barney looked doubtful, but stopped asking questions.

His eyes lit up when he spied the terahertz unit.

Taking a powered torque wrench from his multi-tier utility belt, he quickly cracked the drone casing and delicately applied his own laser cutter, severing a single connection. Pulling out another device, he scanned, then nodded to himself. "There. That takes care of the tracker. Fancy, too – that one was using spread-spectrum comms! But I'll check the others, just in case. You bring me some weird drones, D.G. No toy ones tonight, eh?" he grinned.

Leeth smiled weakly, watching him dive in to her pile of semi-smashed flying pests.

He was soon happily exclaiming over their mil-spec fit-outs and power cell capacities, frowning every now and then at the device on her wrist – which *he'd* built, and traded to her for five drones at their first meeting. She'd thought the pretty, ever-changing display was some kind of artwork, but the boy had eagerly explained it was a spirit detector he was making. Though he'd looked a little sheepish when he admitted it just detected 'everything,' and showed that on its polished crystal display. He figured if there *was* some way to detect spirits, you'd be able to tell by learning what patterns showed when they were nearby.

For Leeth, it made a perfect gadget to wave around to pretend to detect drones. It even kind of did, in a way.

Once you learned how to interpret some of the colorful patterns. *Especially when I can hear them coming, anyway.*

But she'd had to think quickly at that first meeting, when she'd arrived to find Teef 'out' and Barney manning his father's store. She'd dumped the pile of eight drones onto the counter, and the too-wise young ogre had looked at her strangely. "How'd you find so many? Were they all hunting *you?*"

She'd lied, making up a story about a weird sound by the water's edge that the drones had all seemed to be trying to pinpoint. Barney had lapped the story up, but it made her realize it'd be bad if everyone knew she was being hunted so energetically.

She liked Barney, and they chatted for a while. She asked how his micro-manipulator project was coming along, and he proudly showed her his progress on the digit sleeves. He was building the device for when he got older, his fingers grown far too big and clumsy for delicate work.

Yeah, you had to admire Barney.

Soon though, the smell of welding penetrated the shop as Teef, out back, began bonding the new annex, so she said farewell and headed back into the city to try again. *Determined* to get the stuff she needed to make slime.

It took her over an hour to work her way back. *Maybe I should've just bought the Borax and glue from Top Scav, in the Dumps?* But she didn't want to pay ten times what they'd cost at a small store here in Excelsior, and she *did* want to see how hard it'd be to evade detection in the city.

For all she knew, they might've surgically implanted radio beacons inside her somewhere.

Her eyes narrowed. *If they have, I'll just crash a medcenter, force them to X-ray me, then cut them out.* But she didn't think they'd done that. If they had, the Department wouldn't've needed to keep trying to spot her with stupid drones.

She forced herself to walk proudly, shoulders back like she belonged here and was just on her way to a club or something for a night out. Her face-camo attracted curious looks from passersby. She tried to ignore them, forcing a sneer to her face, pretending she was somebody special. Thinking how the disguise would probably work better on a Friday or Saturday.

Passing a MacDonalds, the aromas locked her feet in place, even as the subtle cameras she automatically noted, and the too-bright interior, screamed at her to move on.

Her stomach growled, demanding she go in. On the price board over the wide counter, delicious looking burgers and fries glowed with hypnotic intensity, and she swayed toward the entrance. She wasn't exactly sure what species of rodents and birds she currently had congealing in her stew-pot, but the way her mouth was watering let her know exactly which offering her stomach thought superior. Even though the one time she as Jane had suggested she'd like to try it, Marcie and the other girls had joked about how awful the food there was.

"Try it?" Delta had laughed. "You make it sound like you've never eaten at Maccas!"

She had to tear each foot from the pavement as she turned and walked away, the wonderful smells curling and coiling about her like the arms of invisible seducers.

Stay focused. She wasn't here to stuff herself on fast food, but to get the ingredients to make monster slime for decorating RedSkull corpses.

That thought snapped her back into focus. At the next corner, she checked the street signs. The net had said she wanted the corner of Colby and Sweeney streets, so... yeah. She was sweeping around now toward it, having located the single underground storm-water tunnel entrance, in case she needed to go to ground. She'd found it by studying city maps back in Teef's shop: it was the reason she'd chosen Excelsior for her little test expedition today. In case they came for her, in force. She hadn't studied this area when she'd planned her break-out to save Marcie.

Above and behind her, she heard the familiar high pitched whine of a drone rising up, and adrenaline shocked through her. *Can't they give me a minute's peace?* She faltered, then recovered, fighting the urge to freeze, spin, and whip out her slingshot to knock it from the sky.

I'm in the suburbs. It could just be a kid playing, or a traffic drone. Don't react. Don't jump to conclusions. She didn't turn, though she couldn't get her shoulders to relax. Nor could she seem to loosen her fingers now gripping her red pleather handbag, aching for the weapon hidden inside.

And though the drone moved a little closer, pushing her restraint to the limit, she kept strutting on with her faint limp; kept her face up and her stride assured as the general store finally came into view.

Please let it not be them. Just a few more minutes, and I'll have what I need.

Inside the shop, she kept hearing the drone outside, fading in and out of earshot as it moved around. Like it was scoping the area, or searching for something, the whole time.

Wanting to scream at him to *hurry*, all she could do was bounce on her heels while the elderly shop-keeper scratched his head and tottered between tight-packed shelves. He kept muttering, stopping to smile at her, wondering aloud what kind of party she must be on her way to, for *every single item* on her shopping list!

The instant his register dinged acceptance of the transfer, she snatched her cashstick and bag of supplies and raced for the entrance.

The drone darted to a position across the street as she exited the shop.

She had a bad feeling about this. *I should have shot it down.*

Ahead, a police car turned the corner. Inside, she saw the eyes of two cops fixed on her. She couldn't – quite – hear what the one speaking was saying, but she hardly needed to. Not when it slammed to a stop and the two piled out, drawing tasers while she was still ten meters away.

Looking down at her feet, she started singing, bobbing her head and dancing toward them as if chipped in to a pop tune with a mad beat.

"Miss! Down on the ground, hands behind your head! This is the police. Miss, down on the ground, I said, or we *will* shoot! Miss!"

At five meters away she finally looked up and noticed them. Pretending shock, she turned fully around, putting her back to them, scanning desperately left and right for the threat while backing closer to them for 'safety.' The second cop's reply came as music to her ears.

"She can't hear us, Capper. And look at her. This has to be some kind of fuck-up!"

Still with her back to them, she mimed surprise at seeing no one behind her, just through body language. *Those acting lessons really* had *been useful!* Shutting her eyes, the tiny sounds of their clothing and breathing told her exactly where each stood.

She continued backing toward them, the area between her shoulder-blades feeling horribly exposed.

Now.

Ducking and spinning, she exploded into action.

"Dammit!"

Mother half wished *she* was the one clubbing the inept officers who appeared incapable of understanding a simple order like 'stun on sight.' It was all over within three seconds.

Six, counting the time it took Leeth to draw from her cheap handbag the sleek weapon that Mother had come to detest. Leeth spun and aimed at the drone, killing the feed, which froze her image. It floated in the air, grinning at them like the Cheshire cat.

Damn the girl! Mother wanted to scream. "Just look at that smirk! She knew we were watching."

"Well, she's certainly applying everything we've taught her," Eagle replied, sounding thoroughly unconcerned.

"Are you *enjoying* this?"

"You think I enjoy seeing you fail to recapture an eighteen-year-old girl, Mother? A girl you have assessed as unfit for duty? Why? Do you imagine I see it as a way of making a point?"

"The point is that she's too unpredictable to be of use!"

Eagle turned to Harmon. "What of your vaunted claims of being able to predict her actions, Doctor? Why did she want plastic containers, brass screws, Borax, matches and water-soluble glue?"

Harmon looked unhappy. "I'm afraid-"

"Stop, Doc," Nelson giggled. "Like Eagle said, she did pay attention to some of her lessons. She bought a lot of glue and Borax – several containers – but hardly any screws or matches: those last two items were just to confuse any searches."

Harmon frowned. "And?"

"I just did a search on Borax and glue, alone. Turns out if you add water you can make slime, which sounds like the kinda weird sort of thing she might want to do. How about that?"

Harmon frowned. "Possible. I will need time to consider the implications. In the meantime, let me reiterate the high likelihood that she will visit her friend Marcie. I find it surprising she hasn't done so already. I also predict she is highly likely to attend the upcoming fighting event: *especially* knowing we will try to recover her then. I expect that will only make her all the more determined to compete."

"That's ludicrous, Doctor," Mother said. "What's in it for her?"

Harmon met Eagle's eyes – *this again?* – before turning back to Mother. He tiredly counted off each point with a raised finger. "Thumbing her nose at us; making money; testing herself; 'fun'."

"But she needs money if she plans to bet on herself: and you claim she won't be whoring herself." Mother glared in turn at each of the three older men in the room. "How is she financing herself?"

"My drones," said Nelson, bitter.

"What?"

"There's been nothing left at any of the sites she's shot down a drone."

"You're saying *you're* financing her?" Mother's lips thinned further.

"Hey! It's not like I'm trying to! And you're the one who okayed me finding her with drones."

"*Finding* her, Nelson, not giving them to her. Perhaps we should limit your hours playing computer games – they clearly do not 'improve your reflexes'."

Nelson bristled. Even gone, Leeth was still humiliating him. And she knew it, too: the number of final captures from his downed drones that were an image of her gloating smile and raised middle finger....

"She can't be selling them in the city," Father said.

There was a short silence while they all considered the conflagration they'd set off if they tried to move into the Dumps to catch her selling them.

Harmon watched Mother's expression sour as she also processed that he had correctly predicted she *would* venture into the city. Though it had occurred a week later than he had expected.

Nelson spoke into the silence. "Preacher told me they end the FistFest with a cheered-for vote for 'best performance'. Including the amount. Might be five thou – even higher if there's been a lot of betting, since a percentage goes into a pool. Record's fourteen."

"Does Leeth know this?" Mother demanded.

They all exchanged looks.

"You trained her in social interactions, Mother," Eagle said, "and she *is* there. What do you think?"

"She'll be determined to break that record, won't she, Doctor?"

Harmon nodded, paling as he imagined the risks she would take. Not for the money: for the validation.

Mother and Father were frowning, considering how far and how deep she could disappear with that sum of money. She might even leave the country.

Nelson's expression showed his frustration.

Eagle watched them all. So far the test was proving interesting.

CHAPTER 3

The night she had almost killed him, Marc Disten had converted a tiny portion of capital into coinz. The transfer had completed while the shaking doctor sealed wounds and set bones. Mere hours later, the wisdom of the move had been proven: all financial reserves traceable to Mark Dennis – Disten – had been frozen. Available funds would now support just thirty years of existence at the current meager rate of expenditure.

It should suffice.

But with near-fatal injuries, the need for conscious attention to avoid accidental re-injury, and the necessity to hide from the intense manhunt, Disten's options had been severely limited.

A moldy shack had been found to go to ground in. Hidden beside a submerged jetty on the edge of the West Oakland Dumps, it had been a good place to wait, and heal.

And then, just one week after being thrown from the truck traveling at 100kph, Marc Disten had sensed the resurgence of the Call as the newsment streams went wild. Although, had anyone been watching, they would have seen no sign of each painful tug deep inside. Just seen the tall, unmoving man – watching the live video, internally. In which the girl first tossed the figure from the wheelchair into the rear of the ambulance, then disappeared inside the cabin to eject the driver.

Even before any newsment report identified the young female 'terrorist,' Disten had recognized Jane Baker, her hair now short and blonde.

They were connected. They must join.

When the news feeds lost the ambulance, Disten silenced them and left the shack, still stabbed by the distant girl's emotions. Staring unseeingly across the waters of San Francisco Bay he had stood, planning, as long shadows slid day into night.

He had returned inside to lie down and rest, ignoring each spearing jab of her animalistic impulses. All that night, stabbed by barbed threads that jerked as she danced in mad delight through the collapsed ruins across the Bay.

Crippled, unable to respond, that first night had been torment. Fortunately, it had also been the worst night.

Two days later an attempt had been made to watch her via a drone acquired, laboriously and at great risk, due to the injuries. Only to have her shoot it from the sky.

But drones were not needed to locate her. Not with the constant nagging tug of the Call. Nor did the strange connection need to be understood, to be used.

With a little care, a once-luxurious apartment on the edge of the West Oakland Dumps had been found. Now a vermin-infested, falling down tenement, but it had clear sight lines to her nest across the Bay.

She had been industrious.

But so had this one, carefully acquiring needed equipment. And now, four weeks since the surgeries, healing had progressed to the point that action could soon be considered.

The Link beeped, the medical monitors reminding of the need to move. Back locked solidly in its surgical brace, the signals of pain were assessed. Focusing on the burn of fatigue and the placement of crutches, a path was navigated to the supportive sofa, and the legs in their plaster casts positioned.

To one side, a simple monitoring system connected to a small array of high-powered digital telescopes, each focused on a key exit point around her nest and favored routes. Disten jacked in to the system, shutting eyes to review the activity-flagged recordings from the target area, updating the surveillance charts.

This afternoon's data showed the girl emerge from underground exit five, her face camouflaged and her clothing looking more suited to blending in to the city than the Dumps. The auto-tracking camera followed her until she climbed in through a once upper-floor window of the Millennium II wreckage. She did not reappear at any of her previous exit points.

Her new behavior was considered while the rest of the afternoon's footage was reviewed and annotated. Observing her was a productive use of this enforced period of hiding and recuperation. And as soon as the body had mended fully, the girl would be acquired. Given her performance at the hospital, it was possible her success in their last encounter had not been chance. Waiting was logical.

Soon, though, relocation across the Bay into the Hunters Point Dumps would be possible.

Disten's eyes fell on the array of observation and communication equipment. Automation was good: continued physical presence in this vantage point would not be necessary. It would make many things simpler.

Such as collecting test subjects.

And the girl herself.

This time, she would not be underestimated.

CHAPTER 4

Leeth took extra care on her return journey, listening before emerging from each underground passage. She stayed unmoving, watching from cover for whole minutes at a time before darting quickly across each section of open ground.

Crossing the final exposed stretch, though, she stilled. A prickling up her spine had her diving to the side, dropping her precious plastic bag of slime ingredients. Rolling into cover, she moved only her eyes, searching for tell-tale red laser dots.

But there was nothing.

She scanned the scene. To one side, the jumbled slabs of a collapsed multi-story carpark. Next to it, the sideways sprawl of a shattered office building. The rest, a huddle of broken tenements, tangled in vines and crushed together like a circle of silently wailing women.

Nothing moved. Just the slow shifting of cloud shadows across the broken landscape, her abandoned bag a pale flutter in a wind with winter's bite.

I'm just being silly. No one's watching me. I'm just keyed up 'coz they've started using metro cops. She grimaced, wondering what lies they'd told the cops to make them try to arrest her.

She forced her shoulders down, consciously loosening muscles, and stood. Exposed, but hyper-alert, ears straining. *Could I hear an incoming bullet, if it came from far away?* She hoped to never find out.

Fingers tingling, she darted back to her shopping. Grabbing it, she stilled, then jerked to one side, expecting a shot. She turned slowly then, eyes unfocused, scanning a full three-sixty degrees.

Oakland glared back at her across the dark waters of a Bay lit by the late afternoon sun. She shivered, still skewered by the feeling of being watched.

With a last look around, she shook herself and slid to the entrance to the stormwater tunnel. Scrambling inside, her containers of glue and Borax bumping her shoulders, she headed finally toward her office building's sewers. Ducking under occasional tree roots that had bored through the concrete and slashing through others, she grumbled her way along snaking passages.

She changed out of her city-threads on her return. Mixing

the water, glue and Borax, she thought about the evening's expedition. *I should've taken out the drone: it must've been Nelson. But how'd they know it was me? I'd even altered my gait.* She considered again the possibility they'd implanted a tracker on her. But Barney's 'spirit detector' registered nothing odd when she used it on herself. Besides, if they knew where she was, they'd surround her, not leave her with escape routes.

She shook her head, exhaling heavily.

Had she made any other mistakes? She'd considered finding and smashing the cop-cams, but they recorded to the net, and besides, if they'd been watching through the drone, they already had heaps of vid.

Why had they only used cops, though? Had they really expected I'd be that easy? Why not use real agents, from the main Bureau? She paused, head tilted to one side at a thought. The Department was only a tiny group hidden inside the Bureau for Internal Development – an agency evolved, her lessons had taught her, from the FBI and Homeland Security. But that was basically all she knew about it.

Was that strange? *They'd made me a part of it. Shouldn't they have taught me about what the other, less secret, agents did?*

Her mixture started to congeal, and she focused back on what her hands were doing. You could learn all sorts of cool stuff from the net. And Teef was good about not looking over her shoulder when she paid for access. Though she didn't rely on that, always clearing her search history like Nelson had taught her.

Later, plastic containers tightly sealed, dressed again in her comfy halter and denim shorts, she sighed, delicately spitting a bone into her rubbish cup. Ladling more stew into her enamel bowl, she paused, the smells of the food in the MacDonald's store returning to her in memory. For some reason, her eyes teared up, and she found herself rocking forward and back on her haunches.

Stop it! Don't be such a baby. Tears are for weaklings. That was what her uncle had always said.

For some reason, though, that only made the water well more strongly. *Stop it! If he said it, it was probably a lie. Maybe tears make you* stronger.

Though she hadn't felt strong when Marcie had gazed at her in fear at the hospital. She'd had to turn and flee, the look haunting her even as she'd hauled her uncle down endless hospital corridors.

If I do contact Marcie, will she even want *to talk to me?*

Curling in on herself, ignoring the water welling from tight-closed eyes, she tipped her enamel bowl back into the pot. She knew she had to eat her stew to stay healthy and strong, but right now she just couldn't. Turning off the heating plate and putting the lid back on the pot, she slumped back into her bag-chair, its plastic scrunching as her weight squashed it flat against the floor.

She could try hunting The Breaker – but the trail was pretty cold. Maybe she should try talking to people about it? Just the thought gave her a little lift. *I might even make some new friends.*

Tucking her PowerShot into the rear of her shorts, thinking that she really ought to see if Teef had a holster that'd work, she headed out into the late afternoon. Maybe it was time to start getting known. But not as a fighter: she didn't want to mess up her odds when she entered the Fist-Fest.

The trouble was, none of the reports had bothered to say *where* in the Dumps any of The Breaker's kills had happened. Because normal society didn't care what happened to the CID-less. And it'd probably look suss if she started questioning people about them: they might even think *she* was involved!

She'd just have to be subtle.

Heading south, into the Dumps proper, she decided to start in the Fisher Clan's area. A lot of clans met and mixed there, her studies had said.

Her path twisted through collapsed buildings and over fissured roadways and playing fields, ending at last at a rock shelf that projected above the foreshore. Already, the shadows of the terraces above were stretching out over the wind-swept surface of the Bay. Ahead, and below, came a murmur of conversations – lots of them – all sounding happy. She also scented spices, smoky flavors, and cooked fish. Inhaling deeply, she shut her eyes. Her stomach growled an angry demand, and she licked her lips.

The voices got louder as she moved quietly nearer the

edge. A wisp of smoke curled up, wafting unfamiliar but delicious smells around her. But even at the very edge, she couldn't see anyone. *Must be an overhang.* It was only a few meters high. She considered just jumping down and introducing herself.

At the last moment, she hesitated. *Normal people probably don't jump off cliffs, even small ones.* And she had to seem kinda normal here, too. At least for now. So instead, she backed away, following the ledge south, enjoying the smell of the sea and the hiss and slosh of the small waves rolling in along the shore. Set back from the water's edge, she saw a ragged line of scraggly huts.

It made her smile, and she felt her spirits lift. *I could buy some food for a change,* she decided. *Even talk to people.*

Strangely, the thought brought tears again to her eyes. She wiped them away, shaking her head. *What's the matter with me?*

Rounding the edge of the cliff, the eating area came into view, spread out under an escarpment. As she quietly approached, first one then several of the people seated facing her way noticed her. Circles of stillness radiated out from them as more people turned to watch.

Set back against the small cliff wall sat tubs, tanks, and metal tables with a hodge-podge of cookers. Manning them, a kaleidoscope of people of all breeds and sizes, from blue Avatarians to ogres to perfectly normal un-Altered humans in their more muted browns and blacks and pinks. All kept cooking, but watched her warily as she advanced.

By the time she started weaving between the makeshift tables, all conversation had stopped. *Do I look weird, or something? Am I dressed wrong?* But she kept a smile on her face, and made out the whispers – "Dunno: stranger." "Metro peep." "Forr'nah."

Oh. It's just they don't know me. "Hi! This all smells great – can I buy some food?"

She noticed looks being exchanged, several people nodding, satisfied by her words. But off to her right, a woman hissed under her breath, "I seen her in far; Skulls zone. *Girl* Skull?"

Other voices sucked in breaths, but a second woman's voice answered the first. "Rapin' Skulls don' let 'gash' roam." Leeth turned, to see a black woman spit on the ground, angry eyes meeting her own. "Drown 'em all. We could null 'em, we all band."

"Yeah, Yasmin? 'N how many die, doin'? 'N who next on ya list, after Skulls?"

While the argument continued, Leeth turned back to the food on offer. Her mouth watered at the sight and smells from a wok of jumbled nuts, bright green vegetables, succulent white fish-pieces, and tiny little baby corns almost too cute to eat. She held up her cashstick. "Can I...?"

The cook, a tall thin Asian man, shook his head in amusement, then nodded sideways. After a rapid exchange between him and the stall-holder beside him – in a musical up-down language she couldn't make head or tail of – he indicated she should click sticks with the other cook.

"Can I have a big bowl? Like, this much?" she asked, cupping her hands well apart. The men raised their eyebrows, dueled a second time, then he nodded again. "And some water. And a fork."

Balancing the aged plastic bottle against the red and blue glazed bowl, she made her way carefully to the table where 'Yasmin' and her neighbors had been arguing. "Can I sit with you?"

They all examined her closely, clearly suspicious, but the black woman nodded. "Sho, chica."

"By all means, young lady," declared an older woman with gray hair and eyebrows, a wicked grin, and a long yellow jacket draping bony shoulders. "We would be delighted if you joined us. My name is Jacqueline Stone. But people here call me Miz J."

The woman who hated the RedSkulls, Yasmin, made room. The third person at the table, the one who'd said she'd seen her in the distance, kept her eyes glued to Leeth's hands, except to dart glances aside every now and then, checking lines of approach. As if she thought Leeth might be a scout or something for the Meltie gang. She was a small blonde woman, but with a narrow waist and large round breasts, and deep frown lines around her eyes and mouth.

"Seen ya, Skull terr'. Yo fil? What heah? Who'it?"

"Uh... what?"

"Luce said she's seen you in the RedSkulls territory," Miz J interpreted, "and wonders if you are affiliated with them in some way; she also wonders what you're doing here, and who you're with?"

"I've found a good place *near* the Skulls' territory, I guess." She scowled at Luce. "But I'm certainly *not* affiliated with them-" *I'm planning to kill them.* She stopped herself from saying that aloud. "I like it here, better than home." She started digging into her food, her eyes closing in bliss at the tangy sauce, the crunch of the hot vegetables, and the *mmm* fish. She paused, bent over her bowl, inhaling the delicious steam before cramming in some of the tiny baby corns, too. "Ohhh."

When she opened her eyes again, she saw all three women looking doubtfully at her, then at one another. Luce snorted. "Run to Dumps wit yo man? Tink he protec yo fum Skulls? Where he now, eh?"

Leeth swallowed. "I didn't run here *with* anyone. I'm on my own." Then forked in more food, filling her cheeks. *Mmm, so good!*

The three women weren't moving, she noticed. Miz J spoke first, shaking her head. "My dear, that is most unwise, the RedSkulls-"

"I can loo' a' m'sel." At their blank looks she held up her fork, and swallowed. "Sorry. I can look after myself. I have weapons. The RedSkulls are one thing." She shrugged, then hunched in on herself. "What I *do* worry about is those other attacks I heard about, the ones where people were abducted by the weird robot guy who made them... hurt each other. Before I, um, came here, the newsments said he'd taken people in the Dumps. Sometimes I lie awake at night, wondering if *he's* creeping up on me. Where did he... is he still around? *He* sounds scary."

"Fear Skulls, not Breaker. He gone, tres wiks. Nada. Prob dead."

"I agree with Luce, dear. Whatever it was, it seems to have gone; there have been no attacks now for three weeks. You should be more concerned about the Skulls."

Leeth chewed, then paused in her eating. "Maybe you're right." She reached into a jacket pocket, and unfurled a light cloth. "You guys know Teef?"

They all nodded; even relaxed, slightly.

"Barney printed this map out for me. Maybe you could

mark it with helpful places I should know, and where I should avoid?" She drew out a pencil stub, as she loaded her fork up again and wolfed more of the delicious meal down. "'S *goo!*"

Leeth hugged her new friends goodbye, shaking hands and sharing kisses, before heading off, feeling well pleased with herself. It hadn't been long before a dozen people had crowded around, offering tips and advice, while also trying to find out why she'd 'run away from home,' how she was coping, and where she was nesting. Miz J even offered to bring her into the Fisher Clan, despite Luce's occasional muttered insults.

She'd also managed to get the locations of The Breaker's *seven* attacks marked on her map. It now held a mass of scrawled annotations.

Seven attacks, though: sixteen people, she'd learned. One found, weeks later, dead by thirst, soiled in her own waste. As if she'd just... stopped.

Only one survivor, a teenage boy. Now, more like a zombie. They took her to him, grimly watching on as she spoke to him. She'd tried to get him to talk, or just *react*, in the field he was making out of rubble.

But he simply kept digging the ground, piling each rock into a bucket; carrying the bucket when full to an awfully large pile by the side of the growing plot. Even when she'd held his head so he had to meet her eyes, there'd been nothing there. Just emptiness. When she'd let him go, he simply went back to work, turning a field of debris into a garden plot one rock at a time.

His mother had come with them, looking on, her face stony and frozen – apart from the tears running down her face.

Leeth had gone to her, and hugged her, crying herself, whispering a promise that if she *could* do anything to help, she would.

She shivered, remembering. The thing was far, far worse than the newsments had known.

But when she'd said that, they'd mostly shrugged. 'The Breaker isn't all that dangerous,' they'd said, defending the reputation of their home. These Dumps were much safer than places like the West Oakland Dumps. Or even the Rockies, Yasmin had snorted, telling her of a whole orphanage being abducted by the Brethren of the End of Days to become part of their commune, just yesterday. Hadn't she seen the news?

They'd all looked shocked when she'd said she didn't have a Link, and was just buying net access at Teef's. They'd shared knowing looks, and all become a little more... reserved.

She figured she wasn't the first person to come here, on the run from the authorities.

Though they'd happily shared the story of this latest outrage – which did sound awful. The Brethren of the End of Days was a cult who said the world was going to end soon. 'Shepherd Fox,' their leader, was a kind of religious guru and survivalist, rapidly building a growing number of followers. Most of them lived like guerrillas – which she knew about, now – in and around the Rockies in places where there were no roads, in very difficult terrain. The worst thing about the orphanage abduction, everyone had agreed, was that the majority of the orphans were girls.

The more snippets of news they shared about Shepherd Fox and his followers, the guiltier Leeth felt. She should be *there,* not here. Apparently there were rumors of spooky mind control about the Brethren, too: they said people who joined never wanted to leave. Leeth felt a weird chill shiver through her.

A chill that twisted inside when Miz J added, "Even the women, who they say all automatically marry the Shepherd."

And here she was, hardly even able to go into the city, not even really started yet on her hunt of The Breaker.

As she left the area, her stomach pleasantly full for the first time in three weeks, she thought about all the things she *should* be doing. She had The Breaker to hunt, as well as the RedSkulls; and Mark Dennis – or Marc Disten – just in case he came back after Marcie; and now Shepherd Fox. *Maybe I should make a list. It'd be easy to forget some- one. Oh. Like Robo: it could still be out there.*

She sighed, feeling kind of mixed up. Happy, from a wonderfully full stomach, and meeting a whole bunch of nice people. But also feeling even lonelier than she had, before she'd met them.

She forced her shoulders back. At least now, she knew the locations where The Breaker had attacked people, in the Dumps. And it was only just dark. Consulting her cloth map, she headed off.

Three hours later, she wove a disappointed path back to her 'nest.' She'd found nothing at any of the sites of the seven attacks. Just a fair amount of old, dried blood. No clues. And of course, no sign of any police investigation.

It really did seem like The Breaker had gone away.

She wished the weird prickling at her shoulder blades would too, though. She just couldn't shake the feeling she was being watched.

CHAPTER 5

I need to visit Marcie. That thought was in her mind when she woke the next morning, to the cheerful peeping of bird song. She frowned, remembering yesterday's visit to the city and Nelson spotting her via the drone. How had he done that? She'd camo-ed her face. She was sure they hadn't bugged her. She'd even put stones in her shoes to alter her walk! So how had he picked her out from all the tens of thousands of other girls roughly her size, wandering around in the city?

Her uncle? The Department had taught her about magical tracking. If he was using his Clairvoyance spell, in the city there were heaps of landmarks to recognize – including street signs to read. He might even be hovering around in spirit form. But usually she got a tingly sense of *connection* when he used Clairvoyance, or a kind of *presence* if he was nearby. She paused, shutting her eyes, just... *feeling.*

Nothing.

Unless...? A thrill of certainty ran through her, and moments later, she began dressing, and camo-ing her face again.

There: they'd do. A group of girls passed her hiding spot, heading for the mall. Leeth took a last scan of the sky and surroundings – still clear – and moved quickly to intercept them before they reached the front doors.

"Excuse me...."

Almost as one, they turned, eyeing her up and down, drawing back from her garishly-camouflaged face, visibly trying to work out if she was someone famous. Five girls, all about her own height, similarly slim, and dressed in an interesting mix of styles spanning retro-goth to cyber-mod to rock diva.

Rock-diva was a gorgeous Puerto Rican girl with glossy black hair tumbling down her back. She wore a tight T-shirt with an upright screw beside a finger pointing straight at the reader. Her eyes narrowed as she examined the anti face-recog makeup, then shook her head. "Sorry, no hablamos Inglés, no tenemos dinero," rubbing finger and thumb together and turning away.

Acting time. "I don't want money. I need help. I'm being cyber-stalked. Can I just tag along, walk with you? That's all."

All but the Puerto Rican rock diva closed ranks, the small blonde shaking her head. "Sofia, no, don't-"

The rock diva, Sofia, looked intrigued. "Stalked by who, chica? How would tagging along with us help?"

The blonde groaned. "Sofia, we can't-"

The glare from her suddenly-determined friend stopped her mid-sentence. Sofia turned back to Leeth. "Stalked by who?"

"A boy. A computer genius. I kissed him, once, and now he's stalking me. He uses drones. Hacks camera networks. And he's got money. He sends people to hassle me." She nodded toward the camera by the glass entry doors. "If I walked past that cam, alone.... He knows I've only got one friend in the city, and I'm sure he's watching her place, too. I've got a hunch his software singles out girls my size, who are on their own, then hijacks drones to check closely."

Another girl, a redhead, snorted. "That's crazy."

Leeth met her eyes, wringing her hands while hanging her head, trying to look pitiful. She let her voice sink. "No. It's awful." It wasn't hard to let her lips tremble; and, half surprising herself, she felt water well in her eyes. "Please. Can I just pretend to be with you, and feel normal for one afternoon?"

The five girls exchanged glances.

Leeth flinched as a drone buzzed up, then forced a laugh and reached out to the black-haired girl. "Ha! Good one, Sofia! But could we please go inside now?" On her face, she plastered a look of desperate fear, angling her eyes toward the drone that had now paused behind the group.

Several of the girls looked thoughtful, the goth girl giving a finger to the drone, as if it really was looking at them. "Zip off, pervert!" she called, then held up her Link, aiming it at the hovering device. "Okay, Link: report drone for privacy invasion," she ordered.

For several seconds, the drone hovered, and Leeth could tell it was moving forward and back, like its pilot was uncertain, before buzzing off.

"Hey. That's weird: that fucker ID-ed itself as a carpark security drone. So what was it doing here? Maybe she's telling the truth?"

Leeth felt certain it *had* been Nelson. The girls made

up their minds.

"So, what's your name, chica?" asked Sofia.

Yes! But instead of showing her glee, she was careful to look timid, and grateful. "Thank you so much. It's J-Jenny." *Damn. I almost said Jane. And my hair and eye color haven't changed back much from when I hijacked the ambulance.*

A frustrating but strangely fun hour later, sitting in the food hall, laden with bags, the conversation continued around her.

She'd spent only a fraction of what the others had, just to fit in, wincing when her hard-won cred balance dropped back below a hundred for the first time in weeks.

But if this exercise let her contact Marcie, it'd be worth it.

She plunged into the *delicious* food. Only as her stomach filled did she come back to herself. Frowning as she chewed, she tried to work out if she could ask these girls the questions she'd planned to ask Marcie. But how to explain she knew a super-powerful mage *secretly* locked up by the government; and then ask how to get him released?

The more she thought about the problem, the more it sounded too weird to ask. She'd probably hit them with enough 'weird' for one day....

When at last she couldn't eat another bite, she leaned back from her container of chicken wings, into a silent circle of girls staring at her with variously stunned and amused faces.

Then she noticed her pile of empty food cartons, and compared it to the others'.

They were all watching her. Sofia, Zoe the goth girl – "but call me Zee" – and Jaz, the blonde. Sky, the redhead, and Mai Lyn, a quiet Asian girl, rounded out the group.

Sky was watching her with eyes far too knowing, but it was Zee who spoke. "Are you gonna go and...?" She opened her mouth, pointing her finger into it.

Leeth stared back, trying to decode the message, but Sky rescued her. "That was the first proper meal you've had in a while, Jenny, yeah?"

"No! I had a *delicious* meal just last night! And I've got this stew...." She shut up. These girls would never eat rats and birds, she sensed.

Zee snorted. "Man: that. Was. *Abz.*" She aimed her

Link's camera at 'Jenny' and her stack of empty containers. "I gotta SoBo this-"

Leeth lunged across the table, slamming Zee's wrist down and covering the tiny lens.

"Ow! What the *fuck*-?"

Leeth glared at her. "I. Am being. Stalked." She released Zee and flung herself back into her chair, aware of people suddenly watching with too much interest. Leeth glared at them until they looked away, then turned back to Zee. She took a deep breath, and let it sigh out. "I'm sorry. *Please* don't share me."

Zee was rubbing her wrist, face still twisted in pain. "Geez, girl, you almost snapped my bones. That's some grip." She held up her arm, the skin showing livid finger marks.

"I'm sorry."

"O-kay, but at least let me snap the empties. You don't have to even be in it." She angled her Link again.

Leeth remembered James's words, the time he'd stopped her ordering what she'd wanted at the restaurant, saying that people would recognize her just from the amount of food she ate. And then she thought of Nelson and his *algorithms*.

"No! Please don't. Don't even chat about it, online. I'm sure he scans texts."

Sofia was shaking her head, looking suddenly doubtful. But Mai Lyn's quiet words stopped them all. "It's worse than you're telling us, Jenny, isn't it? Much worse?"

Leeth found herself nodding, slowly. Reluctantly.

"Your name isn't Jenny, is it?"

The others turned to Mai Lyn, reading something in their friend's face, then back to Leeth. Breathlessly watching the strange girl.

Leeth shook her head. "No." She stared at the Asian girl. Was she... *scared? Why would she be...? No. Oh, no!* "You have cyberware, don't you? You've been... online. Searching. What have you done? I need to go. They may already have the mall surrounded." She jumped to her feet.

Mai Lyn held out a hand. "It's okay. I just watched some news footage. That's all."

Leeth hesitated, scanning the area: nothing *looked* wrong – but would it?

"Your friend: her name is Marcie, isn't it?"

Leeth's jaw dropped open, the question confirming *what* news footage Mai Lyn must have found. The other girls watched the exchange, puzzled but intrigued.

Then Zee swore. "Holy cop-thrashing shit – you're *Jane Baker*, that hospital terrorist chick!"

But instead of screaming or calling for help, all five just sat, frozen, watching her.

So much for my undercover skills. She sighed. "The only thing I lied to you about was my name."

A barrage of questions began, but strangely, they were more interested and supportive than hostile. "Did you really force a mage to heal Marcie Dunkirk?" "How'd you knock out those two cops?" "How'd you get away?" "Who was the mage?" "What are mages *like?*" "How'd you do *that?*"

That was Leeth dragging Dr Ranatunga through a hospital hallway one handed, pushing a floppy-hatted person in a wheelchair while simultaneously knocking down three orderlies who tried to stop her. Mai Lyn had aimed her Link down, playing the scene between the tomato sauce bottle and the Dalek-shaped salt and pepper shakers.

"Shut that off!"

Mai Lyn did so.

"And stop accessing any of that stuff. He probably has ways to check up on everyone who watches it."

The girl stared down her cute nose at her. "Ah, eighty million SoZone Likes? 'He'll' be a busy boy."

"Eighty... eighty million...?" Leeth squeezed her eyes shut. *I am so screwed.* She forced the thought aside. Would numbers alone be enough for Nelson to overlook Mai Lyn's access? "He'll narrow it to people in this area. Correlate with possible sightings of me. Then with people who've crossed paths with those possible matches. Like you guys, outside. The drone? Damn, damn, poop and damn! He'll send a drone to check."

They all looked at her like they thought she was mad. But Leeth was certain. She could sense the seconds trickling away.

An idea struck. Looking around, she spotted another girl, sitting with a boy. *She'd do.*

"Come with me. If I *am* right, we'll find out one way or another real soon."

In the Ladies, Abigail Spencer frowned doubtfully. "Fifty creds, just to pretend to be you for fifteen minutes out there with your friends?"

"Yeah," Leeth replied, "my Father's over-protective, and I think a friend of his spotted me outside, and I'm not s'posed to be here."

Side by side in the mirror, Leeth compared the girl's freshly made-up face to hers, the garish patches of color as near to her own as they could manage, and nodded. "We'll need to swap clothes, too."

"Ah ha! *That's* what this scam is! No-"

"No, it's not. Keep your stupid clothes, then. Just wear mine. I'll wait inside here and trust you to return them in fifteen."

The girl wrinkled her nose. "I dunno."

"Please, Abby. Time's running out. I can add another, um, twenty three creds," she said, checking her cashstick's balance.

Sofia and Sky chimed in. "Please?"

Leeth heard the whine of a drone outside, and Mai Lyn's voice speaking clearly, reporting another privacy invasion. The outer door slammed open and Mai Lyn hurried in, eyes wide. "J- Jenny: it's like you warned us. There's a drone out there now! It's from Black Star Fashions, but it was checking out me and Jaz and Zee! It even looked like it wanted to follow me in here! I think it's been hacked!"

At the other girls' looks, Abby rolled her eyes. "Oh, all right!"

Leeth had started stripping at the first syllable. *If this works...!*

She ignored all the women and girls who'd eyed her curiously while she'd waited in the restroom, dressed only in bra and panties. Trying to stay calm while the others all exited to wander around some more stores and be checked out by the drone.

For one overly-helpful grandmother, she made up a story about her clothes being ruined when a friend spilled a whole chocolate milkshake on them, and was now getting her something to wear. But otherwise, people had just kind of looked her up and down either disapprovingly, or amused.

At the sound of six giggling girls bursting through the doors, though, she sensed the news was good.

"That was *sweet,*" gushed Abby as they all crowded in.

Sofia clapped Leeth on the back. "I swear, that drone did a double-take! You should have seen it, the instant Abbz rocked out into the food court: like a bee to honey!"

Leeth considered pointing out that bees didn't actually get attracted to honey, but the others were too excited, buzzing like bees themselves. They explained how they'd chatted together while hitting some more stores. The drone had tried to stay unobtrusive, but they all agreed it was like it couldn't believe that the girl in the camo-makeup was Abigail Turner of North Beach. The whole time, her boyfriend had watched in bemused interest, shaking his head.

When they then added that Mai Lyn had finally sent it buzzing off after capturing its suspicious behavior on her 'StalkerApp' and reporting it, Leeth wrapped the girl in a heartfelt hug, even as she wondered what 'StalkerApp' was.

Five minutes later, they shared kisses and hugs all round. With Abby's face cleaned up so she looked herself once more, and promises to get together again soon, 'Abbz' swayed out, seventy three creds richer and eager to fill her patient boyfriend in on the prank. Leeth and the others waited, then re-emerged into the food court and made their way out of the mall.

All doubts on the parts of her new acquaintances seemed gone, and Leeth tilted her head as the glass doors slid shut behind them, the sun now low on the horizon.

"I don't s'pose any of you live in Oakland? Fruitvale, even?" she asked.

CHAPTER 6

It turned out that Sky lived in Oak Tree, *and* that Mai Lyn had done a report on 'Teen Terrorism' and the 'Baker-Dunkirk Hospital Attack' for her school paper. Leeth just wanted to scout the area, to check out whatever security perimeter and monitoring the Department had set up around and even *inside* Marcie's house. But it was starting to look like her new companions had more ambitious plans.

"Why do we need drinks?" Leeth asked, as they entered the bottle shop at the train station.

Sofia rolled her eyes. "We need a plausible excuse for visiting her, right? What if someone is watching her place?"

If? thought Leeth, distracted as Sky flashed some kind of ID when the store-keeper looked down his nose and demanded "Age?"

"I didn't know you could buy alcohol when you were still in school-"

She deflected Zee's elbow as it headed for her ribs, moving in and locking the arm. But instead of attempting a follow-up blow, Zee just froze. Leeth barely pulled her counter strike, her palm an inch from Zee's face. Then found everyone stopped, mid-action, watching open-mouthed.

"Uh...."

For a second she stood unmoving, her rising blush hidden by her face-camo. Behind the counter, the man shook his head. He clicked 'sticks with Sky, who turned with the 'six pack' and frowned at Zee and her. With a start, Leeth released the girl and shrugged an apology.

She was still trying to work out a plan as they approached the T-intersection at the end of Marcie's street. She noted the parked van with smoked windows and the sign on its side saying 'Highland Pipe Services'.

Really? How obvious can they be? She shut her eyes, focused her hearing, and heard a male voice saying "Eighteen forty three, six young females on foot, entering Sharp Street and proceeding west."

"With booze," a second male voice chuckled.

But Sofia was getting an address from Mai Lyn – Marcie's. It seemed like they were determined to do more than just scout the area. Leeth shook her head. "I'm not sure this is a good idea. And how did you even get that address?

Are you a hacker too, Mai Lyn?"

The other girls nodded, but the Asian girl shook her head, blushing. "The media are like sharks. They get sloppy when they're feeding."

Leeth frowned, wondering what to say if they did just go up and knock on her door or something. It wasn't like she could talk things out with Marcie in front of all of *them*. Besides, Marcie's place was sure to be bugged, so she wouldn't be able to say who she was, or discuss anything useful even if Marcie *was* home and they somehow managed to get inside....

A tramp, stinking of something pungent, lay in ratty clothes in the gutter opposite Marcie's house. Looking remarkably fit and healthy for a bum. *Good grief – how many people do they have watching?*

At least there are no drones. But a careful scan of the trees by Marcie's front door picked out a silent rotor shape peeking through the bushes: a drone perched on a branch. She rolled her eyes. *I bet they also have fixed cameras planted all around. Maybe up and down the street, too.*

She squinted, and at the far end of the road, just as it curved and dipped out of sight, she spied another van with tinted windows parked with a good view of the Dunkirk's front door step.

Which Sofia was already stepping up onto, the others trailing behind. Before Leeth could stop them they were on the porch and ringing the bell of the big, free-standing Queen Anne style house.

Scrabbling desperately now for a plan, she heard Marcie's voice from inside. "You get that, squirt?"

Moments later, Marcie's younger sister, Amanda, was peering at Sofia and the others through the security screen door.

"Yes?"

Sofia hesitated. "Uh, does Marcie Dunkirk live here?"

Amanda frowned, and turned on the porch light so she could see them all better.

Thanks, Amanda, Leeth thought, wincing, hunching deeper into the hood of her jacket.

"Yeah. Why? Who are all you?"

Leeth's new friends just turned and stepped aside, looking at her. Sofia made a 'Well, go on,' gesture with one hand.

Leeth waved a weak little 'Hi' with just her fingers, worried Amanda might blurt something aloud if she recognized her. She whispered in Mai Lyn's ear, who nodded and answered.

"We all go to Oakland Charter High School, and I'm doing a follow-up piece on the weird girl at the hospital for the school paper. I was hoping I could interview – your sister? – for my article."

Amanda's frown deepened, and she looked first at them, and then up and down the street past them, as if searching for people hidden out of sight, or news cameras or something.

"I dunno," she said, but continued examining them. Her eyes paused on the girl with the camo-makeup, hanging back.

Leeth raised her head, risked another tiny wave then mimed the drawing of an arrow, and saw Amanda's eyes widen slightly.

From deeper inside, Marcie's voice came clearly, followed by the sound of approaching steps. Stopping behind her sister, she peered out through the security mesh door. "Who is it, El Squirto?"

Marcie. Leeth could hardly believe how *normally* her friend moved. Not the slightest sign that four weeks earlier she'd been lying with a broken spine in a hospital bed, never expected to walk again. Happy tears welled up, making it hard to see as Amanda turned to her older sister.

Leeth shook herself, waving one hand in a frantic 'Stop', hopefully hidden from any watching cameras.

Amanda tilted her head, puzzled, then made an 'Ohhh' face. She went up on tiptoes to whisper into her older sister's ears. "It's Jane!"

Marcie's eyes widened, and Leeth winced. She didn't *think* the Department had any bugs as sensitive as her ears – after all, they'd never heard her uncle's whispered commands – but had Amanda been quiet enough? Before Marcie could say anything, Leeth stepped up behind Mai Lyn, and whispered to her.

"We're from Oakland Charter High," Mai Lyn relayed, "and I was *Hoping* to interview you for the paper."

But Marcie's eyes narrowed and her expression closed in, not picking up the clue. Or ignoring it? "It'd be normal to message me first, wouldn't it, instead of just turning up on my doorstep at seven pm?" Her eyes stayed fixed on the girl in the hood. "Why didn't you call me?"

"Um, it was kind of a spur of the moment thing? We brought booze," Zee answered.

Marcie's lips stayed pursed shut while she eyed them all up and down, before her gaze locked on to the girl in disguise. "I guess you can come in for a little while. Till my Da gets home."

The others moved forward as if to go in, but Leeth grabbed Mai Lyn's sleeve and whispered again in her ear.

"Uh, we were kind of hoping to interview you in the park down the street?"

Leeth gestured 'silence,' then made walking movements with two fingers, angling her head in the direction of the park.

Behind her, Leeth heard the tramp stir, and then the *cheep* of ultrasonics – a camera focusing mechanism – and winced again. *But not all cameras use that, and Father knows I can hear ultrasonics, even if that's* all *they know. So does that mean the tramp* hasn't *been sent by the Department? Or is it a test, to see if I react to the sound?* She was beginning to feel just a *teensy* bit out of her depth. What should she do if he followed them? As he surely would.

"Marcie," Amanda said, "Da won't be happy if you go out alone. With strangers. Drinking."

It was Mai Lyn who answered. "You can call my teacher to vouch for me. I'll send you the contact."

Mai Lyn did something on her Link, then spoke a message into it. "Miss Mbeki, it's Mai Lyn. I'm talking to Marcie Dunkirk, but she wants to know if I'm really on the school paper. Yeah, Marcie Dunkirk. Will you talk to her, please?" She looked up. "You can also check she's really a teacher at the school."

Marcie looked from Mai Lyn, to the other girls, and finally at Leeth. "Okay, Squirt. Remember what Da says about strangers? Here's what we'll do: you send a snap of the crack reportage team here to Da, while I check out Miss Mbeki and the school, 'kay?" She stared a challenge at the girls standing the other side of the security screen. "I think we can pass on the drinks, though. How'd you even get them?"

Sky and Zee seemed to shrink slightly at the look the

older girl gave them all.

Marcie led the way, stomping down the darkened street, ducking under the occasional low-hanging branch of an exuberant tree. Each time, Leeth winced, hearing Marcie's teeth grind. The five schoolgirls trailed after her, with Leeth following them. And stumbling along behind them all, the fake tramp.

Leeth could hear him muttering to himself – but interspersed with carefully-enunciated whispers like 'Sky River Summers,' as his recognition software ID-ed each girl in turn.

Unaware that to Leeth's ears, he might as well have been reporting to *her*.

Ahead, Marcie suddenly stopped, her expression thunderous. Whipping something pink from her bum-bag, she stalked back toward Leeth scowling like an angel of vengeance.

Dual metal prongs and the cute logo revealed the pink *something* to be a Hello Kitty taser. Marcie brushed past her as she strode directly for the bum staggering along in their wake. Planting herself in his path, she brandished the pink taser in his face.

"Zap off, mister, before I zap *you*. I don't know who you're with, but if you want your damned scoop you're gonna have to get it from Oakland Charter's newsletter."

The man shook his head, swaying. "Dunno wha' cray non- nons-suh, nons-"

"Oh, shut *up*." At a click of her multi-function device, a beam of light blasted his left hand to reveal a tiny vid-cam nestled in loosely-clasped fingers. "Like I wouldn't notice *another* creepy guy lurking around every evening? Or the 'innocent' vans at the ends of the street? Well, piss off: you've missed your chance." She clicked off her light.

The man gaped from her to the other girls behind her, who all watched avidly.

"Yeah, ooze off, douche-wad," Zee added, "before I report you for stalking."

Mai Lyn held up her wrist, light flooding out as she caught the scene. "Creepy men still stalk Marcie Dunkirk, a month after the mass kidnapping," she dictated, tagging and uploading the video.

"Y'ah craze!" With a theatrical flap of his hands, the

man spun, staggered, and stumbled away.

"Woo hoo!" The girls swarmed Marcie, hugging her. "That was awesome. You *rank*, girl!"

"Thanks." But her expression, eyes still fixed on Leeth, stayed grim.

They all moved on, now with Marcie being quizzed about how long she'd been hassled by reporters, and asking if she'd really talk to *them*?

Once again her eyes went to 'Jane.' "Yeah. It's time some questions got proper answers."

Leeth winced. And heard a drone buzzing quietly in the air behind, following.

Oh, come on*! How am I s'posed to take* that *out without giving the game away?*

Turning left at the end of the street, they passed the second van with suspiciously blacked-out windows that Leeth had noted earlier. From inside she heard a male voice ask "Intercept?" The reply was too faint even for her hearing, but several seconds later, she heard the first voice say "Your call," in a tone that somehow held a shrug.

But what was she going to say to Marcie? What even *could* she say, with her uncle's conditioning still very much in operation? *I'll look like a complete pickle if I try to say something I shouldn't.* She chilled at the thought of what might happen if she *did* say enough for Marcie to start guessing. Remembering her uncle's *other* conditioning, that had triggered the time Emma had started putting two and two together. She curled up, inside, knowing that if she started pawing Marcie, she'd lose her friend forever.

The drone buzzed quietly along behind. The whole situation felt like it was spinning out of control.

But it still felt wonderful, seeing Marcie.

CHAPTER 7

"Yeah, Da, I'm in Josie D. Park, being interviewed by some girls from a local school for their newsletter." Marcie scanned her Link around the group, so her father could see where she was and who she was with.

She was careful to omit 'Jane.'

"You be careful, darlin'." Leeth heard the whisper of Mr Dunkirk's reply from Marcie's earbud. "I'll be home in twenty minutes. I love you: be careful."

He said 'love' so it almost rhymed with 'hoof'. It also sounded like he really did love his daughter.

Leeth blinked away tears – *again. Stop being such a baby!*

As they headed to a picnic table, the drone hovered quietly in the background, following. Below it, they crowded in together. Only Leeth tracked the movement as it buzzed quietly closer, stationing itself above the metal awning for concealment.

Mai Lyn set her Link on the table in front of Marcie, its torch function dimmed to provide an intimate light for the 'interview.' With nothing nearby, it was like their faces floated in empty space.

Leeth grimaced. Could no one else hear the drone overhead?

Apparently not: Mai Lyn asked Marcie about the hospital drama. After a long look at Leeth, she answered.

"I didn't see most of it, obviously, being paralyzed and all, but even the stuff in my room... I was kinda sedated at the time. I heard she just grabbed my neurosurgeon, Dr Ranatunga, and was like this unstoppable force, taking out eight orderlies, two nurses, and all six security guards who tried to stop her. Then she and this mage she seemed to have kidnapped, and gagged with one of those black leather red ball bondage things you see pictures of-"

Marcie shut her mouth, giving the still-silent girl an odd look.

"That was the mystery man in the wheelchair, right?" Mai Lyn prodded.

"Yeah," Marcie agreed. "*He* did some kind of psychic surgery that healed my spine, reconnecting all the right nerves."

The girls variously gasped and murmured, while Leeth heard a tiny *tap* as the drone settled onto the awning above them and shut its motor off.

For just a second, the stainless steel roof magnified the sound of the rotors as they slowed, sounding like a wasp buzzing directly over their heads, and everyone gasped.

"What's that?" Mai Lyn squeaked. Several of the others squealed, and ducked.

Leaping onto the table, Leeth grabbed the taser from Marcie's hand and jabbed it into the roof. Electricity arced, making her flinch, as a faint but encouraging *pop* sounded from directly above. Tossing Marcie's now-smoking pink device back to her, she jumped to the ground. *But had that fried the drone, or just 'stunned' it?*

She crouched, then sprang up onto the awning, where a light flashed urgently on a small quad-copter. Ripping off two rotors with intense satisfaction, she hurled it into the darkness. Long seconds of silence were followed by the faint sounds of it crashing through branches. But they wouldn't have long, now, surely? Maybe she should just ask Marcie how they could meet again?

She swallowed. She wasn't at all sure Marcie would *want* to meet her ever again.

Jumping lightly back to the ground, she dusted her hands and turned back to a circle of surprised faces.

"Day-um," Sofia drawled. "You really aren't normal, are you?"

Leeth sat back down, ignoring the question to meet Marcie's eyes.

Who stared at her, that unreadable expression back again. Leeth's heart sank.

No one spoke. Mai Lyn, Sofia and the others were all watching, leaning forward; Zee biting her thumbnail, Jaz with open mouth, and Sky looking from one to the other, eyes wide.

Finally, Marcie shook her head. "I have so many questions I don't even know where to start." Her mouth opened and closed.

And suddenly, Marcie's eyes flooded with tears. "*What the* fuck, *Jane? Just... what the* fuck*!*" She looked ready to jump up and stalk off. Her anguish struck like a knife into Leeth's belly.

About to speak, Leeth stilled at the red 'Recording' light on Mai Lyn's Link. She stabbed a finger toward it, but kept her eyes on Marcie, burning to answer.

No one moved, and Leeth turned slowly toward the

schoolgirl reporter. *If she didn't turn it off right now....*

The girl froze like a rabbit as Leeth's head tracked toward her. But when the odd-colored eyes locked on hers, Mai Lyn felt a physical shock; a sense of imminent-

Slapping her hand at her Link, she stopped the recording, slumping in relief when Leeth's attention turned back to her friend.

Only for the strange girl to fall silent, apparently lost for words. The others watched as she brought her hands up, as if to beg; then began wringing them together.

"I- okay." She was panting. "Okay. But I don't-" She shook her head. "What do you want to know?"

"*Everything!*" Marcie practically screamed. "Who are you? What were you doing? Who was Mark Dennis – *Marc Disten*? Why did he kidnap us all? Who was the *mage*? What did you do to me? They said-." She stopped. "*Why didn't you* contact *me?* Were we ever even really friends, or was that all just an act?" Tears poured down her cheeks. "Oh! These people watching me: they're not watching *me*, are they? They're waiting for *you*; watching for you! They're not reporters at all, are they? They're hunting you!"

Leeth nodded, once. Stunned by Marcie's pain, feeling it herself.

"And Marc Disten – was he after you, too? Did he capture *us* all just because he really wanted *you*?"

Leeth shook her head. "I don't know. I don't think so." At Marcie's look, she reached both hands across the table. "Truly, I don't. Not for sure. There was this Japanese girl...."

She released Marcie's fingers to put her head in her hands, rocking backward and forward as she clawed through her hair. "*I can't remember.* But I don't think he was after me, and I really, truly don't know anything about him!"

"He was a super-rich stockbroker," Mai Lyn volunteered, in a whisper. When no one shouted at her, she added, "The news reports said that four years ago in New York, he just walked off the job and then kind of disappeared."

Marcie waved her to silence. "We know all that." Her eyes locked on Leeth's. "What was he doing?"

"I don't know!"

"You don't know. He kidnaps a whole school, burns down a multi-million cred mansion, breaks my spine and disappears, and... what? *You* disappear, too. And all you can say is-"

She stopped, fists clenched, her face closing in.

Leeth swallowed. "I missed you." Suddenly, she was crying, too. "I think of you every single day. You, and Faith."

Marcie's eyes narrowed, but for some reason she also grew less stiff. "Really. Like, Faith is real."

The girls watched, mouths agape, drinking it all in.

"Faith is real, yeah. Just not, not where I said she was. And I can't go back *there*, either. Unless...?" She shook herself, then began wringing her hands again.

But Marcie's lips were still pursed, her expression grim. She shook her head. "How can I believe that? You lie about everything."

Leeth looked stricken. "I didn't lie about everything! I didn't lie about you." Her eyes flooded, blurring her friend. "Except for Faith, you're the only person... the only person in the world who cares about me. I mean, actually about *me,* not just what they can get from me, or what I can do for them." She shook her eyes clear.

"I cared about Jane, yeah. But you? I don't even know who you are. Jane isn't even your real name, is it?"

Leeth opened her mouth.

Then just shook her head, once.

"So, who are you?"

Leeth froze. "That's... secret."

Marcie's expression soured. "Really. Your name is secret. Like, you have a secret identity?"

Leeth, eyes wide, nodded, silently begging Marcie to understand.

"A secret identity."

Leeth nodded again, fractionally.

"Like a secret agent?" Marcie folded her arms and sat back. Her expression setting in sour lines, she looked away.

Leeth felt like a deer in headlights. *This was all going horribly wrong!* And now the gray confusion was swamping her thoughts. The Doctor's protocols. 'You cannot communicate any information about the Department or its members to anyone outside it.'

She blinked. What had Marcie just asked? *No. Don't think about that: the grayness is there.*

"And what about us?" Marcie asked, sadly. "We weren't ever really friends, were we?"

Leeth gaped at her in shock, her mouth working, tears instantly flooding her eyes, her nose somehow running. "How can you even ask that? Yes! *Yes!* Do you have *any* idea what I gave up to-"

She blinked, teetering on the edge of revealing information she saw would be dangerous to share.

"I ran away. I think they're trying to capture me: take me back. I wanted them to Heal you but they refused, so I ran away to make that happen. But I'm not going back! My-"

A vast wave of gray loomed over her, poised to wash all thought away.

But with Marcie's eyes locked on hers, she fought it. "My uncle... makes...."

The wave crashed down, drowning her, and she was swept away, only Marcie's eyes holding a thread. Still she struggled, no longer remembering what she struggled toward.

Marcie reached out, gently taking her hand. "He makes what? What does he do?"

Leeth felt her uncle's *other* programming stir, and, lost and unable to think, abandoned the battle. The tendrils of confusion retreated, and her mind restarted. All of them now stared at her.

Flushing, she felt the controls vanish. "I'm living in the Dumps," she offered, grabbing for a distraction. Trying not to pant in relief at the girls' reaction.

"The Hunters Point *Dumps?*" Marcie asked, her mouth gaping open. "*Alone?*"

She hadn't expected *that* much surprise. "What? It's nice. The people are interesting." She shrugged, calmer now. "But I need your advice about something important, and I do miss you, so even though I knew they'd be way-way- *waiting-*"

She stopped, her thoughts fuzzing out again.

"Aagh!" She slammed both fists into the table, cracking the wood. And everyone, Marcie included, jerked back, shocked. Maybe even scared. *Oh, nice work, Leeth.*

From the edge of the park, a flashlight swung across

the grass toward them. "Marcie?"

"Here, Da," she called.

Leeth shook her head. "I have to go." She jumped to her feet.

"Wait!" Marcie demanded.

"Baby!" But behind Marcie's Father's footsteps, Leeth heard two sets of heavier treads approaching, quietly. Wanting to smack herself in the head, needing to run, *now*, she paused when Marcie grabbed her hands.

"How can we talk, next?" Marcie demanded.

Leeth felt her face fall. Even coming here tonight had probably been a stupid risk.

Marcie must have read the hopelessness in her eyes. She frowned, her father now visible in the gloom, then her eyes lit up. "I've got a new telescope-" At Leeth's expression, she shook her head. "I can see right into the Candlestick, um, Tower? At the south edge of the Dumps?"

Strangely, Marcie's mouth slammed shut as if regretting her own words, and her expression twisted: kind of horrified, or desperate. But time was running out: Marcie's dad was almost here. Leeth pulled her hands free.

"Get a 'scope," Marcie blurted. "We'll write: *big.*"

There was no more time. Leeth turned away, just as Marcie's Da arrived. The heavier footsteps had separated, one flanking her on her left, the other on her right.

Hunching her shoulders, Leeth moved quickly toward the trees. The heavier steps started running.

She sprinted, dodging and weaving. To both sides, she heard the ultrasonics of augmented muscles. From the way they were following, both could see in the dark, too. And further back, she heard a motorbike roaring.

Ahead, she could see a large tree. *That'll do.*

Once past, a six foot leap took her to the bottom branch. Stabbing both hands into the trunk, she clawed up to the branch above, then crouched, waiting. Below, rounding the tree from from the left and right, each pursuer skidded to a halt. She leaped, kicking out *hard*, knocking both down. Following the first to the ground, she hammered his head again, then rolled to the second, punching straight into his face while he was still bringing his gun to bear.

From behind, she heard the whine of an electric engine,

but closer, a bike. Too close for her to run.

She stopped and turned back, facing the first new threat. The bike skidded to a halt just short of her, Preacher vaulting from it to land lightly, grinning nastily.

She felt her own lips curl up in a delighted smile. "Did you come *alone?*" she asked, pretending not to hear or see the approaching vehicle. It worked, since his expression darkened further.

"Still think this is a game, Leeth?" he shook his head, one leather-gloved hand going to his back pocket and drawing out something like a large scarf.

He'd positioned himself out of her reach, and behind him, the van bounced to a stop, its doors opening. Ignoring Preacher, she sprinted past him, diving feet first in a flying kick and slamming the passenger door into the emerging black-clad male. She heard something break, but took an extra second to slam his head into the metal side pillar. On the other side, she heard the driver exit.

Grasping the roof rail she flung herself up, pivoting over the van, just missing the stocky Asian woman who wove fluidly aside as she landed. The woman clapped silver-gloved hands together, electricity arcing between them.

Dark eyes smiled, and she beckoned Leeth closer.

Leeth obliged.

The woman was trained, and moved well. One hand struck high, the other low. Leeth blocked, forearm to forearm to avoid the sparking gloves. They pivoted, turning, trading blows, establishing a rhythm. Behind her, Leeth heard the ultrasonics of Preacher's augmented musculature as he moved closer, now in full combat mode.

The woman had grown cautious, protecting her center, her head; leaving no openings.

Leeth made one.

Striking fast, straight into her throat, the back of the woman's powerful arm hammered sideways to deflect the blow – and Leeth, expecting that, threw all her strength into countering the force, her arm a rigid bar.

The woman's eyes widened in shock as the blow connected. Gagging, clutching her windpipe, she crumpled.

Leeth flung herself sideways, over the front of the van and out of Preacher's reach, just in time to club the semi-stunned passenger back to the ground as he hauled himself to his feet, a gun in his left hand.

She stalked around the front to face Preacher, dusting her hands. "You should've brought more."

But Preacher's pleased sneer only widened, as did his arms, now spreading a thin... netting...? between them. She had no idea what it was, only that it *wasn't* a distraction: Preacher looked too relaxed.

She circled him, and he turned, keeping his arms wide, leaving himself open, just the fine netting between them.

Intuition warned her not to touch it.

"Did I interrupt an important butterfly hunt, Preacher? You've been promoted?"

His smile only hardened. Seeing him tense, she flung herself backwards, spinning around and then sprinting away, back to the trees. She heard him curse.

With his footsteps pounding behind her, she swiped up at a low branch. Slicing it cleanly, she caught it as it fell and swung back around. Meeting Preacher's charge, she thrust it straight into the netting still held out before him. The branch jerked his arms up, the netting touched his face – and he spasmed, arms and legs thrown out, mouth and eyes opening wide before he collapsed.

She kicked him in the side of the head, hard, but careful to avoid the net. *Just making sure, Preacher.*

Sirens, now, approaching. She spared a quick glance for the woman on her knees, now hunched over and clutching her throat in wheezing breaths. Turning back to Preacher, she looked down at him as he lay stunned, and placed herself to meet his eyes staring up whitely in the darkness.

"That was fun, P! We should play more often. See ya!"

-

Graham Dunkirk, his daughter Marcie, and the younger girls seated at the picnic table had stared as two large, armed men pounded past on either side, pursuing the fleeing girl into the darkness.

Mai Lyn, her arm stretched out, had her Link recording as best she could.

Ears straining, they all listened, staring at one another wide-eyed as sounds like a club striking padded bodies came from the darkness. Only to almost be run down when a brutish, low-hung bike leaped the curb heading straight at them. Hunched low, its scowling leather clad rider stared past them into the trees. Followed, moments later, by the 'Highland Pipe Services Van'.

They heard both vehicles stop. Van doors opening; more cries; the sounds of meaty violence. Someone struggling to breathe. *More* club-like impacts.

Finally, a girl's voice, taunting. Then silence.

"Marcie, take these girls back to the house. I'm thinkin' someone maybe needs help."

Wailing sirens drew closer.

Marcie wrung her hands. "Da, maybe... maybe I should go with you?"

Graham Dunkirk pinned his daughter with a hard stare. "That were Jane bloody Baker, weren't it, M? Sure, and who do *you* think's left standing, daughter?"

CHAPTER 8

Harmon strode down the long corridor, ignoring the pastoral scenes of the Sonoma valley.

Thinking instead of Leeth.

He hid a smile. She continued to surprise: evading Nelson's nerve disruptor, even turning it back on Preacher himself. No doubt the agent would hold that against her, if she returned. Mother would be furious, especially with only six days of her time limit remaining. After that....

After that it would be time to end the game. He had thought it might be possible to cement Leeth's departure and engineer his own. But weeks had passed, and the Department remained impervious to every suggestion to cut their losses. *Why was Leeth so important to them?* Something lay behind that.

So. Leeth would be recaptured, and he would remain here, too. Stuck. At least the Department remained supportive of his research. Not for the first time, he wondered how much Eagle guessed.

Sources of stress.

Considering the man's desire to have an eighteen-year-old girl trained as his assassin, Eagle's ignorance was probably mere pretense: a way to keep his hands clean.

But surely, he did not guess the *details* of her treatment? Harmon flinched, shying away from his own memories.

But if Leeth is to Unfold further, to reach her full potential, she needs stress. And she is so very hard to stress. And harder to contain. So I need to be 'the bad guy.'

All well and good, Alex, a small voice replied. *But did you need to take such pleasure from it?* He grimaced. She had made him fall – *again*.

Once again, I let her undermine my detachment. I need to pull back.

Ahead, the door recognized him and whisked open. Inside, Eagle nodded, and indicated a seat. Harmon wondered for a moment at Mother's absence from the debriefing, then understood she and Eagle were in virtual conference.

Confirming his guess, Eagle spoke aloud as the door closed. "The Doctor is here, Mother, so you may address your remarks to him directly."

A hologram of Mother, seated at her own desk, winked in beside Harmon, glaring. "We now have an agent with nerve damage. I assume you can treat him?"

Harmon spread his hands. "Done."

Mother's eyes narrowed. "A pity your magical abilities fall so strangely short when called on to *locate* our target."

"Magic cannot pass through even formerly living things, Mother. You do recall that on the one occasion I located her lair, I was able to sense that she sleeps on soil, screened by potted plants?"

"Well, that explains it – she has *pot plants* and *dirt!*" Mother spat. "You located her once – why can't you do so again?"

"I did not 'walk' to her location, Mother. Astral travel is more akin to teleportation: I had no path I could retrace."

Mother ground her teeth. "And when she's not sleeping?"

"As I continue to tell you, many parts of the Dumps look alike, so Clairvoyance scarcely helps – unless you can find a willing mage who is local to the area. And as for astral observation, that is both ill-advised, with Leeth, and the... *sensory data* far harder to match to physical reality."

"If by 'ill-advised' you mean you're too frightened-"

"Mother," Eagle interrupted. "My time is valuable. Review the strategic applications of the Doctor's capabilities on your own time. Unless you have a formal complaint to make? Or are you asking me to take over the planning of Leeth's recovery?"

Mother bristled.

"Very well. So what did we learn tonight? Apart from validating Father's prediction of the inherent difficulties in wielding Nelson's neural disruptor?"

Harmon answered. "It means she has finished making herself 'safe' – in her view – and has entered a more proactive phase."

"And therefore?"

"Running and hiding is not for her. At heart she is a huntress."

"Are you suggesting she may start 'hunting' the Department?" Eagle asked.

Harmon paused. "You know I have conditioned her against killing any of us, or even speaking of the Department to anyone except its members. But within those constraints, pushed into a corner? She may surprise us."

"Yes," Eagle murmured, "that does seem a habit."

But as Harmon reasserted his prediction that Leeth still wanted to contact her friend Marcie, hunt 'wrong-do-ers' like The Breaker, and attend the upcoming FistFest, he saw Eagle's attention drift. *Not interested? No*, he decided: *merely that he needed no reminding*. Eagle's attention sharpened as Mother in turn outlined her planned actions; and the meeting wound up.

When Mother winked out, he turned to Harmon, his expression changing. "Shall we discuss what will happen after Mother's four week time limit has expired?"

Harmon schooled his own expression. "Are you implying I am using less than my best efforts to recover Leeth? Let me assure you, use other mages if you wish-"

"Let me re-frame the situation, Doctor. If I offer you the same deal I gave Mother – full control of Leeth if you can return her – how long will you need?"

"I assure you, Eagle, I am using every magical means available to me, to my best ability, to locate Leeth."

"Very well, Doctor, I see I must be blunt. If recovering Leeth becomes *necessary* – no questions asked, no limits – can you bring her to heel?"

Harmon stared into the hazel eyes now burning into his. Sliding his senses to the Imaginal, he confirmed that the offer was no trap. And nodded.

"Then I am content to let the game continue. But don't disappoint me, Doctor."

Eagle rose, and left the meeting room.

CHAPTER 9

On a screen in Teef's shop-shack-home late that night, Leeth called up Earthview, carefully locating Marcie's house, setting it as her POV. From there, she panned the view to see what parts of the Dumps were visible from the upstairs bedroom window.

She sat back. *Well, that'd been easy!* The helpful floating text had even answered her *next* question. She'd been wondering whether it'd be safer to do a net search for Candlestick Tower, or just ask Teef if he knew where it was. But the annotation that appeared as her eyes tracked to the dangerously-leaning structure in the south west had made that unnecessary.

She gestured the displayed map flat, then held one finger over Marcie's house and another over the leaning tower. Ten point three kilometers, the display said.

She noted the compass direction from there to Marcie's house, then jumped around to a few other locations. Not that Teef would snoop, probably, but 'always erase or muddy your digital trail,' Nelson had taught her.

"Yo, Teef: how big a telescope would I need to, um, see something small, ten klicks away?"

The ogre leered at her. "Heh. I c'n give ya show. Don' need 'scope to peep in winduhs."

She sashayed between stacks of old phasion cells, solar tubes, surveillance gear, comp modules, shovels, and distillers. "I'm more a doer than a watcher, Teef." She enjoyed teasing the big male.

His rough lips curled up around his exposed canines as he licked across them with his large tongue. "Happy to let ya prove it ta me, Flit."

They bantered for a while, before Leeth clicked cashsticks with him to pay for the net use, then got serious. "No, really. Could you get me a telescope?"

"How much mag?"

"Magnification? Um... a lot? A hundred times? Would that be enough?"

"Depends. See what?"

She didn't want to describe exactly what she wanted – just in case someone gossiped to someone.

When she didn't answer, he spread his large hands, shaking his head. "Okay, don' say." He shrugged. "If you eyes c'n see so'thing at hunnerd meters, c'n see it ten K wit' hunnerd mag. Unnerstan? You do 'speriment."

"And you can get me a telescope? How much would it cost?"

Teef leered. "More'n all those drones ya brung us. But no one here got one: havta get some'n to goan-get. Ya should just goan city 'n bite ya'sel."

Even knowing that 'bite' was 'buy it,' she giggled at the idea he'd just told her to bite herself. But really, he was angling to find out more about why she didn't like 'goan' into the city. "Nah, guys in the city are just too grabby, you know? I like my lifestyle here much better." She put down the angle grinder she'd been toying with. "Do you have a whiteboard and marker pens?"

She'd do her 'experiment' tomorrow. Would Marcie expect her to have a telescope by the next night? "Oh, and maybe a little stick-on light, too?"

Teef looked at her, grinned, then started heaving boxes out of the way, burrowing back into his three dimensional filing system.

She first called in at her nest to check that nothing had been disturbed. Gulping down some stew, she checked her perimeter. After that, she headed out, the whiteboard tied to her back. She kept to the upper terraces where fewer people ventured as she made her way south.

Wondering why Marcie had looked *scared*.

The ground twisted in crazy folds, jumbled, looking somehow still tortured. At the water's edge she gazed to her right, trying to see how far this waterway speared into the city from South Basin. Farther than she could see, in the dark. *I could just swim across: it's only fifty meters wide.*

It was close to midnight now: would Marcie even still be awake? *And it's not like I actually have a telescope yet.*

The smell of muddy, marshy land was strong as she stood, recalling the map from the net. There hadn't been any bridges.

Her shoulders rose and fell. A quick fifty meter swim through cold water, or a long, long walk?

Rolling her eyes, she started stripping, then wrapped her meager equipment in her clothes. Piling the bundle onto the small whiteboard, she slid and slipped into the cold. Holding the board one-handed above the small waves, she side-stroked to the other slimy bank.

Some exploring was fun; some less so.

Twenty minutes later she gazed around at the desolate, scrunched-up grounds, all the colors of ash in the gloom. No trees; here, even the kudzu vines struggled, looking thin and withered; just an occasional sickly runner instead of the usual thick green mat in the areas they'd invaded. A sliver of moon gave plenty of light for her to see by. She stood on the ridge of one of the kilometers-long folds in the land, studying the landscape.

It was really, really quiet here. Strangely so.

There was also a strong tidal smell of salt, and mud. A few hardy plants clung to life. Nothing moved. In the distance, to her left, waves lapped at sodden soil. Ahead, a few hundred meters away, Candlestick Tower angled drunkenly up from the ground.

Her skin prickled as she studied the building, her nose twitching.

It was an odd design. Only about seven stories tall, maybe fifty meters wide, and on this side, just three columns of windows stretching vertically up the otherwise blank walls. As she moved closer, she could make out large cracks and gaps zig-zagging up the walls. All the windows were broken.

Something about it felt wrong. There was an unpleasant smell in the air, too, that made her want to leave. It smelled... unhealthy. Almost rotten. But only faintly.

She got out her PowerShot, loading the cup – with a ball-bearing, not just a stone – and crept closer.

The hairs on the back of her neck were standing up. No light at all from the building, no movement, no sound. She circled round, looking for a ground floor entrance.

CHAPTER 10

"I still fail to believe, Doctor," Mother said, "that you cannot locate your ward, considering your abilities and your thorough understanding of her."

Mother's thoughts were difficult to read, and not just due to her tight mental controls. She had frighteningly extensive cerebral implants: Harmon suspected much of her thinking happened in the cybernetic portions of her brain, beyond the reach of any magic.

And, as usual, their meeting was devolving into an interrogation session. He suppressed a sigh.

"How can so many of your 'Sendings' fail to work, Doctor?"

Harmon shrugged, but took care to look Mother directly in the eye. "Emotionally disturbed states can alter auras sufficiently to prevent the spell 'locking on.' She sleeps surrounded by organic matter. She may travel through wooden-lined corridors, or underground; or underwater. Though since Leeth has no gills, we can probably rule that out."

Mother didn't smile. "Even when your Sendings do work, your descriptions of her physical surroundings are rarely useful."

He tapped the esheet on the pristine desk between them, knowing his preference for the physical media annoyed her. "There are no street signs in the Dumps, Mother. And at night it's pointless, as I cannot see in the dark." He tapped the report again. "She also moves around a great deal." Tap-tap. "Frequently underground, I surmise. And *no* magic can penetrate 'living earth'."

Mother's lips pursed. "The tunnels themselves are not full of *living earth*. Why don't you follow her?"

This *again?* "Yes, unlike a spell, I don't need to take the shortest path, so I *could* follow her – if I wished to risk having her cage me in a simple physical enclosure, locking me out of my body. I would die within hours." *Or minutes, if Leeth were present, too.* He shuddered at the thought. "I fully expect Leeth will have prepared several traps exactly like that. You do recall the Department had me instruct her on magical surveillance?"

Tap-tap. "And the frequency with which you insist I attempt to locate her... we are merely training her at avoiding scrying and astral tracking."

"Really, Doctor? You yourself admit she is no mage.

Yet now you claim she can sense astral presences, even spells?" Mother rolled her eyes.

"When I approach close enough to 'see' her, her aura shifts and she begins *hunting*." And Leeth, he suspected, was very, very dangerous to any astral body.

"How very frightening for you: and you in spirit form, able to move only at the speed of thought."

That decided him: a demonstration of Leeth's capabilities would serve a double purpose. *So.* "I assure you, another mage would do no better."

Harmon *saw* Mother take the bait.

The verbal sparring continued. But all the while, he knew that *he* was the key obstacle to Leeth's return. Ironically, though, his control over her also provided the simplest solution to their problem.

And now, despite the necessity to conceal that secret, he had found a plausible way to use it. With the right timing, it would even return her *after* Mother's deadline had expired. He concealed his smile.

"But to return to the point of our meeting, Mother, I believe I can make *her* come to *us*." *Provided I meet with her, of course, to 'explain it'.* "Leeth has larger dreams than eating rats and brawling with petty criminals in a worthless no man's land. If we offer her an important mission, a 'heroic' mission to save many lives, it will motivate her to return. And a recent event offers a suitable target." He sat forward. "I propose having Leeth assassinate Shepherd Fox of the Brethren of the End of Days."

Mother went utterly still; and Harmon watched, astonished, as her thoughts vanished, one by one, until her mind was empty. *What on Earth...?*

"Why did you pick that target, Doctor?"

She must be thinking entirely with the electronic parts of her brain! He shook himself. "A charismatic lunatic abducting people, converting his victims into survivalist followers of his fantasy that Judgment Day is nigh? It reeks of magical influence. Not to mention the Brethren's treatment of women. Leeth would be ideally suited to getting in, killing him, and evading pursuit until we extracted her. My analysis of the social dynamics of the group indicates it would fall apart within a month without Fox. Perhaps weeks."

For a long time Mother didn't move; just sat, watching

him, thinking cybernetic thoughts while her will clamped down on her fore-brain.

"Is there something about the Brethren you should perhaps tell me, Mother?" he prodded.

"Yes, Doctor. There is. But not unless, and until, Leeth deals successfully with the Fox Situation. It will be safer for all concerned, that way. How did you research the topic?"

Harmon frowned, while noting how her mind still remained clamped in its disciplined lock-down. "Just the news media. Did you know his followers kidnapped an entire orphanage in Bannock County, Idaho recently? I imagine that would resonate strongly with Leeth."

Mother looked cautiously approving. "Good," she nodded, "that is safe enough. You need to discuss the matter with Eagle: I have informed him you are on your way."

Harmon blinked. "Now?"

"Yes. And Doctor: be very, very careful. In this area, the Department *itself* walks on thin ice. Eagle will tell you what you need to know."

Mother's thoughts remained opaque as he rose and let himself out of her office. Yet he felt sure she was unaware of his mental probe. Who, then, had she been shielding her thoughts against?

He wondered what he might be getting Leeth into.

CHAPTER 11

Inside Candlestick Tower, the smell was worse, and the building stranger. For a full minute she looked around, not moving. Just listening. Hearing the wind sighing around it.

The ground floor had once boasted an impressively open area, with polished floor. Decades later, the illusion of wealth was as shattered as the marble veneer piled in the lower edge of the sloping floor. The whole building leaned toward the Bay.

The entry area, especially in the ghostly light of the moon, seemed more like the set of a horror film. The large arc of a once-impressive reception desk now swelled like a cancerous growth. Water had exposed the wood as cheap particleboard, at some point invaded by fungus and now dried out into a repellent mass that looked somehow infectious.

Corroded brass lettering a foot tall set in the wall above it spelled out 'Welcome to Your New Paradise.'

She shuddered as a stronger whiff of the unpleasant stink rose and fell. It was impossible to move silently over the crumbling and crackling rubble.

Of course the lifts weren't working.

Perhaps the creepiest thing of all, though, was that nothing had been scavenged.

A sweep of tilted stairs led up to a sagging, curved inner balcony that followed the circular walls. She ascended gingerly.

At least the stairs didn't creak, though the shattered marble veneer made for uncertain footing.

The longer she was here, the less she wanted to explore. *Don't be stupid*, she scolded herself. *I'm not in a horror film!*

She circled the wide balcony, noting the small lift, and a weird number of corridors angling off from it – she counted twenty. Against her better judgment, she headed down a random one, the feeling of wrongness intensifying. Each corridor was lined with *handles,* on panels about a meter square, and each panel had a corroded brass plaque, with a name and a code under it. She read, 'Patterson, A. D., F, H2372'; 'Vasquez, S., M, H2374'; 'Jeffers, J. B., M, H2376.'

Each handle was stainless steel.

And no one had scavenged any of them.

She swallowed, her throat dry, all the nerves in her fingers tingling, as she carefully tucked her PowerShot into the band of her shorts and gripped the handle for 'Jeffers'; then tugged.

An inhuman groaning made her skin prickle, before she recognized the sound as metal grating on metal, and the... drawer slid open.

Inside....

Her head tilted to one side: inside was a kind of human-shaped molding – space for arms, legs, torso, head – and a whole bunch of crumbling plastic, with corroded wires threaded through it, as well as all kinds of tubing.

She slid it shut, having to shove hard, her feet braced, as metal groaned and wailed again, resisting. Even then, she couldn't close it all the way.

Frowning, she stepped to the right, gripped the handle of 'Davies, M. E., F, H2378,' and started tugging. But as the seal broke, gas puffed out, enveloping her in a cloud of stomach-heaving rottenness, like nothing she'd ever smelled before. Something dead, she instinctively knew.

Involuntarily, she took a step back, trying to purge the air she'd just breathed in; trying to control her stomach.

It smelled like something Faith had buried, and dug up long after.

Wincing, turning her head away, she darted forward to it and forced the pallet closed as hard as she could, seeing the dark shape it contained, shift. Looking up, eyeing the handles above, and all the handles to left and right, she backed out of the corridor.

Trying to guess the number of dead people who might be resting in here.

Suddenly understanding the weird look of horror on Marcie's face. But it *was* the only tall building for miles.

Back at the circular balcony, in the 'clear' air and with the moonlight splashing through the shattered glass doors below, she considered leaving. Clenching her jaw, she circled around to find the fire stairs instead.

Climbing up, and around, and up, and around, she very carefully didn't do sums. Didn't count rows; didn't guess numbers of handles along corridors; didn't multiply that large number by twenty corridors; didn't think what seven stories tall meant.

She just climbed, in the extraordinarily cheerful glow of her three-LED lamp. Up and around the wonderfully ordinary cement stairwell, with its dust-rich non-slip treads and plain brown painted metal handrail.

At the top, hoping it would open onto the roof, and clear air, she twisted the handle down, metal grating on metal, and wrestled the heavy door open. Circling left and right, a dark passageway, while a corridor of stainless steel handles branched off before her.

A gentle wind blew the scent of death toward her, stirring eddies of dust on the stairs. Still trying not to think about how many rotting bodies surrounded her, she turned off her torch and stepped out. She'd be able to see well enough without it, and shook her head at the thought of people seeing a light moving inside the mausoleum. She eased the door closed behind her.

But she had to test she could open it again, before she could bring herself to step away.

Coward, she berated herself. *They're just dead bodies. Not zombies or something.* She licked dry lips, wondering if there was a way up onto the roof. Then realized it'd be better, assuming she understood Marcie's plan, to set up her whiteboard at the end of a corridor. But which one faced Marcie's house?

With a strange prickling feeling running up her spine, she pulled out her new compass. Keeping close to the central wall with the fire stairs and lift, she followed the sloping inner corridor around the tilted building, checking the shivering compass needle at each radiating branch.

When she found the hallway facing the distant lights of Oakland, her spirits lifted. From there, she'd be able to see Marcie. And Marcie would be able to see her.

But for some reason it felt worst of all creeping down the sloping corridor. Like she might slip and fall, sliding down to plummet out the broken floor-to-ceiling window at the end. She found herself digging her toes into rotted carpet, reluctant to grab any of the helpful shiny handles crowding both corridor walls.

She was breathing hard – panting, but unable to stop herself, despite the awful, penetrating smell leaching from the drawers.

The first *one I opened was empty. Maybe lots of them*

are empty? Maybe I just happened to open the only one that wasn't. But her nose rejected the lie.

Not normally scared of heights, for some reason she couldn't quite bring herself to go right to the edge of the building and poke her head through the emptiness of the window-space.

It's just because the rain, and weather, and mold, might've made the carpet slippery, so I'd shoot out into space. Besides, if I set up the whiteboard back here, with the light shining on it, only Marcie will be able to see it.

Only, of course, she didn't know exactly which house was Marcie's, from here. Or exactly how far into the corridor Marcie could see. Not without a telescope, and probably hours of looking.

Why couldn't they have built some other *tall buildings here? What* is *this awful place, anyway?*

In the end, she just wrote 'Hope' on the whiteboard in the biggest black letters she could, and stuck the lamp to it so it shone down on the writing. Then started cursing when she realized she had no way to prop it up so a strong wind wouldn't just blow it straight out the window.

Fists clenching, she looked around for anything to tie it in place. Maybe downstairs? Would they have string, or tape, somewhere? But if this place had ended when the Big One struck, in '44, it'd be as old as she was.

She felt like screaming aloud, or smashing something. Then rolled her eyes to the heavens, there in the moldy, rotting corridor, and saw the answer.

Ten minutes later, filthy with greasy dust, her hair matted and filthy, she tightened the last twist of copper wiring around the whiteboard. Then stared out across the dark waters to the twinkling lights of Fruitvale, Oakland. One of those was Marcie's bedroom window. She might even be watching, right now, through her telescope.

The thought brought a welcome, if wry smile to her lips, and she waved, just in case, before heading back to the inner stairs.

Outside, the air smelled so sweet and pure she had to stop and fill her lungs.

A cloud drifted across the slender moon, and the night seemed to grow colder. Her shoulders prickled, the sensation of being watched very strong all of a sudden. She slowly turned, confronting the ominous tower looming behind her, half expecting to see desiccated figures crawling down the walls toward her... but there was nothing.

She found herself turning slowly back around, facing Oakland again, and the shimmering trails of light it dusted toward her across the dark waters of the Bay.

Shaking herself, she pushed the feeling down. *I'm just getting tired. I need to sleep.* Actually, even if it was a little later than that, a midnight run was probably exactly what she needed to blow the spooky cobwebs from her mind.

Shaking her arms and legs, she set off at a fast run, over the undulating troughs of the desolate and abandoned flats.

-

Through the telescope, Marc Disten tracked the distant shadow, dimly illuminated for several seconds every few minutes, as it sped across the night lands. Certain it was Jane Baker, the source of The Call, as he flexed almost-healed arms, and fully-healed fingers.

Wondering what the code 'Hope' meant, and who it was intended for.

CHAPTER 12

The walk to Eagle's office proved an unsettling experience, retracing for the first time the path through empty concrete passages as he climbed the institutional stairwells back toward the surface. *Apparently I'm now trusted enough to be allowed up to sub-basement five*, he thought, sourly. It seemed a much greater distance today, 'escorted' this time merely by guidance arrows projected on the walls, rather than the threatening squad of weaponized arthrobots that had escorted him and Leeth below that first time.

Alone, too. No Leeth, jogging beside him as she studied the anti-spell bindings.

The door to the buried office whisked into the wall, and he blinked as he stepped out into a sleek and sterile space apparently perched atop a sunny, snowy mountain peak, blue sky above.

"Come in, Doctor. You had a productive meeting with Mother." The *finally* was left unsaid.

Eagle was seated, turned toward him, but Harmon frowned as he entered, noting an old man. Wisps of white hair clung to a bare and liver-spotted scalp, the man's spine curled in a wheelchair before Eagle's alabaster desk.

A strange sensation shot through him as the man's intense green eyes met his. As if the world had subtly shifted, or time had missed a beat. While the man gazed into his soul, studying him.

The bald head turned to Eagle. "Yes. It's as we thought." The old man's voice, unlike his frail body, was firm and sure.

Harmon felt a premonition of doom.

"And...?" Eagle looked from his visitor, to Harmon, then back to his visitor.

"We should feel pleased." He glanced at Harmon. "Next time, show me them both. Together. But let's discuss it later, at the club. There are still threads we haven't traced."

"Take a seat, Doctor."

At Eagle's gesture, Harmon realized he still stood, frozen to the spot, just inside the office's inner door. This time, as he circled the desk, he noted its solidity. He had the sudden impression the unit was not so much a piece of furniture as some kind of densely-packed machine. Still frowning, he sat, one eye on the elderly visitor.

As soon as he did, the man backed up his wheelchair a short distance, fumbling at a side pocket to slide out a short tube of amber. Fingers shaking, he twisted it, telescoping it out into a one meter rod.

It was only then that Harmon registered the man's aura was that of a mage. Strangely, he found it hard to judge anything further: on the Imaginal, the patterns were unlike anything he'd seen before – a certainty of self that rivaled Leeth's, or the Dragon Lord of China's; the fluidity normally seen only in children; and a subtlety that reminded him uncomfortably of Godsson.

"How long can you shield us?" Eagle asked, nodding toward Harmon as a narrow strip of smooth white flooring irised open, encircling his desk and revealing a gleaming umber-gold metallic band. A concealed ritual circle.

"I'm not sure. A few minutes, at least." The man backed his chair further away, waiting.

"Very well." Eagle turned to Harmon. "Your plan to motivate Leeth to return to us?" he prompted.

Harmon eyed the stranger, considered asking if he had clearance – then realized he'd look foolish, asking that of Eagle.

Setting aside all the confusing mummery, he considered Eagle's question. "You don't approve?"

"On the contrary: I think your idea is excellent." Eagle watched him with a curious intensity. "Do you have any reservations?"

"Leeth will relish the challenge, if properly presented. The mission would have to be well planned, of course. There would be an element of danger."

"Really?"

"I see no call for sarcasm, Eagle. I am fully aware we would be sending Leeth to assassinate the leader of a paranoid cult which abducts and perhaps magically brainwashes people into joining them. I suspect something odd is going on – perhaps magic, perhaps new technology – given both the speed of the conversions and the low recidivism rate."

Eagle leaned forward, elbows on his desk, and linked his fingers. He looked pleased. Harmon's eyes drifted to the curved glass vase with its twist of aquamarine, holding pale orchids on graceful green stems, and shuddered at the memory of his previous visit. Once again with the feeling he had stepped out of his depth.

Eagle smiled, and Harmon winced. *Still monitoring his visitors' emotional states, of course.*

"My assessment matches your own. I also feel Leeth may be ideally suited to tackling the mission you propose. A suitable test before we risk her on the real threat, behind Fox. The operation will require care in planning, swift action, and a solid cover identity. How sure are you the mission will provide sufficient motivation for Leeth to rejoin us?"

Harmon knew *he* was the real obstacle to Leeth's return. But if he were the one who recovered her, he saw no real impediments. Unfortunately, to hide all that, he needed the pretense of some other motivation.

So he explained how the autocratic nature of the Brethren of the End of Days, their brainwashing, and in particular their recent capture of an entire orphanage, would be particularly motivating for Leeth.

He had the distinct impression that none of it was news: when he finished, Eagle simply waited.

Odd. "But Mother indicated there was something else I should know, something deeper – but not until after Leeth had dealt with Fox. She also appeared worried about how I had researched the topic. Why is that?"

Eagle nodded, pleased. "Key questions, Doctor." He looked across to his visitor. "I think now, old friend."

The end of the amber wand quivered down. The moment it touched the red-gold circle a translucent turquoise dome flooded up from it, meeting over Harmon and Eagle's heads.

Harmon gaped from the old man, clearly now expending effort to raise the odd magical circle, to Eagle, who had closed his eyes. Harmon took the opportunity to quickly cast a Mindmeld – only to have it lash back at him, jerking him back in his seat.

Eagle opened his eyes, raising one eyebrow at Harmon. "Don't distract me, Doctor. To *safely* answer your question requires mental discipline." He again shut his eyes, holding up one finger in a 'Wait' gesture.

It gave Harmon time to compose himself. Percepting carefully, this time he saw subtle signs of an active spell bound to Eagle. *A mobile spell shield?* So Eagle wore some kind of magical protection.

The green and blue dome was more interesting. The only thing he'd ever seen even vaguely like it was Godsson's golden Barrier spell.

Finally, Eagle lowered his finger and opened his eyes.

Harmon, lips pursed, waited for an explanation of the bizarre actions.

"You are aware of stories in which the naming of an evil summons that evil?" At Harmon's frowning nod he continued. "Have you heard of quantum entanglement? Good. The Department is aware of a problem, perhaps *too* aware. This 'problem' has magical means of sensing and locating people who are aware of... it. Able to sense people talking about it: even *thinking* about it, we suspect."

A cold prickle ran up Harmon's spine. He studied the turquoise Barrier when Eagle paused and closed his eyes, once more holding up a hand. When he opened his eyes again, his expression was jarringly calm. "You know the famous quote: 'if thou gaze long into an abyss, the abyss will also gaze into thee'?"

Harmon blinked; then, as the implications sank in, felt the prickle at his neck spread, his skin crawling.

Eagle inclined his head. "Shepherd Fox is... *associated* with that larger problem. Its servant. For him, that connection is a strength; for us, a trap. So in future, should you have further questions about him, it will be safer for us all if you submit them to me. I will have them answered without anyone gazing into any abysses."

"Sweet buttered hell. So... if I ask the wrong question, I might... magically connect to this 'problem'?"

"In essence, yes. Though it's not so much asking the wrong questions, as learning the *answers* to them."

Harmon stared at him, recalling Mother's thoughts *retreating* from her brain into her digital computing enhancements. "So... *not* knowing these facts provides protection?"

"Exactly. Ignorance really is bliss in this instance. The longer you, and Leeth, can be kept innocent of certain key pieces of knowledge, the better you will both be able to deal with the threat."

"How long-?"

Eagle held up a hand. "Please. I have told you exactly as much as you should know at this stage. And it is a strain to have this conversation. Let us move on to another topic.

One I find interesting that you have not raised, yourself."

At a gesture from Eagle, the Barrier fell. Harmon swiveled in his seat to see the visitor looking relieved, tired – yet alert, and now watching him very closely indeed.

Harmon wanted to consider what he'd just been told, but then realized just *thinking* about it might be dangerous in itself. *Sweet buttered hell on rye.* He took a grip on himself, feeling shaken to the core. It was like being told not to think about white rabbits.

He hoped Eagle's new topic would be sufficiently distracting. He turned away from the old man.

"This new, third kind of incorporeal spirit which Leeth and Godsson fought, and destroyed, at the Institute for Paranormal Dysfunction," Eagle said.

Harmon swallowed, feeling his skin prickle once again in goosebumps. *Yes, that should suffice,* he tried to joke to himself, feeling suddenly cut adrift from solid ground.

"We now believe Lao Pi Shen dropped David Benson – Godsson – in our hands *because* Shen knew this third kind of spirit had been magically bound to Benson, through their killing of Melisande d'Artelle, yes? Yet Benson, despite his enormous magical knowledge and power, and the Dragon Lord's magical Barriers, had barely been able to defend himself from it during *fifteen years* of 'visitations.' Nor is it clear the Dragon Lord himself could have dealt with that threat. Yes?"

"Yes." Harmon glanced at the older man, who looked as if none of this was news to him, and was instead studying him intently.

"Yet Leeth and Benson together were able to kill it."

"Yes."

"And I understand Leeth seemed able to sense it – *Her*, she called it, I gather? – and even harm it somehow, even without Godsson's aid?"

Harmon nodded.

"So Leeth may be the only sane person on the planet with some chance of dealing with what may be a new kind of magical threat."

Laid out like that, the logic was rather... appalling. And the knowledge that he had been putting the girl under extreme pressure – to induce further magical Unfolding – struck him suddenly as something awful. But had that not been crucial to the development of her unique magic? Had perhaps been the very thing that enabled Leeth to handle *Her?* "I... had not framed the events quite that way. I will need to research the question."

He thought about it. The discovery was ground-breaking. Why was it only now that he considered the implications? Was it just to avoid recognizing he had blithely exposed a child to monstrous, unknown spirits? Or because once again he'd become so obsessed with asserting his dominance he'd lost sight of the goal? He felt his face flushing.

"Fine," Eagle replied. It took Harmon seconds to remember *what* was fine. "But make it a priority – second only to recovering Leeth herself. I think you begin to grasp the full significance of the situation."

Harmon felt stunned. "Do I assume your friend will be assisting me in that research?" he asked, glancing to the side.

The man's snort of laughter took him by surprise. "Heh! Perhaps, Doctor. I look forward to hearing what you discover. Always room for more on my plate, in Eagle's view!"

The look he turned on Eagle held both anger and pleasure. Harmon set that aside to consider this new dimension to their immediate problem. "Mother is not entirely enthusiastic about Leeth's return. I shall inform her of Leeth's potential importance, and the events at the Institute: it will improve her attitude to Leeth."

"No."

Harmon sat up, doubting what he'd just heard.

"You *want* Mother to be unsupportive of-"

"No, Doctor. I would be very happy for Mother to change her views of Leeth."

"Then why-" Harmon stared at Eagle, the hazel eyes under those salt and pepper eyebrows watching him, waiting.... "You don't trust Mother." He closed his eyes, massaged the bridge of his nose, and opened them again, to see Eagle once again looking pleased.

A glance at the stranger showed him nodding with the same pleasure.

"But why haven't you been more involved, then, in planning how to motivate Leeth... ah. Because you believe Mother will feel more agency in Leeth's return if she is responsible for it? As well as giving Leeth a chance to earn

Mother's respect, the longer she evades recapture? Perhaps, also, a test of Mother? Or a lesson. As well as a test for Leeth."

"We should talk more often, Doctor. It's pleasant not to have to spell things out."

Which made Harmon wonder: were there *other* reasons, too, or had that comment just been a piece of psychological manipulation to make him think there *might* be more? *Damn the man.*

Eagle smiled.

"You do know Mother is unhappy with my attempts to locate Leeth magically? She feels I am not giving it my best efforts."

"Then you need to convince her that you are, Doctor, don't you?"

Their visitor chuckled. "I see you have things well in hand, Eagle. Chair: take me to the car. Dr Harmon. Good to see you looking so well."

The wheelchair spun on the spot, the outer door whisking aside for it as it left the office.

Harmon felt the oxygen return to the room. And a feeling that the man's peculiar aura was familiar – that he had met the fellow before.

"Who was that?"

"An old friend. Like me, he appreciates the long view."

Harmon waited, but clearly, nothing further would be forthcoming. "Who was he referring to, earlier, when he said 'show me them both, together'? Myself and Leeth?"

"Yes, Doctor." Eagle's expression chilled. "But we will leave that discussion for another day. I've given you enough to absorb, for now."

Harmon rose, then paused. "One more thing. You will need to promote Leeth to a full agent. I see no reason you could not call all this," he waved one hand, "her graduation test."

Eagle's expression did not change, but Harmon sensed amusement. *It* had *been a test! Sweet buttered hell!* He saw Eagle register that shock, and sensed the amusement deepen. Still with no change in the man's expression.

Harmon collected his wits. "She will want to feel that she won. She will not accept a return to her lowly trainee rank, if she continues to outmaneuver the best that Preacher, Nelson and Mother can throw at her."

"No need to exclude yourself, Doctor," Eagle murmured.

Harmon ignored the gibe. "Returning as a trainee would feel like a defeat to her. She would fight us forever rather than admit defeat. She will return to us in victory or not at all."

"Oh? Are you claiming that if we do succeed in capturing her, we will no longer have her loyalty? Or is this an excuse for your continued failure to return her to us, Doctor?"

"I mean she must return *voluntarily*. She would see recapture as a personal failure."

"Very well, Doctor. Proceed. It will be interesting to see *who* will fail this test."

CHAPTER 13

Leeth woke to a gray dawn light and birdsong – and the sensation of being watched.

Rolling over in her bedding, eyes still shut, she curled up, hugging the warmth to herself and just listening. But a slow prickling up her spine warned her that someone stood over her, just outside the woven branches of her den – within arm's reach.

But silent: no sound of cloth scratching on cloth or skin; no soft breathing; no heartbeat. Something warned her not to react, though. Not to even think about it.

She yawned, wriggled through the branches of her small nest and stood slowly, stretching. Then leaped, fingers slashing through cold morning air. She felt her invisible blades slice *something*.

Uncle. But the instant of fiery elation drowned under an immediate flood of dismay. Her fingers cut deeper as the presence jerked free, vanishing.

She stood in stunned shock at the implications.

Did I just kill Keepie? She shook her head, denying the guilt. *Good! He deserved it – and more.*

But still, somehow, she felt her face flush first hot and then cold as memories, both good and bad, deluged her. She remembered laughing with him, when she was little. Recalled the desperate expression in his eyes when she'd staggered from Godsson's cell.

Saw him healing Faith as she lay dying from her own rocket blasts, having saved them all.

Oh, Uncle. Why?

She considered herself – her healthy skin, her fit body, nicely revealed by her figure-hugging clothes. *Was it my fault? Because I dress to show off my body?*

No. That was the sort of clothing *he'd* bought for her. He was the one who'd told her it was important to set an example for others.

It was him. Not me.

Gradually, though, panting, she calmed as she replayed the whole thing in her head; realizing it hadn't *felt* like... the Doctor.

Her eyes narrowed. She flexed fingers, sensing the echoes of death at their tips, reading the psychic echoes. Tasting, almost.

She shook her head.

No, that hadn't been her uncle.

So, who was looking for her now?

She waited, alert... then with a shrug moved to her stew-pot and activated the heat-plate, frowning down at the energy reading. Time to swap cells.

She'd climb up to the solar panel after eating.

Picking her way to her waste bucket she sighed as she contemplated the dawn. Squatting down, the precious toilet paper nearby, she wondered if Marcie had seen her message; if Teef had found any telescopes; if she should try to find out more about the creepy Candlestick Tower? Then there was her plan to hunt the RedSkulls; and she really should try again to track down The Breaker. And her cooking pot was almost empty: she should go out on another hunt.

Looked like another busy day.

After breakfast, and tracing a severed wire from the solar panels – a bit more of the roof had fallen in, and cut it – she sat down with pencil and paper to color in the word 'Hope' again in ten centimeter tall letters. She learned she needed the full length of the floor before the letters got hard to read. A distance of about eighty meters, she figured, after pacing it out.

Let's see; Marcie is ten K from the Tower. 10,000 divided by 80 is 1,000 by 8... halving that sum a few times gave her the answer: 125. So she needed a '125 mag' telescope. Or bigger, so Marcie could write smaller. *I wonder how big Marcie's is?*

She drank her fill of water, checked the pipes and filters from the roof drains, then considered. She *should* hunt some more rats and birds. She sighed, remembering yesterday's feast with Sofia, Mai Lyn, and the others, licking her lips.

But the 'Landwave' eating spot was just as nice. Besides, she might not have time to hunt for food today: Teef might've gotten her a telescope already! She headed for his tech-shack.

"*How* much?" she demanded, not sure she'd heard the ogre correctly.

"Thousand two hunnerd. That 'cludes prop' stand. 'Sa big unit!" He gestured with large, callused hands. "Six inch lens, 300 mag! 'S serious gear, Flit."

She frowned. She had less than two hundred in her cashstick. And *if* she didn't damage a drone too badly, Teef gave her fifty for it. She'd need... twenty four drones! And most days now, she hardly even saw one. Let alone any Teras – Teef gave her two fifty for a terahertz drone. She'd only need... five of those.

Briefly, she considered going into the city, with a big bag – maybe grab some food there, too – but shook her head. *That'd be pushing my luck.* Tranq gun drones were bad, but the web-gun ones were worse – and though she had more clothes since her expedition with Sofia and the others yesterday, that didn't mean she could waste them. She pictured her wardrobe full of beautiful clothes, left behind at the Department.... But she could imagine her uncle advising them she'd want to buy clothes, too, and to be ready to trap her if she tried. Or even...

She stiffened.

What if they sent *Uncle* himself in? If he shouted 'Leeth, Mode One. Come here....'

It'd all be over.

"Hey, girl, you 'k?" Teef was snapping his fingers in her face. "Meb could drop to thousand one fitty, f'you. Or...." His features settled into a curiously vulnerable expression. "Meb we make other 'rrangements. Ya could share my space. Share my bed...?"

She focused back on him, and smiled. "I don't think so, Teef." She looked him up and down. He certainly was fit, his chest like a barrel, strong arms, large hands, and large *feet*. She smiled again. "Though I *was* considering something like that, that first night, when I woke you up to buy water, and buckets, and food." *That, or killing you.* Though she felt strangely uncomfortable at the memory.

Teef's bony eyebrows rose, and his lips twitched open.

"But the FistFest is only eight days away, and I plan to make a lot of money there. Could I get it on credit? You know, get it now, and pay you back later?"

Teef shook his head, but looked interested. "You gonna ennertain? What you act?"

"Act?" She considered the question. She *would* be underplaying her fighting skills, at least to start with. "Kind of, yeah."

Teef looked intrigued. "You sexertain?"

She snorted. "No!"

"Then what? Only sexers 'n fighters earn big."

"Yeah, that's what I'd heard," she said, fighting to keep from grinning. "How about you get it for me on credit, and I'll pay you *fourteen hundred* creds after."

"'Nif you not earn so much? You make up difference, working *under* me, here?" Crude finger gestures made it crystal clear what he meant.

She smiled lazily. *He might be kinda fun.* For an ogre, Teef had a kind of brute appeal. Not that she'd fail to earn fourteen hundred, and more.

"Sure," she agreed. "It's a deal!"

They shook, and she pretended to wince when Teef gently squeezed her hand; though she had to fight the urge to squeeze back and see just how strong ogre bones were.

Instead she smiled up at him, batting her eyelashes.

But when she left, excited afresh at the thought of the upcoming Fest, she considered that she'd gotten the Department to agree to send her there, as a test. Would they realize she still planned to attend?

And if they did send her uncle to recapture her? She couldn't kill him: she'd tried, once, and her muscles just locked up, frozen, at the attempt.

Well, if I can't kill him, I need to find a way to neutralize *him,* she decided. *Neutralize the Doctor.*

CHAPTER 14

A demanding buzz and Mother's voice woke Harmon.

"Doctor: you're needed in the infirmary at once!"

Adrenaline flooded his system. "Is it Leeth? What's happened?"

"No, it is not Leeth. You have a patient." There was a moment's pause, then Mother added, "a mage."

Harmon smiled.

"Fascinating." He was conscious of James and Mother following his every movement as he examined the well-dressed male lying motionless on the gurney. James seemed agitated; Mother annoyed.

He considered the glacial pulse: six beats per minute made little medical sense. Beside the patient, the med-bot waited for Harmon's decision to begin treatment.

"Quite fascinating." The more he examined the aura, the more certain he grew that the man was indeed a mage; probably quite a strong one, too. "I don't think he'll die if you proceed with the suggested drugs, but let me look inside first for other injuries."

Shifting his focus, he summoned the pattern of the healing spell and sank it into the unconscious fellow. Intriguing: the heart was damaged; as you might expect from some massive trauma, or electric shock. But the more he looked, the more pervasive the disruption appeared: chemical messengers running haywire, electrical activity disorganized. What *had* she done to him?

At last he disengaged, and met Mother's eyes. "He was astrally tracking Leeth, I assume?" Casually, he set the robot into operation, eyeing the first injector as it extruded and oriented itself. The needle slid delicately into the man's arm. "His heart should withstand standard treatment now, but I must say I've not seen anything like it before. Although I have read of similar, ah, 'injuries'." *But from attacks by powerful spirits, not by a human being.* He fought to keep a pleased expression from his face. "What happened?"

Mother nodded to James, who answered. "We contracted for a mage to help locate Leeth. He set out 'astrally' a little before dawn, using one of the ritual circles in the Bureau." He jerked his head upward, indicating the building many levels above them. "A little after dawn, without warning, he screamed, jolted upright, eyes staring, then collapsed in cardiac arrest."

Harmon nodded and turned to Mother. "It would be useful if I could question him. What does he know of us? He could return to consciousness soon; or it might take days."

Mother pursed her lips. "How injured is he? How functional will he be, when he awakens?"

Harmon shrugged. "Impossible to say. Some kind of massive shock sent his neurochemical systems haywire."

"Take him back up to the Bureau's sick bay, James. Have him monitored. We'll send you up, Doctor, in the guise of a trauma counselor when he comes round."

"*AAH!*" They all jumped as the mage screamed and sat up. "Get her away! Fuck, fuck, no!" He started flailing at empty air.

Harmon shifted his senses to the Imaginal, half-expecting to see some kind of spirit-Leeth present in the room, but it was instantly clear the man was merely terrified.

"Or I could perhaps counsel him right here," Harmon murmured.

-

James stuck to the explanation the Doctor had suggested, as he briefed the next mage they seconded from the BID, the Bureau for Internal Development. "We have a small team investigating reports of a new shamanic street drug." He slid over an envelope. "There's a few strands of hair from one of the users, a nineteen year old girl," he lied, "who we want to locate, to bring in for questioning."

The mage, Agent Tom Henson, a brown-haired man in his early thirties, shrugged. "Okay."

"She's living in the Hunters Point Dumps, but you need to keep your distance. The drug makes her dangerous to you."

Tom Henson sniggered. "Sh'yeah. Got it."

"I'm serious. She put Brad Stevens in hospital this morning, when he got too close. *Astrally.*"

Henson looked interested. "Yeah? What happened? What'd she do?"

"We don't know, exactly. But it sent him into cardiac arrest."

Henson shook his head, smiling. "You know how much exercise Stevens does? None. No exercise." He shrugged. "One big scare: bam! Look, *maybe* there's some new street drug, but unless Stevens for some reason decided to stand there and go toe to toe with her like he was wrestling some hostile Inorganic Being...." He shook his head. "It'd be like you trying to puncture a balloon by slapping it in mid air. Astrally, mages move with the speed of thought."

"Henson, I just want you to tell me where she is. Find her, look around, come back, and we'll try to match up your impressions to a physical location. *She is danger-ous*." James eased back. "I mean, the drug makes its users dangerous."

"Sure, bud. No worries. I'll be careful."

But Henson was smiling as he said it.

Five minutes later, a very shaken Agent Henson sat up in the ritual circle. "Holy hells." He looked down at his chest, probing as if to check he was in one piece, pulling out a dull coppery-gold nugget on a leather cord from under his shirt. "What the fuck?"

"What happened?" James asked.

"Distance in the Imaginal isn't the same as in the physi-cal. You have to get close enough so that stuff 'near' her Imaginally is near her physically. *Then* you just have the problem of matching emotional objects to physical land-marks. But when I got close, she lashed out. Without warning! One moment she's walking along, oblivious, the next moment – bam! – she's somehow stabbing my fuck-ing focus!"

He held up the tarnished-looking nugget angrily. "This is drained. Dead." Then he stared past it, once again feel-ing his chest. "God knows what would've happened if she'd hit me, rather than it," he muttered.

He looked up at the guy from the Accounts Department who was coordinating the team investigating the street drug.

"Well, at least now you know you need to be careful. You need a break, or you ready to try again?"

Henson winced. "I can try again," he said, shaking his head. "But I dunno: I'm not sure I can get 'near' enough her to say where in the Dumps she is.

"I'm sure as shit not going close to her again, I can tell you!"

CHAPTER 15

By now, she was a regular face at the Landwave, and had learned it was much more normal to trade for food than to buy it. She'd also learned that the rodents and birds she'd hunted, and shyly offered, were gratefully accepted – and turned into much tastier meals than she could cook herself. And when she could bring in a duck or two – or even better, a goose – the joy that greeted her arrival made her feel like a hero. Which was a bit silly, since the bigger birds were actually the easiest to shoot.

Yesterday though had been another fruitless day of searching for The Breaker. If she didn't find any traces today, she might finally change over to hunting the Red-Skulls instead.

Teef should have her telescope, today. She'd climbed back into the eerie tower last night and updated her message to say 'Maybe tomorrow.' But she hadn't stayed there.

Today, she'd checked for news of The Breaker, on the net at Teef's shack. Then she'd re-visited five of his murder sites in the Dumps, again with no luck. She was returning to the popular spot for a top-up second breakfast. This long after dawn, there were few people eating. Out on the Bay, one of the Fisher Clan's raggedy vessels rocked on the small waves.

"Heya, City," called a colorfully-dressed figure.

She still just shrugged when people asked her name – sticking to the original plan for reasons she herself couldn't explain. That meant, though, that every second person felt entitled to make up their own name for her. 'City' was apparently because her clothes weren't what people here normally wore. But there was no way she was going to dress in shawls or skirts or trousers.

"Hey, Tricksy." Leeth steered her burning hot bowl of spicy octopus, shellfish and seaweed over to the slim blonde. 'She' was finishing a fired-soy and seared vegetable breakfast, sipping a herbal tea. The cold morning wind flattened Tricksy's rainbow-dyed shift against her chest, revealing small mounds – but Leeth knew she also had a small bulge between her legs. When she'd asked Tricksy if she was a man or a woman, she'd received a smile and a 'No' in response.

Leeth took a seat beside her, so she could see who came and went, digging into her meal with relish. She'd pick up her telescope this afternoon, and would keep hunting for

The Breaker till then. She'd been thinking about how no one ever saw the victims taken, so figured that scouting lonelier areas of the Dumps, where people were few and far between, might lead to something.

Tricksy rested a slender hand on Leeth's bare thigh. "I'm vision questing tonight, with Beebee. Meb you come too? I hunch you'd Learn."

Tricksy nurtured and supplied a vast range of exotic plants from all over the world – Nepal, the Amazon, Siberia, Africa, Mexico. In her little hothouse, she harvested odd compounds which Leeth was pretty sure were really drugs.

She felt an odd shiver run through her at the suggestion. The temptation made her shake her head. "Nope." 'Drugs are for weaklings,' her uncle had always said. And Tricksy did seem kind of soft. Though maybe she'd be interesting for sex, especially since she was old – at least thirty. But Leeth had other plans for tonight. Which reminded her. "Hey, you've lived here a long time, right, so you might know. I saw an odd place in the distance the other day. Kind of creepy. I think it's called Candlestick Tower. What-"

"Stay away from there!" Tricksy shuddered, her long blonde hair trembling around her. "That place got bad mojo."

"Why? What was it?"

"Uploaders. Transhumes. More money 'n brains. Out of their skulls, livin' virt life, wheelin', dealin'..." she shook her head, and her voice sank, her dark green eyes burning into Leeth's. "Then the Big One hit, an' most of 'em died, trapped in their life-support pods. They say their minds are still there, tied to their uploads still running in the net. Tied to the building, and everything inside."

Leeth shivered again. So it was just a ghost story? Ghosts weren't real. But the place had felt... odd. Still: it probably meant she'd be undisturbed when she chatted to Marcie. And that her telescope would also stay undisturbed if she set it up there and left it.

Tricksy patted her thigh again, drained her tea – urging her once more to stay away from 'Corpse-stick Tower' – and left. Leeth chewed her octopus, frowning.

Four hours later, tired, dusty, and a little thirsty, Leeth

scowled around her. *Not one sign of the stupid Breaker. And* she was being hunted by someone from the Department, she was pretty sure. Several times she'd heard someone following her, or felt she was being watched. But they were good. She never caught sight of them even once. Though she *had* found tracks: a few narrow boot-prints in the dust caking the floor of an empty, tilted tenement, the one time she'd gotten sufficiently annoyed to back-track.

The back-tracking had scared them off. A bit odd, for someone from the Department, but probably they'd been ordered to follow her and find out where she slept. She'd be especially careful when she made her way home tonight.

Though the prints had been too large to be Emma's, and too small for any of the men. And strangely few, con-sidering how much dusty floor there'd been. Just two prints, by the broken window that had allowed the watcher to look down at where she'd been. And the smudged-clean windowsill, like someone had perched there.

She felt a strange certainty that her tracker had been female, and a little shiver ran through her.

But now, even her mysterious tracker had abandoned her. *This was annoying – where was The Breaker?* Maybe he really had left the area entirely, and moved on to somewhere else? Or somebody else had already killed him. *Which would be good, really*, she told herself. *Even if it sucked.*

She flicked a stone with a toe, then stood on one leg shaking her left foot to dislodge several small pebbles that had wedged under the stik-sole. Around her, tumbled down shops and former tenements made small urban canyons. She wove a path between them, wearing a face mask and wishing she had goggles or something, too, to keep the wind-blown dust and grit from her eyes.

She'd headed this way after hearing faint screams, but then been baffled by the maze of ruins.

A noise in the distance – quiet voices, male – had her picking a path in that direction, and she stepped out onto the wider, tilted concrete surface of what had been a main road. Here, the shops and offices spilled out to block only half its width.

To her right, maybe fifty meters away, a rough looking bunch of four men in hard worn jeans and jackets rose to their feet as they caught sight of her, eyeing her up and down with gap-toothed smiles a hair too wide and a touch too hungry. Two of them looked gene-altered, judging by the long fingers and sharp teeth. She saw scraped and bloodied knuckles, and a wild, fevered light in their eyes. She recognized that light – they saw her as prey, not a person.

Her lips thinned.

One had still-bleeding scratches on his face, she saw. She felt the tingle unfurl at her fingertips.

It took a conscious effort to dismiss it. None of them had guns, she saw. One, with tangled brown hair, looked a little ill, but the other three all seemed fit and strong.

Were these guys RedSkulls? But they had no skull tatts, and were all human, with a sort of rabid, feral look to them. Not the hostile tribal feel of 'Skulls.

She stopped ten meters from them, setting her fists on her hips. Not that they'd have anything useful to tell her, but she had to ask.

"You guys seen anyone strange round here?"

The three healthy ones began spreading out in an arc across the tilted street before moving closer. The ill-looking one answered her, stepping forward. "Ya. *You* look pretty strange." His friends laughed, then he spread his hands. "Ya lost, chica? We help?"

Did they think she was stupid? She frowned while she considered it all: the way they were looking at her; the screams she'd heard earlier.

What they'd just been doing, and the way they leered at her, made their plans as clear as if they wore signs round their necks. Her fingers tingled again; but what if one got away, and spread the word that she could fight?

She pulled out her PowerShot, slotted in a ball bearing – for maximum penetration – then sighted and drew. The one in the middle licked a long tongue over sharp teeth, grinning. Held up both hands as he advanced. "Please, no shoot poor boys who-"

He thinks this is a toy? She loosed, the shot hammering through his forehead. She palmed a second iron sphere, sighting and reloading while he fell.

For several seconds they gaped, then turned from him to her, muscles tensing.

She twitched her weapon. "Next?"

They paused. Looked at one another.

"Back away, now. Leave." She shrugged. "I can't let any of you come a step closer." Which wasn't true – she'd actually relish it – but they didn't need to know that.

She met each of their eyes, half hoping they'd make a move, but instead, cursing and muttering, they backed away, leaving their 'friend' lying face down in the dirt.

She heard them hissing about her in angry Street which she couldn't fully understand, but from the venom lacing every... curse, she didn't really need to. Once out of sight, they stopped moving, and she heard them whispering, clearly planning a counter-attack.

She moved past their hiding spot, still heading in the direction of the scream she'd heard earlier, but now listening with all her might.

The sobbing led her to them. A young woman not much older than her, naked, bruised, and bloodied, curled into a man lying on his back, blood soaking into the hard packed earth. As Leeth approached, the woman started, flinching away but clutching... the one she loved? Refusing to leave him.

Leeth met her eyes, holding them as she crouched down, resting a hand on one bare and scraped shoulder before feeling for a pulse in her partner's neck. He'd been stabbed in the side. But he was still warm....

Behind her, moving quietly, she heard the remaining three members of the rape pack returning.

"Wait here," she told the woman. "I just have something I need to do. I'll be back in a minute."

Several kilometers later, when Leeth staggered into the Sustainer's camp with the young woman, Jaycee, limping beside her in her ruined clothes, her husband Alan's dead weight around her neck in a fireman's lift, it caused a small sensation.

"Bring your Healer, fast," she gasped, as many strong hands took the burden from her shoulders, while women enveloped Jaycee.

She gratefully accepted water, and food, but had to leave. It was almost sunset, and Teef should have her telescope. They didn't seem to want to let her go, especially after Jaycee told the gathering community how the 'animals' who'd killed her husband wouldn't be hurting anyone ever again.

"Jaycee," Leeth told her, "a strong healer can revive someone if they've been dead less than an hour. Don't give up on Alan yet." She knew the Sustainers had a shaman – it'd been in the material she'd studied.

But then she had to leave, much as she wanted to see a happy ending. She didn't want Teef thinking she was playing some sort of stupid trick on him.

She lugged the surprisingly bulky and heavy telescope back to her place, then wiped herself down with a damp cloth. After a quick meal she set off south for Candlestick Tower, armed with her compass, an exact bearing for Marcie's house, a new whiteboard eraser, battery, and extra-thick black marker pens. And the telescope, of course – '*spotter* scope,' Teef had corrected her. He'd seemed to enjoy her expression after he'd explained, with gestures, how it wouldn't reverse or invert the image.

It did look beautiful – all shiny white, with special caps to protect the ends and the 'finder scope,' and not too many scratches. It came with a special stand, and Teef had even included a chain and lock. Teef was so thoughtful. She'd kissed him, properly, much to his surprise.

She circled the building, standing under the overhanging facade and craning her neck up to the corridor she'd left her whiteboard in, the night before last. To her, the lighted corridor high above was pretty bright, but for people who couldn't see in the dark, she suspected it'd be hard to pick out. Unless they were looking at it from directly across the Bay with a telescope, she hoped!

Re-positioning her 'scope and the rest of her gear on her back, she turned and headed to the entrance to the silent, gaping tower. She wasn't sure if it felt more creepy, or less, now she knew what it was.

Either way, she moved extra silently, listening with complete concentration as she entered. Growing excited as she wondered if Marcie'd be ready; if they'd actually be able to see each other, and write to each other.

Wondering if Marcie'd have ideas about how to free Godsson.

CHAPTER 16

She had the exact bearing, and a powerful telescope, and knew just what Marcie's house looked like; she hadn't expected it'd take so long to just *find* it! A fifteen centimeter scope really made everything big, she discovered. She was glad Teef had shown her how to use the small finder scope attached to it.

But when she saw the window with a poster clearly visible on the far wall, with its large yellow 'diamond' outlined in red, inscribed with the stylized red 'S', she knew she'd found her! Heart pounding in her chest, she fine-tuned the focus – then read the numbers on a card stuck below the poster with a sinking heart: '23:oo.' That had to mean Marcie wouldn't be looking until eleven pm.

She spent several minutes checking out the room beyond the window, recognizing Marcie's wardrobe, her other posters, even the family picture of her and her dad and her sister Amanda – and a telescope that looked even more special than the one Teef had gotten for her – but puzzled by the lack of a whiteboard for Marcie to write on.

Probably she had it hidden away.

Rubbing out 'Hope' from her board, she wrote 'I'm here' instead, in thick black letters fifteen centimeters tall. *Now what?* Wincing at the smell, she scraped away an area of rotted and moldy carpet – or maybe fungus – until she'd exposed the concrete floor to sit on. But eyeing the repellent sludge underneath, she changed her mind, pacing up and down the slightly squelchy corridor in the dark instead.

She also remembered to change the dying power cell in the lamp stuck to her whiteboard. Then stood blinking in the awful brightness once she'd set it to shine down on the gleaming board.

At ten to eleven, she couldn't keep away from the eyepiece any longer, watching the distant empty room, jigging on the spot. Then squealed, and waved, and generally danced around like a goof when Marcie entered and bent to her eyepiece. When she went back to *her* eyepiece, she saw Marcie now jumping up and down and waving, and couldn't help but join in!

After they'd both settled down, a bright rectangle appeared on the bedroom wall behind Marcie. Leeth had a sinking feeling, which only deepened as she saw Marcie's lips move, large black letters appearing behind her: "How cool is this?"

Leeth dove to her whiteboard – "No! Stop!" she wrote – and then bent to her eyepiece. Marcie stood up from her telescope, hands on hips, her body language very clearly demanding to know why.

How was she supposed to summarize all she'd learned about surveillance and electronic eavesdropping from Nelson, in twenty five words or less?

She rubbed out the old words and wrote: "Don't use tech!!", and waited for Marcie to read it. Then rubbed it out and wrote "Just whiteboard!", underlining it twice.

From ten kilometers away, Marcie glared at her, hands on hips. Leeth stood up, then bent so her head was in front of her own whiteboard, and nodded a vigorous Yes.

Back at the eyepiece, she saw Marcie fume, then stalk from her room. A geological age passed, then Marcie's younger sister, Amanda, burst into the room, looking around as if she expected to see someone hiding in there. Noting the telescope, she tiptoed toward it.

Leeth winced, considered moving out of sight, then bent down to her eyepiece and waved weakly. Amanda jumped like she'd been tasered, almost knocking the telescope over. Leeth cringed, then watched the drama unfold when Marcie re-entered with a whiteboard mostly covered in notes and fridge magnets. She followed the showdown, which moved from cross words to shouting, when Marcie found the telescope had been moved. Leeth wished she could magically jump the distance and calm them down, tell them it was alright.

Instead, the two sisters' moved closer, until their faces were inches apart, getting redder and redder. Then she saw Amanda's face crumple, her bottom lip trembling, and Leeth reached out before realizing she could do nothing. Tears welled in the distant face, Amanda spitting words that seemed to include the word 'Da'; and Marcie froze.

"Don't be mean," Leeth urged her friend, under her breath. "Amanda's cool, just hug her." She chewed at her bottom lip, grimacing.

Soon, though, the two were hugging and making up. Leeth felt a strange ache in her heart. Marcie moved back to her telescope, adjusting and muttering. Amanda dashed from her sister's bedroom, returning with an easel. Shutting the door behind her, she set the whiteboard on it.

Soon, their secure communication channel was re-established. This time with Amanda included.

"How's Ur spine?" Leeth asked.

"<u>Perfect!</u> Who was that mage?" *who healed me,* clearly.

Good question. Leeth shook her head. Even if she was allowed to answer that, she didn't know what to say. She herself hardly knew. Had he changed so much, or had he always been like that?

In the end, she just wrote "A healer." Then asked the next most important question. "R U + me ok?"

She watched as Marcie leaned back from the 'scope and gave the question some serious thought, while Amanda peered into the eyepiece and started saying something, only for Marcie to hush her and then write on the whiteboard in letters far too small for Leeth to read. Amanda jerked upright, then started nervously looking around the room, wide-eyed and searching. Like Marcie had written down that they were being listened to. Leeth watched the distant communication, wishing she could rap on the window to remind them she was still here. *Eventually,* Marcie rubbed the blurry block of text out and wrote a single word in large letters, that had Leeth blinking away fresh tears: "Yes."

Marcie followed that with: "How's Tower? Creepy?" She added a frownie face.

Leeth thought of lying, but there'd been too much of that. So she just wrote: "Yes." Then stuck her face in front of it, and smiled, and shrugged.

But what should she ask next? Might Marcie have some advice about her uncle? Just thinking about how to ask, though, left her standing confused, and when she finally snapped out of it and looked back through the eyepiece, she saw Marcie and Amanda looking very worried. "R <u>U</u> OK?"

Oops. "<u>Yes!</u>"

Marcie: "?? True?"

"<u>Yes!!</u>"

She saw the two girls penciling notes to each other, Marcie finally looking doubtful before nodding, then *Amanda* wrote "Did U do something-" waited, then "bad? R U in troub-"

How to answer that? But Amanda was still writing. "-

le? Can't U go back?"

Leeth drew in a deep breath, standing up from the eyepiece. Could she? One day? They'd been teaching her so much she needed to know. And they were doing super important work, for the whole country. At least, that's what they told her. But they *hadn't* let her uncle heal Marcie.

But what *she* wanted didn't matter – she couldn't go back even if she wanted to. Not until she'd solved the problem of her uncle's control. And even then, she wasn't sure if she should. The question was complicated. She still wasn't one hundred percent sure they were the good guys. She trusted Father, and Eagle. Dojo, of course. And James and Emma were real nice. But the rest of them.... She shook her head.

In the end, she just wrote. "So-so. Maybe."

Finally, though, they got to the subject she wanted to ask about: how to rescue Godsson. Spelled out, painfully slowly, a few words at a time. "Get Ur advice? Friend – 'X' – in jail. Secret jail. I promised tell no-one. Promised: no jail break. All who know, don't want X out. So: how to free X?"

"Convince people who know, free X?"

"Tried. Tried. Tried. No." She gave them time to absorb that, then rubbed it out and wrote, "Promise unfair? Break promise?"

"Free X = break law?"

"Yes."

"Get U in trouble?"

"<u>BIG.</u>" Leeth remembered the expression on Prof Sanders's face, saying she'd go to jail for a long, long time if she even tried.

They talked about it, in awkward choppy sentences, till she saw Marcie growing frustrated. Then Marcie wrote: "Can U ask X? U can visit, yes? X solve puzzle? Or: renegotiate promise?"

Leeth sat back, a little bit stunned. The more she thought about it, the more she liked both suggestions. And maybe she could find out more about Godsson: gather her own evidence, maybe act like a lawyer and make a proper case to Professor Sanders? *Yeah!*

"THANKS, M! Great ideas!"

For her part, Marcie had seemed real impressed she'd taken down five attackers, the other night. Leeth had to reassure her that she hadn't been hurt at all – Marcie hardly seemed to believe it. "Wish I could have seen. Twice now I missed out."

She must have told her younger sister about it, since Amanda then wrote "R U <u>Sleena</u>?!" The cartoon pixie warrior. Leeth had blushed in pleasure.

Marcie had also wanted to know what Leeth had done to the biker – "Da said: biker mad as Hell." So, Preacher had been angry? Excellent!

They chatted on for a bit, until both sisters jumped. Marcie quickly waved goodbye and Amanda dived for the whiteboard. Knocking it over, she began frantically erasing it while Marcie shoved the telescope into a corner. Seconds later, Leeth saw Amanda tiptoe to the door and open it. Their father peered in and around suspiciously, and spoke sternly before sending the younger girl from the room. A few more words to Marcie, then he shut the door.

Marcie looked at her telescope, looked back to Leeth, then wrote on her whiteboard and held it up. "Tomorrow. 9pm." Then waved a sheepish goodbye.

Grinning, Leeth straightened up, wrote "OK" on her board, and then after some thought, turned the torch off and unstuck it; Marcie probably wouldn't see it until tomorrow. She moved the telescope to point in a random direction before capping all the lenses and locking it to one of the VR pod-coffins, shuddering as she touched the stainless steel handle. Then headed back to the deep dark black of the stairwell.

I should probably explore this place properly. But she couldn't summon up the enthusiasm to do it. Not now, anyway. Instead, she savored the memories of tonight – of today.

She hugged herself. What a great day! It was awesome to not feel useless for once. Like she'd done something worthwhile. Sure, she hadn't found The Breaker, but she *had* ended a rape-gang and rescued one, hopefully two people, *and* reconnected with her best friend. She even had the start of a plan now for Godsson.

-

Across the Bay, Marc Disten considered the odd half conversation just observed. Trying to puzzle out what it meant. Who had been at the other end.

Questioning that one would complete the information.

Flexing fingers, concentrating on the sensations, the absence of pain was noted. The fingers were now fully healed. In a few days, the arm and leg casts were due to be removed. Even careful examination of their movement yielded only tiny indications of injury.

Soon.

CHAPTER 17

The next day's hunt for The Breaker was just as dusty, frustrating and fruitless as that of the day before, but it was great checking in on the Sustainers camp to learn their shaman *had* been able to heal Alan.

They'd wanted to make a big deal of it, so she'd quickly made her escape. The last thing she wanted was questions about herself, especially with the 'Fest only a week away now.

Teef had clearly been pleased by just how happy she was! They'd even made out, just a little, just for fun. "But don't get your hopes up, big guy – I'll be paying you back shortly from my w- uh, earnings."

Now though, back at her home in the early afternoon, well fed and watered, she felt at a loose end. Like there was something she should be doing, but was avoiding.

Thinking about visiting Godsson brought it back to the front of her mind. She didn't think they'd expect her to break in to visit him. *But might they have allowed for the chance I'd break in to* free *him? Or visit Faith?* She frowned. *Maybe.*

I'll just have to be careful, she decided. Especially since it'd only take her uncle's presence and three whispered words to put her back in his control; back into the Department.

The Department. Did she *want* to go back?

She'd been learning so much from Dojo. She wondered whether he still thought about her, like she did him.

And James and Emma had been teaching her how to be an actual spy, so she could uncover plots and kill bad guys and stuff.

If they'd ever planned on letting me go on an actual mission! They hadn't let her uncle heal Marcie, when they could've. It wouldn't've been hard to give her and the Doctor secret identities for the task.

Suppose I did *go back? What would happen, say, if I said I wanted to rescue all those orphanage kids the End of Days guys kidnapped?*

Her heart lifted at the thought. That'd be a real mission! But finding where they were... even without the Department hunting *her,* that sounded hard to do on her own. *With* the Department, it'd be a piece of cake. *Then I could just sneak in, kill Shepherd Fox and his henchmen, and lead all the kids home!*

But would they let her? Even though Godsson had saved *everybody*, they were keeping *him* locked up. Was the Department even really the good guys? Her uncle had never really seemed happy there.

Uncle.

She felt her face fall. *He* was the real problem. Whether or not she went back to the Department, he could always just take control of her.

She thought about it all, getting angrier and angrier. The big problem was Uncle. But maybe even without him, the decision wasn't so clear cut.

I need to talk to Eagle, she realized. *Ask him directly, why they wouldn't let Uncle heal Marcie.* She cast her mind back to that conversation with Eagle, trying to re-member exactly what he'd said when he'd refused her re-quest. She remembered the peculiar look he'd given her, as she'd left his office. Like he'd expected her to say some-thing, or do something.

Slowly, a thought formed. *Had he... had he* wanted *me to do what I did? Had he been testing me, to see what I could do?* The more she thought about it, the more con-vinced she grew.

But if he did want me to do it, why are they hunting me now? Are they still *testing me?*

She frowned, finally admitting to herself something that she'd been burying. The attempts to recapture her: the fact they *hadn't* sent her uncle after her; that they kept underestimating her.... She shook her head. That wasn't Eagle; or her uncle. *Mother* was behind the attempts to re-capture her, and maybe Father. Not Eagle; not her uncle.

What did that mean? Had Mother and Father taken control, imprisoned Eagle and her uncle? Could you *do* that kind of thing when you worked for the government? Or were Eagle and her uncle just not co-operating? Maybe using *her* as a test for Mother and Father?

Her head was starting to ache. She flung herself back onto her padded plastic bags and stared out between the branches of her little circle of shrubs. Pursing her lips, she made two decisions. With or without the Department, she was gonna hunt down and destroy bad guys – *powerful* bad guys who hurt a lot of people.

And she'd talk to Eagle to work out if they were really the good guys or not.

And work out a way to neutralize the Doctor. He was the real problem. But that sounded tricky.

In the meantime, she'd see if she could find out more about Godsson.

Sunset found her back in Teef's shop-shack, hunched over a small screen in a corner, doing net searches. But queries for 'Godsson' kept turning up all these pages about a guy called Jesus, instead. Which turned out to be just the tip of a hu-u-uge iceberg. She started finding page after page of all sorts of weird information, using heaps of the words she'd never been able to find definitions of before, back at the Institute. Words she'd had to ask her uncle about.

And the whole, horrible truth dawned.

He's been hiding all this stuff from me. Blocking it somehow so she couldn't see it. How had he done that? *Why? Wasn't it enough, torturing me?*

Somehow, though, that he'd been deceiving her for her whole childhood, seemed worse. *Lying to me since I was only little, and trusting. The* whole *time. Why?*

She sat back, on the stool in Teef's tiny shack, stunned.

And then remembered looking up some of those words a couple of times at the Department, too, and failing. She felt her eyes go round. That meant *they* were in on it *too!*

She bent back to her search, wiping away angry tears, growling at Teef when he asked if she was okay. Sniffling, she pursued her search for the real Godsson. It was almost a welcome distraction.

But searching the net for Godsson wasn't helping. She remembered once trying to find out if Emma knew about him. What had Emma called him?

Or Melisande's weird spirit, the first time the eerie thing had talked to her about Godsson? *Think, Leeth!* What was the joking name *She* had called him....

Bent son! *She* had called him Bent son when She was saying he was mean, and cruel, trying to turn 'Sara' against her friend. *Benson! That was what Emma had called him!*

She bent back to the keyboard, dimly aware of Teef watching with interest.

She left Teef's home fighting the urge to break into the Institute *now*, tonight. Only the knowledge that Marcie waited to chat at nine pm held her back.

Godsson was *good*, not bad. Even the people who blamed him for that billionaire's death didn't suggest he'd *hired* the assassins, only that his conspiracy theories about Newtopia and its boss *encouraged* them. Besides, it was Godsson – when he still called himself David Benson – who'd first warned the whole world about Melisande d'Artelle! And later risked his life to help slay her.

And what was his reward? To get locked away, just because he'd gone a bit mad. Had her uncle really even tried to cure him? It couldn't have helped, having people who slowly turned creepy and weird locked up in the cells next to him. Maybe her uncle put them there pretending it was for *Godsson's* own good?

She blinked, looking around, suddenly noticing it was full night, and that she had no idea at all what time it was. And she was starving. Could it be nine already?

She ran for the Landwave. It was on the way, anyway. She didn't even sit to eat, though – just wolfed down a bowl of stir fry before charging off.

This time she barreled straight through the broken glass doors to the creepy tower. She sprinted up the stairs, tummy protesting at all the running since her fast refueling.

She made it to the telescope in time, though. Marcie had only just set things up on her end.

But Leeth was distracted, and couldn't properly enjoy their chat.

She asked Marcie a few questions, but it was quickly obvious that she *did* know about Jesus, and that yeah, pretty much *everybody* did, and it was freaking her out that 'Jane' was even asking.

Yeah, the chat wasn't so great, tonight. After she'd changed the subject, Marcie started to ask her about her combat skills. Leeth admitted she'd learned a little kung fu. But it took ages to get Marcie off the subject. She'd been strangely persistent – Leeth asked if Marcie was thinking of learning some martial arts. She'd said she wasn't, but Leeth had the uncomfortable feeling Marcie was planning something. It was only after she asked that, directly, that Marcie changed the subject, back to Leeth's friend, X.

She'd felt a weird kind of relief when Marcie stopped

grilling her about her fighting. Before she signed off, though, she warned Marcie she probably wouldn't be able to speak to her the next night, since she might need to use the 'evening visiting hours' to see X.

And then, for some reason, she'd started feeling a little bit nervous about the whole expedition. Like there might be even bigger, awfuller surprises ahead of her.

She made her way out, puzzling over how to get in to see Godsson. In the end she decided the simplest and best approach would be to just kidnap Professor Sanders and force him to take her down to visit Godsson. That'd also make it clear she wasn't breaking her word and trying to break him out.

Yeah, she decided, nodding to herself. *That'd work well.*

That just left the problem of how to get there, and into the grounds, undetected.

CHAPTER 18

Since she hadn't been troubled by drones, she guessed the Department hadn't expected her to travel by bicycle. Her long shadow slid ahead and down the hill as she crested the last rise before the Institute. Switching off the electric motor, she slowed to ten kilometers per hour when the curving stone wall came into view.

She'd be really annoyed, though, if something happened to stop her returning the bike to the rental place. The deposit had almost emptied her cashstick. And she'd need that money to bet on herself in the 'Fest in six days time.

Had the bike guy increased the cost because he'd had to give her lessons? She'd spent hundreds of hours on the VR exercise bike back at the Department. But riding a real one wasn't quite the same, she'd soon discovered.

Eyes narrowing, she spied a suitable place to hide the bike, a good distance from where the ground started getting too rocky.

A minute later, after checking the gear packed into her small bucket, she slung it on her back again and shouldered the bike. Then began hiking up to where the brambles grew close to the wall, keeping alert for the sound of drones.

Behind her, the sun edged to the horizon.

Two hours later, inside the tall stone walls of the Institute for Paranormal Dysfunction, a patch of earth trembled, shifted, then crumbled upwards. Soil spilled from a dirty brown hand. A second hand appeared, tearing the hole wider, then a filthy, muddy arm emerged. Finally, clumps of earth fell from short, once-blonde hair as a head forced its way through. Leeth, cursing under her breath and spitting out dirt, wriggled free.

She inched slowly and quietly further from the wall, aware of the sensors on top of it.

When she was far enough away, she unpacked her gear and wiped herself clean, then unwrapped the cleverest part of her plan. Stretching the elastic band over her head, she settled the smiling ovoid shell of a real Tik Tek gynoid's face over her own. Shaking out the white 'sexy nurse-bot' uniform, she wriggled into it. Teef had made all sorts of weird remarks while they'd been scouring his shop to put the costume together, but she'd just played along with him as if she knew what he was talking about. Something to do with sex, obviously.

But the Institute's security system had probably been told to be alert for her. So disguising herself as one of Mr Shanahan's roving bot guards was the best way she'd been able to think of for passing as normal. She was pretty sure her 'repair-girl' disguise wouldn't still work.

Okay. She looked around, breathing in the air and soaking up the sight of her woods – *the Jungle*, she used to call it, when she was little. It had seemed endless, back then. She felt her shoulders relax from a tension she hadn't known she'd been carrying. She felt a stupid smile spread across her face.

Not that she cared – and not because it was hidden behind the dumb robot mask.

I'm home. But only for a little while. Just for part of a single night.

The smile slipped.

But then blossomed afresh: Faith would be around, somewhere. That had to be first – before dealing with Mr Shanahan or kidnapping Prof Sanders. Briefly, she reviewed her memory of where the cameras were placed. Would they have bothered moving them after Jax's upgrades? Especially since he must've reported that she'd stayed with him, watching him undo years of her work?

Whatever. First thing was to find Faith.

She crept through the woods in the clear night air, considering the time, and where Faith would likely be in her nightly patrol. *She always does it clockwise, so I'd better head right. Otherwise she'll find my tunnel before I've had a chance to tell her to keep it secret!*

What she heard in the end, though, wasn't what she'd expected.

A whole lot of *somethings* were moving swiftly toward her through the woods, a mix of panting and ultrasonics and a quieter, somehow more powerful humming she'd not heard before. She stilled, uncertain, moving to shield herself behind the trunk of an oak, even though that took her off Faith's patrol route.

But then she heard excited, quiet yips and growls – a whole pack of them – and cursed her stupidity. *I'm upwind!*

The yips turned to growls, and then the pack burst from the bushes... but her heart swelled when she saw her old friend leading the charge! Without thinking, she squealed in joy and dived from cover to race *toward* her.

"Faith!"

Faith's expression showed an almost comical doggy surprise as the two slammed into one another, Leeth clutching her and burying her face in her fur, laughing. "Oh, Faith, I missed you *so* much!" she breathed into the shaggy coat.

Suddenly Faith arched her whole body, growling in fury, cyber legs planted like pylons. She snarled and snapped at the other, younger dogs who came to a screeching halt, circling them both a hand's breadth away, weapons clicking into place.

Leeth dropped to all fours, then flung herself somersaulting over the red targeting beams. Grabbing both guns of the largest dog, she hoist him upside down over head as her feet hit the ground.

And *growled,* glaring into the bewildered doggy face inverted above her. She lowered the stunned animal, using its weight to flip herself back over it and land beside Faith.

It righted itself, its tail curling between its legs. The others bumped against each other, milling around or panting, ears flattened, a few making small 'yips.' Looking somehow confused.

"Bad dog!" she growled, in her deepest voice, before dropping back into a crouch beside her truest friend, so the two of them faced...?

"Faith? Is this *your* pack?"

The dogs quieted, sniffing and circling in closer. The one she'd flipped and held over her head, a brindled Alsatian with strangely bulky legs, shook himself then nosed right up to her, whining and smelling her while Faith rumbled a warning. The seven others milled around, keeping their distance.

Leeth held out a dirt-streaked hand to the braver one while coaxing the others closer, admiring them as her friend's pack took her scent. "Wow. They're lovely, Faith!"

Introductions over, Leeth and Faith trotted together, back on Faith and her pack's rounds. They paused at the freshly dug tunnel she'd emerged from, inside. Faith whined at her doubtfully, but she bent down and cuddled her. "It's okay. You can smell that that was me, right?" She held her hand up to her friend's excellent nose.

She was filthy under her white 'sexy nurse' outfit, but nothing like she would've been if she hadn't found that her magic was *amazing* at cutting through the soil. What *had* taken all the time, was shoveling it back out behind her, one bucket at a time.

She and Faith's crew made their way to the main buildings while she discovered the eight new members of the team were a bit undisciplined; they didn't even understand 'shush,' nor the idea of 'stay,' either. Which was a bit of a worry, as the security building was now coming in sight, and she needed-

"Good girl, Faith!"

Leeth stopped moving as a torch beam shone over her. Mr Shanahan stepped off his front porch, shaking his head and smiling at Faith and her pack. "You're amazing, girl. The system only flagged this bot as behaving abnormally five minutes ago!"

He was playing the light up and down her tight white uniform. But the movement slowed, by degrees, finally stopping at her exposed cleavage. Then...

"Holy mother of god!" Turning, he ran back up the steps.

Leeth dived after him, tackling him to the ground in the doorway and elbowing him in the side of his head as he struggled in her grip. Behind her, Faith charged, shouldering her way through the closing door, leaving her pack yelping and barking outside.

As Mr Shanahan slumped, Faith stalked up, growling, looking accusingly at her while sniffing and nuzzling the man on the wooden floor of the corridor.

"It's okay, he just, uh, fell, and, um, something kind of hit his head. He'll be all right." She got to her knees, slipped her hands under him and rose smoothly to her feet, turning sideways so she could carry him down to his bedroom.

"You don't need to worry, Faith, we're just kind of, you know, playing. Sort of."

Faith padded behind her, uncertain, all the way to his bedroom at the back, where Leeth gently laid him down. He wouldn't be out long, though. She considered, eyeing the bed, before shooing Faith from the room. "I don't think Mr Shanahan would want you watching what happens next," she chuckled, dropping again to her knees to give her friend a big cuddle and to breathe in her wonderful electric dog smells.

Faith licked her up-side the face, showing she was still glad she was back.

"Me too. You have *no idea* how good it is to be back." Then felt her smile slip. "But I can't stay long," she said, squeezing her friend. "I'm not really s'posed to be here." Standing, she led Faith to the front door. "You'd better go out and quiet down your pack – who look pretty impressive, by the way, but I think they need some more training." She hit the door open button, and the younger dogs all swarmed forward, surrounding the older cyborg animal. Faith set about quieting them down, then looked back up at her, head tilted to one side.

"It's okay. I'm not gonna do anything bad. Especially not to Mr Shanahan!" Faith looked doubtful, but just watched as she went back inside.

She hurried back through to his bedroom and began tearing the sheets into strips to tie him to his bed. She stuffed his mouth with a wad, checking he was breathing okay, then tied a strip round that to keep it in place.

That done, she trotted down to his security room – only to find that he'd changed his security codes. She looked around for clues – notes that might let her guess what he'd changed it to – but drew a blank.

She did note an iris scanner mounted to the side of the bank of monitors, though. That was new.

Outside, one of the dogs had started howling.

Leaving the room, she went to the front glass door to wave reassurance to Faith, who still watched, uncertain. The howling dog was the brindled Alsatian she'd had to lift overhead. She opened the door and stuck her head out. "You!" she said, pointing at it, angry. "Stop it!" She added a growl for good measure. The dog stopped, its tail drooping as it looked across to Faith.

"That's better. Now be good, and do what Faith tells you." With that, she closed the door and walked slowly back to the bedroom, pulling off the nurse-bot face mask.

Mr Shanahan was straining, red-faced, trying to break the twisted strips of sheets. He stilled as she came in and sat on his bed.

"Sorry. But I just knew you were going to raise the alarm."

His eyes, looking a bit glazed, widened in fear and he shook his head.

"Don't worry," she said, "I made a promise to Prof Sanders. I'm not here to break Godsson out."

He looked relieved, then questioning.

"I want to talk to Godsson, and Professor Sanders too. I'm not sure the promise he made me make's a fair one."

The fear returned.

"Well, how is it fair? Hardly anyone knows Godsson's here, and he made me promise not to tell anyone who doesn't already know about him. So how am I supposed to know who I can talk to about getting him *legally* released? I did some searches. Did you know, there was no trial? Just people saying he was mad. I think they were just angry. Did you know people claimed he'd done all sorts of sneaky stuff ages before that? Including getting the head of the Newtopia Consortium killed?" She shook her head. "They even made up a mean name for him: the Manipulator. I think they just didn't like that he kept outsmarting everybody, and so they locked him up, saying 'how sad, after he'd been all heroic *helping* the Dragon Lord defeat the Enemy of Mankind. *I* bet he was the one who really defeated Her, with help from the other two!"

Mr Shanahan's eyes had gone really wide, and he was shaking his head, clearly begging to speak.

"If I let you talk, you have to promise not to start shouting and calling for help, 'kay?"

He nodded. Against her better judgment, she untied his gag, fishing the soggy rag from his mouth for him.

He swallowed. "Sara, yeh don't want to be speaking to Godsson. He's not your friend, he's nobody's *friend!*"

"He is too! It's just none of you understand him."

Mr S visibly took hold of himself, his accent fading. "Anyway, you can't see him, and you can't talk to the Professor, since he's away tonight."

"Away? No!"

He nodded, smug.

"Then I really need to talk to Godsson."

He shook his head. "Best you just leave." He frowned. "How'd you... oh. You tunneled under the wall, didn't you?" But there was still puzzlement in his eyes, like she shouldn't have been able to do that. He didn't ask her any questions about it, though.

"Why don't you just give up on talking to Godsson? Go out and do a patrol with Faith and her new cyberpack, instead? Be like old times for you, eh? I won't set off any alarms, on my word."

She tilted her head. "I'm not *stupid,* Mr Shanahan. I know you'd *have to* set off alarms. And I know I can't stay to play with Faith. I'd get captured."

"Captured? D'ye mean 'arrested'? No, you mean captured, don't you?" He shook his head. "What sort of trouble are you in now, girl?" He looked, then, pointedly at his arms and legs stretched to the four corners of his bed. "Apart from assaulting people and tying them up."

"I need your new password."

He just smiled and closed his mouth tight.

She sighed. "I noticed you're using iris scanners, Mr Shanahan."

"Sara, no!"

"Sara, yes!" She started looping more of his bed-sheets around his lower legs, in case he kicked while she tied them together.

"Wait," he said, quietly.

She paused. "What?"

"I can see I can't stop you, so best I go with you."

She eyed him sideways. For some reason, she felt he looked somehow sly. "You give me your word, *truly* this time, you're not just going to shout for help, or try to escape? Or set Faith's pack on me?"

"I promise."

"*Truly* promise?"

"Truly promise."

Though she thought he now looked kind of sad. So he *was* up to something. She'd just have to be alert. "I'm going to keep your hands tied, though, behind your back." She *could* carry him, but there was no reason to let him see just how strong she was. 'Specially not since he was planning some kind of trick.

She was glad she'd brought him, since now even the front doors, set back from the wide stone steps, needed a palm scan to open them. But it was out of his reach, with his hands behind his back. She considered undoing them. Instead, she just steadied him, helping him step one leg then the other back through his arms so he could bring his wrists up in front of him. It was a little awkward with his hands tied, but he was able to activate the scanner.

As the door whisked open, she paused at the sound of many voices talking, from further inside, in the canteen. She whipped around in front of the security officer, ready to knock him out if he tried to shout, but he just looked at her steadily. If a bit groggy, still.

She frowned behind her nurse-bot mask, trying to work out what he was up to. Faith was looking up at her with a confused and worried expression. Crouching down while keeping one hand on the ties binding Mr Shanahan's wrists, she hugged her friend awkwardly. "It's okay. I won't be long. It'll be fine. I'm just going to talk to Godsson."

Faith growled at the name, but Leeth just ruffled the fur behind her ears, then stood and pushed Mr Shanahan forward, as the doors started to close.

"Come on," she snapped, "and remember your promise."

The door to the basement hadn't changed, though it too now had a palm scanner. He raised his wrists, silently asking her to undo them. She snorted and shook her head – then belatedly realized she should have checked him for weapons. But time was running out: someone might leave the cafeteria at any moment, and then there'd be real trouble. And she didn't want to hurt anyone here.

"Nice try, Mr S," she whispered. Awkwardly, he again pressed a palm to the scanner.

The door didn't open.

"I have to enter a code, too."

At least that much hadn't changed. She watched carefully as he punched in the code on the keypad, memorizing the sequence as the lock clicked. But there were two more doors, yet.

She pushed the metal door open and urged him through. Inside, she waited till the door closed, then searched him carefully, pocketing his netlink, wincing at having not done so earlier. *Chit! Anyone'd think I hadn't been trained in this kind of stuff!*

He let her do all that, patiently, then they descended

the stairs to B1 and the second security door. He scanned his palm, again, and entered a code.

She frowned. "That's not very good security, Mr S. You should use a different code for each different thing. Even if you have to use some tricky pattern to make them a bit different."

If anything, his expression grew even sadder. But he said nothing.

She pushed that door open, and he stepped through. She followed, then thought to stop it closing. All she had was the dirty cloth she'd used to wipe her face.

But as she bent down, he spoke. "You're truly not going to try to release him, are yeh? It'd be very, very bad if yeh did."

She looked up at him, from her haunches. There was sweat at his brow, and he looked super, super nervous. Which was silly: Godsson wasn't that bad. Why did everyone keep insisting he was so terrible? Plus she *wasn't* going to let him out. She didn't even know the code for Godsson's cell, and she was certain Mr Shanahan would never tell her.

She placed the wad of cloth and let the door squeeze against it.

"I wouldn't do that, Sara. If the door doesn't shut, alarms go off."

She looked down at the cloth, then back up at him.

He elevated one eyebrow.

Scowling, she snatched the cloth away and let the door snick shut. But why had he told her that? It would've been an easy way to set off an alarm.

From his strange expression, she was still missing something.

But in the end, unwilling to turn away when she was this close, she rose and they headed down to the third and final door.

At her questioning look, he shrugged. *Go ahead.* Frowning, she entered the same code, he pressed his palm to the scanner, and the final door unlocked.

Something about that bad piece of security worried her, especially at his strange expression when it closed behind them; but she'd figure it out later.

Finally, they'd reached the bottom level. Ahead lay Godsson's cell. Off to their left was the large empty space they'd made, to fit all the FBI agents and soldiers, for Her final attack.

Only months ago, but it seemed half a lifetime. There was even the chair that her uncle had brought down, to sit in. She made Mr S sit, tying him to it, then made her way toward Godsson's cell door. But first she looked warily through the narrow window of the cell to its right, wondering what horrible person they'd installed there this time.

It was empty.

She moved to the window of Godsson's cell door, pulled off her nurse-bot face mask, and looked inside.

CHAPTER 19

Ripped from his bed in the middle of the night, Harmon flailed at his assailant, only recognizing James as he was dragged into the night-lit corridor.

"What's the meaning-"

The agent ignored him. Picking him up as if he were a mere child, James accelerated down the corridor, spinning around corners with frightening speed.

"What's going on?" Harmon's mind leaped. "What has Leeth done?"

Ahead, inside a lift with its doors open, Dojo stood with arms folded. The moment James slammed to a halt in the carriage, it fell, the doors closing overhead as it descended far too fast.

Metal screeched and the lift hammered to a stop, Harmon suddenly glad he was being held by the augmented agent, who stood with legs braced. James leaped out through once again already-open doors, decanting him into the cramped rear seat of a sleek vehicle idling an arm's length away. Agent Emma was already buckled in to the passenger seat. "Where are we going? What exactly is going on?"

Dojo folded himself in beside Harmon, pushing him to one side.

"Go, code nine," James ordered the car as he braced one hand on the dash and buckled himself in with the other. The vehicle surged forward with insane power, and Harmon felt he might have been left behind had Dojo not been pressing him down into the seat.

He buckled in, then shut his eyes as the car slid sideways toward a concrete wall. Harmon felt them shoot forward up the first concrete ramp.

In the Accounts Department, alarms had alerted Eagle, Mother, and Father. Thrown left and right now inside James's hurtling Windsteed, Harmon spoke to them via clunky tele-presence goggles, feeling nauseous.

Leeth moved to Godsson's cell. They saw and heard her knock on the thick crystal set into the door, then wave. *I should have seen this coming.*

Beside him, Harmon felt Dojo, similarly goggled, lean forwards. They were seeing Leeth from behind. Harmon could see she was speaking, but couldn't hear her. The sound appeared to have cut out.

"What happened? We've lost audio, Nelson!" Mother snarled.

"Dunno, audio channel's clear."

Beside Harmon in the VR space, Eagle turned to him. "What is she discussing with him, Doctor? What are the two of them planning?" There was an edge in Eagle's voice that Harmon had not heard before.

He took his eyes from his... ward... with reluctance. "Leeth is not planning anything, Eagle. And despite his reputation, Godsson is clinically insane. Nor have they spoken together since the night she broke him free. So-"

"*Red bloody plagues!*" Emma swore. Beside him, he felt Dojo stiffen. The car jerked, drifting most unpleasantly for a moment before moving strangely, as automated systems cut or increased power to each wheel to restore traction.

"Sorry," James muttered. "But bleeding gods, Doctor...!"

Instantly regretting his unguarded words, Harmon could only continue. "They have not spoken since, so there can be no deep 'Benson plot' at work here. Unfortunately, where Godsson is concerned, Leeth is hopelessly naive. There is a chance that..." he paused, then with heavy sarcasm, added, "I trust everyone is sitting down, this time? There is a possibility she has returned to try to 'rescue him' again."

The look Eagle turned on him made Harmon want to tear his VR goggles off. "God help you all, and this Department, if she succeeds in the twenty minutes before you get there, Doctor.

"But what if there is even more to it than that? You say she is a hunter, not a hider. What if this is her method of hunting the Department? You say she can't kill Department agents herself. But what is to stop her unleashing somebody who can? Have you any psychic blocks in place to prevent that, Doctor?"

Harmon's expression was answer enough.

"Good God," said Mother. "They're striking a deal. She'll release him if he takes us out. Then they'd both be on the loose! I told you we needed to have lethal force approved."

Eagle spoke. "We can afford no mistakes, tonight. Thanks to Leeth freeing Benson last year, he is now aware of our final deterrent. My fear is that forewarned, he might somehow survive even that."

There was a very long silence. Ahead, traffic lights turned obligingly green. The car braked, slid around the corner, then jerked straight and leaped forward again.

"What do you estimate the likelihood that your ward is there to release him?" Eagle demanded.

"Low. She gave her word to Professor Sanders that she would not. Her word means a lot to her. Nor do I believe Leeth feels herself cornered, which *might* push her to some extreme act."

Eagle stared at him, and Harmon knew he was considering both Leeth's talent for thinking outside the box and the qualifier attached to that promise: 'not by illegal means.' Harmon shook his head. "It is far more likely she has gone to discuss something particular with Godsson." And then sat back in shock as the likely topic occurred to him: asking Godsson to remove her magical conditioning.

He wanted to groan aloud. Staying silent was the hardest feat of self control he'd ever managed.

Father spoke. "The secondary team will be in position by the time you arrive. They will wait, just a minute away should they be needed."

"With shoot-to-kill orders for Godsson, and to stun Leeth on sight should she somehow get past Dojo, James, Emma, and the Doctor?" Eagle asked.

"*Stun?*" demanded Mother.

"Yes. *If* she somehow releases Benson, it will be essential to question her, to learn what they discussed. And if she has *not* freed him...."

Mother nodded, reluctantly.

"She won't get past us," Harmon stated. *Three words are all I need.*

All eyes turned to him. Then as one, the others all turned to Eagle.

"That's good to know, Doctor. She's just gone for a chat with her old friend, has she?"

He's furious, Harmon belatedly realized.

"On the off chance you're right, and you all survive the next hour, this ends tonight. *Bring her in.* Alive, if possible – but not if it introduces any risk of Godsson's escape. Clear?"

Harmon smelled the salt of the sea, and the car began

weaving insanely. *We must be crossing the Golden Gate Bridge*, he realized. He heard James swear, then the car jolted and swerved, before shooting forward even faster. Around them, horns blared.

"Have you revised your estimate of Leeth's effectiveness as an agent, Mother?" Eagle asked.

"It's not her *effectiveness* I question, it's her sanity. If she somehow spirits Benson out of the grounds before the Doctor can take her, how do you plan to explain the nuclear Incident internationally?"

Eagle scowled at Harmon. "Most countries would be relieved to know the 'Benson threat' has finally ended. The *local* reaction would require more finesse. But with the example of India's God Wars, I would frame it as a measured and sensible 'sterilization' response."

"We're evacuating the building now," Father told them, eyes focusing back on the others. "All except our three main actors of course; and the Poison Witch. A containment vehicle for *her* will not be available for forty-five minutes. Professor Sanders has left the awards dinner and should arrive at roughly the same time."

Eagle turned back to Harmon. "Would you care to explain why you did not predict that Leeth might drop in on the most dangerous mage on the planet?"

This time, Harmon looked faintly ill. "Unfortunately, she considers him a good friend. But I will soon be finding out for myself."

"So your omission was simply a mistake on your part? A miscalculation?"

Harmon saw Mother's smile. But he *should* have seen this possibility. "Indeed."

"I'm willing to forgive such an error once, Doctor. Once." Eagle turned away. "You're sure your selected team can take her this time, Mother?"

"The code Shanahan entered has them locked in behind three sets of steel doors, Eagle. Even your pet whirlwind won't escape from that. And the Doctor assures me he can convince her to rejoin us."

Eagle studied the expression on Harmon's face – who was now very carefully saying nothing – and leaned back in his chair, looking grim.

CHAPTER 20

Leeth rapped at the inches-thick glass window. She saw Godsson turn, and then go still.

She gave a little wave, smiling.

Looking as surprised as she'd ever seen him, he made his greeting gesture – spell – slowly, as if in a dream. Equally slowly, he then moved to the window.

"*Sara?*" he said, before his expression grew stern. "Or should I say, L'ith?" He eyed her up and down, one eyebrow raising so high she thought it would touch his hair. She realized he was taking in her filthy, mud-stained appearance. For some reason, a smile twitched at his lips.

She pursed her own in annoyance, and found herself brushing futilely at her soiled clothes. Running her fingers through her hair, she felt her face flush as lumps of dirt fell out onto the floor.

"Stop it! It wasn't easy getting in to talk to you! Stop being mean."

He smiled. "Stand back a little, let me look at you."

She did, turning around, waiting for the complaints about how she was dressed, or jokes about how grubby she was. She shook more dirt from her hair – but he simply studied her, intensely, his eyes *kind of* seeing her, but also looking *through* her. Like her uncle sometimes did. It was almost like he'd done a time or two before, except *this* had no force behind it; no ache.

He had a complicated expression on his face as he slowly shook his head. Some mix of pleased and annoyed. All he said, though, was that she was looking very well. "And are you staying to chat, this time, or will your colorful serpent friend be dragging you away once again?"

"What serpent friend?" she asked, wondering if Godsson had *really* gone mad, like everyone said he was. But instead of answering, he seemed to relax slightly and changed the subject.

"What can I do for you, L'ith?"

She rolled her eyes at his slightly odd pronunciation of her name, but had long since given up trying to correct it. "What makes you think I came to ask for a favor?"

He just looked down his nose at her.

How rude! "If you must know, I came here to help *you*. Well, to be exact, to ask if you had any ideas *how* I could help you. After last time, I had to promise Prof Sanders not to talk to anyone about you being here, who didn't already know, and not to break any laws in getting you out-"

"How remarkably law-abiding of you."

Her eyes narrowed. "I *promised*. But now I'm wondering, was it really a fair promise? I thought – well, a friend suggested, maybe *you* might have some ideas about how I could get you set free? Legally."

"A friend? A girl, I assume?"

"That's not imp- how'd you know it was a girl?"

Godsson just smiled, but for some reason it made her uneasy.

"Anyway, do you? Have any ideas? You must've thought about it from time to time, right?"

He blinked. "Perhaps a time or two, yes."

"Well?"

He frowned. "I thought public pressure would be sufficient to end my illegal imprisonment. But apparently, mankind feels so little gratitude for my sacrifices that they... wait. What did you mean when you said you had promised to tell only those who 'already knew'?"

"I think hardly anyone knows you're here. Why does that matter?"

For just a moment, she saw a flash of anger. But when he answered, his tone was mild. "Oh, it matters, Sara. Fifteen years of imprisonment *matters*."

"Fifteen-! Oh, Godsson, I'm sorr-"

He waved her apology aside, smiling. "It does, however, mean the solution is simple. The religious pure, those strong in faith, must be told of my Second Coming. My rebirth. Who I am. You, Sara – L'ith," he amended, smiling strangely, "can be my new Peter."

"What? Look, I'm not changing my name – 'specially not to a boy's one. And people don't get born twice. And even if they did, people must've already known who you were, before you got locked up here."

His eyes fastened on hers. "But that's just it, Sara: I didn't know, myself. Not until I traveled to the Deeps, to the place beneath even the Imaginal, underpinning Reality. It was only in the fight there, against the Enemy of Mankind, that I saw the Light and the Truth, and remembered Myself."

He'd started glowing. Which was very impressive, the first few times you saw it, but after that it was just kind of annoying. She blinked, scrinching up her eyes so she could see him. "Okay, so you're saying you just want me to tell a bunch of people you're here? That's all?"

He smiled. "Yes. It will suffice to tell those who wait for my return that I am here. I have Risen."

"Okay, okay. Can you stop glowing, please? Thank you! So you're saying, it wasn't a fair promise, and it's okay to tell people you're here?"

"Yes. Professor Sanders tricked you, by having you agree to impossible conditions. How is that fair? You are a grown woman, now, Sara – L'ith. You must have heard of the right to free speech."

"Yeah." Still, though, she had the sneaking feeling she was missing something. Could the solution to saving Godsson really be that easy?

"But let's talk about you for a while. You seem a little sad. How are things between you and your uncle? He's treating you as kindly as ever, is he?"

She flushed as she remembered that Godsson and her uncle had never really got on. And as it turned out, Godsson had been right, all along. Nobody else had ever warned her about her uncle. She blinked. Maybe he could even help? Though how could she explain? Just thinking about her uncle's magical controls-?

"I'm sorry, Sara, I shouldn't tease you. I could see at once that you have had... alterations made to you. Terrible alterations. Yes?" He stared at her, but vaguely; *inside* her. Triggering a tickle of discomfort.

"Terrible. Yes," he said.

She felt strangely naked.

He nodded. "Yes, I could help. I could remove his control."

She stared at him in shock: he *knew?* How could he know? She felt a rush of desire, a hunger to enter the cell, to kiss him, to take him – but the instant arousal was so unexpected, so surprising, and *his* reaction showed so little surprise, it penetrated the fever. She remembered, then, throwing herself onto Emma, when Emma had begun to suspect. She felt her limbs trembling with need; a need *imposed.*

But that vast urge to throw herself onto Godsson, making her want to take him: instead of making her want to agree, to say '*Yes,*' it made her wary instead.

You know? she tried to ask, but the gray confusion rose before the words reached her lips.

And Godsson watched. "Fascinating. Yes, I can help. I can remove Harmon's control."

Something about the way he said that made her uncomfortable. "What would I have to do?"

"Just trust me. Open yourself."

Those were almost exactly the words her uncle had said, before he'd done *it*. Maybe she could trust Godsson inside her mind, though? She shook her head. *No. Letting someone in, to tamper with her mind....* "No."

"I understand. How could you trust anyone, even me, after a betrayal like that? It's wise of you, Sara, though sad. You were magnificent, the night we vanquished the Enemy of Mankind's creature, together. So brave. You are that rare person, who understands the value of personal sacrifice for the greater good." His eyes met hers. "I had hopes we would work together, to right other wrongs.

"Yet I cannot imagine how your uncle's betrayal made you feel. Fortunately, you are strong, and have your own powers. You have even escaped his immediate influence, I gather, or you would not be here now. But what of others: how will you stop him doing to other girls, the same thing he has done to you? If you only knew how they suffer – out there on the streets, preyed on by men like him, or worse. But your uncle, he at least you should stop, before he finds another to twist, torment and torture."

She'd never thought of that. Staring past Godsson, once again she came back to that dark place, to the obvious solution: kill... not Keepie. *Keepie* was already dead. Kill the Doctor.

She blinked, meeting Godsson's sad eyes. He nodded. "I see it in your face: the knowledge of what you must do. But you will also need to end his other creation."

"What other creation?"

"His creature, the one you had him Call, when we battled Her together, in my cell. His 'invisible monster,' you named him."

"Robo?" She gawped at him. "Uncle *made* Robo?"

"You and Harmon, together, made... *Robo*." He smiled, just faintly. "What an apt name. Robo," he repeated, as if trying it out, before smiling kindly at her again.

She shivered, suddenly cold. Feeling her skin prickle,

as if it was trying to flinch away at just the memory of being near Robo. A Robo that had changed, over the years,
getting colder, and bigger. Scarier.

"What do you mean, *Uncle* and I made Robo? I didn't
make anything! I'm not magic – at least, not like that.
And besides, I was only little, and Uncle told me about
Robo almost as soon as I got here, and I first Hunted him."

"Harmon, through you, has reached Deep. He somehow harnessed the power of a child's imagination. Your
profound and sure belief fed Harmon's creation. Gave it
reality." He met her eyes, trapped them. "And now it tortures, and kills, and only you can stop it."

She felt her mouth gape open.

"You didn't know, L'ith? Even I, locked away here, am
allowed to receive world and local news. Have you not realized that The Breaker is your Robo?"

She just stared at him, in shock. The Breaker... all his
tortures; like her uncle did to her – only worse? "But- but,
The Breaker is a *man,* or a... ro... bot...."

"Or some strange blending of the two, yes." Schooling
his expression, he added "I suspect that somehow, through
some mechanism I don't understand, 'Robo' has bonded to
a vulnerable human, creating a disturbed killer. One who
will be attracted to you, as its creator. It will seek you out."

He waited, while she stared off into space, stunned. He
let her absorb the implications. "But as its creator, L'ith,
your touch...."

His words brought her attention back.

"Given your part in its creation, your touch, with a
Blessing from me, will allow you to end its torment."
Godsson's eyes were alight.

"My... touch? You mean, like stabbing it, right?"

"No, no. If its host is killed, it will merely find another.
Besides, much of what it does now is because it suffers. It
is in pain – feeling emptiness at your rejection of it: at being cast away by the female half of its conception. Abandoned, if you like, by its mother."

An awful pain surged inside her.

"No, you need to hold it to you, soothe it. Change it.
Be yourself, let it mold itself to your spirit, instead of to its
father's, your uncle's."

She found herself shaking her head, even though it
made a dismaying kind of sense. She just couldn't...

"You are afraid. A pity. How sad for your child. Would it help you gather your courage to know that with my help, my Blessing, I can arm you so you may complete its evolution: allow it to flower as it should?"

If his eyes had been alight before, now eagerness *poured* off him in waves.

"I dunno. It's killing people. Torturing them. That's wrong. I think I need to kill it."

"Because it kills?" His eyes burned into hers. "Is it so different from its mother?"

It is! I'm not cruel. She glared back, defiant.

His look softened. "Yes, destroy it if you wish. The choice will be yours. My blessing will simply empower you."

"What do you mean by a blessing? Is that a kind of magic?" she asked, increasingly suspicious. "How can you do that? Magic can't go through the barriers around your cell."

"A blessing is far more powerful than magic, L'ith, and far more subtle. Especially for one such as you. And I. No magical barrier can obstruct a blessing. Place both your hands on the window."

She frowned, wondering if she should; remembering the transparent smoke coiling and curling around her hand and arm when she'd done a similar thing at his request, all those years ago. He'd said it was just an illusion – but how could he make even an illusion go through the magical barriers? It didn't make sense. Was Godsson tricking her? Did *everyone* she know, lie to her and trick her all the time?

Godsson chuckled. "I do believe you're afraid, L'ith. What has happened to change you so much from the brave young girl I knew?"

Uncle, was the answer that sprang to mind. She shook the thought away. Godsson still waited, one eyebrow slightly raised and a gentle smile on his lips. She had to force herself not to look away.

Putting one hand, only, on the thick glass, she pressed it flat. "If a blessing's so powerful, you shouldn't need both hands."

Off to her right, tied in his chair, Mr Shanahan called out, so faintly she had to strain to hear him, like he was a *long* way away. "Sara? What are yeh doing, girl?" He sounded scared.

She turned toward him. "It's okay, Mr S." *I think.* "Godsson's giving me a blessing. To fight The Breaker."

He frowned, his eyes moving down to her lips then back up to her eyes. She watched the color drain from his face, a look of horror dawning.

She looked down at herself, then around, trying to see what had frightened him so much.

"Sara, I can't hear yeh," he said, but only faintly. "But you hear me, aye?"

She nodded. "Yeah, though a bit... muffled?"

He shook his head. "It means Godsson's working magic outside his cell!"

"Who are you talking to, L'ith?" Godsson demanded. "Did you bring someone else with you?"

She turned back to him. Let her hand fall from the window. "Maybe."

"Oh, L'ith. I fear you have been tricked. Who was it? Did this person help you get here, to see me?"

She nodded.

"Why? Why did... he...? offer to help?"

She frowned. It'd been help, or be dragged here. But why had he entered the code? She could have forced him to use a palm scanner, or an iris one, had there been one... but she couldn't've forced him to enter the code. *So why had he?*

Uh oh.

"I fear you have been trapped down here, L'ith, almost as I am." He shook his head. "I am so sorry you put yourself in this position, for me. But I can still perform a quick blessing. If you one day regain your freedom, and have the courage, it will be enough to defeat Robo. But decide quickly, there may be little time. This may be the last we ever speak together."

What to do? Was Godsson tricking her, or had Mr Shanahan? Or both? But she remembered Mr S's sly look. She stepped over to him, staring down at him, hearing his harsh breathing. "Am I locked in here, Mr Shanahan? Is that why you stopped me propping the door open?"

He didn't answer; just looked sick. It was answer enough.

Striding back to Godsson's cell, she met his soft, sad brown eyes; and made her decision. Though as she placed her hand flat on the glass, she tensed, ready for some new, horrid deceit.

But Godsson only bent his head slightly, meeting her eyes, and said "Oh Father, bless this servant of your will so her hands may grip the spirit she calls Robo, and defeat him when they meet." Then lifted his head.

"That's it? That's all?"

He smiled. "It will be enough, I assure you. But I sense your time is running out. I will pray for your swift release: who knows how many more people Robo will ruin, while you are locked away as I am."

"No one's gonna lock me away." She dropped her hand. "Bye, Godsson. And thank you. Till next time."

Turning, she stalked to Mr Shanahan.

Each step away from the door to Godsson's cell added a layer of sound. First Mr S's panicked questions, then the scrape of the chair legs on the concrete floor as he struggled to get free, then the rustle of his clothes and the rush of his breaths.

He stared at her, an awful fear in his face as he watched her approach. Like he thought she was going to do something terrible to him.

"Will that code *unlock* the doors too, Mr Shanahan?"

His eyes widened, but he lifted his chin while bracing his spine against the chair back. "No. But I figured it'd be better for yeh to be arrested by the FBI than recaptured by whoever's hunting yeh."

He thought that would be *better?* "Oh, Mr S." She shook her head, and he tensed.

"I have to leave. Look after Faith, okay?"

He blinked, then un-tensed. "I'm sorry, Sara girl, but yeh can't leave. We're stuck down her, with *him,*" he shuddered, "until they come for you."

"*You* may be, Mr S. But I'm not staying here," she swore, hearing iron in her own voice. "I have things I have to do."

She paced to the door, then stood, just breathing, in, then out, shoulders relaxing, gathering the force inside herself. Feeling the shadow of her need coil through her muscles. Visualizing the lock, and the strike. The force needed. Setting aside thoughts of time running out, of need, of chance. Seeing the lock shatter.

She turned partly away, gathering her force, then

struck.

"Holy Mother of Christ!" she heard behind her, when her heel slammed into the target, the steel door buckling to the harsh sound of metal snapping.

Wedging both hands into the gap she'd created, she *pulled.* One sharp *crack* as metal fractured, the upper section shifting a hand's span toward her. She heaved again, feeling every sinew like steel cables-

Crack. With a lurch, the bottom of the door broke free, and she hurled it open as alarms started sounding.

"Holy bloody Mother of Christ!"

She turned back to Mr Shanahan. *"See?"*

Then charged up the stairs to the next door, leaving Mr S gaping, astonished, behind her.

"Sara?" she heard, his voice fading behind her. "Don't be leavin' me down here wit' *him!* Sara?"

She ignored him. It was just another trick. Godsson was still locked in. Probably they had some kind of noise canceler thing in the corridor outside his cell.

She had to smash the hardened glass of the front door to leave the now utterly silent Institute.

The area was completely deserted – except for one shaggy figure who rose to all fours the moment she appeared inside the foyer.

"Faith!" She bounded down the stairs, grabbing her friend who jumped up on her hind legs. They both sank back down, Leeth suffering the extravagant, relieved licks with delight. She hugged her friend tightly in return, breathing in the strong scents. Storing them up.

For one glorious, glowing moment, she imagined Faith by her side, loping alongside her as she raced back into New Francisco and then into the Dumps....

But the tunnel was too small. She'd only made it big enough for herself. And there was no time to widen it, now. *Stupid! Stupid girl!* She felt tears falling.

"I'm sorry, Faith, I didn't plan this out properly! I didn't know you'd made a pack that could protect everyone here, so you could come with me. I'm so stupid, I didn't think how *you* would've gotten ready, too, so you could come with me. I'm so sorry!" She buried her face in Faith's fur.

But time was running out.

"I'll be back, I promise." She pulled away, then stood, hugging herself. In the distance, she could hear a murmur of voices, and faint *yips*. She looked up, around. "Did they evacuate? Why'd they do *that?*"

Faith looked at her, but for once she couldn't work out what Faith was trying to tell her.

"I'm sorry. I have to go. But I *will* be back. You'd better go and help your pack guard everyone from whatever they're worried about. Go on. Go, Faith!"

But Faith insisted on running with her, all the way to her tunnel, whining as Leeth squeezed back into it.

Behind her, as she wormed her way through the moist earth, she heard Faith tearing at it with her paws, the sounds tearing equally at her heart. For long seconds, she had to stop, letting tears fall into the soil.

Then, bracing her elbows and her resolve, she wriggled on through the short burrow.

She was a body length into the tunnel when she heard her uncle's voice, behind her.

CHAPTER 21

It was no surprise to Harmon that, unlike the lift doors back at the Department, the gates to the Institute did not lie open and waiting for them. Although they *did* begin swinging apart the moment they braked to a stop. He unbuckled himself. Fifty meters inside, a small crowd had gathered – patients, staff, and a contingent of humanoid robots, both nurses and patrol bots. All surrounded by a pack of cyborg guard dogs.

"What are you doing, Doctor?" James demanded.

"If we don't waste time arguing," he said, levering himself out of the cramped rear seat, "I can astrally scan the complete perimeter within a minute. And unlike the Dumps, *this* area, I know well."

Dojo leaped out. "I will stay with the Doctor."

James and Emma exchanged a brief look, then zoomed up the curved road through the woods, the gates closing behind the car.

"Perhaps you could ensure the gates will open quickly, Dojo, when I have finished?" Without waiting for an answer, Harmon lay down at the edge of the road. Composing himself, he slipped effortlessly from his body. Beside him, a Barrier with the spiritual weight of a mountain arced ahead and behind. With lightning speed he darted off, skimming its edge, alert for any sense of Leeth's presence.

As he completed his circuit, he noted the clean lines of his Japanese companion's aura, who stood guard over his body, alert but chafing at the delay. Without allowing himself time to adjust, Harmon slipped back into his body and stood, swaying slightly as the gates swung open a second time. "Nothing. Let's go in, so I can check inside."

Ignoring Dojo's outstretched hand, he moved the few steps needed to cross the Barrier as the gates closed behind them. Lying down again, he slid his spirit free once more.

Inside, conditions were different. Decades sealed under a magically-impenetrable dome, psychically severed from the surrounding countryside, had led to strange changes in the area. Pockets of dreamlike tranquility, stands of moss-draped trees with dark branches clawing skyward, paths laced with pastel twinkling energies. He shot off, again following the mountain-like Barrier curving now overhead.

He could feel the worried knot of tension that was the

crowd of evacuees, but couldn't directly Percept them from this distance. Skirting past them, he flashed forward, following the edge of the Barrier; the wall.

And *Saw* Leeth, blazing bright. She was on her knees, clasping the paradoxically bright aura of the cyborg wardog. He drew nearer, studying the bond, the way the two auras mingled. Remembering how hers had coiled toward his own – once.

He saw the agony it caused Leeth to tear herself free. For a moment, she stiffened, her head turning in his direction. Faith, her aura in sync, turned toward him too – but then Leeth shook herself and plunged *into the earth*. The dog dived after her, clawing at the soil in anguish, digging frantically.

He swayed, buffeted by the raw emotions, and drew back, astral senses probing. No sign of Godsson. She hadn't released him! And her aura had been unchanged. His controls remained intact, undisturbed. His spirit swelled.

For long seconds he hovered, watching. Then flashed to the inner Ward that encircled just the buildings. Spiraling outwards, he made a perfunctory search for Godsson, just in case he was free but not with Leeth.

By the time he sat back up in his body, he had fully regained his composure. Standing, he brushed off his trousers. "Leeth is not within the grounds outside the Institute proper. Nor is Godsson. I'm quite safe – if you wish to run ahead, I will join you at my best pace."

Dojo sprinted off.

Harmon also ran; into the trees, ordering his Link's torch function on.

He heard the dog, Faith, first. When he arrived at the tunnel mouth, the animal was half buried, only its hindquarters visible.

Sensing him, it wriggled backwards, squirming free. He saw its jaws open, then the animal went still, just watching him. Looking somehow surprised.

She will still be able to hear me, he felt sure. He could take her, now.

The wardog studied him. Not moving.

He made his decision.

"If you can hear me, Leeth, you need to hurry. Backup

forces will have the whole area cordoned off within...” he checked his watch. “Two minutes.”

And then he walked to the main building.

CHAPTER 22

There was total silence in the Department's largest briefing room as they watched the footage from the camera in the corridor. Emma drew in her breath as she saw for herself the metal door suddenly buckle outward.

Small fingers poked through the gap to first grip it – then seconds later, rip the door wide open. Leeth raced through. Eagle watched, expressionless, as she repeated it twice more before once again suborning the cyborg patrol dog, the two of them disappearing into the trees.

"Were the doors defective? Did you examine them, on site?" Mother asked.

James answered. "No. The doors were strong. Not equal to what we have here, but I couldn't have done what she did, Mother, and I have level three augmentation. *That* was something like level four. Nor do I understand how the flesh of her fingers survived the pressure she applied to tear each door open."

"Doctor?"

Harmon shrugged. "Transient hypertonia? Hysterical strength? As I have said on numerous occasions, her magic is directed inward, affecting her body."

"And Shanahan?" Mother demanded, turning to Emma. "Tell me that *he* at least heard what she spoke to David Benson about, for five minutes?"

"No, Mother," Emma said, grimacing. "Although he *was* able to tell us she said she hadn't come to free Benson. But he was unconscious when we found him, and remembers nothing after she tied him to the chair."

"Once again we see how she treats her 'friends'," Mother said, glaring at the Doctor. "I suppose we should be grateful she decided not to kill him."

Harmon shook his head. "I must correct Emma: he was *asleep*, not unconscious. Minimal physical injury, too, just a mild concussion, easily healed, and bruising on the side of his temple. She had obviously taken care with her blow. If that was what happened."

Mother stared at him in disbelief. "'*If that was what happened?*' We saw Shanahan on camera, Doctor, opening the doors and leading her into the trap. And James and Emma found him 'asleep,' tied to a chair when they arrived on scene – too late. Who else could have rendered him unconscious – Godsson?"

Harmon frowned. A dismaying possibility. It might be

wise to examine Shanahan magically, a second time. More carefully. Even assuming the worst, he could not credit even Godsson as able to do more than erase a few fresh memories, in the minutes the two had been alone. But better to be paranoid than take a risk.

Mother had turned to James. "And *you* failed to close the perimeter: allowed her to escape, despite a cordon being thrown around the area within minutes. Can anyone explain that? We knew she was there, people! How did she evade capture *again*? I swear, it's like trying to hunt a shadow! Can she go invisible, Doctor?"

"No. Absolutely not." Harmon saw Eagle was watching him closely.

"Then how?"

Nelson holographically joined the meeting. "I can answer that. Look."

On the wall to their left, footage appeared: a female cyclist speeding past a camera on a winding road.

"Back-casting based on her speed, and estimating from where we found her burrow, I'd say she had a bicycle ready, and rode off about a minute after the backup team had passed her starting point. Two minutes after team one had passed that same location. Which puts the timing at about two minutes *before* the drone cordon was set up. By the time it was deployed, she'd left the area."

There was a brief silence.

"*A bicycle.* You're telling me she escaped the *Department* because she had a *bicycle?* Clearly, we'll need to increase our budget substantially if our opponents have *bicycles* at their disposal." She glared at Nelson. "Why was that possibility not factored in?"

He shrugged. "Cycling isn't one of her listed skills. The Doctor said she'd never ridden, and she'd only ever used the VR exercise unit here."

"We know she's a fast learner, Mother," Father pointed out, after a look at Eagle.

Who had still not spoken, his attention entirely fixed on Harmon.

"Irrelevant," Mother said. "The key question is, what drove her to this reckless incursion into the Institute? Even Leeth must have considered it risky. What was so important to her? What about Benson himself – were you able to learn anything from him directly, Doctor? He was your patient there for over ten years."

Harmon looked even unhappier than he had previously. He watched Emma, who had overheard his exchange with Godsson while she questioned Shanahan. "In my expert opinion," he began, then paused at Mother's reaction. When she merely pursed her lips, he continued. "Godsson appeared extremely pleased with himself. If I could describe his attitude in a single word, I would say 'smug'. I would go so far as to say he feels that whatever happened tonight was partial 'payment' for being rendered helpless and recaptured, last year."

James and Emma both sucked in their breath, but Harmon could tell that this time it was due to their old fear that Godsson had manipulated Leeth when she was younger. "On that occasion, he got little further than the front drive before he was neutralized," he reassured them.

Emma watched him carefully. Then raised one eyebrow.

He glared at her, but could see that if *he* didn't volunteer the rest of it, she would. "Godsson also thanked me for preparing such an exquisite tool for the final correction," he reluctantly added.

Without moving a muscle, without changing his expression, Eagle's presence seemed to fill the room.

Apart from flicking a glance to him, Mother did not allow it to distract her. "Correction to what?"

"I don't know. Tonight was the first time he had put a name to the plan he's been dropping mysterious hints about for fifteen years. I would say he chose to do so *because* he knew there were others in earshot, while I spoke with him. I have no reason to assume that is what he calls his fantasy, even to himself. He probably picked the name simply to sound ominous and threatening. I remind you, he is locked in a cell; behind metaphysical barriers through which no magic should be able to escape."

Mother looked horrified. "'*Should?*' Taken with your earlier remarks about Shanahan's unconsciousness, are you suggesting those barriers are failing?"

The idea was beyond dreadful. *Am I really so certain Leeth had not simply knocked Shanahan unconscious?* She had done so before. But these circumstances were different. The bruising had not been fresh enough. The recording had also shown Leeth turn and appear to speak to Shanahan, before briefly leaving and then reappearing in camera shot.

"I fear it is a distinct possibility, yes." Appalled expressions met that remark.

"Chipshit!" Nelson blurted. "Should we maybe get the Dragon here, to inspect them? Check his Wards aren't rotting, or something?"

Mother closed her eyes. "Nelson, I would expect a remark like that from Leeth, not you. I will schedule a refresher course on politics for you. You just suggested that the world's most powerful mage, the devious head of a hostile state, might take time from his schedule to inspect a situation that he himself set up fifteen years earlier, giving him a chance to prod it along."

"All the same," Harmon added, "had Leeth not taken her 'reckless' action tonight, we would still be blissfully ignorant of the possible danger."

"Enough." Eagle's voice fell like a clap of thunder into the room.

Harmon noticed all the others ease away from the line of sight between himself and Eagle.

"Do you recall my orders tonight? End it: bring her in. Tonight."

Harmon's skin crawled. *Eagle knew.*

"Now we're *lucky* that Leeth broke into a secure facility to chat with the most dangerous mage on the planet? You and I will discuss that further, Doctor, in just a minute.

"But first: I no longer care who is responsible for bringing her in. Just get it done. *I* will decide what is done with her at that time." He looked from Harmon to Mother. "And just to ensure there are no conflicts of interest in our efforts to return her, all previous deals are terminated as of now.

"Despite his failure to predict tonight's fiasco, I still believe the Doctor's idea of the 'Bad News' narrowcasts into the Dumps is worth trying. On the assumption she'll feel guilt at her lack of contribution in catching 'big bad guys,' bombard the local news feeds with stories of home grown and overseas threats. Begin them at once. And if that plan also fails, Doctor, I may have you personally canvas the Dumps on foot with James, until you are successful.

"James, Emma: you will review the security arrangements at the Institute for Paranormal Dysfunction. I do not want her able to reach Godsson ever again. But *should* she try, I want her trapped.

"Any questions?" He looked around. "No? Dismissed. All but the Doctor."

Those physically present left, almost as swiftly as the merely-virtual attendees.

Eagle stared at Harmon. Not speaking. Expression grim.

"So Leeth merely went to chat with her old friend? And we're lucky she did so? How very tidy. Unless, perhaps, there was some other plan involved? Perhaps set up even before Leeth's dramatic 'escape' from us. Perhaps the mastermind behind all Leeth's recent actions lies closer at hand."

"That's ridiculous! She knocked me out and *kidnapped* me-"

"Before you launch into the retelling of Leeth's dramatic escape, Doctor, I'd like you to view *this*."

A hologram sprang up between Eagle and Harmon, whose heart instantly sank. Darkness that brightened to a wildly pivoting viewpoint that oriented on himself, standing between the trees of the Institute. The camera angle was low to the ground.

He watched himself speak.

'If you can hear me, Leeth, you need to hurry. Backup forces will have the whole area cordoned off within two minutes.' In the hologram, he turned and walked away.

The image vanished. "I believe it may be in the Department's best interests to retire you."

For Harmon, time stopped: frozen between one beat of his heart and the next. His skin chilled.

Time re-started. Harmon felt his heart beat again. "I see. No act of kindness shall go unpunished," he murmured, then met Eagle's glare. "But more than that, hearing her claw her escape through the earth, I was more certain than ever that dragging her back in chains is not the way to return her to us, to restore her faith in this Department. As I noted recently. I will also remind you that I recommended, *before* the incident which incited Leeth's departure, that I should be allowed to attempt the healing of her friend. I warned you that your refusal could lead to unexpected results. This whole affair is of the Department's making, not mine.

"In the circumstances, I had to make a decision. I acted."

Eagle considered him. Eventually, he spoke again.

"Very plausible, Doctor. But I no longer have confidence in your judgment where your ward is concerned. I even question your value to the Department. You have clearly demonstrated where your loyalties lie. But no one is perfect: perhaps your spectacularly unsuccessful predictions of her behavior tonight were merely bad luck. Perhaps you can *restore* her to us yet. I will give you forty-eight hours to prove to me you are working in this Department's interest, rather than against us.

"Forty-eight hours, Harmon: prove your commitment."

But once alone, Eagle settled back, continuing to consider the event that had most surprised him: the Doctor's actions. Harmon had risked his position here, his access to Leeth, and even his personal safety, for her freedom. Extraordinary. Could he really value the girl more than himself?

If so, it would provide a lever which could be used to control him – as long as Harmon himself remained unconscious of his own feelings. The man's blindness, considering both his intelligence and his profession, was quite remarkable.

Or was it as he half suspected – part of a plot between the two of them? It remained a distinct possibility. But as yet, he had no idea what their goal might be.

Either way, it was definitely time for him to step in and take charge of Leeth, personally.

CHAPTER 23

Carrying a bicycle for kilometers through the Dumps wasn't fun. She dumped the stupid thing by her bedding, still grumbling that the guy she'd hired it from hadn't been around.

Not long after she'd started racing back to the city, she'd heard a faint, strange sound in the background and stopped to listen. She eventually recognized it as a whole swarm of drones, spread out back in the direction of the Institute. *Like Uncle warned me.* She'd jumped back on her bike and pedaled away as fast as she could.

Why did *he warn me? Why didn't he 'Mode One' me?*

That question preyed on her the whole ride home, trying to distract her. One more thing piled on top of everything else.... Instead, she'd put her head down and just *pedaled,* losing herself in fierce exertion. The rush of the cold night wind. The sweeping curves. Dodging idiots in manual-drive cars....

Only to reach the transportation shop and finding it closed, dark and locked up! For a moment she'd pictured spearing the dumb bike through the tiny store window and just leaving it there for him to find in the morning. But she needed that deposit back for her stake in the Fest, less than a week away now. And what if Nelson had spotted her on her ride back? *Could* she even safely return it to him tomorrow, without them trying to grab her as usual?

She'd ripped off her nurse-bot disguise as soon as she'd squirmed from the tunnel. Now she stripped off the rest of her clothes. Snatching up a rag, she soaked it and started rubbing angrily at the ingrained dirt. "I don't even have a stupid shower," she muttered. "Or soap. And now I'm talking to myself! *Aloud!*"

I'm distracting myself, she realized, and stopped washing.

She shook her head. Being with Faith again... but then having to abandon her? *Again.* And what Godsson had told her: *Robo was The Breaker.* She shook her head. *And me and Uncle made it, somehow. Or had we? Had Godsson just made that up?*

Godsson telling her she had to stop her uncle. Stop him hurting other girls. *Kill him.* She swallowed.

Then hearing her uncle, even through a couple of feet of earth. *Talking to me. Knowing I was there, but not taking control. Even* warning *me, helping me get away.*

What did it mean? Was it just to make her think he was on her side? Confuse her?

Yes. It was some kind of trick. A trap. It wasn't like *he* was the one in trouble, and needed her help to escape the Department. He was a mage. He was too valuable to them. They probably had *all sorts* of plans for him, like reading enemy agents' minds, and taking control of them.

No, he didn't need her help. He was still her enemy. She had to *deal* with him.

There was one tiny positive: she knew now how to help Godsson. At least *that* part of the plan had gone as well as she'd hoped. She'd have to thank Marcie. She laughed aloud, though her voice sounded a bit strange even to her. High. Breathless.

She started washing herself again, forcing herself to calm down.

By the time she'd finished, her stomach rumbled. *I wonder what time it is?* It felt like one a.m. Too late to go and buy food.

She eyed her stew pot, considering the congealed mass inside it. Then sniffed, and grimaced. *Uh oh.*

So now she had some garbage disposal to do, and if she wanted to appease the growing emptiness in her stomach, she needed to hunt down something.

Rats again, probably. And her with no herbs.

Damn them!

She headed out.

Standing, staring at her catch, she tried to summon up the enthusiasm to cook them. *Barbecuing them'd be fastest: then I wouldn't have to skin them.* But there was precious little wood in the Dumps – certainly none for burning – and she hadn't yet bartered for that roaster from the Sustainers.

Sighing, she squatted down to skin and prepare the first of the six little bodies, starting with the plumpest of the rodents. Knowing they'd be worth more, and taste better, if she traded them for food at any eatery in the Dumps instead.

She found herself suddenly hunching forward in the dark, tears falling, feeling sorry for herself. *I shouldn't have to live like this! It's all* his *fault! Dammit!*

Tossing the rat down, wiping her face with the backs of

her hands, she rinsed them, then drank several mugs of water to fill her growling stomach. Curling into a ball, she lay down to sleep. Her stupid stomach could just wait until dawn.

She sniffled, with eyes shut, remembering Faith's smell; the feel of her warm fur; and fell asleep, pretending she wasn't alone.

The next morning she was the first customer at the Landwave, everything still all grays and blacks, the sun just a faint peach glow below the horizon. Boris, a large beefy guy with a strange accent, quizzed her about her catch – where, when – sniffed them, then took her order and added five creds to her stick.

Breakfast and five creds profit for an hour's hunting. *Yay, Leeth: you're really making a difference to the world!*

She hunched in on herself, devouring the battered fish before licking her fingers clean and considering the problem of her uncle. In the background, a radio broadcast was going on about a terrorist attack in Seattle last night.

'*Government agents last night broke a massive drug ring, amidst controversial claims the foreign gang was funded by Chinese interests, a claim robustly denied by the Imperial Palace. "Stories like these always surface when the international balance of trade figures are released. The US needs to stop looking outside its own borders for the sources of its considerable social problems."*

'*An FBI spokeswoman said the timing of the raid had been due to intelligence gathered after penetration of the group's communications channels. "We knew where they'd be at nine pm, so that was when we had to act".*'

Nine pm. *About the time I'd been tunneling in to the Institute.* She wondered if Commander Stone had been the FBI agent in charge. *I should be doing cool missions like that!*

Thanking Boris, she stood and stretched, then for once just sauntered off, head down, kicking at stones, thinking.

Her uncle, and his Mode One, was the problem. Even if he'd chosen not to use it, once. *Especially* if she was going to need his help to deal with The Breaker. Though Godsson said she could do it on her own, thanks to his blessing.

But the thought of *holding* Robo felt deeply wrong. She shuddered. Once she'd dealt with her uncle, she'd make him tell her what he'd done; what Robo even *was*. Find some other way of ending Robo. The Breaker.

How could she be Robo's *mother?*

No. She couldn't think about that now. First problems first: Uncle.

But do I really need to? He hadn't take control of her last night, when he easily could have. *No. Don't be stupid: that was just a trick.* Images flashed: the ugly twist of his lips as he watched her struggle not to slice herself; the triumph in his eyes as he thrust from behind....

Just a trick.

Chemical castration? But that'd just mean he couldn't sex her. That was the least of her worries.

Rip out his voice box? But even if she *could* hurt him physically that badly – and she knew from bitter experience her muscles just locked up, if she tried – he'd just heal himself up.

Could I maybe just squish his larynx, and somehow stop him healing magically, so his body repaired itself but made the injury permanent? Like Marcie's would've been?

She shuddered. Shook her head. *No. That'd make me as bad as him.* She shook her head again. *Just.... No. Besides – I* can't *properly hurt him. He did something to me so I* can't. *And I'm not going to* torture *him. I'll never torture* anyone!

She paced on, just wandering, for once on no special mission. The sun rose, and people began leaving their squats and shelters, starting the daily business of living. She heard laughter, and a young girl singing, her voice light and happy, and she turned away, heading into quieter areas.

But would whatever magical command he'd set inside her, stop her from getting someone *else* to kill him, for her?

She felt her lip curl in distaste. If she did that, he'd have won: beaten her. *I have to save myself, not get someone else to do it for me.*

Anyway, how could I explain that *to the Department? I can't tell anyone what he does to me, so I couldn't justify my actions. Mother already thinks I'm some sort of crazy person who likes killing things. It's why I let him... change me. Why I trusted him. To make it so I couldn't hurt anyone who worked for the Department. So they could trust me.*

And how well had that worked out?

What she really wanted was her old Keepie back. The good Keepie. She felt tears well up in her eyes, again, and shook them angrily away. That person was dead, and gone. If he'd ever really existed.

Why had he done it all? 'This is for your good, Leeth,' he'd say. 'It will make you stronger, inside. Where it counts.'

Liar.

What about if I just talk *to him? Make him see that what he's doing is wrong? Somehow stop him from being able to talk, then just explain it to him?*

Something about that idea appealed. But how could she know if he'd really change? *He'd probably just lie to me. Like always.*

Could she involve some third party? But she couldn't see how she could: she *physically* couldn't explain to any-one what was going on. So that was a dead end.

Yet even so, that idea – getting someone, Marcie maybe, to help – also felt like a possibility. Despite know-ing it wasn't.

Godsson said he *could do it: break Uncle's controls.* Should she go back, accept his offer?

No. Something told her she'd made the right decision last night. Even if she could get back in. Though she'd al-ready thought of a way; and they probably wouldn't expect her to go back tonight, so she'd probably even get away again. She giggled. *I hope Mother had been furious!*

But Godsson's offer, to remove her uncle's controls... no. She shook her head.

Then *what?* There had to be *some* solution!

Feeling like screaming, she wandered the Dumps.

It was at noon, her hands thrust deep in the tight pock-ets of her shorts, her head down and kicking through the rubble, that the idea came to her. She frowned, thinking through all the problems; but also seeing solutions. She'd need to spend even more money, and she'd need Teef's help, and Barney's. Marcie's, too. And she'd have to somehow get her uncle out of the Department, to neutral ground.

But it would work. She was sure.

She turned the idea around in her head, fitting all the pieces together. *I'm so glad I didn't kill Teef for his water that first night, before I knew him. He's turned out to be a real friend.* That thought seemed important, somehow.

With the borrowed Link from Teef, she checked all the approaches, and her escape routes, and then made the call, contacting the Bureau for Internal Development. "I want to speak to Eagle, please."

"Is that a first name, or last?" the woman asked.

"He *runs* the Bureau. *That* Eagle."

"I'm sorry, we have no one-"

"May I please speak to your superior?"

"I would need the subject of your call."

"I have information about a dangerous person on your Wanted list."

"What is the name of the person on the Wanted list?"

"Look, just put me through to your superior."

"I'm sorry, I need-"

"It involves a break-in at the Institute for Paranormal Dysfunction last night."

"I'm-" The woman stopped. Seconds passed. She sounded more alert when next she spoke. "Can you tell me the time of the break-in?"

"I- It would have been between nine and ten pm."

"Transferring you now. Please hold."

"Eagle?"

"Hah!" a male voice answered. "No. You have information about a break-in. Can I ask how you know of that?"

"Because *I* broke in. And I know Eagle will want to talk to me, so if you don't at least ping him, you're gonna be in big trouble."

"You do know it's a federal offense to waste-"

"What's your name?"

There was a pause. "Agent Jacob Reynolds."

She bit her tongue. What she *wanted* to find out was where Agent Jacob Reynolds was, so she could go there and shove his Link- "Look, if I'm right, if you text the following message to Eagle it will get an immediate response-"

"I'm not going to... you're calling from the Hunters Point Dumps?"

"Yes, and I know perfectly well you're tracing this, but I don't care. Text this...." She thought quickly: she'd better not use her real name! "'It's 'Sara' calling about the Institute break-in last night.' If you don't get a response immediately, I'll hang up."

"Immediately?" He laughed, but she heard typing. "I don't know what-"

There was a sudden silence at the other end; then, a second later, without her activating it, the pico-projector built into Teef's link activated, and she saw Eagle. He raised one finger before she could even speak. "Wait."

She stared at his dim and flickering image on the cracked plaster wall of her temporary location, then the projection flashed and stopped. She twisted the Link around, seeing lights pulsing in weird patterns on the band, then blinked as its projector powered on again. Wincing, she aimed it back at the wall, where a whole bunch of messages and codes flashed briefly up.

A large and curly 'N' appeared, swelling larger before bursting apart to morph into a short animation of dancing robots. Finally that cleared and Eagle reappeared.

"Thank you, Nelson. Now, clear the line. I mean it. This conversation is private, between myself and Leeth."

His eyes focused on her again. "The line is now secure." Then he just waited, watching her steadily.

He doesn't look happy to see me. "We need to talk."

"Indeed."

"I want to make a deal."

"I'm listening."

"You're probably wondering why I went to talk to Godsson last night."

"True."

"It was about getting him out: I really wanted to talk to Professor Sanders, but he wasn't there. I want to renegotiate my promise. I think it's unfair I can't tell people about him being there. You don't have a right to keep him locked up in secret!"

"I like you, Leeth. But I cannot allow you to free Godsson. I have a duty to the people of this nation; to humanity as a whole."

"But Prof Sanders promised I could, so long as I did it

legally! He promised!"

Eagle blinked. "Are you claiming you have no plans to break him free?"

"Of course not! I *promised*. What kind of hero breaks her promises? But what's the point of Prof Sanders saying I *can* try to get him out – legally – if you say I can't? You're higher up than Professor Sanders, aren't you? Maybe even... *his boss!* That was *you*, wasn't it? That night in the Professor's office, after *She* tricked all those soldiers and FBI guys. The disguised voice on the speaker. Even cranky Mr Smith had been scared of you. *You* were the person talking about me befriending Godsson, and telling me to remember the Dragon was the head of a foreign superpower. That was *you!*"

Even though his expression didn't change, she could tell she'd pleased him, somehow. "So will you stick by the deal I made with Professor Sanders? Except this time, I'm allowed to tell people who don't know he's there. That part of the deal wasn't fair."

"Do you swear on your honor that you will not attempt to free Godsson by any illegal means?"

"If you agree I don't have to keep it secret that he's locked up."

"Let's first discuss the consequences of publicizing his imprisonment. What do you think it would mean for the others now being treated there? For all the new doctors and carers? They won't be able to do their work with crowds of people trying to scale the walls. We would have to move Godsson. Probably retire Faith and the new guard dogs: we could not risk having them wound or kill an innocent person who broke in, because you had stirred them to some kind of righteous anger. I will need your promise to properly study the situation before you take any action. And then I will leave the decision up to you.

"Let me make a counter offer, Leeth. I am prepared to agree to those conditions, if you rejoin the Department, working directly under me. I will make you a full agent. You can continue your training, to improve your skills and enable you to undertake missions of real importance: national importance. Even global importance. Become a true hero, a force for good."

She felt her mouth fall open. The idea was tempting. Very tempting. *But were they really the good guys?* She *wanted* to believe they were, she suddenly realized.

"I won't do bad things for you. And *I* want to be allowed to propose missions, too."

"Certainly. Though they will have to pass the same feasibility tests we apply to any other operation."

"Alright. But I also don't want Mother constantly on my back about stupid stuff, like the clothes I wear or the places I go."

Eagle inclined his head.

And now, finally, I can get to the real point of this conversation. "But I need to speak to Uncle, first."

Eagle considered her. For some reason, she felt her demand had secretly pleased him. "If you wish to tell me something, about your uncle, I will listen."

If only I could! "No. I just need to talk to him. On neutral ground. Somewhere I choose."

"A private matter, no doubt?"

She nodded.

"Then perhaps it will help if I say you can consider the Doctor no longer a part of the Department, for your meeting. I will be interested in the Doctor's condition, following your discussion."

Huh? Is he suggesting it's okay if I kill *him*? Or was it another test? "Uh, okay. Thanks."

"But how can I know you won't just run off with him? That this isn't a plan for both you and he to flee?"

"As if. We both know it'd be a hundred times easier to capture me if I had Uncle with me. He couldn't outrun a one-legged bot." She shrugged. "Make him swallow a tracking device or something. I don't know. I promise I'm not trying to run away with him. And I promise that if you let me talk to him, for... a half an hour, then I'll return to the Department."

"To work for us again. Following *my* orders."

"Yeah. Unless the orders are *wrong*." She stared a challenge at him, expecting him to argue, or get angry, but instead he looked amused. Maybe even pleased, again.

"Why did you run from us, Leeth? Why didn't you just return to us immediately after your impressive performance in saving your friend Marcie?" He nodded at her, encouraging her to speak.

If only she could have! If only she could tell Eagle *now* what Uncle had been doing to her. How much better, how *perfect* would everything be?

But she *couldn't* answer that question. The Doctor's conditioning wouldn't let her. Instead, her eyes narrowed. "Is that what you wanted me to do? Was it all... is *this* all, a test?"

Eagle smiled outright. "We learn and grow by overcoming obstacles, Leeth."

She waited, but he offered nothing further. "So, can I meet with the Doctor?"

The corners of his mouth lifted, microscopically. "I am happy to arrange that, yes. And you promise you will return, after you speak with him? You give your word?"

"Yes."

"Where and when do you want to meet him?"

"I, I haven't worked that out. Can I call you again? Tomorrow?"

"Yes. I would appreciate it if you returned to us at your earliest convenience. You are needed." He gave her a special link address to call. And a code to say. "What else did you and Godsson discuss, last night?"

She almost blurted out the shocking news: how her uncle, with her help, had created Robo. The Breaker. But that seemed like too awful an admission to make without first talking to her... to *the Doctor*, first.

She shrugged.

"Does it involve the invisible spirits from the Institute?"

Off-balanced by his guess, she nodded, hesitantly. Then, inspired, added, "But I need to talk about it with the Doctor, first."

Eagle stared at her so hard it made her want to squirm.

"Um, what Nelson did to this link – is it ruined, or can I give it back to its owner?"

"You don't wish to keep it, to communicate with us again?"

She just looked at him. "I'm not stupid, Eagle."

He chuckled. "I'll have Nelson reload its previous OS. I look forward to your call, tomorrow."

Then his face grew serious, his eyes drilling into her soul. "I need you, Leeth. There is a mission of great importance I wish you to undertake. And the sooner, the better."

Heart swelling, feeling her lips clamp together in deter-

mination, she nodded; one sharp nod. "I understand. Sir."
She was about to sign off when she remembered his opening words. "Did you mean what you said, before?"

"I meant everything I said. But what specifically?"

"That you like me?"

Eagle saw the raw hunger, which triggered an uncharacteristic surge of anger, directed at the Doctor. But he did like her; which made the answer easy. "I do, Leeth. Perhaps more than I should, given our roles and the dangers I will have to put you in. Can you accept that?"

"*Yes*," she said, with a depth of feeling that gave him second thoughts. "Leeth out."

Returning Teef's link, she shuffled her feet as she explained that its data had sort of gotten erased. He lifted one bony eyebrow, his expression clearly saying he thought that unlikely, but it only grew more bemused as she explained the equipment she needed. Not so much for the tranq gun, but at the other items, like the recording device.

He frowned. "So, like a bug. 'N capture."

She stared at him, shocked. Slowly shook her head. "No, I'll handle the capture."

Now he seemed *really* interested. "Meant *audio* capture, Flit. Who you-"

"Wait, no. It's got to be super sensitive. And the, *capture*, has to be real short. Like, ten seconds." She described in more detail how it had to work, and the other bits she'd need, to much head shaking from Teef. But not because it couldn't be done – he said it'd be easy, in fact, for Barney – but just because it made so little sense.

But it wouldn't be cheap.

"What about if I trade in my telescope? That was fourteen hundred."

"Still owe t'ousand. And's used, now."

"It was *used* when you sold it to me!"

"Not the point. Y'only had't tree nights – don' need't anymore?"

Not after this; not if her plan worked. She could visit Marcie *easily* if she wasn't being hunted.

Probably.

"Leave witme."

"Why? Where are we going?"

"Not-" He started again. "Leave it wit me," he enunciated.

"Oh. Right."

"Ask quesch?"

"Uh, sure, go ahead."

"Why you carryin' bike?"

She craned her neck round to check it was still there, propped outside his shack. "I'm returning it to get my deposit back." At his look, she added, "I went for a ride last night." Then had to add, "To visit some old friends."

He stared at her steadily. "You 'k, girl? In trub? Need help?"

"No, but somebody is," she grinned. She leaned in to hug him, hard. "You're all right, Teef, you know that?" He grunted in surprise, and she heard his ribs creak, and hurriedly loosened her grip. *Oops.* "When can Barney put it together? Tonight?"

"Nah. Past's bedtime. But meb t'morr. Other stuff b'easier."

She ducked her head in thanks, then let herself out and hoisted the bike back up on her shoulder for the long walk and climb to the hire shop. Then she just had to work out a few last details. Like what to say to Marcie, tonight.

And how to keep her safe.

CHAPTER 24

"It's obviously a trap," Mother declared to Harmon, Father, and a silent Eagle.

"Really?" asked the Doctor. "To what end?"

Mother scowled. She had no solid suggestion, but knew there was more to the demand than met the eye. Her inability to justify her remark dredged up a memory of the girl, po-faced, advising her to trust her hunches. *The girl doesn't even need to be present, to be irritating.*

She also failed to see how Eagle felt so sure the Doctor would convince the girl to return. Nor how Eagle had convinced her to meet a representative of the Department at all. She eyed the man, but there would be no point in asking him. Father sat, equally quiet, just listening. She turned back to the Doctor.

"The girl is disturbed. How can we be sure she doesn't plan to abduct you, and thinks to trade you back to us for her freedom?"

Harmon smiled. "You find Leeth unpredictable?"

"And you don't? You failed spectacularly to predict her actions last night." Mother felt her hands tighten, and consciously relaxed them. "I find it a little suspicious she contacts Eagle within hours of the first narrowcasts of enticing problems she could be dealing with. Have *you* been in communication with her, Doctor?"

In a sense, yes, Harmon thought. Leeth would have been all too aware he could have taken control of her last night, but had instead chosen to help her escape. No doubt, it was a significant factor in her request to meet him.

"There is no need to look for complex explanations, Mother. Leeth *yearns* to be a hero, and is feeling highly frustrated at being forced to hide out in the Dumps." *Did Mother not see that?* Harmon stared at the woman with deepening interest. *She must really have quite a strange mind – to be so lacking in empathy, yet still able to perform her duties.*

"How can you be so sure you can convince her to return?"

Harmon leaned back in his chair. "I understand her, Mother. It was the Department's ill-advised refusal to allow me to heal her friend that drove her away," he said confidently. "But I believe I will be able to convince her that we still represent 'the good guys,' and that we have a suitably important mission for her."

"And you feel sure she won't harm you?"

Harmon laced his fingers, relaxed in his chair. "Quite sure. Do you think I would offer to meet her if I thought she posed any real danger to me?" He steepled his fingers. "No, I will return, unharmed, with Leeth once again happy to work for us. Though she may well *put* me in danger – she does have a tendency to underestimate threats and overestimate her capabilities. Some backup would be appreciated. I don't want to be wandering the Dumps alone."

Privately, though, he wondered how she thought she could silence him. Fortunately, she still had no idea of the extent of his controls. He almost felt sorry for her. If she *did* try to kill him, however, she would deserve the consequences.

"Yes, we wouldn't want you getting lost, would we?" Mother agreed. "Also, she may not be acting on her own. You seem to assume she feels the need to accomplish this all herself. What about her friend, Marcie Dunkirk?"

"A frightening thought – Leeth teaming up with a nineteen-year-old wannabe actress," Harmon murmured.

Mother pointedly ignored him. "Since her visit to Dunkirk's house, has she attempted to contact her friend again? Message boards, social media? Personal ads? Direct messages?"

Father answered. "Not really, although you too may have noticed one odd thing. A few nights ago, Miss Dunkirk projected the message 'How cool is this?' on her bedroom wall, in letters two hundred millimeters tall. For approximately thirty seconds."

Eagle began staring quizzically into space.

"And?"

"That's all."

"Steganography?" Mother asked.

"No. Although we didn't have the res to fully analyze the image itself, Nelson was able to tell us the signal was generated from a text API, not image, so there could have been no hidden messages buried in it. And she *sent* it nowhere, merely displayed it."

At that, Eagle finally smiled. But said nothing.

Father noticed, wondering what significance he'd seen. But, deferring to Eagle's judgment, didn't ask.

Mother frowned, turning back to the Doctor. "Very

well. I will send James to shadow you. And we'll implant trackers. And bio-monitors. I suggest you keep that in mind. Assuming Leeth does indeed even bother to contact us to arrange a mutually agreeable meeting point."

Eagle cleared his throat, while silently messaging James. *«James: tomorrow night, you will shadow Marcie Dunkirk. Just to be on the safe side. Step in if things get out of hand.»* Aloud, he said, "I'm sorry, Mother, I have a small mission for James at that time. Dojo would be a better choice in this instance."

Dojo and Eagle exchanged inscrutable looks.

Mother visibly chewed on several responses, before finally shaking her head. "Very well. But if this plan works, and you allow Leeth to return, are you seriously considering using her against... the Brethren? An eighteen-year-old girl?"

"An eighteen-year-old *agent,* Mother," Eagle said.

Harmon watched with amusement as Mother's lips thinned.

"Agent? You can't be serious! She is not ready. She may never be ready. Her lack of discipline, her complete disrespect for authority, her-"

"Her unusual qualities are what I need, Mother," Eagle said. "If she holds up her end of the bargain, she *will* be promoted to active agent status, and will report directly to me."

Harmon's growing good humor vanished, at that last comment.

"And none of our other approaches has worked for our Brethren problem, let alone the far larger one behind that. I think she has a chance. So if she succeeds...."

Eagle and Dojo's eyes met.

"She is the one," said Dojo, his voice certain. "One day, she and I will face the *demon.*" Both of his hands curled into fists; one by one, each knuckle cracked. "Together."

CHAPTER 25

Leeth had gone again, the previous night, to 'chat' to Marcie. Candlestick Tower had seemed especially creepy, now she knew Robo was The Breaker. She hadn't been able to shake the feeling he'd been watching her.

Which was just silly. She hoped.

She was asking a lot of Marcie – too much, she knew – but Marcie seemed truly happy to be helping. Although Leeth, even from ten kilometers away, had felt that several times she'd freaked her friend out. Especially the bit about the tranquilizer gun.

Her biggest problem had been where to set the meet, though. It had to be on open ground, and bordering the Dumps, but far enough away for Marcie to be safe – especially if something went wrong.

The solution had come from Marcie herself, suggesting they meet at the 'Youngblood-Coleman playground,' a little bit inland from India Basin. Leeth half remembered the name from her study of the Dumps area, weeks ago.

"I'll B there," she'd written. "8 PM? 9?"

"Make it 11," Marcie responded.

"Can't wait 2 C U 2 morrow nite," Leeth replied. Feeling that finally, things were going her way.

The next day, after trading in her telescope, she visited Teef's shack several times. Well, maybe a *few* more times than that, but that'd been no reason to throw her out. She'd only been trying to help, tidying up some of his piles of stuff. It had taken less than a minute to dig his customer out. He shouldn't stack things up so precariously.

But she couldn't stay away. She spent the next four hours circling the shop at a distance of a hundred meters, until finally, around four pm, she heard Barney, inside, mutter 'Done!'

Teef had told her to stay away until he gave the signal – an actual cloth flag with a sort of tick mark, they'd run up their spindly buckytube pole. So what was the hold up?

The moment the flag started its jerky ascent she sprinted back, slowing to a casual saunter as she knocked politely on the perspex-windowed door.

"Thaz quick," Teef said. "Bin hangin'?" His wide grin revealed all his huge teeth.

She blushed, unable to deny it. But forgave him for the teasing when she saw Barney beaming, his work proudly spread out before him on the counter. She moved over, slowly, taking it all in.

Barney turned pink at her delight, proudly demonstrating each tiny gadget. And they didn't just work great, they looked cute, too! Barney had exceeded all her expectations. When she kissed him, his cheeks glowed rosier still.

The tranq gun even had a holster. Grinning like an idiot, though starting to feel a bit nervous too, Leeth secreted the gear carefully on herself: the tiny earbud, the micro-speakers, one stuck under her armpit and one at her waist; the super-sensitive microphone, the acoustic switch. Thrilled, she paid gladly, then danced outside.

Only to dart back inside a minute later to borrow Teef's old Link, again, to make her call to Eagle.

Barney and Teef both eyed her doubtfully.

-

Disten pulled the hoodie further forward, keeping his features hidden from cameras. Moving through the suburbs was a risk, but the reward would be worth it.

Marcie Dunkirk would recognize the face, so straightforward approaches were ruled out. And unfortunately, the Dunkirk house was both under guard, and under surveillance.

Following the girl to the school had been simple, as the destination was expected. But Dunkirk appeared to have acquired an armed bodyguard. And at a very generous distance, a drone.

At the school, too, changes had been made, with weapon-registered arthrobots painted in warning colors at the front gates and roaming the grounds.

For now, it appeared that questioning Marcie Dunkirk might present too great a risk.

No matter.

The Call, the painful, itching Call, was stronger than ever. The Call would be followed, instead.

Hours were spent, waiting at the edge of the Hunters Point Dumps for the Call to settle in one place. It did not. Except briefly, in a far too populated area where a long rock formation cut across the Dumps at the water's edge. At 20:05 it began moving again. But by 21:00 it had still not settled at the unknown meeting place. The messages were recalled. '8 PM? 9?' and 'Can't wait 2 C U 2 morrow nite.'

Apparently some other meeting time had been agreed.

Disten followed. Patient.

At 22:33 the Call – the girl – began moving more purposefully. North, and west. But along an erratic route. Rarely in sight, and then, only briefly. Increasingly, underground. Did she suspect she was followed?

Unfortunately, when the girl left the Dumps, her pace dramatically increased.

Disten followed, breaking into a tireless run.

Ahead, now, lay the Youngblood-Coleman playground. The Call had been steady for over ten minutes. Disten walked, hands in jacket pocket, head down, by the side of the empty road, sure now of the prey.

A vehicle swept up from behind, then past. Inside, Marcie Dunkirk peered out the window.

Disten walked faster.

A minute later, a second vehicle – the only other vehicle seen on this road so far tonight – whispered up and past: a low-slung, gunmetal colored extravagance. A Windsteed.

The driver was not visible. The car drove with no lights.

Disten followed it around the curve. The park was less than two hundred meters ahead, a sprawling gash of vegetation that had spread like an infection, creeping over the remains of landslip-buried housing.

Moving slowly and staying concealed, Marc Disten arrived at the park's edge in time to see Marcie Dunkirk leave the car and enter the deserted park. The car departed.

Convenient.

What was not convenient was the placement of the following vehicle, the Windsteed. It had stopped a short distance from the current hiding spot.

Disten moved slowly closer, crouching down so the city light threw the occupant into relief.

It was a male figure. It watched the Dunkirk girl. The profile registered as familiar – but was not the Dunkirk girl's bodyguard. Disten accessed the memory. It was the male who had intervened, months ago, the night of the Japanese girl in the opera house restaurant. Whose spirit had fled at a touch.

That male had been well-balanced, moving and speaking with stability and certainty. A threat.

Disten waited, considering.
Trying to fit the pieces of the puzzle together.
Patient.

-

It was *great* being with Marcie again. But it was strange, catching up on all the latest from the Drama School. Tara and Co were still pickles, Marcie said, but maybe not quite as bad as they'd been before. Security at the school had been tightened. Ms Sorensen and Mr Beckman were having an affair.

They'd graduated.

Which made Leeth feel weird. Like she'd become a shadow in Marcie's world. Not really real anymore.

Marcie had even come top of the class, she admitted. Leeth could sense the fierce pride behind the shy statement.

Which was great, but made her feel still worse. Like Marcie was slipping away from her, even though she was right here.

"I wish I could've been there to see Tara's face when they announced that."

Marcie grinned. "Yeah, her lips pursed up so tight, it made her mouth look like a cat's bum."

Leeth giggled.

So did Marcie, but then she gasped. "You *giggled!* I didn't even know you *could!*"

Which only set them off again.

Marcie also had a role in a small, one-night production, and she'd heard Joss R. Martin might attend.

But it all seemed somehow distant. As if it was happening a long way off, or down a well or something. Fogged.

"How was your dad the other night? He didn't realize it was me, did he?"

Marcie just looked at her.

"Oh. What'd he say? Did he really guess it was me?" At Marcie's nod, she winced. "Was he angry?"

"Yeah. Kinda. But he's also still pretty amazed at what you did for me." Marcie looked uncomfortable. "He thinks you're dangerous as hell, and that I should keep away from you."

Leeth met Marcie's eyes. Noted her short, well-cared-for brown hair, soft skin and body. So vulnerable. She sighed. "He's probably right," she agreed. "You don't have to do this. I could probably find someone else." *Teef would do it. For the right incentive.*

"No way! And you say, this guy is the same mage who healed me?"

"Yeah, but he's dangerous. Especially...." She had to warn Marcie. Godsson said her uncle would do it to other girls. "Don't let him...." *No-o-o!* She felt the gray slide in, pushing the thought out.

Marcie waited. And waited. "Uh, Jane?"

She took Marcie's hands. "He... I..."

Marcie hands gripped hers back. "He what? You tried to explain the other night, didn't you? He makes you *do* things? It's only us here, this time. You can tell me."

Leeth tried to think. *Word. Say?* Marcie's eyes bored into hers, her expression stricken. And then language itself vanished.

Purely on instinct, sensing somehow it was right, Leeth nodded, against neck muscles that suddenly tried to resist. It only confirmed the impulse, and she fought harder, nodding again, more firmly.

The gray churned in anger, lashing.

"You mean he... he's abused you, hasn't he?" Marcie's face paled. "And he's a healer," she whispered, her eyes widening. "So that means if he hurts you... oh, Jane, I'm so sorry."

Marcie's words vanished in a roaring maelstrom, their meaning plucked away. A wave of affection for her friend rose up. Affection, and more.

Leeth stopped fighting, feeling like she'd won, though unable to say why. The affection swelled.... Leeth felt her uncle's *other* programming stir. She snatched her hands free, and shut her eyes.

She emptied her mind, swimming *with* the current. Someone had taught her that. Tried to show her it was important.

She let her breathing slow.

Easing back from the brink, gradually, cautiously, she tried to remember what they'd been talking about. Rejecting the rising heat, which tried to cling.

Finally, she opened her eyes. "Right! So, this plan. Will you help me?"

Marcie was staring at her strangely, with tears in her

eyes. Then her lips pressed into firm lines.

"Count me in," she said, her expression grim.

Marcie seemed worried, watching her, but Leeth shook herself. "Okay, so here's what we'll do. You'll need this," she said, handing the gun to her friend and seeing her eyes go big and round. "It's okay, it just shoots tranquilizers. This is what you have to do, and it's *real* important you do it, okay?

"First, if I start acting... funny, you ask me 'Do pigs fly?', right? Then...."

CHAPTER 26

When Marcie was comfortable with the plan, she moved off to hide.

Leeth watched her go, lighting her way by the torch in her Link, then switching it off. Leeth saw her make herself comfortable behind the bush, and turned away to call Eagle, using the special code he'd given her. Somehow, she felt sure she wouldn't have to wait long.

She *wouldn't* wait long. She wouldn't give them time to prepare a trap.

Eagle answered at once: said the Doctor would be there in eight minutes. The words sent a weird thrill through her, from scalp to fingers to toes.

She started pacing, waiting.

Hoping her plan would work.

At the distant sound of rubber on road, she spun around, sure from the timing it must be him. For a moment, she felt like turning and fleeing.

But then it stopped. Ears straining, she heard a car door open, then close. She tilted her head. Maybe three hundred meters away.

She heard nothing for several seconds, then the sound of tires on the roughened road surface. It sounded like the same car, only moving slower. So why had it stopped? To let someone out?

Finally, she saw the headlights, and soon after that the car pulled up, not fifty meters away on the edge of the disused park. Her stomach turned upside down, a huge emptiness opening up as she recognized her uncle climbing out.

She saw him look around, before turning on a small torch and panning it around. It flashed past her, blinding her, then quickly returned. She shut her eyes against its glare; half expecting him to say the words that would steal her will from her. She tucked her thumb casually into the band of her shorts, her thumb brushing Barney's tiny speaker, for reassurance. Flexed her shoulder to feel the backup one, stuck in her armpit.

Seconds trickled past before the flashlight swung down off her face and he started walking toward her.

At arm's length he stopped, adjusting the beam to a soft, diffuse glow. They stared at one another for long seconds, neither speaking. She couldn't read his expression, but just for a moment thought she saw tiredness; maybe even regret.

He opened his mouth.

She raised one finger. "Stop. Just listen. I know you can... you know... and that's probably your plan." She struggled, the suspicion that others were listening forcing her to steer her thoughts between the forbidding reefs of the words she *wanted* to stab him with.

Harmon inclined his head, and said nothing, his expression one of calm superiority.

He so deserves this. "First: did they bug you?"

"They wanted to; but Eagle overrode Mother. I told them you would want that," he said, his smile sly.

"Not half as much as *you* do." That was enough to throw her thoughts into confusion again. She blinked, struggling to remember what she wanted to say. With an effort, she collected herself, her hands clenching into fists. She had the vague feeling he'd spoken.

He saw, and smiled wider, repeating himself for her benefit. "I said, they might have bugged you too."

She shook herself. "I don't think so. And if they did, it's a risk I'm prepared to take. Of course they bugged you. So strip."

His eyes narrowed.

"I'm not a baby. Not a child. I'm grown up, Uncle. And I'm not stupid. I know what you did to me."

He stilled.

She saw his fingers twitch, then stop. "Go ahead. Cast your mind reading spell. I'd actually *like* you to know what I'm thinking."

His smile turned predatory. But he just waited, radiating patience.

"*Strip!*"

"Very well." He turned off his light.

She watched, in the dark, as he began removing his clothes, folding each item neatly; piling jacket, then shirt, then trousers, on his shiny black leather shoes.

"Everything."

He continued: socks, undershirt. Underwear.

Even naked, he looked comfortable; sure of himself. Sure of her.

She hated him *so much*.

She circled him, noted the small tab between his shoulder-blades, and peeled it off. Another in an armpit. One under the arch of his left foot. She crushed each one as she found it.

It wasn't until she had him bend down, and ran her fingers through his hair, that he reacted. She saw him squeeze his eyes shut, at her touch. For some reason, water welled in her own eyes. She quickly wiped them dry after she'd pulled the tiny device free.

She could see he was angry; and embarrassed, too. *Good.* His hand fumbled toward hers, in the dark, and she paused, seeing where his attention was directed.

"We had an agreement, Mother," he said, speaking toward her wrist and the microphone she'd removed from his hair. "What signal does this lack of trust send to Leeth?" He nodded, and she crushed the wafer thin bug.

She found two more trackers, or bugs, in his hair, dropping each tiny carcass onto the neat pile of his clothes. "Okay," she told him. "Probably they have other stuff, internal, but they'll just be locators."

She saw him take a breath, no longer smiling so smugly. "May I get dressed again, now?"

"No. If they've got stuff woven into your clothes I'd never find them. Let's step over here so we can talk privately. No: leave the torch. That'd be easiest of all to bug."

"I won't be able to see."

"I don't care." She carefully eyed the trees, and led him toward the spot she and Marcie had selected earlier. Her skin crawled with the tension, hoping he wouldn't steal control just yet.

Again, they stood in silence. A whisper of motion in the distance made her spin to one side, peering into the darkness. She thought she saw an object – a person? – drop to the ground, to crouch like a bundle. Not moving. She wondered who it was. Whoever had gotten out of the car, earlier?

She turned back to him. "You didn't come alone like I said to, did you?"

"This is not an entirely safe area for me, and I don't have your deadly skills. Yes, Eagle provided me some backup. Is that a problem?"

"Not if they stay out of it."

Neither of them spoke, then, but she saw him relax, and guessed he was watching her 'Imaginally.' Watching her emotions, reading her. But if he was, the way they were burning in *her,* she didn't see why he'd be relaxing.

Oh. He'd see she wasn't planning to kill him. But that reminded her.

"We really need this talk, Doctor." She saw him flinch slightly at the use of his title, and felt a tiny flare of satisfaction. "And I wasn't kidding when I said I'd *prefer* you to cast your mind reading."

"I think I would prefer not-"

"*Cast your mind-reading!*"

Shaking, she fought for calm, surprised by how hard she was breathing. Watching his superior little smile return, somehow helped.

She knew she was taking a gamble, but felt sure she'd have no trouble keeping both of them focused on what was in the front of her mind. She'd had years of practice, after all.

She watched the hated finger-wiggle. "Now we can talk." But suddenly, she hardly knew where to start; suddenly, felt so, so tired.

"Why did you do it, Keepie? *How* could you do it? Do you hate me so much? You were there when I needed you: but not to *help* me. Instead, you tricked me into helping you make a cage, and then threw me inside.

"Weren't we s'posed to be a *team?* You said we were a team; I thought you cared about me. Once upon a time, I even thought you loved me. But you never did, did you? Do you even know *how* to?"

Water smeared her vision; she shook it angrily away. "All the awful things you've done: I don't know why. I think you *do* have a reason, you tell yourself. But was it worth the price, Keepie?" She felt her bottom lip trembling, and suddenly tears flooded her eyes. "*Was it worth the price?* I trusted you."

He was no longer smiling; his pained expression, his continued silence, helped her take hold of herself again, brushing angrily at her eyes. "You could have asked me. I'm no coward. You know that. You know I want to be special. To be good enough for your-"

Love. Her throat closed up so she couldn't talk, and her stupid eyes started running with tears again so she had to look away. And she didn't want his love, anyway. Not anymore. He didn't deserve it.

She swallowed.

"To be good enough."

When she could see well enough to see him, he looked stricken. She saw him shake his head, and his shoulders hunch, as if bowed under an oppressive weight.

Her eyes locked on his, wondering what he was thinking. Wondering if she'd gotten through to him....

Harmon reeled in shock. Yes, he knew what he'd done. All too well. But it had all been for her own good. He should end this nonsense now. Take control of her and return with her. What would she be if he hadn't stressed her, trained her, *created* her?

But as he opened his mouth to speak the words, a sick feeling in his stomach surged, and he paused. Paused, watching her falling tears, each a drop of flaming magma to his Imaginal senses.

And it was only in that moment, as he gazed down at her in the dark, seeing her pain, her thoughts churning in his mind, that he truly felt her anguish.

And learned that knowing it, and feeling it, were two different things. The truth hammered him, freezing the words in his mouth. Was she right? Was he incapable of love?

He was certainly capable of guilt, though, he discovered, as her thoughts and emotions deluged him. *Clever of her to make me read her mind,* the clinical side of him sneered. But it didn't change the truth of what she'd said.

All the things he'd done to her in recent months, with the control he'd gained? That she hadn't thrown *that* in his face – strangely, it was the loss of her faith in him that hurt now the most.

And to what end? She had not Unfolded further, as far as he could tell. Merely matured, emotionally.

But, sickly, even as he thought that, he saw the signs of some new potential, lying buried within her. Gestating. He had miscalculated, however. He had lost her trust and lost her faith.

Had it been worth it?

But already, part of him was coolly recalculating and re-planning. Seeing how a less inhumane approach could work. *Let's be honest, Alex, shall we? A less cruel approach; less sickly self-indulgent.*

Even now, determined to continue the experiment. After all, had she not been so recalcitrant, he would never have been driven to such extreme measures. All he had asked was an ounce of co-operation.

"You're right," he finally told her, and heard her indrawn breath. "And I will change, Leeth: I promise. Truly, I want you to be the best you can be." In her emotions, he read both her hope and her distrust. He wished he could see her face, too.

"You won't treat me like a, a *puppet* anymore? A toy to play with? You'll treat me like a real person – with respect?"

He bowed his head. "I will." Hoping he could keep that promise. But that meant he now had to *convince* her to return, not force her to do so.

The curious mix of hope and distrust in her aura strengthened. But then, as she prepared to speak again, he saw fear blossom.

"I spoke to Godsson, last night, Uncle. He told me what you did."

Her words struck like a premonition of doom. He saw her aura change as she, with her night vision, saw his reaction. He braced for the worst.

"*You* made Robo. With my help."

Harmon blinked, stunned.

"Ha! You didn't think I'd find out, did you? You thought I'd never get to talk to Godsson again."

Stars above! What fresh madness is this? "Leeth, no, I had nothing to do with Robo. *You* had nothing-"

"There's no point lying about it anymore, Uncle. I know the rest of it, too."

"There's *more?*"

"Don't act like you don't know." He heard the sneer in her tone. "Godsson told me the rest: what Robo's become. *Who.* The Breaker."

Harmon gaped. Was that even *possible?*

"Yeah, your secret's out. What did you do to Robo? To make *him* go mad and start torturing people? Or does he just take after his father?"

"Leeth, this is nonsense. Just another of Godsson's mad fantasies. More of his lies."

"He's not the one who lies."

She was ignoring his words. The certainty he read in

her aura only firmed. *Dear stars above, she trusts Gods-son more than* me, *now!* He felt the situation spiraling out of control.

"But why did you make Robo, Uncle? You and me, together," she whispered.

"That's absurd. *You* know that's not true, Leeth. I truly thought, all those years-." He stopped himself, on the brink of admitting he thought it had just been a figment of her imagination; a way to induce the right kind of dread, of stress. But that admission would put the final nail in their perhaps not irretrievably-broken relationship.

He saw her misinterpret his hesitation, and felt like striking her. He could have groaned, but even *that* would only reinforce her mistaken belief. *'Godsson told me.'* He closed his eyes, pained. *David Benson. The Manipulator.* He opened them again, seeing the elegance of Benson's trap. Damned if he did, and damned if he didn't. How delighted the madman would be, if he could see his carefully crafted psychological bomb exploding.

Well, he had one trick up his sleeve that Godsson couldn't know about. With its help, he could still salvage the situation.

Cursing Godsson even as he said it, he whispered the words. "Leeth: Mode One."

"No!" she gasped. "You *promised!*" He saw disbelief crackle through her aura; saw her hope crumble, vanishing under a tsunami of betrayal. He felt sick. But in this mode, he had time and a chance to make her see the truth. He would explain; then release her.

"Leeth, Godsson lied to you. *I* did not create 'Robo.' Nor did you. *I don't even know what Robo is!* And *you* have never had the sort of magic to invoke it, whatever place it came from; nor create it."

She stood paralyzed; trying to break his control; trying to hurt him. Just seeing that intent was a pain in itself. "Wait there, quietly."

Shaken, feeling sickened, he walked back to his clothes, dressing by feel before turning the torch back on, dimly – he would prefer to avoid Dojo's observation, unsure how much he could see through light intensifier goggles. Planning how to change her mind, and expose Godsson's lies.

He walked back to her. But just as she became visible in his dim light, he heard a tiny sound. And Leeth collapsed to the ground.

Asleep, he read, as he ran forward, then saw Marcie Dunkirk emerge from the tree line, pointing some kind of gun at him.

He halted. Smiled. "Don't be foolish, child. You have no idea-"

She fired.

He stared down in disbelief at the dart sticking out of his chest.

The last thing he saw, as his torch slipped from his fingers, was the young woman stalking forward.

CHAPTER 27

"What did you *do* to her?"

Harmon's head swam. Blinking and nauseous, he tried to get up, only to realize his hands and feet were bound. *Where's Dojo? Is he waiting to see if I can still gain the upper hand?*

Leeth, looking stricken, sat off to one side, cross-legged, hands pressed under her thighs. On the other side stood her friend Marcie, still pointing what must be a tranquilizer gun at him.

"What did you do to her?" she demanded, again.

Harmon sensed that little time had passed. For them both to be awake so soon, and from the unpleasant racing of his heart, he realized the two must have planned for this; must have brought an antidote for the sedative.

He smiled, bowing his head. «*Leeth,*» he whispered, «*capture Marcie Dunkirk. Revive me with the antidote if she shoots me again.*»

Leeth rose lazily to her feet.

"Jane? What are you doing?"

«*Quickly,*» he ordered her.

"Jane? Do pigs fly, Jane?" Marcie started backing away. "*Do pigs fly?*"

Leeth still moved slowly, and Harmon cursed her. «*Capture Marcie quickly,*» he clarified.

But Marcie Dunkirk had already fired again. Leeth turned, smiling at him even as she fell.

And the girl shot *him,* again.

This time, he rolled on his side and vomited, heart pounding and gripped by nausea as he regained consciousness. *Fools! Were they unaware of the danger of overdosing on tranquilizers, or their antagonists? He had to be careful. Not spook them.*

His hands and feet were still bound. Twisting away from the vomit brought him face to face with Marcie Dunkirk, who now sat cross-legged herself, waiting.

With an effort, he sat up. And saw, by the soft glow of his own torch, Leeth lying nearby, unconscious and bound now, too.

"What did you do to her?" she demanded.

He ignored her.

"What did you do to Jane? Fix her!"

A perfect time for a Suggestion. He tried to move his

fingers, then found she had bound them together. Had Leeth told her to do that? Clever. *Still. I'm facing two naive young women. One already under my mental control.*

"Has she explained our relationship?"

"I don't care about your bloody relationship. I asked what you did to her? When I brought her round, she tried to grab me again. Only she vomited, and I tranqued her. *What's wrong with her?*"

"So you have tranquilized her three times, now? You could have killed her." He couldn't even cast a mind meld, with his fingers immobilized. "She is likely to be even more ill if you administer a further dose." He saw her eyes narrow. "But in answer to your question, 'Jane' is rather unusual. I am, effectively, her keeper. She is quite dangerous."

"Yeah, funny that. Why did she try to grab me?"

"She is unstable. It is why-"

"You're lying. *You* did something to her."

He shook his head, sadly. "I'm sorry. But sometimes, she has psychotic-"

"QUIT LYING TO ME!"

Harmon, focusing on her aura, saw the unshakable faith, and stopped. If he could read her mind, he would know what Leeth had told her. Interesting that Marcie had not asked who he was; nor Jane's real name; nor where either of them worked. Because she already knew the answers? Surely, even Leeth would know not to do that. So... more likely she had simply warned Marcie that the less she knew, the better. There seemed to be a lot of that, going around.

Where was Dojo? Surely the fool realized he should intervene?

The girl still waited for her answer.

"I may be able to restore her to herself when she comes around."

"Which will take how long?"

"I don't know. *I* don't know what drugs you've been shooting her – both of us – with. It could take ten minutes. It could take half an hour. But do not shoot her again: you're very likely to stop her breathing."

"Then why don't you explain *how* you'll 'restore her,' while-"

Leeth groaned, dry-retching, and they both turned to her. Harmon, surprised, took a moment before whispering *«Leeth, free yourself, quickly, and knock out Marcie. Then free me.»*

Leeth retched, again, but he saw her hands slash obediently between her feet, her bonds falling away.

"Shit!" swore Marcie, scrambling to her feet and then shooting her again.

"No! You little *fool!*"

He felt real fear as Leeth slumped unconscious, yet again. Squirming over to her, he set his fingertips to her neck and felt for a pulse.

Nothing. Fearing the worst-

Throb.

He exhaled, in relief. "I told you, if you sedated her again, you could kill her!"

"Yeah. I got that."

Her eyes were full of tears, he saw; tears, and blazing anger. What had Leeth told her to do? He felt a chill: something extreme, no doubt. It appeared her friend was quite prepared to kill her. How in all the stars had Leeth persuaded her to do that? How much did she know? Surely, a mere teenage girl would not have the... *spirit* needed for such an extreme act?

More likely, Leeth expected – perhaps they both expected – that he could revive her if she died. But could he? He honestly didn't know. Clearing an excess of sedation was not a normal part of the healing process.

He sighed. Two stupid, young girls. And what was the business about pigs flying? Why had her friend asked that, as Leeth had advanced on her the first time? Some sort of code phrase?

If he could read Leeth's mind, he could learn what precautions she'd taken, and work around each one. But without knowing that, any command might backfire. Leeth would not survive her next sedation.

Damn the girl!

He saw Marcie swallow as she studied the ropes that had tied Leeth's ankles, before crouching down to search her. She found no knives, of course. The girl stared again at the severed ends – quite remarkably cleanly cut, then looked at *him* in horror.

He watched her unbind Leeth's arms and rebind them

across her back, forearm to forearm; then retie her legs.

He also realized another problem: when Leeth came round, she would still be under orders to capture Marcie quickly. With potentially disastrous results. He would have to observe Leeth closely, ready to cancel his orders promptly if her friend was too alert. Unless Leeth acted with subtlety.

Not a likely prospect.

"She may have told you I can heal her, even if she dies. But I am very unsure I can. Physical trauma, yes, up to a point. The healing spell works by supercharging the body's own healing abilities. But over-sedation? Do not shoot her again, unless you intend to kill her."

From Marcie's expression, and from her aura, he saw she recognized his sincerity.

But what she said was, "You'd better fix her then, hadn't you?"

Unfortunately, he could also see she wasn't bluffing.

He saw Leeth, once again, come around far earlier than she should, instantly squirming in her bonds before discovering it was fruitless. Twisting her legs under her, she angled herself so she could see her friend Marcie, who she stared at intently.

He needed to distract her friend from Leeth's actions. "Marcie, I need a little privacy to... restore Jane to herself."

Marcie laughed bitterly, and turned to him in disbelief. "As if."

He stared back, willing her to keep her eyes on his. Leeth, he could see, had not given up. She was still looking for a way to carry out his last order. Slowly, she got her bound feet beneath her and somehow began rising to her feet, balancing. *Hardly subtle. Damn the girl. She's doing that deliberately.* He watched, in disbelief, as Leeth swayed, gathering herself. "You seem to assume I am the wrongdoer here, Miss Dunkirk," he blathered, trying to distract her.

It didn't work. Marcie saw Leeth's movement. She began scrabbling backward, raising the gun again with an expression of dawning horror.

«*Leeth, stop. Lie back down,*» he whispered.

Light blinded him as he spoke. "What did you just do? I saw your lips move! You did a spell, didn't you?"

He looked down, tried to hide his mouth. *I can still do this: I just need to order Leeth to* pretend, *to deceive her friend...* but the bright beam of her flashlight followed him. Damn the girl. Damn them both.

If this continued, Marcie Dunkirk would start asking questions which would lead to answers she would be killed for knowing. He knew Leeth would never, ever forgive him that.

So instead, he whispered the string of nonsense syllables that ended her obedience mode. For now. *«Seshoostus desstussten.»*

Strangely, he heard Leeth's teeth bite together, hard, twice, before she seemed to relax.

"I saw that! Stop doing spells!" The girl raised the gun again, the barrel now weaving between him and Leeth.

"It's okay, Marcie: I'm okay. You can untie me."

"Sh'yeah, like that's gonna happen. Do pigs fly?"

"They do in pig season."

Harmon hid a smile. *Excellent. I simply need to order Leeth to deceive her friend, once she is untied.*

Marcie exhaled in relief, dropping to her knees beside her friend to untie her ankles. Then held up the ropes Leeth had previously sliced through. "How'd you do *that?*"

"That's another one of those questions you don't want to ask."

Marcie said nothing.

"Um, my arms, too? Please?"

"Maybe later," Marcie said, but helped her to her feet. Leeth hesitated, but then let her. Both girls turned to him. "Now what?" Marcie asked.

Leeth nudged her, and began walking off a little way. "Come over here."

No doubt setting up a new code-phrase. He shook his head. She was still so naive. *She should have gagged me.* Harmon smiled.

Frowning back at him, her friend followed, though turning so as to keep him in sight, while keeping what she obviously thought was a safe distance from Leeth. He considered taking control again and ordering Leeth to kick her unconscious. But he had seen no sign that her friend had a knife to cut Leeth free, so instead he waited.

The two whispered together for a while, Leeth at last convincing her friend to untie her.

He waited until she had finished. Considered, even, not doing it. But it had to be done. *«Leeth, Mode One. Behave normally, for now.»*

She stilled, then moved to her friend and hugged her before returning to him. Marcie followed, still worried.

"Help me up," he ordered Leeth.

She did so, of course.

Though with a strange smile on her lips and her head tilted to the side, looking up into his face.

«Deceive Marcie Dunkirk. Get the gun from her,» he whispered. She turned toward her friend, her aura awash in bruised purples... and then a flare of golden exultation burst across it, like the sun coming up.

'Get the gun from her.' Leeth bit at the air as she turned to Marcie, the sound conducted through her flesh and bone. *«Seshoostus desstussten,»* whispered Barney's speakers at her waist and in her armpit. She grasped at the syllables, as always, straining to remember them... but as ever, they vanished like a dream.

No matter. They'd done their job. She turned back to her uncle, feeling powerful. *It worked! It had actually worked!*

Now for the next part. Which, really, didn't require much acting.

"We all face tests in life, Uncle. *You* taught me that. But you just failed yours." At his expression, she couldn't help giggling; even clapped her hands. "Oh, Uncle, don't you see what you've just done? Truly? By trying to..." she skated around saying *order me,* or *make me,* "do what you just did, you *did* make me stronger, inside! 'Where it counts.'" His eyes widened as she parroted his own words back at him. She grinned in delight at his reaction. *That'd worked even better than I expected!* "Truly, you can't *See?*" Her smile widened, as she saw the shift in his focus that meant he was seeing her Imaginally. Her aura would be excited; energized; maybe even subtly different. But she had to interrupt his examination. "I broke your...."

Even as her thoughts swam and she lost track of what she'd been trying to say, she kept the smile on her face, certain it was important to look confident.

He was falling for it!

«Leeth, Mode One,» he whispered, trying again. He watched, sure it had worked, though her expression didn't change. He looked: nor was there any feeling of dismay. Impossible. Suddenly he was just as sure it *hadn't* worked. "Untie me, 'Jane.' I need to explain something to you. In private."

She *danced* back to him, crouching down on her heels – but instead of cutting his bonds, she put a finger to his lips and giggled. "*Now* do you believe me, Uncle? You're not the boss of me any more."

«Leeth, MODE ONE. Don't let your friend shoot again. Quickly now, take the gun and tranquilize her.»

She rose, turning to her friend – then back to him. And *grinned.* "Hah! Got you!"

But the playfulness abruptly fell from her expression. "And I guess we now know how much your promises are worth, don't we?" She blinked, rapidly, then her lips pressed into a thin line.

Reaching down, she hauled him to his feet and glared up at him. "Oh, and Uncle?" she sneered. "*Do* keep trespassing," she placed one finger to the side of her head, meeting his gaze full on. "In here."

He felt his eyes narrow fractionally.

"I reckon I'm close to learning how to do to your mind, when you intrude, what I can already do to an astral body."

She let her teeth show, making the evil pixie smile she'd perfected by age ten. A shiver of dread ran through him – had she also broken his other conditioning, the prohibitions? – and swayed back in her grasp, seeing the sincerity in her aura.

Had she planned all this? Despite his dismay, he felt a strange pride at her resourcefulness. Once again, she had surprised him. The question now was... what was her goal, here? Just her freedom?

Could he still motivate her to return? Time was running out.

And why the devil hadn't Dojo intervened? With her friend disarmed, I could at least have been persuading her to return. Instead, both Leeth and I spent who knows how long, bound and unconscious on the ground!

It made no sense. Unless... had Leeth really accomplished all this on her own? He sensed Eagle's hand at play. A chill ran through him: there had been other indicators that Eagle *suspected*....

He swallowed. Beginning to feel desperate. *Bring her in,* Eagle had commanded.

Before he could speak, though, her hands twitched behind him, and his bonds fell free. Marcie gasped, but Leeth just turned to her, keeping her eyes on her friend's as she dropped down to his feet to slice, shrugging as she bounced back up. He felt the ropes part, and kicked them off.

Things were moving too fast. "L- *Jane,* I'm sorry, but I grew desperate when you refused to listen. I just wanted you to hear me out. You have only heard one side of the story."

"Yeah, yeah. You're going to blah on that Godsson lied, and that you'll tell me the truth."

Harmon grimaced, as much at hearing her name Godsson in front of her friend – who was listening with fascination, he noted – as at the impossibility now of convincing her to believe him. *Damn* Godsson*!*

"He may be mad," she continued, "but at least *he* doesn't lie to me."

But, watching her aura, he could see that she herself didn't entirely believe that.

He let his shoulders fall. "That you should say that... well, I deserve your distrust. I have earned it. But don't let that distrust drive you to accept a madman's fantasy just to spite me." He shook his head. "His story doesn't even make sense! And I swear I did not create... those things. I did not even believe they existed, until you proved to me they did! Remember, too, what he did to you and Faith, when it suited him."

Her friend was watching, even more avidly, and he winced, but had to speak. "We need to discuss this – but in private. These are not topics to endanger innocent civilians with, by involving them."

That hit home, he saw, as Leeth turned to her friend.

"I'm not an innocent civilian," Marcie declared, "I'm a *friend.* And that's what friends do: they get involved. Besides, I can protect myself." She pulled a small, pink... *taser?* from her pocket.

At the sick expression on Leeth's face, Harmon could have smiled. *Thank you, Miss Dunkirk.* He spoke quickly, before Leeth could interject. "But none of this is why I agreed to meet you tonight, Jane. We need you. Your Father and Mother need you. They see now they were wrong to prevent me from attempting to heal Miss Dunkirk. And there is a job, an important job, that only you can do. A job that will help a lot of people. Please come back home with me."

Leeth stared at him. Thinking. *That* at least was true, matching what Eagle had told her.

Harmon could see her wavering. He considered casting a mind meld... but he needed to re-earn her trust.

He shook his head, sadly. "This meeting has not proceeded at all as I had envisaged. Perhaps I should have stopped you last night. Your Mother and Father were very angry that I helped you run off again."

Leeth understood his coded message. Her aura shifted again: puzzlement, pleasure, and a thin thread of hope. He turned toward her friend. "I must say, Miss Dunkirk, I am glad to see my healing has left you so fit and well. Although I had not expected you to use your restored mobility quite as you have, tonight." His eyes moved from her face, to the tranquilizer gun she still held, pointed at him. "I'm sure you'll understand when I say I hope we won't meet again."

The two girls gaped at him as if his remark had been unexpected. He gestured Leeth ahead of him, toward the waiting car. "Will you return with me? We have much to discuss. We can make a fresh start, you and I. We all see great things in your future, if you return home."

He held out his hand, and hoped. Feeling oddly light, even adrift, envisaging her returning with him, tonight, nestled beside him in the car.

She stared at his hand.

"Nah. But I'll have my people call your people."

Her words shredded the foolish image – though her aura was less negative, and gave him some hope.

"It'd help if you could stop cousin drone-stealer perving on me. Oh, and how about one other little test? Can I trust you with Marcie, while I go and say hi to your bodyguard?"

Harmon blinked.

Marcie looked doubtful. Leeth gently took her gun hand and raised it so it was pointing back at her uncle. "Just shoot him again if he gets out of line."

She waited for Marcie's uncertain nod before running off into the dark.

Leaving Harmon and Marcie standing in awkward silence.

She screeched to a halt an arm's length from Dojo, who doffed his night vision goggles, blinking, and bowed slightly in response to her own deep bow.

"Leeth."

"Sensei. Um. I just wanted to say sorry, for, um, you know...."

Dojo waited; then allowed himself a small smile. "A warrior does not need to apologize for a victory. I look forward to continuing your instruction. There is much, yet, for you to learn."

As he had expected, Leeth blurred forward, and in the next instant, had wrapped herself around him. He patted her on the back, waiting. Her arms hugged him, hard, for long seconds, before she drew herself together and released him. She stepped back, and in the dim light he made out her lips pressed determinedly together, midway between tears and joy.

"Do I take it your business with your uncle has been successfully concluded? You have accepted Eagle's offer?"

She wiped at one eye with the back of her hand, and straightened. "Yeah, I have. But let's not tell the Doctor. I don't think he even knew about it – is Eagle cross with him?"

"Yes. We saw him warn you, last night."

Leeth's mouth fell open.

"What you did last night was very foolish. You must not trust Godsson. He deceives."

She put her shoulders back. "How do you know that? Have you even met him?"

"No. I know him only by reputation. But I know the power of a clever lie."

She frowned. "I guess we have a lot to talk about. Like this mission Eagle wants me to do: is it *really* important?"

"Hai. It is also dangerous. And time runs short."

Dojo looked super serious, and she felt a tingle of excitement, feeling suddenly *lighter*. "I'll make my own way in, okay? I'll race you!"

For a moment, it looked like Dojo almost smiled.

"Hai."

"I guess I shouldn't introduce you to Marcie though, should I?"

He inclined his head. "A wise decision."

"Okay. Well. Maybe you and the Doctor could follow her, make sure she gets home safely?"

"Sore wa sōdarou. It will be so."

Marcie called a ride. "I'll phone in a little while to check you get home safely, okay?" Leeth said, her eyes locked to Harmon's. After a crushing hug, she ran off into the dark.

Leaving James, hidden, waiting to follow Marcie home, and Alex Harmon and Marcie Dunkirk once again standing, ignoring one another. Dojo, his light intensifier goggles back in place, stayed out of sight – puzzled, briefly, by a movement across the road, heading in the same direction Leeth had taken.

CHAPTER 28

"No Leeth, Doctor?" Eagle, seated, with Father and Mother beside him, had him standing before them like a schoolboy sent to the Principal's office.

Mother radiated 'smug'.

Harmon ignored her. "If Dojo had intervened to prevent Marcie Dunkirk from tranquilizing me, Leeth would be standing here right now."

Eagle leaned forward. "Dojo's instructions were to keep you alive," he lied, "not to inflame the situation further by attacking Leeth's friend. I am more a diplomat, but perhaps you as a psychologist can explain how that would have helped cement her trust?"

Harmon fumed, but had no answer.

"Once again you have demonstrated your lack of understanding of your own ward, Doctor. I shall take over directly, from this point on, where Leeth is concerned."

And that simply, Harmon felt Leeth slip from his control. But mixed with the fury, and dismay, was a tinge of relief. *Let's see how* you *cope with her*, he thought. *For now*, he added, knowing how circumstances changed, when Leeth was involved.

"Did you make any progress at all in convincing her to return?" Eagle asked.

Harmon calmed himself. "She requested a show of faith, saying it would help: having Nelson stop trying to track her down with drones. But perhaps you should ask Dojo. She spoke quite happily to him for some minutes." Despite his best effort, he heard the edge of bitterness beneath the words.

"What of her friend, Marcie Dunkirk?" Mother asked. "How much did Leeth reveal to her? Is she a loose end that needs tidying up?"

"I anticipated that question, Mother. I also know how Leeth would react were some 'accident' to occur to her friend. While Leeth and Dojo were having their very friendly chat I used the time to read Miss Dunkirk's thoughts. I was pleasantly surprised at how little Leeth shared. I will prepare a detailed report if you wish."

Mother snorted as if surprised by his foresight.

"A good idea, Doctor," Eagle agreed, in mild tones. "Do that, while Dojo gives us his debrief."

"I think it would be best if I-"

"Dismissed, Doctor. Leeth is my concern now, not

yours. Apart from providing healing as needed, of course."

With ill grace, Harmon turned to leave the room.

"And Doctor? I would like to receive your report on Marcie Dunkirk *tonight*."

«Eagle!»

«Yes, Nelson?»

«I've found her! But we've got a major problemo – you'll never guess *where* she is, and *who* she's with!»

«Would you care to bet on that, Nelson?»

For several seconds, Nelson just stared at him via the virtual link, then started laughing. «You frickin *knew* she was coming? And sent Dojo back out to escort her?»

«Correct. But from the timing, I gather your systems did not identify her until she met Dojo at entrance seven-C?»

«Uh, yeah. She had a walking stick, see, and she'd painted.... Oh. *Chip*shit.» *Another point to Eagle.* «Lemme guess: don't alert anyone else? Not even Mother, or Father?»

«Why would you assume that, Nelson? *Their* roles do not include monitoring our security systems, just their oversight. No, inform them at once, and have them join us in my office. The Doctor, too.»

Father arrived first. He frowned, but said nothing, as he noted Leeth standing to one side of the alabaster expanse of desk, wiping her face free of zigzag splashes of color. At the farthest 'window', his back to the room, Dojo stood gazing out into the light field rendering of a rugged mountain pine forest.

Father picked up a walking stick that rested against Eagle's desk.

Mother entered next. Her eyes narrowed as she saw Leeth, and paused in the doorway. After a brief look across the room to Dojo standing at ease, she continued in.

For long seconds, Eagle's four guests stood as motionless as a high-res printed sculpture of a tension-laced scene. "The prodigal returns," Mother finally muttered, her expression sour, and settled herself into the contours of the rightmost chair.

Leeth, assuming that was some kind of insult, just smiled back at her. "Yeah, Eagle said you guys needed my help."

Mother looked as if she'd just bitten into a lemon, but said nothing.

Leeth finished wiping her face, and folded the cloth back into a small square. Moving around the desk toward Eagle she paused, tilting her head a fraction, then passed it to him. "Thanks."

Father, in the meantime, had been examining the plain bamboo walking stick for concealed weapons or other devices. Still frowning, he placed it back on the desk and took the seat one along from Mother.

Fresh orchids curled from the aquamarine vase, and Leeth touched one delicate petal, letting a finger trace down the graceful arc of glass. But as she did, her expression hardened. *A trap?* She took a step back, her head lifting, looking into a far corner of the room, then angrily turned on Eagle. "I thought-"

At that moment, Harmon burst into the room. "Leeth!"

She wheeled around to face him, tensing, her fingers stretching out... then suddenly relaxed, standing straighter. She turned away from him.

"What's *he* doing here?" she demanded of Eagle. "You said I'd be working for *you*."

The door slid shut behind Harmon. Whose expression transitioned from pleasure, to pain, to withdrawn, before he'd taken his next step across the room. Automatically noting the positioning of the separated seats, he ignored Leeth and sat down on Father's left.

Eagle inclined his head to the space remaining, between Father and Mother.

"Thanks," Leeth said, with heavy sarcasm. "I think I'll stand. *Considering*."

Mother raised one elegant eyebrow. "I don't think you need fear restraints springing from the seats of these chairs, Leeth."

Leeth spared only a glance at Mother before turning back to Eagle. "Nah, it's the invisible guy in the corner I'm worried about," she said, grabbing the vase, her arm flashing back to throw it.

"Ha! Ha, ha, excellent!"

In the far corner, hunched in a wheelchair, a liver-spotted old man abruptly materialized, chortling. One hand lifted in a shaky gesture that might have meant 'peace'.

Everyone, except Eagle, startled at the sudden appearance from thin air.

"I concede – she surprised me!" he said, grinning at Eagle, then back to Leeth. "I'm not often surprised, dear."

Leeth scowled, then put the vase back down, with a soft *clink,* shaking water from her hand. "Who's *he?*"

"Mr Abrams, the Department of Games," Mother answered, looking extremely annoyed. "You should be flattered. Mr Abrams prides himself on never being surprised."

Leeth sniffed. "He must get awfully bored."

"Mother exaggerates," the old man answered, zipping his wheelchair forward to join Eagle.

Leeth jumped suddenly back from the desk. A moment later, a section of floor began irising apart around them all. She crouched down, ready to attack, or flee, as an umbergold band was exposed, encircling the entire room.

"It's all right, Leeth," Eagle told her.

She saw Dojo take two paces toward the center then stop, his hands clasped behind his back.

"For what we are about to discuss," Eagle continued, "we need magical shielding. Please, take a seat. I apologize for not warning you in advance."

"I thought you liked surprises!" the old man teased her.

She pursed her lips, working them from side to side, unsure what to make of him. Her uncle, she saw, was staring at him intently, with that unfocused look that meant he was looking at stuff only mages could see. She wrinkled her nose, then met Dojo's eyes.

He nodded, once.

Leeth sat, easing herself between Father and Mother. "So, what's this important mission? It's not about Godsson, is it? Or, um, the special stuff, about the Institute?"

A greeny-blue dome of translucent light sprang up around them. Leeth noticed the old guy, Mr Abrams, now had his head bowed, and his eyes shut.

"No," Eagle said. "It's not about the Institute, or Godsson." Without giving any outward sign, Eagle focused his monitors on Mother. "No. You, me, the Doctor and our visitor will discuss that shortly. Now that I have granted you full Agent status."

Now it was *Father's* turn to look annoyed. "Really, sir, how can you reinstate Leeth – even *promote* her! She should be punished." He turned to her. "Every agent needs to learn to follow orders."

Her return stare could have cut steel. *If you only knew. But I already told Eagle I wouldn't follow* wrong *orders.* She waited for Eagle to respond; but he didn't. Sensing undercurrents, she spoke for herself. "More important than achieving the objective?"

"What punishment did you have in mind, Father?" Mother answered. "A cut in pay? Reduction of leave? *Physical chastisement?*"

It took Leeth a moment to realize that Mother was speaking in her defense!

Father blinked.

"I get pay?" Leeth asked. "And 'leave'? What's that?"

They all stared at her.

"Dear god," said Mother, turning to Eagle. "And you plan to send her to retire Shepherd Fox?"

For the first time since Leeth had met her, Mother looked uncertain. Worried. *On* my *behalf?* Mother? *Just how bad* is *this mission gonna be?* "Um, how long will it take? I was really looking forward to competing in the FistFest, four days from now. Can't I kill him after that?"

"No," Eagle answered. "We have a narrow window. Right now, we know the general area where Fox and his survivalist cult are operating. You'll need to leave early tomorrow." He, Mother, and Father began calling up displays and outlining the mission. But for some reason, Mother and Father grew increasingly nervous; they spent a lot of time thinking, and doing breathing exercises, while they briefed her.

Her uncle looked worried, too. Or *pretended* to.

But when they showed her the heavily forested mountain terrain she'd be operating in, her eyes lit up. "Oh, I just had a *great* idea: you said you have to send me in alone, yeah?"

The others nodded, wary, her uncle looking... unhappy. *At not having any say in what I do.*

"I should take *Faith* with me!"

After they had all left, Abrams took a deep breath, and opened his eyes.

Eagle, checking his monitoring systems, frowned and held up a hand. "Would you mind waiting here, old friend, while I follow the others? I won't be long, I just need to fetch something up from below."

On the feed from the hidden camera, Eagle watched Leeth jerk up from the door and run silently down the corridor. *Well, well, well.* He blinked, considering the door's *extensive* sound insulation. *Well, well, well.*

Eagle waved a hand. "No, never mind," he added, on the inconceivable chance that Leeth could *still* hear him. "So: now that you've seen them together?"

Abrams ignored the question, intrigued. Then he clapped his hands. "Hah! The girl was listening at your door, wasn't she? Successfully, too!"

Eagle suppressed his annoyance. But Abrams was a two-edged sword. Without that supernatural ability to recreate a whole jigsaw from a handful of pieces, their loose alliance would not have been so valuable; worth the risk of involving the outsider.

Abrams cackled in delight at Eagle's irritation. "But to answer your question: yes, it was Harmon who Connected her to the Deeps. Impressive. I will need to work with him, to decide whether he knows what he has done, but I suspect he has some inkling."

His expression grew serious. "But there is something more. Astral 'echoes', as if she is multiply Connected. To what, I cannot say, at this stage." One bushy white eyebrow quirked upward. "Did you know, she also yearns to kill the Doctor?"

Eagle did not look surprised.

"She *is* one. A wild card. I cannot predict her." Abrams smiled, opening both hands and shaking his head. "The threads condense at the Fist Fest – a singularity. But I'm troubled. One of those Connections is like nothing I've ever sensed before. Something young. As impossible to predict as your girl, but..." he shook his head, "cold? Intricate?"

"A new player?" asked Eagle, frowning.

"It's very possible. My intuition tells me it ties to the Blankness. Or might, one day."

Eagle looked worried. "And how is the Blankness?"

"Still spreading. Slowly. Nelson and his Ghost device remain key, there." Abrams shook his head. "But I see little choice. How does it feel, holding three nuclear weapons, now? Counting Nelson and his toy as two."

Eagle stared steadily back. "You'll be glad you uncovered them for me, if we're right about the powers at work in the world."

Neither man smiled.

CHAPTER 29

Just knowing Faith was nearby cheered her.

But Shepherd Fox and his cult followers were skilled woodsmen *and* paranoid and suspicious, so the two of them weren't allowed to travel together, in case their trail was back-tracked. It'd be a pretty short mission if they saw Faith's paw prints. It'd be hard to explain traveling with a cyborg wardog.

She surreptitiously blew a loud and painful *'peep'* on the long jade pendant – actually an ultrasonic whistle – and smiled when she heard Faith's answering *yip*. From about half a kilometer off to her left, and slightly ahead. She had a fresh pair of Nelson's special glasses, and checked the high altitude drone feed, confirming Faith's location. They also noted three more possible sightings of members of the Brethren – the nearest, only a few ridges over, maybe a couple of kilometers.

She settled her backpack on her shoulders, pushing off from the steep slope following a 'rest.' She rolled her eyes. She could've been twice as deep into the Gros Ventre Wilderness by now if she could've moved at her own pace. But Father had impressed on her that at any moment she could be under observation – by *telescope*, for example – so she had to appear unexceptional at all times, or risk blowing her cover.

Nor was she to rescue any of the orphans.

"Neither before nor after you retire Fox," Mother had added.

Eagle had correctly read her expression. "Your mission is to retire Fox, Leeth. I have FBI teams ready to pour in to rescue the innocent, if you can do that."

"How can you be so sure that killing the boss'll be enough?" she'd asked. "Mightn't someone else just as horrible take over?"

Instead of answering, they'd all just looked at one another, behaving really strange again – doing their deep breathing exercises. Mother even shut her eyes.

There was something real weird about this mission. Like being briefed inside a glowing Barrier spell, with the strange old magician: Mr Abrams. From the *games* department. 'Games' was probably a code name for something extra secret. Like how the Accounts Department was its own special group.

Mr Abrams's spell had reminded her of the golden

Ward spell that Godsson used to use, to try to keep *Her* out.

That'd been the first indication there was something odd about this mission.

The second thing had been how Mother, Father, and even Eagle, had stopped several times in the mission briefing for a 'meditation pause.'

After that, there'd been a three-way discussion between her and Eagle and Mr Abrams. Though first he'd had a rest. While the Doctor fumed and waited. She'd made herself useful by putting Eagle's flowers back in the vase. Then admired the 'scenery,' pointedly ignoring the Doctor.

Finally, they'd closed the big circle and opened up a smaller one, and she told them about the invisible spirits at the Institute: *Her*, and Robo, and how she'd used to hunt them. How *She* had used to talk to her, and pretend to be her friend. *She* had called herself Lily, and wanted 'rides.' Mr Abrams seemed both real worried by that, and relieved that Leeth had never given in.

The Doctor had tried to join in, but she'd just pretended she couldn't hear him. She'd been pleased to see that Eagle and Mr Abrams also seemed real cross with him.

And after *that,* after the Doctor had left, Eagle had explained a little bit more about the Fox mission. "We face an unusual magical threat, Leeth. There are certain thoughts we have to avoid thinking."

"Why?"

Eagle raised one eyebrow. "The threat is able to sense the spread of its secrets."

"But..." she circled one hand in the air. "Aren't we behind magic Barriers? Like *this* one?" she said, indicating the dome – though a bit worried, as it started looking *thinner,* the old man hunched up tense with effort, and sweating.

Eagle looked unhappy. "Not as secure as those around Godsson. And now we know Godsson is able to at least partly breach them. As was the meta-spirit you call '*Her*'."

When she'd told them about Her, earlier, Leeth had thought her uncle was going to faint. She'd heard his heart racing. *At least that meant he had one.*

"Shouldn't you tell Leeth something of what you informed me, earlier-"

"You are not here to speak, Doctor, but to listen. And I am providing Leeth exactly enough information to give her the best chance of completing this mission. Unlike you, she is highly intuitive. Perhaps you could usefully use your time to study Mr Abrams's unusual shield."

Leeth smiled at Eagle. *That was telling him!* It was good they'd found some magic research for him to do. It'd be safest for *him* if he kept his mind off her. Maybe they'd even send him back to the Institute? He could study Godsson from the cell next door.

Her smile had vanished when the magical dome *flickered*. She needed to be thinking about her upcoming mission, not her uncle. The Doctor. What had Eagle been saying? "But if this new threat knows when its secrets are uncovered...?"

"Good: you see the implications. So I need to take great care with what I tell you. And the last thing you should do is use your intuition to guess what might lie behind Fox: if you guessed correctly, that too would put you in danger." Eagle wanted to warn her more explicitly that Fox was not the real threat – that he was a mere acolyte of a far more insidious Power – but feared even this hint might have endangered her.

Then Eagle changed the subject to Leeth's discussion with Godsson, the night before last.

She'd taken no pleasure in telling them how he'd said her uncle had created Robo. With her help.

Mr Abrams had grimaced at that, but she hadn't been able to tell whether it was because of what she'd said, or the strain of holding up his protective spell.

"Um, should we finish up? Mr Abrams doesn't look so good."

But he'd shaken his balding head and gestured for her to continue.

They'd all listened, as she retold what Godsson had said about Robo, and The Breaker. Eagle had assured her that he and the Doctor would discuss it further, and that the whole subject was now the Doctor's only priority. And added that *she* might indeed be the key to the problem. Which had made her feel warm inside, and special; but then Eagle went on to say she shouldn't trust Godsson; that he'd been nicknamed 'The Manipulator' for good reason.

Mr Abrams had let the shield drop, and then just *drooped* in his wheelchair, fallen asleep. Various motors and injectors had started up, along with a warm pink glow from something hidden under his shirt.

And Eagle had ordered her uncle to leave! She'd kept her eyes on her new boss, nodding her thanks that he'd kept his word. Hoping that he always would, and *this* wasn't just some new trick. Her uncle, she ignored, even though she could hear his heart pounding, no doubt in anger, as he stalked from the room.

Life was good! She'd made backup copies of the Doctor's 'Mode One' ending phrase, and separately, had Little Brother making her a few special 'music players', in case Barney's device got damaged.

It'd do, for now.

And now this, her first mission – a proper, good assassination! – Eagle had added to his earlier warning. "There is a lot more to this than we can safely tell you, Leeth. Ignorance is your best shield. But stay alert, and trust your instincts."

So here she was – a real agent, on her first mission. And it was a big one. An important one. One that other agents had tried to execute, and failed. The target, Eagle had added, also had magical protection against bullets.

The snipers had not survived.

But for now, she had to put all those thoughts aside and concentrate on just being 'Katy Bennett, teenage runaway.' So she stretched up an arm now to carefully miss grabbing a pine branch and fall forward onto her knees, pretending to slip. The trickiest part was deciding how many grazes and scratches to cause. She didn't want too many, cause she only had a small tube of antiseptic, and every scrape hurt. It was also tricky to control the exact severity of each graze while making each accident appear natural, just in case someone *was* watching her.

She whimpered as she pushed herself back upright from the slope – mainly to stay in character, not because anyone could get close enough to hear her before she heard them. *I hope my camp tonight attracts a cult search party. I'll use extra smoky pines when I start my fire.*

She blew a couple more ear-piercing 'peeps' from the carved jade 'tooth' around her neck – the signal to Faith that all was well, and to let her know where she was. She hid a smile at Faith's barely-audible answering bark.

The biggest disappointment was that she was going to miss the 'Fest. They'd said she'd likely need a week to be noticed by Shepherd Fox and be able to get him alone. The FistFest was tomorrow night: she'd been 'running away from home' through the woods for two days now, after getting off the bus in Jackson, where US Highway 26 turned north; since she had to head east.

She hadn't liked the way the man in the general store had looked at her, either, while she bought the cheap backpack and camping stuff. Pestering her with questions about what a 'Purdy lil thing like her was doin', hikin' alone? Didn't she know there were 'bars' in them hills?'

She would rather've been dropped off with Faith, from the auto-drive car. But, again, 'in case anyone backtracked your trail....'

It'd been weird, walking through a city – or a town, really, she guessed – so completely untouched by the quake of '44, or even the World Storm. Which didn't make much sense to her, since this whole area must have been buried deep under snow for over six months. She wondered how they'd all survived.

As she'd headed down the wide, straight, two lane road heading east, the businesses had vanished first, then the houses started thinning out. A few people even said 'Hello,' and wanted to talk, which was also weird. From their questions, she quickly got the feeling they were worried about her, which also made her feel funny; strangely sad and happy at the same time.

She got the impression some of them might even report her to authorities, from the way they'd eyed her backpack, and clothes, and the questions they'd asked. She just said she was going for a small hike, and meeting some friends 'tomorrow.'

At the final bend in the road, where Elk Refuge Road started – the true beginning of her mission – she turned back. The last two people still watched her, doubtfully. She waved to the old couple and thought the woman shook her head. Settling her pack, she headed on and out of their sight.

Now, two days later, she finished setting up her tiny tent, rolling out the too-warm sleeping bag inside it and putting together the fire. Remembering to add plenty of

green wood, and getting it going well before sundown.
They took her that night.

CHAPTER 30

Of course, they were careful to make it look like that wasn't what they were doing, and Leeth was just as careful to remain in character as Katy Bennett, acting a little overwhelmed by the realities of her flight and overjoyed at her 'rescue.' If a little nervous about the big, scary men.

Though it had been pretty obviously a capture, from the way her Link signal failed shortly before she heard them creeping up on her. But she just smiled and handed it over, when 'Jake' examined it then snorted at her use of a Tik Tek comm-band in the Rockies. "Chinese shit don't work like nothin'n these hills. Give us, I'll get our Spock to add a proper antenna for ya. Might take a day'r two, but – he's a busy man."

They'd checked her glasses – which had made her tense, until it was clear that Nelson's security worked. Just like at the acting school, they only operated when *she* was wearing them.

But they hadn't given them back. "Women don't need to be seein' any more'n what's right in front of 'em! You got menfolk lookin' after you now, little lady."

They wanted to know who she was and what she was doing here, all alone.

She hedged, and avoided, but let them worm her cover story out of her. Katy Bennett, teen runaway, actively seeking out the Brethren. Did they know how to find them?

The men had grinned. "Yore in luck, little lady – you done found 'em!"

They packed up her meager possessions while she looked on. She'd offered to carry something, but again, they'd just laughed and shouldered her small backpack, after making jokes at having to lengthen the straps.

While they led her down the steeply-angled slope and then along, and up another, she thought back to her final briefing, with Mother. The plan had been simple and direct. 'You fit Fox's profile,' they'd told her, when she'd asked how she was supposed to get noticed by Fox and gain his trust.

"What does that mean?" she'd asked.

They'd exchanged looks. Mother's expression, in particular, looked sour.

"He likes young girls," Father explained, grimly. "You will need to seduce him. Is that a problem?"

She'd studied the image again, pursing her lips. A similar build to her uncle – lean – though he looked taller and much fitter. Dark brown eyes, almost black; heavy black eyebrows that joined up in the middle; a strong nose and large jaw; large hands. His hair, too, was very black, and cropped short. He held a rifle tucked under his arm in the picture.

She'd pursed her lips. Shrugged. "I guess he'll do."

They'd exchanged more funny looks, and turned to her uncle, who looked defensive but said nothing.

She was to find an excuse to be alone with him, at night, so she could silently kill him and get away, then slip out under cover of darkness. But because it was only five days from a full moon, they'd also made her memorize a week of moon-rises and moon-sets.

It'd been super weird, meeting Mr Shanahan to borrow Faith. A bit uncomfortable, actually, even after she'd apologized for knocking him out and stuff.

Though when she asked him what he and Godsson had talked about, after she'd left, he'd just shrugged, and calmly said 'Nothing.' It was the *calmly* that kind of worried her. Mr S had never been *calm* when the subject of Godsson came up, before. She should maybe mention it to Eagle, later.

But he'd been his normal self when they explained the reason they'd come. Of course, after they'd first met Professor Sanders. James, who had gone with her, had been super suave and helpful in that awkward meeting. Plus, he had that *sleek* Windsteed!

Anyway, Mr S had even given her the special whistle, now disguised as a jade tooth, to let Faith know where she was. He'd also taught her the sequence he used to use to signal Faith to attack, when the two of them had fought the guerrillas in the eco wars.

He seemed surprised she learned the sequence on her first attempt at blowing it. He *didn't* seem to notice her wince at the piercing sound. In fact, she saw that *only* she and Faith had reacted, at all, and realized none of them could hear it.

So she'd pretended she couldn't, either. But she and Faith had grinned at each other – another secret communication system. But only from some people: she saw that James had noticed her reaction. He'd winked.

Mr Shanahan had looked worried, though, when she'd asked if there were other instructions Faith understood. And not answered. Something to investigate, later.

Anyway, that had been the plan.

But tonight, with the two men with the hungry but somehow haunted eyes helping her pack her tiny tent and camping gear and 'escorting' her through the steep fir forest, it no longer felt like a game. The two wore dark camo clothes and carried rifles with an easy familiarity. Two more, who she had to pretend not to hear, flanked them in the darkness.

Then, after only a couple of kilometers trek, she noticed a dark mesh spread above their heads through the trees, and soon after that, saw the glow of fires and heard the murmur of voices. A lot of voices. Mostly men, though a few women too.

When they brought her into their camp, 'the Patriarch' was waiting. He'd looked around as her two escorts brought her out of the woods, and their eyes met. In his eyes, gleaming in the firelight, she saw first an admiration of her body, then the awareness of his own power, and her lack of it.

But something else shot between them. She saw him see *her* recognize that power difference. She recognized the glint in his eye; saw him see her tiny flinch, which no one else had. And she saw the dark pleasure that roiled behind those eyes.

And she knew – *knew* with sick certainty – that something far darker than the Department understood, lurked here. Waited now in delight until it could be alone with her. Like her uncle.

She couldn't take it. She *wouldn't* take it.

Eyes downcast, trembling, drawing deep on her acting skills, she took a single hesitant step toward him. As if reluctant. As if she knew she shouldn't, but couldn't help herself. And, horror above all others, she felt a dark pleasure spark inside herself. Felt a part of her that *wanted* to give in.

She glanced up, then, and saw him see that, too. His lips parted, and as she crept closer, a tiny moth to a raging bonfire, he put out a hand to stop those who had stepped forward to intercept her.

No one else moved, no one spoke, as she approached

him, one faltering step at a time. Nervously playing with the jade tooth on its thin leather cord. Kissing it, like it was a talisman that could keep her safe. *Blowing it.*

And when she stood before him, eyes still downcast, seeing the silver chasing on his shiny black leather boots.... She lifted her gaze slowly, past the thickening bulge below the ornate silver belt buckle, raising her eyes fearfully at last to look deep into his.

She rested one hand on his broad chest, the other touching below his taut stomach, fluttering nervously, like a butterfly.... She moved her body closer, and whispered, too low for him to hear. He bent down over her, bringing their bodies even closer.

She called the sharpness to her fingertips and slashed them through his neck, grabbing his head by the curly black hair as it fell and stepping sideways to avoid the first arterial geyser.

But while one hand reached for his holster, before his death had registered on his own mind, she sensed *something* trying to approach. Trying to move *towards*, from elsewhere. Something unutterably cruel. She slashed at it, too, and felt it recoil in pain and shock. But even as Fox died, and the door began closing, something slid through it, this time radiating sorrowfulness, offering...

In her mind's eye, her claws *glowed,* exposing the lie, and she stabbed deeper. The door snapped shut. Turning and smoothly drawing his silver six shooter, she began rolling and firing.

And the first of Faith's rockets roared in, blowing three men into the air, rifles flying from their hands.

Screaming people dived for cover, drawing or raising their own weapons as the second of Faith's rockets exploded and Leeth plunged into the bushes.

Then a fourth, fifth, and sixth rocket detonated behind her, followed by a long burst of machine gun fire from low to the ground, amongst the trees.

Whistling 'withdraw' and circling toward her, Leeth dodged between the trees. The two met in the dark, the glow of Faith's red eyes a welcoming sight.

Then they ran, full pelt, around and between the trees, over the ridge and down into the next valley, grinning at one another in the dark as bullets flew around them and the fires leaped higher, behind.

Together, they *flew*.

PART II

Fight

CHAPTER 31

"Fifteen seconds," Mother muttered again. "With not a single word exchanged?"

"Eagle said to trust my instincts. And as soon as our eyes met...." Leeth shook her head. "I had to kill him. He was... poisonous."

"You realize Faith's signal scrambled the team mere hours after their arrival in the general area? *Interrupting* their initial briefing meeting?"

"Cool! I bet *Eagle* timed that, yeah? Anyway, since I finished the mission early, I'll be going to the FistFest tonight, okay?"

Mother and Father just blinked at her.

"You jest." Mother said.

"Don't worry, I slept on the plane coming back. Curled up with Faith." She smiled, hugging herself at the memory. "Did you know they'd mounted these extended rocket pods to her, specially for this mission? She was *so* good – you should have seen her!"

Mother waved that aside. "It's not your alertness I'm concerned about. Why do you wish to attend this... *brawl*? So you can run off again?"

Father had harrumphed, agreeing. "Taking a side job just to earn cash is an unnecessary-"

Eagle cut him off, even as he waited to hear from Abrams about the patterns the man had sensed, that would coalesce tonight. "We have no fresh missions planned for Leeth, and the exercise can be used to build up her Dumps-dwelling persona into a useful cover identity. A 'young runaway' ID could prove useful to us in the future."

Leeth resisted the urge to poke her tongue out at Mother and Father.

"Do you know where it will be held?"

Leeth sat back. "Uh...."

Eagle gave her a pointed look. "Preacher does. Perhaps you could be looking to join his gang, and wish to use the Fist Fest to prove your capabilities."

Join Preacher? She felt her face twist.

"Very well. You may attend: a reward for a successful first mission," Eagle said. He even smiled at her! "I expect tonight's small test of your abilities to proceed equally smoothly. But try to keep a low profile, eh?"

"Yes sir! And maybe Faith and I can work together again, in the future? We make a great team!"

At that moment, Eagle saw an incoming call from Abrams. *Priority.*

"I will consider it," Eagle told Leeth.

«I've just cast the yarrow stalks for your small force of nature.» Abrams said.

«And?» Eagle prompted.

«I threw *Ming Yi*, hexagram 36 – *Darkening of the Light*. I'm also looking at *The Tower* and *Death*, in her Tarot reading.»

Eagle kept his expression neutral, while the girl beamed delightedly at him.

«Are you saying I should stop her attending the 'Fest?» Eagle asked.

He heard the puff of a wheezing laugh. «You couldn't!» Abrams declared; then continued, more seriously. «No, deep currents move tonight. And we need to let them flow, wherever they lead us. Trust your girl, Eagle.»

Eagle was looking at her strangely, Leeth saw. "Is everything all right?"

He didn't answer straight away.

"Remember all you've learned, Leeth. I expect your very best effort, tonight. Do not take anything for granted."

"Um, okay. I mean, sure. Yes sir." *Another test, I bet.* She felt a shiver of anticipation.

But after that, the debriefing basically ended. They actually cut her off when she started trying to explain what she'd sensed *behind* Fox. "Put it into your report," Mother had said. Looking *nervous.*

Emma ambushed her outside the meeting room, slipping one arm under Leeth's and wrapping the smaller girl in an enveloping hug. Leeth melted into it.

Then Emma sniffed, and eased away. "Whew! Where did *you* sleep last night, a dog kennel?"

Leeth bristled. "Faith is my best friend!" Or was Marcie? Maybe she had two best friends? She shook herself. "Are you saying I smell?"

Emma, with one arm around her waist, wrinkled her nose. "No. You stink! You don't mind if you shower while you fill me in on all the goss? I want to know all! You caused quite a disruption to operations. And *what* did you do to Preacher?"

So Leeth had washed herself clean of days of hiking, blood, smoke, and even Faith's familiar doggy odors, talking through the glass door while Emma sat on her bed, asking questions and occasionally snorting with unladylike laughter.

She'd been very intrigued by Barney's 'drone detector,' and the society of the Dumps. She seemed genuinely interested in all the people Leeth had met.

And after Leeth was clean, she invited her to try the sauna, to ease any remaining aches.

"We have a sauna? I've heard of those, but never had one."

"Come on, you'll love it. I do. And you can keep filling me in on your news."

Leeth did love it. And hadn't realized how soothing such intense heat could be.

Emma shook her head, fondly, as she watched Leeth slumped, bonelessly asleep. *So young.* So innocent. It was good to have her back.

She had expected Leeth to waken as the pale green sheets shimmered in the dark and cedar-scented room. But the young agent just lay, head lolling back on the curved wooden support, exposing her neck, her chest rising and sinking with each slow breath.

Emma rolled her shoulders, enjoying the soothing beauty of the simulated aurora, then sighed. *I may as well get some work done. I've had some of my best ideas, here.*

She ladled more mentholated water over the stones, breathing deeper as the steam flooded out. The heat penetrated her unmodified muscles, and felt nano-pores open, to flush out days of accumulated cellular rubbish.

She lay back, eyes and mind gorging on the lush auroral display. But before she too slipped into sleep, she linked to the room's trid projectors and began constructing a 3D visualization of Tik Tek's acquisitions – public and obfuscated – and the associated research areas, building a mind map. Somewhere there, she knew, was the pattern that disturbed her.

Leeth woke from aquamarine dreams of swimming through the Forest, dancing with the spirits. Only this time, they were green, fairy-like, and she could see them as they and she skated through shimmering curtains of shifting sapphire and emerald. But strange doll houses were scattered through the Forest, miniature labs, factories, and medical assembly plants connected one to another by glowing, gemstone-colored cords.

Green blood pulsed along some cords, the flows running thicker to some of the key *businesses,* she realized, reading their hovering names. And above them all, two convoluted structures linked to them by wisp-faint threads that made her think of puppet strings.

She blinked, startling properly awake, to chartreuse lights in the air and a swirl of opalescent butterfly wings vanishing in a fall of twinkling light.

"Beautiful," she whispered as they faded, leaving just the ghost-fire green curtains and the floating gem-like net.

Emma looked across at her. "Awake? Sorry, I've just been trying to see what Tik Tek and Newtopia are up to." As she spoke each name, first one node of puppet strings, then the second, glowed brighter. "I've been beating my head against the problem for years. It's more than just business, but I haven't found the right way of looking at it."

Leeth frowned. "It's super complicated. There must be thousands of them. I don't see how *anyone* could properly juggle all those. You'd have to have a brain like a computer."

For some reason, Leeth's words sent a shiver through Emma.

CHAPTER 32

Leeth paced her rooms, waiting for Preacher. It was hard to believe six hours could seem so long. She'd spent one whole hour just on her description of killing Shepherd Fox, and the evil thing she'd injured the moment before he'd died. And especially, her impression that it was hidden behind him, and still out there somewhere. Lurking. Not like Robo, though. It had felt more like *Her*, somehow. But grown up: old, not young. Very old. Wise, too, and sneaky.

She felt certain she'd face it again, one day. *I bet it's to do with the stuff they didn't want to tell me about Fox.*

She took a recording bead from its resting place in the trid player, and placed it on her makeup table, moving back under the light. For thirty seconds she turned and posed, then beamed it back to the trid to check herself once more. The lithe form in the tight, shiny black outfit turned and moved in replay. Black leather choker, studded, to match the wristbands. Savage! She'd show them how fierce a 'city girl' could be!

She tried a smile. Her face was finally starting to look more like her own. Mostly-blue eyes stared back at her from still-bleached skin. Staring at the weird speckled irises, she willed her proper orangey-brown color to fight back harder. And the treatment to her hair roots, a month ago, would keep her hair this stupid blonde color for weeks yet. She scowled at it.

At least it means all the friends I've made in the Dumps will still recognize me. She wondered if Barney and Teef would be there tonight. *I bet I amaze them!* She snorted. *Sexertainer – as if!*

Carefully wiping the vidder's storage, just as she'd been taught, she neatly put the unit back onto the trid.

She was glad the Department hadn't tried doing any of those weird "personality overlays" since that awful night of the Opera. She shuddered. She still had nightmares about being trapped deep down a well inside her own mind.

She picked up Barney's spirit detector, smiling fondly as she turned it over. But she'd better not wear it, tonight – it might get broken in a fight. *Besides, I'm not on the run any more!* She put it back down, then began pacing.

What is taking Preacher so long?

There'd also been a news report of some violence in the Dumps, just that morning. The Breaker? It'd been sketchy, though. *I'll need to investigate.*

Tomorrow, she told herself. *I deserve* one *night of fun, just for myself.*

At that moment, an odd chime from her wristlink stopped her. That meant something unusual...

A pleasant synthetic voice from the more powerful comm unit on her desk accompanied the appearance of an image on the wall facing it. "Incoming call, insecure, from Marcie Dunkirk, for persona Jane Baker."

Leeth blushed, ashamed. *I should have called Marcie again, after I got back!*

"Baker appearance match, ninety percent," the female voice continued. An option appeared, to 'Enable image processing?' She dismissed it. "Please select a response option," the voice prompted. On the wall, four choices were shown: herself with a vaguely-rustic bedroom suitable for a farm behind her; herself in an office with people moving to and fro in the background; a window that said 'ignore'; and a final one that said 'voice only.'

Leeth moved, her Jane-face moving identically. But was that a *spot* on her nose? And did she really look a bit cross-eyed?

A glance in a mirror made her growl. More stupid tricks by Nelson!

But why was Marcie calling now, of all times? She was about to reluctantly select the 'ignore' window, when an awful certainty struck her: *The Breaker had taken Amanda!*

Despite the press of time, she hurriedly sat down, gesturing at the office background option. She just had time to school her expression, before a window opened for her friend, while the one showing 'Jane' in her office setting shrank.

"Jane! It's so good to see you! I was just about to give up."

"What's the matter? Amanda's missing, isn't she?"

Marcie looked puzzled. "No. Amanda's fine. Why wouldn't she be?"

"Are you sure? You know where she is right now?"

Marcie pursed her lips, saying nothing. Then turned her head slightly. "Hey! Kidling!" she called out. "Jane wants to say 'hi'."

Leeth heard running feet, a slamming door, then Marcie's kid sister charged across the room to lean against her, waving. "Hi Jane! Whatcha doin'?"

Leeth, heart pounding in relief, watched her Jane face blink stupidly. She forced herself to stop looking at it. Was Nelson's software exaggerating her expressions in the simulated image? "Uh. Hi Amanda. Great to see you!"

"Okay, scoot, Squirt. I got big girl stuff to talk about with Jane."

They both waited while Amanda left the room; much more slowly than she'd entered it.

"Okay. Spill. What was that all about?"

"Uh, nothing. I just... I was just reading about an... uh, assault, in the, um, city, and I guess it made me a little jumpy."

Marcie looked unconvinced, peering curiously at the office background then back to her friend. "Your mother and father are okay? You didn't, um, get in trouble?" From her expression, she was dying to ask more, but knew not to.

Leeth thought back over the last couple of days, unable to keep a dopey smile off her face, remembering her time with Faith. And ending Shepherd Fox. *Who'd been super creepy.* She sat up straighter.

"Did you hear about the Brethren of the End of Days? The net's crazy with stories. The FBI rounded up the whole cult – the survivors, that is. People are saying there was this ninja girl cutting off people's heads and shooting rockets!"

Leeth felt her eyes widen before she could wrestle her expression under control. "Uh, really?" *Does she suspect it was me?* "That sounds pretty chill. Wish I'd been there!"

Marcie smiled. "Looks like you're back at work?"

Leeth nodded.

Marcie waited for her to volunteer something. "Do you miss the Dumps? Ever think you might go back?"

Yeah: tonight! "Um, sure. Some time, I guess."

Marcie leaned forward. "But isn't it dangerous?"

"No! Not really. People exaggerate. Some places are dangerous, sure, but most of the people there are really nice. Like they band together a lot more than people in the city, you know? Help each other."

The ends of Marcie's lips twitched up fractionally.

"Yeah. I'd heard that. So. Doing anything interesting tonight?"

Marcie was looking straight into her eyes. She tried to lie, but found she just couldn't. "Uh, yeah, I am. It should be fun, actually. But I shouldn't talk about it."

"I could do with a little fun. Maybe I could go with you? I have some news."

"Um, I don't think that'd be allowed." She imagined asking Eagle if she could take Marcie with her into the Dumps, tonight – then pictured Eagle's reaction. Marcie would stand out like a... like a duck in a dojo. "What's your news? Is that why you called?"

"I've got an audition on Monday, for a *great* part! But I wanted to catch up with you, maybe get some tips."

"*Me?* Tips? What kind of part is it for?"

Marcie looked smug. "Just something my dangerous friend might know something about. When do you finish your 'fun' tonight? Maybe we could meet up, after?"

"Sorry, I think it'll go quite late. And there's... a little traveling time, too."

Instead of looking disappointed, though, Marcie just smiled. And a little later, refusing to say more about her mysterious audition, signed off.

Leeth sat staring at the wall where Marcie's face had been projected, feeling like she'd missed something. *Had the* Department *decided to hire Marcie?* She shook her head. *No. That's crazy.* But Marcie clearly had *some* secret they needed to talk about.

She checked the time again, frowning. Juice! Where *was* he? She resumed pacing the room, growing more angry with each passing minute. Finally, hearing his footsteps out in the corridor, she thrust the door open as he touched the entry panel. "Come on, let's go!"

Preacher blocked the doorway. "Hey, hey! Not 'fore you're ready, bim."

With an effort of will that bared her teeth, she held herself still. "What. Do you. Mean?"

He held up a dark, smelly bundle and smiled. "You're not *dressed* yet."

She took a step back.

He nodded, following her into her room. "Brung ya some street threads."

Five minutes later Leeth stared at her reflection, wrinkling her nose in disgust. *Was this some dumb revenge for paralyzing him with his own stupid weapon, when he'd tried to grab me last week?* The ratty denim jacket was kind of chill. But the ugly black leather trousers: how could anyone see her legs? The shirt, though, was the worst – at one time it'd probably been a check pattern. Now, murky yellows and greens struggled against the dirt overwhelming its muddy colors. She couldn't even name half the stains on it! Plus it was making her sweat.

In a fit of revulsion she tore it open. Struggling out of it, she flung it across the room, breathing heavily.

Come on, she told herself at last. *It's not that important.*

But somehow, it was.

She put the denim jacket back on, by itself, liking how it left her waist bare. She was proud of her stomach muscles: they looked good. She poked them. The trouble was, the jacket had no buttons.

Her eyes fell on the remains of the disgusting shirt.

-

Preacher tried to ignore the oddly-dressed figure beside him as he led the way generally upward through bleak concrete corridors, finally nearing one of the main exits. The Department filled deeply-buried twentieth century shelters. In the aftermath of the Big One, at Eagle's directive, they'd been restored and refurbished. Leeth and Preacher worked their way up and across, and now walked through a 'disused' service tunnel connecting the forgotten warren to the business district above.

Leeth was once again examining her clothes. "How'd they get the leather so soft? I still think I could've kept the heels."

Preacher sighed. At last they came to a drab gray door. "Okay, this is it. We're about to enter the back of the mall's service complex here – this opens onto basement level eight of its car park." He checked the screen displaying a wide-angle view of the empty expanse beyond, and then the log of the motion sensors. All clear.

He turned to the girl. "All clear," she told him, her expression shading toward smug as she read his annoyance.

He eyed her up and down. Gods knew how she'd turned the trousers into shorts. By the look of it, probably ripped the legs off with her teeth. But the tatty, torn strips of shirt holding the denim jacket *mostly* closed – knotted ends replacing the missing buttons – was the sort of fashion touch that might even take off. The swelling curves revealed by the interesting gaps....

He snarled as he dragged his attention back, annoyed at himself. So. Maybe she had smeared the dirt on her face a little too artistically; but maybe he thought that just because he'd watched her daintily apply it.

Bare feet, dirty. He'd let her keep the studded leather choker. And she'd loved the deadly sharp knife, now concealed up one sleeve. She'd do.

"Okay, give me fifteen beats to double check the area's clear."

She rolled her eyes.

"We'll take the BART into Mission, as far as the 24th Street station." He frowned. "You know what the BART is, right, the-"

"Bay Area Rapid Transit, almost a hundred years old, blah, blah, blah. Yes! I used it every day for two weeks, with Emma! I'm not a total null."

"From 24th Street I'll make my way on foot to the Dumps; I gather you're such an expert you'll choose your own route. Prob' best: mine's tricky, you'd prob' get lost. Or attacked." The remark ruffled her feathers, as he'd hoped. "Unless meb you'd like a wager – you try to shadow me after I leave the station, but if I sight ya, ya lose."

"Hah! I could follow you, easy!"

"Yah, so, you on?"

He saw her grow wary. "What do you get if I lose?"

He shrugged. "All ya winnin's, tonight? *If* ya make any. Or we sex. You c'n choose."

"And when I win?"

He smiled. "I double ya winnin's."

He watched her think about that; she obviously expected to win big, and she could see *he* thought he risked little.

But she shook her head. "No. When I win, I want you to pretend you don't hate me."

He blinked. Almost, felt guilty. *Almost.* But he remembered her final kick to his head, as he lay paralyzed in agony from Nelson's damned neural disruptor. Instead, he schooled his expression. "I don't hate ya, kid. Just think you're a bit big for ya boots. But hell, yeah, I c'n do that. So: game on?"

They shook on it, and he lightly punched her shoulder. That was the signal. Now Nelson knew he'd get the 'accidental' shot of her they needed. "Ya gonna lose."

She shook her head, lips pursed.

But maybe he could lure her into more trouble? Considering her curiosity, and her attitude toward orders... "Mother and Father've told ya ta stay out've my biz, yeah? Don't ask questions. My op's need to know. Even James and Emma aren't in the loop."

He tried to read her expression, but this time he couldn't tell whether she'd taken the bait or not. "Okay. And don't lose your cashstick or you'll have nothing to stake yourself into a fight. 'Cause we wouldn't want that to happen, would we?"

She just stared at him.

"And remember-"

"I know, I know. You're called 'Dad' and you've got your own gang, the Crazers; and don't go on full in the first fight, to improve the odds; and, and, *and!* Can we just *go*?"

"Right. Just try not to get mugged. I won't be able to help you out, it'd wipe the cover."

She raised her eyes to heaven, ignoring the jibe, and waited while he opened the door and stalked off, shutting the door in her face. She counted heartbeats as she heard his quiet footsteps slowly fade.

Then stepped out. *Finally.* Tonight was gonna be so much fun!

CHAPTER 33

Nelson smiled when Preacher poked Leeth's shoulder. Time to grab a drone and move it into place.

He followed her via video feed as she climbed the stairs to street level. While she headed down Market Street toward the station, he jumped to a traffic cam. He would've liked to bug her, but didn't want to be *too* obvious.

How badly would she react if she learned what Preacher did? He giggled. Knowing how she'd reacted when he'd introduced her to a perfectly harmless 'training' stimsense, the explosion should be spectacular. Did Preacher realize his danger? Probably not. But if Leeth did retire Preacher, it'd make pretty compelling footage. Eagle couldn't let her get away with that! *Though if the Doc's right, she* can't *kill any of us anymore. Not that he's been right about much, lately.*

It'd be good to test that; see if he'd been telling the truth. He shivered, touching his chest, seeing again the psycho bitch snarling down into his face, her invisible claws poised over his heart. He forced the memory aside, his skin prickling uncomfortably, and shuddered.

He'd learned a lot about her since she'd attacked him. A lot and a little – the data he'd found had raised more questions than it answered. When he'd discovered she'd come from the Institute for Paranormal Dysfunction, he'd been sure at first he'd found the dirt he was looking for. But it'd turned out the Doctor and Leeth weren't there as inmates. *Un*fortunately. Also annoying was that James and Emma had both apparently uncovered that fact some months ago.

But what he *did* find out was that every time she went into New Francisco, someone died. Violently. Which sounded good, considering she was being trained as an assassin – until you learned that none of the kills had been authorized.

It had started last year, before she'd even joined the Department, when she'd killed two guys, Simon J. Gallagher and Scott Barrymore, in Golden Gate Park. After that, three CID-less people on the fringes of the desperate nightclub scene down in SoMa, and another the same evening, in the broken-down old General Hospital. A good effort, even by her standards.

Then her highest-profile victim, the opera singer, Maria Lempriere. Leeth had somehow killed her without

James knowing, too, which was kind of impressive, he had to admit. A twofer night, also – she'd killed another CID-less guy down in the Tenderloin, after the show. Though *that* one, she'd done right in front of James!

There *was* one time she hadn't killed anyone when she'd been allowed out – the night she'd had the breakdown during the opera, and almost gotten James's membership revoked. Nelson chuckled. So the one time she hadn't killed anyone, she'd had a mental breakdown. Probably from frustration. Unless that had just been an act? Had she and the Doc *together* worked to erase the Jennifer persona he'd labored over and implanted for her?

Hmm. He put that thought aside, for later.

He was on shakier ground tracking her kills after that. Later on, during her disastrous 'socialization' training at the drama school, there'd been the guy who'd 'accidentally' fallen to his death down the stairs in Emma's apartment while Leeth had been staying with her. He snorted. But there wasn't any solid link between Leeth and the violence that had flared up in the Hunter's Point Dumps at that time. Except the timing: the locals stirred up, like you'd expect if some quietly nasty predator was down there hunting and killing them. It seemed pretty obvious who was doing it, although Leeth probably thought she was being real sleek.

Some newsfeeds were reporting some of those deaths as being the work of The Breaker. Nelson mulled over the idea. Not really her style, when she was her normal self. But she'd been scary as hell in Psycho Bitch mode. Though some of the deaths attributed to The Breaker were from earlier, before she'd been allowed out. That wouldn't stop her copying them, though, during a psychotic break. He'd noticed her interest in those reports. She'd even made a map of the murder sites. Trust her to idolize a serial killer.

It was kind of frustrating that he didn't know how many she'd killed while she'd been AWOL and off-cam. But fewer than his stats had predicted: probably 'cause she was too busy just surviving. He snickered at the idea of her hunting and eating rats and insects in a rubbish dump. Then his expression soured, thinking of the number of drones whose last image was Leeth's face, either close up or whipping out that damned slingshot of hers. Or giving him the finger. She'd made him look like an idiot in front of Mother and Father. *'You're funding her?'*

He would've liked more time to study that 'drone detector' the baby hacker had built for her. As far as he could tell, it detected light, heat, hard rad, pressure, sound, smells – you name it – *and* their deltas, and deltas of those deltas. It then did some sort of weird cross-correlation of them all, everything fed into a deep neural net. He still wasn't sure it wasn't some kind of personal performance art-piece. His best guess was that it recognized the *sound* the drones made.

He shook himself. *Right, Leeth's death toll....*

She'd apparently been on her best behavior while being hunted: she'd only lightly injured the cops and agents sent against her.

By *her* standards.

Anyway, it was time to set Agent Adam Garland on her trail. He sniggered at the irony of Eagle making the former PASWAT dude who'd already arrested her once, into a Bureau agent. This could get *poetic*.

Garland even had an ongoing search running for violent events in the Hunters Point Dumps, he saw, and the FistFest fitted that! It'd be tasty to send *all* his data to Garland, but he couldn't do that without tipping his hand – there was no way Leeth's movements would be known to anyone outside the Department.

He grabbed a drone, positioning it so it'd catch a short clip of Preacher when he 'bumped into' one of his gangers any minute now. The two would discuss the FistFest so a busybody 'concerned citizen' could learn about the illegal event and report it. Leeth would be positioned somewhere in the background, for Garland to spot, thanks to her bet with Preacher. Fortunately, even though Leeth didn't look like herself at the moment, she still *moved* like herself; and Garland seemed pretty smart, for a grunt. Heh. The citizen could just happen to zoom in on the girl in the background, too. Maybe finish off with a cleavage shot.

Yeah.

He considered what text to add, apart from the 'Fest tip-off. Maybe something like 'Check out the girl. The way she moves: could she be a fighter?'

Two minutes later it was all done. Nelson leaned back in his chair, looking at the problem from other angles; for other avenues of attack.

But the only new thing he'd learned when he'd finally summoned the nerve to crack her personnel records was that after the night she'd killed Lempriere at the opera, she'd been explicitly ordered to stick to just her nominated targets. Disappointing, really. There should've been more data. Lots more. Like *something* that would've led back to her parents.

Had Eagle *expected* him to crack their records? He put that thought carefully to one side. At least it meant Eagle knew of some of her kills, and didn't sanction them.

Leaning back in his command chair he steepled his fingers, watching from the station's platform cam as she followed agent Hall – *Oops, Preacher: not s'posed to know the agents' real names* – onto the train and out of his view.

Would the FistFest be enough to satisfy her? From the material he'd seen, fights to the death weren't all *that* common. But if she didn't manage to kill at least one of her opponents tonight, he was sure she'd find someone else. Maybe someone she'd really get slammed for. He hoped so. If she did, it'd be a good time to dump what he'd found to Mother and Father.

He wondered who she'd kill tonight. Or rather, how many.

CHAPTER 34

Leeth peeked into the next carriage, noting the ease with which Preacher rode the rocking motions, standing. He had a sour expression on his face, like he was annoyed he hadn't gotten a seat. She eased back into her seat smiling.

Beside her, the old woman got up as the cabin lurched and slowed, and a big, well-built young guy in leathers and torn jeans slid in beside her. He'd silvered his short fuzz of hair, and had a sleek gash of scar arrowing diagonally up his cheek. The jacket smelled strongly of leather, but the wear and tear was clean, and he himself smelled of fresh pine, cedar, and soap. The whole look was just too carefully put together for him to be a genuine ganger.

He turned toward her, one hand sliding under her jacket, tugging it so the grubby checkered ties danced in the revealing gap, his breath in her ear.

"Cute buttons, girl. Meb' ya'd look slicier in silver chains, but? I know a place."

She twisted around, snaking her own hand through the tight waistband of his jeans and down between his legs, brushing her lips up against his ear as her fingers slid beneath the stiffening rod, encircling the sac. An arrogant grin blossomed as his own hand stroked up the side of her breast.

She imagined Preacher's expression, if he saw it.

That helped.

She closed her fist and pulled, following the punk forward as he hunched over, jerking like he'd been tasered. She clamped her teeth onto his earlobe, then just Growled, low and angry.

Releasing him and leaning back, she ignored him as he jumped up and practically ran for the carriage doors.

She thought about Preacher, just as they'd left the Department; how his expression seemed to somehow say 'I know something you don't.'

She wondered what he was planning.

She was still wondering, when she felt a sudden weird sense of nervousness. A kind of tugging. She looked around the compartment, scowling, wondering if someone had just tried to put a spell on her. It didn't really feel exactly like that though. More like when Mark Dennis had been following her, when she was Jane Baker.

She looked around, but didn't see him. *What hap-*

pened to him? I should check; add him to my list if he's still out there.

The train slowed, coming into the 24th Street Mission station, and she shrugged the sensation off. Time to get moving.

As she exited, some massive weirdo in a trench-coat and what looked an antique *smog* mask, of all things, looked for a moment like he was going to bump into her, but she dodged aside.

A scratchy whisper at her collar made her whip around, hunting for the source. Her eyes narrowed as the big weirdo, now hunched over, limped past her toward the exit gate.

She stood staring, watching, *listening*, trying to work out what it was about Mr Trenchcoat that set her nerves on edge. If he wasn't bent over, he'd be big, that was for sure. Like, two meters tall big.

So, not Mark Dennis.

With a start, she realized Preacher was almost out of sight, already leaving the station, and she ran to catch up a little, darting past the hulking figure. She could worry about him later.

From the new heights of Bayview, she followed Preacher by the sound of his soft footsteps, with their characteristic twisting upward scuff from his right foot. Down they headed, into the wrecked streets of the Hunters Point Dumps, skirting black puddles of ash-laced rainwater. Far below, a fog rolled in off the Bay, partly cloaking the smashed and charred houses. She kept to the middle of the old main road. Here, the rusted and burnt out wrecks were fewest, although it made her more visible, backlit by the night-glow of New Francisco. To either side, shops and offices stared slack-jawed into the desolation.

The Big One of '44 had thrust this whole region up, making a terraced ruin cut off from the city proper. Still following Preacher, she paused for a moment to look back and up at the first escarpment now massing above her. Six more of the cliffs stretched out below her, a giant's steps. Far in the distance on the bottom-most terrace, a few dotted orange fire-lights glowed.

A fair way down and a little to the left sat what had been her home for the last four weeks. She wasn't sure

how she felt about that. It had been a good time. Mostly.
She sighed, picturing her abandoned nest, empty now on
the edge of the RedSkulls territory. Had anyone found it?
Dared to move in?

A long way to the right, south of her, the creepy Candlestick Tower loomed darkly out toward the water of San
Francisco Bay. She frowned, wondering why they hadn't
renamed the Bay when they renamed the city.

She stretched her arms wide, wishing she could grab
the ruins and the darkness, the *reality* of the broken landscape, and just hug it. She fitted, here. It was a place she
could belong. She shivered in delight. Far ahead, the
sound of Preacher's soft steps faded. *Stop being silly*, she
scolded herself. *This isn't a game!* But she couldn't keep
the grin off her face as she trotted on again.

By the fourth tier, a rusted wreck told her she'd crossed
into the inhabited part of the Dumps. It was the first one
she'd seen tonight that'd been reduced to a skeleton. Tires
crudely hacked away for shoe-soles, every part that could
take an edge or serve a purpose, unscrewed or prised off. A
carcass stripped to the bone.

She looked around. There was little rubbish – only the
burned, the ruined, or the absolutely worthless. She shook
her head in admiration. The people here didn't waste anything.

Below her, Preacher called a distant greeting, and she
heard his pace speed up. She couldn't make much sense of
the words, but thought they meant 'hello.' She quietly increased her pace, frowning. She hadn't realized Preacher
spoke *Street* so fluently. She stopped, head tilted to one
side, and concentrated. Sounded like she now followed a
group of four people.

Continuing on, she began hearing other movements.
Sometimes far behind, sometimes off to the sides. But just
the regular sounds she'd come to expect – vermin burrowing and foraging, insect buzzes, the night wings of bats,
and birds too, adapted to the light from the nearby city.
And people, locals, nesting down for the night – or traveling to the Fest!

By the time she'd descended to the seventh and final
terrace, she was into the clammy fog, and visibility had
dropped to thirty meters. Off to her right and up on a
higher terrace she heard a distant rumble, growing quickly

to a thunder of internal combustion bikes. They skidded, careening into sight down an impossibly steep rut of dirt between tumbled concrete blocks, then along a rusted metal girder before dropping to the merely rough ground. *Juice, they could ride!*

She leapt to the roof of a van, flattening herself out on the rusted surface, watching the outlandishly dressed figures sweep past. She'd thought she'd hidden, but one hooked his fist up into the air in greeting as he sped past.

She frowned at the disappearing forms, then hurried to stay within earshot of Preacher and his friends. Who headed left now, northwards along the Bay.

Fifteen minutes later, the trickle of people scrambling through the rubble had swelled to a stream, a carnival fever lacing the air. It'd got so crowded she'd had to stay within ten meters of Preacher to keep him in earshot, easily close enough for him to see her and win the bet – if she'd been taller.

From up ahead came the smell of smoke from a massive building where orange red firelight flickered from the lower floors. Music beat out in waves, with a heavy, driving rhythm, speeding her pulse. Warmth radiated from it, pushing back the fog.

She paused by a darkened side passage, hearing something large and heavy move, growling. The rules of the Truce only applied to the lit areas. She paused, tempted to investigate. Down there, in the private places of the people and things who lived here, she might find a better test than the 'Fest itself.

But imagining Mother sneering at her for getting distracted, she continued on.

The main passage opened out into a bustling area. On tiptoe, craning her head, she sifted the crowds for 'Dad.' *Funt! He was gone!* But did it matter? They'd arrived, so surely their bet was over, and she'd won? Food stalls to her right; past them, even denser crowds. Further ahead.... Ah! She caught a glimpse of him and his companions. One of them, a tall, weedy guy, was nodding earnestly as Dad said something to him with hand gestures that made her think Preacher was describing some woman. She met his eyes and cocked a finger and thumb – got you! He stopped, then spoke a few words under his hand. The thin guy went to turn toward her but she'd swear Dad stopped him. Like he was protecting her identity. *Huh.* That was more than she'd expected; but all the same, she wasn't going to let her guard down. She'd won their bet, but suddenly doubted the wisdom of it. Would it really be better to have him *pretending* to be her friend?

The weedy guy moved off and she nodded a reluctant 'thanks' to Dad before sinking back down off tiptoe. Dad and his other companions continued on ahead. It wasn't too hard, now, to follow them along the fire-lit walkways, through the lingering wisps of fog. She even started to relax a little.

She'd deliberately stayed on the fringes while she'd been living here. She'd had no idea there were so many types of people all crammed into the area. Did they all live here, or had some come from other places, just for the Fest? It really was like she'd stepped into a bizarre dream-world. At least half the people were mutants. Trolls, ogres – all victims of the terrible Melt retrovirus, in all their strange combinations. But lots more of the Altered, too, than she'd seen before. There were Furries of all sorts: *Bast*ean, Dogmen, Wolven, and others she couldn't name.

People strode or sneaked or staggered around, singly or in groups, dressed in leathers or chromes, kevlar or rags. Smoking, drinking, popping or chipping. Dancing, talking, buying, selling. She passed a juggler of blue-flamed acetylene burners, whose audience half-blocked the passageway; and a male and female artistically coupling further on. A smaller crowd watched, throwing tokens and suggestions in equal numbers.

Leeth smiled and moved on. Yeah, Dumps people weren't sheep!

The central atrium of the plaza had long been open to the sky, and four bonfires threw flames and sparks up soot-stained walls. A portable phasion furnace mounted higher up poured a more powerful wall of heat into the open central area. It'd probably been pumped by an energy raid sometime recently. A band of Dumpers would've tapped the nearby city's power grid for tonight's event, hauling energy cells back before the citycops or one of Phasion Corp's tactical response groups located them.

She looked around. Streams of people continued to

swell the crowds seated on the wide steps surrounding the entertainment dais, food sellers and intoxers squeezing through the area screeching their sales.

On all four sides, six floors rose up, each balcony crammed with people, all overlooking the same courtyard. Here, the jungle beat pounded, strong and insistent. At the edges of the plaza, former shop fronts had been barricaded or just hung with curtains, turning them into homes. The small shapes of almost-feral children darted through the crowd, playing. She watched them disappear, with envious eyes.

Across the way, she spied Pr- *Dad* seated in a good position, arms draped across two young but dirty-looking women. He was laughing and grinning with the people around him. She looked around, deciding her next step.

A puff of smoky wind brought scents of fat, spices, gamy meats, and fish. A roasting beef smell wafted from one of several food stalls pressed against one wall. A lean male turned from the counter, passing her with a grilled gerbil, maybe, jammed on a stick. Biting into the crisp skin, he tore off a succulent hunk. Licking her lips, she forced her way over to join the small crowd.

Smoke from grease-caked stainless steel vats of simmering fatty oil warmed trays of fried insects and spiders racked above. A small girl exchanged a token for a scoop full, dumped rattling into a dirty styrofoam cup. *Eww.* Leeth saw a tab for a cashstick and tapped hers to it, catching the cook's eye and pointing to one of the slowly turning vermin.

A minute later she bit into it, and a smoky, gamy flavor flooded her mouth. She paused, fatty juices running down her chin. *Wow! Better than the Landwave!* She began moving again, teasing flesh from the small bones. A whine and a wet nudge against her bare shin made her look down into the furry muzzle and pleading brown eyes of a rangy, thin dog.

"No way," she told it, trying hard to ignore its hopeful, begging expression. It whined again as she forced her way back into the main press of people.

I wonder what Faith's doing tonight? But Faith *really* wouldn't fit her cover: a weaponized security dog would probably make a lot of people uncomfortable. She smiled though, remembering last night, the two of them racing together through the fir trees, explosions and fire at their back.

She'd have to make sure they got to do more missions like that together.

Meeting the sad eyes of her hopeful four-legged shadow, she felt her shoulders slump. "Fine. You look like you need it more than I do." She tossed the small carcass reluctantly down, where it disappeared in a single snap. She was still licking her fingers clean when a throaty voice spoke at her side.

"Cool skins."

"What?" She looked up, and up, into a high-cheek-boned face half-hidden by a cascade of auburn hair. Dark eyes and red, red lips.

"'Miring your covers," the woman explained, sliding her fingertips under the edges of Leeth's tight-fitting shorts, feeling the soft leather. She looked deeply into Leeth's eyes. "So young. So diff. Where you from, special-girl?"

"Nowhere you'd know," Leeth retorted, forcing down a shiver of attraction. She shoved past. When she looked back, the tall woman was gone.

CHAPTER 35

The anonymous tip-off about the illegal combat festival appeared in the data feed of Agent Adam Garland's 'violence predictors' query. The attached video was fresh, only minutes old. He shook his head at the cleavage in the vid's thumbnail. But something about the tagged comment from the anonymous nunce – 'check the girl in the background: a fighter?' – decided him to open it anyway.

Playing the clip, he was struck by the feeling he knew the girl with the cleavage, in the background, clearly eavesdropping on the two foreground gangers. That impression only deepened as she bounced impatiently just in shot.

Judging by the way the drone's cam zoomed in on her chest after the two men had moved off, his tipster was a teenage boy – especially when the view then followed her, focusing in on her admittedly taut ass. And it was while watching those nicely-muscled legs stalking gracefully down Market Street that he shocked upright in his chair.

She moved like the girl his team had arrested months earlier at the mental institute! With the mage, Harrison, no, Harmon. The pair they'd had to hand over to Eagle – and who had both then fallen off the radar. Despite the charges: illegal drugs and underage sex for Harmon; assaulting police officers, for the girl. It would've been charges of multiple homicide if his team members hadn't been Healed. Including his ex-partner, Berlusconi.

His mind drifted to *another* morning; a crueler morning. Standing with Diego at the base of Lash Lighter cliffs, an hour before sunrise. Police divers emerging from the chill, dark water, with Marta Sanchez's body.

Seeing Berlusconi break down.

He glared now at the image of this girl. She was the right height, right build, and right age. He forwarded her image with the footage's GPS co-ordinates to the police city-watch system, quickly getting a lock. While his conscious mind caught up – reasoning that hair could be dyed and eye color faked – he was up and moving, already certain. Ordering his car to meet him at the rear exit, to save a minute, he took the express lift to the ground floor. Even in the worst case – if she were heading for the BART rather than staying on foot – a quick check of its timetable showed he should intercept her in good time. The real question was: what to do *then*?

The thing was, DNA evidence or no DNA evidence, his

gut told him she was responsible for the murders that day at the Golden Gate Park. Which meant she, in fact, was probably the serial killer he and his ex-partner were now separately tracking. The person who'd murdered Detectives Richard Henderson and Marta Sanchez – Berlusconi's ex-wife. Hard to believe an eighteen-year-old girl was The Breaker.

If so, this time, he'd make sure she'd face the courts. Unlike their last run-in, when no convictions had been recorded for either of them. *Eagle's handiwork.*

He could still taste the gall of bringing the girl – Sara – to Eagle. Seeing her throw herself at her abuser, wrapping her arms around her 'uncle.' And Eagle's cool admission that he'd thrown himself and his team at her as a *test.* Of Sara.

If his hunch was right, Eagle *did* have a use for her – *assassin.* His mouth turned down in distaste. But why was she in disguise, tonight? There hadn't been time for her to be properly trained and deployed yet. And even Eagle wouldn't set her torturing then killing ordinary civilians.

Which meant that even Eagle wouldn't be able to protect her, if he could only get the evidence.

He found himself thinking of the incoherent statements buzzing around the undernet after the take-down of the Brethren of the End of Days – about some girl who'd somehow cut off the head of their leader, Shepherd Fox, in plain view, with...! *Fuck! Idiot!* With someone – or some*thing*, like a cyborg wardog? – firing rockets into the melee?

Shit. That had been *her.* Eagle *had* made her an assassin, and *was* using her on American soil! He found himself shaking his head. Though taking out that sick fuck, Fox, was probably a point in her favor.

But why was she heading to the FistFest? Hunting more victims? Or just let out to get her jollies, a thank you for a job well done?

Something told him he'd find out tonight. But this time she wouldn't wriggle free. Eagle or no Eagle. No one could order executions without even a trial.

Or kill cops.

Exiting the building, he wondered if he should call Berlusconi. Diego'd be pissed if he didn't. But Garland was all too aware of what he was risking, following her. Knowing that Eagle had taken her in, and she acted for him... who knew what kind of shit'd come down on him, and Berlusconi if he got involved too?

Nah, he had to do this solo. Besides, Diego had a short fuse at the best of times, and if he thought Garland was on her trail.... Instead, he just fired off a note: 'Let's meet, a.m. Coffee. Catch up re Breaker.'

City-watch automatically tracked the girl as she moved, and it did look as if she was heading for the station. But as usual for this time of night, traffic status was green. He considered how to cover his face. If he could recognize *her*, disguised, he felt sure she'd recognize *him*. At six foot six, he tended to stand out.

As he exited the building, his car pulled in. Popping the trunk, a quick rummage produced both the unnecessary and out-of-fashion smog mask he thought he'd left in there, and the grubby overcoat. He ordered the car to drop him at the station, then follow him as best it could after that.

By the time he'd shrugged into the trenchcoat and cleaned out and pulled on the dusty smog mask, he'd arrived at the station. He hurried inside.

He caught up in time, entering the carriage and watching her from behind his mask. He saw her assault a youth who got too friendly with her, sending him fleeing. He grimaced. She hadn't changed.

He'd also spotted the older guy she'd been following in the vid, in the next carriage. A facial search on him failed to provide a match. He certainly *looked* CID-less. A search on his colors and markers was more successful, however: apparently the blagg was a member of a local gang called the Crazers, suspected of dealing addictive chips.

Maybe tonight'd be a twofer? He hoped she hadn't been sent to assassinate the chip-dealer. Arresting her for *that* crime wouldn't justify pissing off Eagle.

When the train stopped at the 24th Street station, the Crazer ganger left. Garland waited, hanging back before he too disembarked, palming a locator roach and slipping in behind Sara as she got off. Activated by the harsh light of the underground station, the microchip cut in and took control of the tiny insect brain, snapping it out of dormancy. Although she'd dodged when he'd tried to bump into her, he flicked the modified insect onto her jacket, where it scurried for the deeper darkness under her collar.

Strangely, she spun around a moment after it had scuttled from sight, her eyes on him as he ignored her, hunching past to the exit.

The roach was primarily a passive tracker, with only enough power for five minutes of active audio broadcast. As he crossed the broken tiles of the concourse he keyed it for a quick check, then set it back into idle mode.

Footsteps echoing off plascrete-patched walls, he trailed the other passengers, finally exiting onto the street. Stepping into the shadows, he activated the surveillance co-opt he'd registered earlier. Halving the scene on his Tik Tek retina, he assigned the view from his eyes to the lower half, reserving the top half for a remote view. Assuming he could get one.

The chip-dealer moved off up Mission, threading his way through the night-time crowds. Garland waited patiently, carefully hunched over, while his security co-opt was processed. Complex aromas of Mexican and other foods made his stomach rumble.

The mil-sat network, of course, responded with a flat 'access refused.' He considered making an official request using his new Bureau credentials, but if her escapade tonight did involve Eagle, that'd be unwise. The low-altitude traffic drone system responded soon after with a 'no monitor available in your current location.' He registered Sara merge into the crowds as he stood staring blankly, until finally, good old city-watch came back with an affirmative. Not that it'd be useful for long if they were heading into the Dumps.

He followed up with the necessary auth codes and directed the camera temporarily assigned to him to orient on his location. The picture was poor – it *was* night – but recognizable, as long as he didn't lose lock for too long. He walked the view forward until he saw Sara, then keyed it to track her automatically. He followed behind, stopping to grab a spicy vegetarian burrito and a bottle of water. Funny how so many parts of the city had died away from the effects of the Big One and the World Storms, but some of the older, poorer areas like the Mission had just shrugged it off. Maybe because they'd had to cope with so much other shit in their time.

As he trailed her out of the district, working his way higher into the up-heaved area of Bayview, the streets grew steadily darker and less-traveled. His digital retinas smoothly adjusted to the lower light levels. She seemed to be heading in the direction of the Dumps, and he thanked his lucky stars: his crappy, stained and crumpled old trenchcoat would blend better into the under-society of the Hunters Point Dumps no-go zone than it did in this low-rent part of the quake-altered town.

He idly pinged the locator on the girl, mapping its co-ordinates onto his retina, too. Good. It matched.

He followed, well back, keeping the city-watch view in the upper half of his field of vision. That left the bottom half displaying the streets he walked, as the landscape segued steadily into decay.

CHAPTER 36

Joss R. Martin was looking for someone very particular to play Stryker Zaxx, the alien bounty hunter in the new season of his *Underworld* net series. The more Marcie read about the role of the young female alien, the more certain she grew that *she* could do it. She'd faced hardship, and overcome it. She had a feel for how magic could change your life. And she'd impressed him, last night – otherwise she wouldn't have her audition, Monday. More than that, though, she *understood* acting. She had a knack for getting into a role, for becoming the character she was playing.

She even knew someone who seemed to live the role she was to try out for.

She'd watched the footage of Jane storming the hospital till she knew every moment. She was still in awe that the video was real, undoctored. Not some special-effects production.

A lot of people on the net said it *was* a fake – that a girl like that couldn't've taken down all those security guards, and interns. And the cops, outside.

But Marcie knew better.

She wished she could've *seen* Jane in action against those heavy-duty mercs the other night. It would've really helped for her upcoming audition. *Well, tonight I* will *see her fight!* She shut her eyes, remembering Jane casually heaving Mark Dennis out of the truck.

Shivering, she felt again the brutal strength of his grip. He'd plucked her up by the neck, tossed her-

Stop! Don't think about it! But Mark Dennis – aka Marc Disten – was still out there, somewhere. Luckily, she'd found Cutter to keep her safe.

She checked the boots and other clothes she'd put together for her performance tonight. *This'll be a real life test of my acting skills!* But she'd done all that painstaking research, getting a feel for how they lived, what they ate, where they slept, what they wore. She picked up her new collection of piercings. Squinting doubtfully, she eyed the tiny gaps in the silvery metal, grimacing at the hair-thin filaments that *should* allow painless insertion – and easy removal.

It was amazing how much you could learn, and the services you could hire, in two days searching the net – and undernet.

She'd wanted to film Jane's fights tonight, but 'Cutter,' her secret bodyguard and guide for tonight, had warned against it. If she did, and people realized – especially if they then spotted her as an outsider – even his cyber enhancements might not be enough to keep her safe.

She'd 'met' Cutter on the undernet, when she'd learned of the FistFest events in the Dumps. She'd been researching the brutal but strangely honest sub-culture that existed just across the Bay from her own home. Partly, that had been due to worry about Jane – but also because the culture sounded similar to that of Zaxx's home planet. Cutter had been really helpful. But still, it'd been good to hear Jane confirm what he'd said about how safe the lawless area really was – *if* you understood the people, and had a guide.

It was interesting, that no vids existed of any FistFests – they'd rate like crazy. She'd read that it was a measure of just how much anger the area's inhabitants held against the society that had rejected them. They weren't going to let themselves be made into entertainment.

So: no recordings, tonight. Which was fine, really. She'd live the moment, absorb the experience, instead of insulating herself behind a lens.

Besides, if Jane really was some kind of secret agent, her boss probably wouldn't be happy to have her recorded.

Why was Jane going to the FistFest, though? It was purely a local event. Though one of its functions was like her own upcoming audition, except for mercenaries. A way for someone with no reputation to show their skills to others, like Cutter's mysterious crew, the 'Buzzers'; or Happy Joe Holliday's team, who he always said were just old friends he hung out with.

Marcie sat, and began applying the makeup to blend in with the 'Festies,' the young girls and guys who idolized the fighters. She wondered if Nightslice'd be there, tonight? He looked *deadly*.

But she'd better slip out. The 'Fest'd be starting soon.

CHAPTER 37

The crowd had thinned as Leeth moved away from the food stalls.

She was standing there, absorbing it all – the confusion of sounds and smells, shadows and movements – when she felt a man staring at her. For just a moment, she thought his expression looked calculating, but then he smiled in approval and pushed his way closer.

She checked him as he approached. No markings of Dad's gang, so he probably wasn't working against her. Stockily built, his head was just a fuzz of brown hair, except for a long braided rats-tail draped over one shoulder. His clothes looked several steps up from the locals' usual scavenged and pieced-together coverings. His teeth, as he smiled, were filed to points.

They looked chill.

"You're new here, aren't ya?" he said. "I would'a marked ya fore now, else." She thought he was going to ask how she'd come here, but instead he said, "Name's Crack. Show ya round?"

"I guess," she agreed, not letting him see how grateful she felt. This was nothing like the sober and serious Dumps she'd come to know.

"C'mon. Follow close 'hind me. Show ya best roost in house." He forged a way through the still-increasing crowds. Leeth looked around at 'Dad.' He'd just accepted a hunk of food, and looked solidly in place.

She followed Crack's compact, well-muscled body as he cleaved a path up densely packed stairs, barging and forcing his way up several flights and then over to a balcony. He hopped up into what had once been a corner rockery, now a miniature wasteland of rubble, dirt and smashed pottery. Jammed into one corner, a sloping cement slab made an awkward perch for one person right at the edge. Further back, people crowded together on once-decorative boulders. "Yo, Tapper," Crack called to one of these, getting a friendly wave in return. He threaded a path over to another guy, whose feet rested casually on the handrail, preventing him from slipping over the edge.

"Ya, Bandersnatch. Couldn' find Luce, but hey – no Luce's good nooz, I'm thinkin' right nano."

Bandersnatch snorted. "Less she spot ya."

Crack bent forward. "Lissen, compadre. I scan it's really sproutin', down-b'low, but..."

His friend rolled his eyes.

"But c'n ya slot me a big one? Let me'n m' little caro here some room to *move*, you scan?"

At the word *move*, Crack's large hand gripped her buttock and tugged her against him possessively. She wasn't sure how she felt about that.

Bandersnatch screwed up his face, looking from Crack to the girl, and stopped. He eyed her carefully up, then down, then up again. "Y'owe me huge, Crack," he muttered, but got up and left. He thumped Crack's shoulder as he moved past, looking down the gap in the front of Leeth's jacket.

Crack gestured for her to slide into the vacated space, then crammed in alongside as she sat. Leeth leaned out and over, looking down three floors to the plaza below while Crack draped a meaty arm across her shoulders. She leaned into him, enjoying the contact. Bonfires burned fiercely at the four corners of the raised dais, the music now settled into something raw, unpolished, but compelling.

"Hard or soft?"

"What?" She turned to face Crack.

"You want hard chem, or just alc?"

"No drugs *or* alcohol."

Her companion laughed, rolling his eyes to heaven. "Flick, chick, loosen up."

She just stared back at him.

He sighed. "I'll get you a sweetwater'n buzz, then. Straight enough?"

She chewed her bottom lip. Her eyes narrowed. "What is-"

More rolling of eyes. "Kaff, chick. Kaff'n sacch. Coffee. Sweet, like you," he carefully enunciated. "Or it zone you out you'll be eyes till late?"

"Uh...."

The last eyes-roll did it.

"Sure. Thanks."

Crack bellowed, making her wince. "Toxer!"

Across the long-ago cafeteria, an arm raised, waving acknowledgment. Crack turned to her. "Where ya from?"

"Here in New Francisco. I made myself a little nest a bit north of here; just been scoping things out, you know? But I haven't been on the streets long-"

He snorted. "Knew that."

"I left Mother and Father. Proving I can make it on my own."

He stared at her. "You sayin' ya *chose* ta come here?"

She lifted her chin. "Yeah. Why shouldn't I?"

At that moment, the toxer arrived, bottles, canisters, tubing and dispenser nozzles looping and bulging under his coat. He was an ogre, with the usual leathery, hairless skin and rough features, and large frame. *I wonder if Teef came, tonight?* She'd have to keep an eye open for him and Barney – it'd be nice to have friends watching her fight.

"What'll it be, frens?" the toxer rumbled.

"Black Velvet, 'n a sugarwater Buzz. 'N two cups."

"Five ten."

Crack held out another cashstick, set the amount, and the man tapped his own against it. He reached under his long jacket, passing them each a thin and crude plastic cup. He dropped pellets – saccharin, he explained, at her sharp look – into a metal shaker, then a couple of black cubes. Tugging down a tube, he pressed a faucet at the end. "Agua," he said, as the water flowed. He capped it, shook it, and with a final disdainful air poured it into the cup Leeth held. Crack's drink came from a bottle; black as ink.

Leeth sniffed her cup suspiciously as the toxer strode off. At least it *smelled* like coffee. She looked at her companion, who slitted his eyes in pleasure as he eased down a single mouthful of his brew.

"I want you to drink half of mine," she demanded.

Crack laughed. "Ah, caro! Wisdom?" He wrinkled his nose, but drank deeply from her cup. Swallowing, he made a face, then handed it back.

"Safe now!" he said, then started laughing.

Leeth blushed, and took a drink. It was bitter and sweet. But okay. Definitely coffee.

"So, tell me about all this," she demanded, putting her thin cup down carefully.

Crack beamed, leaned back further against their boulder, sweeping one arm in an expansive arc. "This-" he began, then abruptly stopped. Slowly, his head turned further to the right, the arrogant smile sliding from his face as all his attention seemed to focus there. Leeth craned around, and saw the tall red-headed woman who'd spoken to her earlier. Who just stood there, watching.

"Crack. Whose seat, dealer?" the woman called.

His voice was shaky when he spoke. "*Tash?*" He shuddered. "Yours. All yours. C'mon bim, let's rat off." He urged Leeth up, grabbing her arm and sliding off the rock then down onto the ground.

Tash stepped forward. She raised one hand and the man stopped dead, flinching away from it.

Leeth scowled at Crack. "What's the matter with you? Why are you running away? We were here first."

Tash raised an eyebrow. "Well, Crack?"

"*C'mon*, ya little sluk!" he swore, pulling at Leeth.

She tugged her arm out of his grasp.

"You scan what she *is*?" He seemed frantic.

"Oh? What am I, Crack?"

Tash's tone had been mild, but Crack backtracked, avoiding the question as he focused on the girl, grabbing at her. "Come *on!*"

She fended off his grasp again. "*I'm* not scared."

"Well, frag you, halfdeck!" he said – and ran off!

Leeth looked around. No one else seemed to have reacted – though they wouldn't have been able to hear much of the exchange over the sound of the music. She looked back at the woman, who studied her with a lazy smile. Predatory.

Leeth bristled. "So what are you? Why was Crack so scared?"

"I... watch the little people. The kinda people Crack slices." She smiled, wolfishly. "And it's been awhile since I been here. Seein' me must've 'freshed some old tales."

"You slice guys like Crack?"

Tash just smiled.

Leeth sized her up. Tash looked strong, capable, and moved with an easy grace. "Well, since you just scared off Crack, if you want to *share* my seat you have to tell me about all this, first," she demanded.

Tash's elegant eyebrow arched again. "That'll take awhile."

Leeth considered, but finally nodded. The woman looked like she might be... interesting.

"I'm Tash," she said, sliding in beside her.

Leeth nodded. Across the central space, down on the ground, she saw Preacher still sandwiched between the same two grubby but curvy women not much older than herself. As if feeling her eyes on him, he looked up. His smile deepened, with something of anticipation in it, only to slide from his face like he'd just realized something awful.

Good. That means I'm doing something right. He seemed to be staring at the woman beside her.

"Your name?"

Leeth's lips set stubbornly. "I haven't picked one yet." Her uncle's advice, several ages ago, back when she'd first learned of the 'Fest. Before she'd left the Department and forced him to heal Marcie. So long ago. But it *was* revealing, what each person named her. She wondered what Tash would call her.

But for now, Tash's eyebrows just raised ironically.

Leeth frowned at her. "So. Tell me about this."

Tash told: about fights for money, or honor, or justice. For recognition and a new start, or a swift end. About money, and bets. About the fighters, and the declaration and ranking system. About the blood.

It would go till they ran out of fighters, Tash said.

But during the whole explanation, a slow wave of heat had been surreptitiously building. It suddenly crested, bursting over her with an unpleasant prickling sensation. All her nerves snapped taut.

No! Not this! Not now! Twice before she'd felt this, and both times it'd lasted for hours, raging through her until she collapsed exhausted. *Can I* will *it away?* She clenched her hands, trying to hold them still.

Instead, the tendrils of itchy tension spread further, till even her teeth felt jittery.

"Lemme buy you," asked Tash.

"What?"

"What're ya drinking?"

"Uh. I'm okay. I've still got some left," she said, jerking up the plastic cup from where she'd placed it earlier.

Tash stroked one cool finger down Leeth's neck. "So, sweetwater, what you do here?"

"Came to make some money."

Tash eyed her up and down. "Maybe you start with

me."

Leeth considered it, with a return of that little shiver. "No." She shook her head. "I plan to earn a lot more than you'd wanna pay."

Tash looked intrigued, but said nothing.

The bone-deep rhythm returned, insistent and demanding, dominating all other sounds. Blood pounding in her forehead, Leeth found herself standing, looking down over the balcony at the scene below.

Two men stood at opposite corners of the dais. One was young, the other really old – older than her uncle. Maybe sixty, she guessed. The old one, a blond bearded giant in light impact armor, had a tanglestick and a knife, while the young one lashed something too fine to be seen. Razorwhip. Her lips parted, wondering what the old one would do. Dojo had warned her of these: strike the man, swiftly, and take the wound, he'd advised. Or be cut into small pieces.

Maybe the tanglestick would suffice.

A huge troll stepped up onto the fighting platform, and silence descended. Nine feet tall, massive build and leathery gray skin like an elephant's. Canines protruded like small tusks from his mouth. He wore an enormous tailored black dinner jacket and torn blue jeans.

"Uno!" he bellowed, voice reverberating around the arena. He pointed at the old one, the bearded one. "Thor! Muscles. Eyes. Fast." Turned to the younger, unscarred challenger. "Flick!" A mutter of laughter. "Fast. Mono whip." From his belt, where Leeth now noticed a whole bunch of colored cloths, he drew out a square of black, and held it high.

The crowd *aahed*.

The black cloth fluttered to the ground, and the troll moved ponderously off the dais. Five long, slow, loud, bass beats tolled.

And then they were moving.

"Black means to the death," Tash said, standing pressed against Leeth as she too now gazed down at the scene below. There was such a strange, heavy finality to her words it was almost enough to distract Leeth from the dark dance below.

Flick darted in, his right hand slashing sharply. Up flashed the tangler in Thor's left hand, stabbing with the knife in his right. But Flick danced back, and the crowd sighed as blood flowed. He'd scored a deep cut: Thor would bleed out in minutes.

But instead of waiting, Flick attacked. Again the slash of the barely visible weapon as Thor responded, striking hard with his knife. But Flick folded, flipping and rolling away. Thor followed, parrying another whip-strike with his tanglestick, twisting viciously. Flick, still on the ground, let it go. Thor descended on his fallen enemy, his knife plunging down. But Flick struck viciously up, first, with a booted foot.

To Leeth's ears, the sound of a blade punching through meat and gristle was clear.

Flick rolled sideways as Thor toppled to his knees, the knife slipping from his fingers. Seconds passed; then he crashed forward. Flick staggered up and away, clutching his slashed side, slipping once in the blood that gleamed like black water in the firelight.

"Why did Flick move in when his enemy was already bleeding to death?" she asked Tash, hands still clenched, eyes glued to the scene below.

Three people – the troll, an ogre, and an ordinary-looking man – hurried onto the dais. The troll bent down, asking the dying man something which even Leeth's hearing couldn't pick out. Thor shook his head, eyes clamped shut in pain. Across the dais, Flick bent down, resetting the spring blade in his boot.

At last Tash answered, in flat tones. "To be scanned well. To show courage."

One of the other figures, the ogre, now knelt by the old one's side. Found a hand and gripped it hard. Spoke urgently.

"... heal ya!" Leeth heard.

But again, the head shook.

Heat shivered through her, the knot of tension tightening in her stomach. As the young Flick, grinning wolfishly, bought himself healing from the ordinary-looking man, she turned to face Tash. "You said black meant 'to the death.' But healing's allowed?"

Tash shrugged. "Not if peep don' 'gree."

Leeth decoded that as 'Not if people don't agree.' She looked around. People looked tense: but no one was objecting. "Why won't Thor let himself be healed?"

Tash stared past her. "Cuz he'd begun makin' mistakes. Didn't want to drag any with him." Her next words were a whisper. *"Warrior's ending."*

"You knew him?"

Tash still stared down at the scene below.

"Yeah. We Raided together. When he was young."

Leeth studied Tash intently. *When* he *was young?* What about Tash herself? She finished her drink, clenching her teeth as another prickling wave flashed along her nerves. She looked back down in time to see Thor go still. It was a good way to die, actually.

Maybe I'll come here if I get old.

The troll lifted the body, and a roar of approval shook the air. Then Flick stepped to the center and raised his arms. The response to this was less complete, and a scowl spread over his face. Defiantly, he shook his fists in the air before striding off.

Leeth felt the urge to attack him. Suddenly she needed to move, but there were too many people crowded in around them, below them. The whole balcony was now packed solid.

Two men threw buckets of water over the arena and began sweeping the blood away, steam rising from the canvas covering. The music started again, with a harsh edge that made her grind her teeth together. She checked her cash-stick.

"Who takes bets from the fighters?"

"Sit down," urged Tash, tugging at her. "Come *on*."

Leeth sat, clenching her teeth. She should be down there!

"The ringmaster."

At Leeth's blank look, Tash added, "Robbie. The troll."

"The troll is really called *Robbie*?"

Tash nodded.

"How come?"

"Cuz he wants to be."

Suddenly the bellow again. "Two!" She jumped back up, looking down to where the troll once more occupied the center of the platform. "Deezer! Troll! Good!" The crowd laughed. 'Robbie' the giant troll turned away from a smaller version of himself to indicate a large human. "Skulls. Megs."

A whisper ran through the crowd. Someone started

chanting "Zonie," heckling, and much of the crowd picked it up.

As the troll ringmaster drew out a dark splotched cloth from his belt, Leeth spun to Tash. "What's all that about?"

"Skulls be jerked up on Megs. Zoned out. MegaPulse. Prob stronger'n Deezer, till he crash. Cost him a K, prob screw'm in knots, after – cuts deep. Must be total desper."

The five long beats sounded.

Tash noted Leeth's confusion. "Desperate."

"Oh."

The two figures moved together. This was a bare-hands job, more brutal than the first fight. It lasted longer, too. No finesse, either. Leeth muttered criticisms and twisted in frustration. Deezer won. Both chose healing.

"Buy you again?" offered Tash.

"No." Leeth wrung her hands. She jumped to her feet. "I've gotta get down there. Place my bet."

"You can do it from here – anyone'll bet ya. Or see a greener, ya wannabe formal."

"A greener?"

"Yeah – the bods with the green LEDs. They take any's bets."

"But you said Robbie takes the fighters' bets. And when do I get to fight?"

Tash frowned. "Fight who?"

"I don't care. Rank me and put me on."

"Rank *you*?"

"Yes, *me*. That's why I came tonight. To fight. Prove myself. Make some creds." Eagle had agreed she may as well develop this identity into a real cover.

"*You*?"

"Who. Do I. See?" grated out Leeth.

"Sweetling. You don' wan' do that. Look, I buy you for eve'. Five hundred creds."

"Who do I see?"

"You too late, now. Robbie prob got whole 'Fest slot-ted. You shoulda gone to fighters' balcony, 'cross on level two, any, 'fore start."

Leeth stared at Tash, stunned and horrified. Began to wriggle her way past her companion, looking toward the stairs. Tash grabbed her arm, with surprising strength.

"You too late, sweetling. Can't get to Robbie now. Down there, no one let you force through to fighters.

Crowd be set like plascrete."

She shook her head in dismay. *No!* She scourged herself for being an idiot. After all this, to fail before she'd even started.

The five long beats sounded: a new bout. She forced herself back to the railing, looking down unseeingly as two more fighters faced off.

Then saw the way.

She placed one leg over the railing.

Tash's hand returned, grabbing her shoulder from behind. "Sweet, no!"

For Leeth, it was like sparks firing off behind her eyes. With difficulty, she wrenched her shoulder free, and spun round, growling at the surprised woman.

Tash flinched back. One glimpse of her startled expression, then Leeth vaulted the rail into space.

She landed on the narrow brick retaining wall of an old planter box built out from one of the supporting piers of the mall's levels; the once-decorative embellishment filled now with broken bottles and thrown rubbish.

Turning to face the pillar in front of her, she stepped backwards into space, eyes down, utterly focused. Where her feet had just rested, her palms slapped down, taking her weight. Looking up, the simple joy of being alive, being *here,* burned through her, and she met Tash's eyes.

Looking down, she swung out slightly, dropping as she started to pendulum back in. Landing with cat-grace on the edge of the planter box three meters below, she paused, wincing, to shift the sheathed knife from her sleeve into a pocket of her jacket. Her next leap brought her to the last box, over the heads of the people seated on the top of the wide stairs down to the central dais.

Glancing across into the ring, she saw one of the fighters looking up at her, just as his opponent's cyberspurs took him in the throat.

Ouch. Briefly, she wondered what had distracted him, but scanned the ground for a good place to land. Some of the people immediately below her had turned, now watching her instead of the fighters. She gestured for them to make room.

They ignored her instead, pointing and laughing.

She saw Robbie, the troll, almost at the dais now, watching her as he moved.

Glaring down at the obstruction below her, she judged distances and angles. Then with a hungry grin leapt straight into the middle of them.

A few were fast enough to shift away, but she knocked two off their feet as she dropped between them.

She took enormous pleasure in the swift blow to the one behind her, kicking the nearest fallen one hard, before he could retaliate. The third raised his hands in mute surrender from the ground.

She looked around.

No one moved to interfere, and she began forcing her way between them, making her way to the dais amidst a rising murmur, hoping for trouble. None materialized.

The small leap up to the fighting platform was made with economical grace. The razorguy eyed her warily while the ringmaster and the scummy-looking healing mage stared at her with undisguised interest.

Robbie seemed to be thinking.

"You fight?" he asked at last.

CHAPTER 39

You fight?

Leeth nodded, emphatically.

Robbie the troll was even larger, face to face. She stared up at him, wondering if she'd be able to touch the top of his head if she jumped...?

"You weapon?"

She straightened, shocked. "How could you tell? It's that obvious?"

The troll's brow wrinkled in heavy corrugations. "Tell what?"

It was her turn to frown. "Tell that I'm a weapon."

Long seconds passed while Robbie blinked, looking her up and down. "Fest not joke. Fights be real. You just little girl, break easy."

She snorted, before she could stop herself. "As if."

"You cop, meb? Corp agent? Some trick?"

From off to her left, a boy's voice piped up. "Go D.G!" She winced. Barney bounced excitedly on Teef's shoulders, who stood with his back against the wall, watching her worriedly.

She waved briefly before turning back to Robbie, shaking her head violently. "No! I promise! I just- I just *need* to fight! It's really important to me." He looked from Teef and Barney back to her, still doubtful.

Stepping right up to him, she pressed one finger firmly into his belly, at her eye level. She felt tough hide and tougher muscles bend, resisting the force. She pushed harder.

Robbie's eyes narrowed, and she pulled her finger away, seeing him sway forward when she did. "Worry about your fighters, not me."

Robbie snorted, and it made her burn. "Will I get into trouble if I accidentally kill any of them?"

"Kill... fighters? You?"

Again, Robbie blinked, like he thought she was joking. *Chit!* This was taking forever! "Just let me fight. You won't regret it, I promise. Let me show you what I can do."

Robbie worked his jaw, looking her up and down again. Nearby, onlookers yelled rude encouragement and ruder suggestions. With an effort, she ignored them, despite the urge to sweep through them and slice the smiles from their faces.

"You name?"

They were supposed to pick her name. That was the plan. She grimaced: her uncle's plan. But then, on the brink of answering, she remembered Amanda's question, on the whiteboard. "Call me *Sleena*," she blurted, instead.

Robbie just stared at her. At last he nodded, inclining his head toward the stairs leading to the fighters' area.

Yes!

Strutting down the narrow stretch of cleared path in the direction he'd indicated, she ignored the curious onlookers' stares and questions.

But Robbie wasn't following. At the bottom of the flight of stairs she looked back, seeing the troll conferring with the mage, who shook his head. It was hard even for *her* to hear. She had to shut her eyes and focus everything she had, to filter his words from the music and the noise of the crowd.

"No cyber. Not a mage. Normal human," and then, it was hard to say, but she thought he was trying to stop Robbie from letting her fight.

She was about to storm back, when Robbie shook his head and dismissed the gray-haired mage.

Five minutes later, Leeth's anger was growing. *How dare they!* They thought she was a *joke*, did they? She'd show them. She'd show them all.

Staring at the pink ribbon dangling from the troll's pocket, furious at the bet it signified, she stalked behind him and her ugly opponent.

At the raised dais, she leapt up, stomping to her corner while her opponent swaggered to his, one hand in his pants making jerking gestures, which half the crowd seemed to find hilarious. She glanced over to Barney, who was now pestering his father with questions. Teef looked embarrassed, glaring at her like it was *her* fault.

Robbie bellowed for silence and the crowd gradually settled. "Five! 'Sleena.'" But, with the match number given, his tusks moved in thoughtful chewing motions as he considered his next words.

The name caused both muttering in the crowd, and laughter. Someone yelled out "Ya wuz smaller on trids, pixie! Ya put on weight?"

Someone else called out "Where's ya wings?"

Robbie held up hand. "Sleena: hand to hand. Null cyber. Null spells. Null tox." He turned to the ogre. "Hag-jabber. Strong. Tough. *Hand*-some."

The crowd went wild in its appreciation of this last witticism. Hagjabber grabbed his crotch again, beaming.

Leeth *burned*.

Robbie pulled out an orange cloth – signifying a normal, knockout bout – then more slowly, the long length of pale pink ribbon.

"Sleena bet extra! Bet self to Hagjabber for rest of night!"

The announcement brought cheers and jeers. As the troll ringmaster bowed and lumbered off, the music flared out in a circus tune instead of the normal five deep beats.

Leeth looked up, briefly, at the balcony where she'd sat with Tash, seeing her lean forward eagerly as Hagjabber stomped casually forward. She turned back to him, tilting her head to one side, studying him. What, did he think that would intimidate her? She straightened, shook her shoulders to unknot them, and stalked stiffly forward. Furious, yet deadly calm.

Hagjabber stopped, grinning down at her like she was his curvy little gift, and gestured her closer. She took one step forward and arced a leg straight up into his crotch. The big ogre's smile froze. He toppled forward.

Not quite believing he'd simply *let* her do that, alert for some last-minute trick, she pivoted to the side, hammering her knee into his descending head.

He crashed to the mat and lay unmoving, knocked cold.

There was a moment's surprised silence, then the crowd erupted in hoots of laughter and cheers.

Hands clenching and unclenching in fury, she stared down at him. She'd promised herself she'd pound the smug leer off his bony face. And now he'd cheated her of even that! Electricity surged along her nerves.

Gritting her teeth, she bowed stiffly to the crowd, her skin pricking and burning, unable to enjoy her victory even when Robbie raised her hand to the crowd. How could she, when the stupid fight had only lasted two seconds? The next one had better be more satisfying. An awful thought occurred to her: *what if all their fighters are equally useless?* She blushed. *What if the* whole night *is a waste of time!*

Up on the balcony, she saw Tash cross her cashstick

with one of the betting guys – the 'greeners' – with a smile on her face. Well, at least one person had been smart enough to bet on *her*, not the stupid ogre. Teef looked surprised; Barney, ecstatic, pounding his father's muscled shoulders. Most of the other people she saw in the crowd didn't look happy at all. *Good.*

Maybe this would turn out all right, after all.

You just wait, she promised the grumbling crowd.

CHAPTER 40

Marc Disten had abandoned the Oakland dwelling three days ago, finding a new place near her, in the Hunters Point Dumps. The same day that had ended with the confusing performance in the empty park. Disten had followed when she left, planning to take her – but she had moved too fast. And at South Van Ness, twenty minutes later, the Call had vanished. Standing unblinking in the dark, washed in the headlights of passing cars and all too aware of the outstanding arrest warrants, a retreat had been necessary.

If pursuit was required again, it would be best to commandeer a vehicle.

The Call had returned and faded several times; flaring once, briefly, to a painful intensity despite its distance.

Disten sat with legs braced on the twisted metal fencing, leaning against the tilted cement slab of the collapsed car park's upper floor. From here most of the city could be viewed. Across the dark waters of the Bay, Oakland's distant lights shone forth, radioactive tracers marking diseased flesh. Large sections of West Oakland still lay dark, shattered in succession by earthquake, the de-populations of the Red Plague, and finally, the World Storms.

It had been a good place to hide and heal.

Below, and a few klicks north and east, fires burned from some event in the Dumps. Even from this distance the jagged chaos of another animalistic gathering was clearly sensed, a constant, distant pain. It would make a good hunting ground.

But that distant discomfort faded into the background as the far more compelling presence made itself felt once more.

The hunted female, Jane Baker, had returned to the area. Again. Disten considered. This morning's subjects had proven to be failures.

Moving surely down the shattered cliff face, a path was set northward. Toward the female: the key.

Some terrain had permitted jogging, other areas, where the twisted ground made the path impassable, had required circling around. But moving steadily north and east.

Never had her presence felt so painfully sharp and clear. Tonight. Tonight she would be Perfected. Ending the pain.

The direction of the target steadily shifted. Too late to intercept her, it became obvious she headed toward the distant stinking gush of humanity, swarming moth-like to the fires of lust and greed. In hindsight, it was obvious the chaotic female key would journey toward that seething discord.

After crushing the pick-pocket's hand Disten moved like a cold current through the fringes of the swarm. Just a gaze at their fevered scurryings quelled them; generated space. Somehow, they recognized a difference.

None approached.

It was difficult to sense the female's presence through the painful jangle of chaos pressing in all around. The girl was the key. Perfecting the girl would do more than just end the pain. Through her, a circuit would be completed, creating something new, and pure. Something fundamental.

The experiments of those earlier months in the Dumps, before the unfortunate mass abduction, had been instructive but not dramatically productive. The newly-Perfected did not fare well in this lawless area. Most of those few Perfected had been killed before they could become comfortable in their new capabilities, recognized as something alien by the locals and destroyed by the feral human packs.

Numbers were needed for survival, it had become clear. Yesterday, as a test of healed limbs, another had been Perfected. That made just two others, now, who still lived. But that man and woman were the start. They would wait safely, hidden, as instructed.

Disten looked ahead, into the jarring tumult that must be entered. Physical pain was nothing, but the discordance, building all around, repelled. Reluctance was strong.

But she was close.

It required a conscious effort to move forward into that diseased torture. Not for the first time, the idea that some kind of magic was involved was considered. The connection made no sense otherwise. Yet the collection of skills, flesh and will that formed the *perfected* Marc Disten performed no magic. There was even evidence that magic collapsed in on itself rather than interact with such Perfection.

It was a puzzle, but one that did not require consideration now. The crowds thickened as forward progress continued, but Disten was determined that the female would not evade capture tonight.

The sense of presence flared, a jab of pain that jerked Disten's attention to a disturbance far ahead, perhaps in the main arena. A fresh stirring of the crowd there, chaotic animal emotions swelling like an ocean wave. Then a young female leaped from above, into the crowd.

She was the one. Jane Baker. The girl who had disrupted the abduction and caused the month long convalescence.

Disten forced a way deeper into the tightly-set living mass, but it reacted angrily, cells rejecting an invading organism. Apparently the destination ahead was generally desirable, even fought over.

Disten didn't care.

Pushing between two lumbering, acromegalic ogres, their skulls trying to grow out through their skin, an even larger form impeded further progress. One massive arm swung to block progress as the behemoth turned, its broken-tusked face snarling.

It looked the human up and down, disbelief dawning on its face. "*Worm* dare push Bem?"

As the troll's tusked mouth huffed angry breath into Disten's face, it seemed plausible that interactions like this had killed the newly-Perfected, in the disorientation of their first awakening. Diplomacy might be more effective. Reaching for memories of social interactions, Disten stretched the mouth into the shape of a smile.

The troll growled. Disten sensed its anger spread like an infection to the two ogres just pushed past.

"Bem crush worm!" One huge club-like arm crashed down like a falling tree.

Disten's up-stretched hand stopped it.

The troll stared in disbelief, long enough for Disten to conclude that diplomacy had failed. Reaching into the creature's anger, Disten grasped the source, and severed it.

The troll blinked, confused, fighting to understand what had been done to it. Sandwiched between it and the two hulking forms pressing from behind, Disten sensed the anger take root in them, growing swiftly. Some kind of physical action would puncture the build-up.

The troll's arm continued to press down, but less strongly. Disten's own left arm still stretched up, fingers splayed out against the huge fist. It would make a suitable demonstration. Disten twisted the wrist convulsively, with the peculiar focus possible to the Perfected. Tendons tightened to steel, and troll bones flexed, then cracked.

But pressure that could snap troll bones was more than human flesh could stand. Disten's own fingers split. The creature cried out and tried to pull away.

Disten released the beast. It backed away, fear now in its eyes. Ignoring the pain, Disten turned, bloody handed, to the two ogres behind.

Their eyes flickered from Disten's cold, dead eyes to the shocked hulk cradling its broken wrist. Their anger drained away, fear flooding in to replace it. Whispered exclamations blossomed, and suddenly space grew.

It would suffice.

Flexing the injured left hand experimentally, Disten began working forwards again.

Disten was close enough to see, now. It was the one. Her emotions blazed: powerful and dangerous, intertwining with the squirming organic chaos of the crowd's mood, stabbing and tugging at all those around her, weaving through them all in an unpredictable tangle.

Painfully intense, but so familiar. This was what had been calling, for years. Yet it was not the girl from the opera restaurant. That one had been Asian. Nor the dead girl in the alley, many months earlier. That one had had long black hair. This was Jane Baker, with her blue eyes and pale skin, who had caused the loss of forty five subjects.

Watching the girl as she swept aside her opponent, the question arose: were there more than one of them, or did some spirit *possess* suitable hosts? Youthful females?

Tonight, the truth would be revealed. This girl would be taken. Tonight. And unless her spirit once again fled, she would be Perfected. With the equation completed, the dominoes would begin their fall, each bringing the animal fires of the next under control.

Starting tonight.

CHAPTER 41

The next half hour was a slow torment. *Finally* it was her turn again. She trotted along behind her second opponent, Maneater, and the troll ringmaster, bouncing up and down as she moved. Wanting to push the two lumbering giants in front of her to move them along faster. She danced to the music, trying to burn off some of the itchy energy.

It didn't help.

Maneater was a big woman, looking like she'd be a match for Robbie himself – hormones and fanatical training had seen to that. She also had a mean temper. At least, according to the little Leeth had learned after introducing herself and talking to the other fighters.

At last they were at the arena. Looking up, she waved to Tash on the balcony, then to Teef and Barney, then to the rest of the crowd. A girl on the balcony below Tash waved frantically.

Springing up onto the dais she hugged herself, bouncing, waiting, while Robbie announced the fight.

Robbie's voice boomed out. "'Leven. Sleena. Fighter." The troll shrugged in apology as mutters ran through the crowd. "Maneater. Strong. Tough. Nat 'roids."

Listening, and watching, especially to the annoyed reaction of the greeners taking bets, she gradually worked out that *fighter* wasn't a common 'ranking' term. The betting slowed as people tried to work out what it meant. Finally, just when she was deciding she should maybe take a little jog around the ring, Robbie drew out the orange cloth and held it high.

Someone in the crowd yelled out "where's the ribbon?" and laughter again erupted. Grimly, she ignored it.

The five slow beats tolled as the ringmaster lumbered from the stage. The crowd went silent.

Maneater, breasts reduced to pectorals from massive muscle building, flexed for the crowd and then faced her. The leopard-pattern body suit left little hidden. "Gonna eat you up, chickie!"

For her part, Leeth had to fight the urge to simply sweep in and attack. The big woman seemed slow, but that might be just a trick. Besides, she'd had to wait *eons* for this fight, and Dojo had said not to go all out from the very start; to pace herself. He'd advised her to hold back: not to reveal more of her abilities than she had to. Only gradually show some of what she could do.

But she wanted to *move!* Hands clenching into fists, muscles straining at the leash of her will, she suddenly saw a way. She stilled, even pasted a scared expression on her face to lure Maneater closer. The woman obligingly struck, one massive fist careening toward Leeth's head.

Swaying back at the last instant she let it whisper past her nose. It passed, and she moved forward, but only slowly, swinging her right arm in its own small arc, drawing Maneater's massive left arm across in a block. Darting forward, she twisted as she hammered her left fist into the woman's kidney in the 'one inch punch' Dojo had taught her, before jumping away.

For a second, the massive woman staggered, then shook herself. Leeth blinked, impressed. Maneater stared at her: no longer seeing her as a joke.

Maybe it was time for *her* to play? Pay back some of the mockery? As Maneater slowed, becoming more cautious, so did she: excessively so, until she moved like a slow motion video, a parody of reduced-speed martial arts moves. Before blurring forward, pounding one, two, three, four, five blows into Maneater's heavily-muscled eight-pack.

She shouldn't have tried for the sixth. The giantess's arms descended like sides of beef, and she couldn't quite dodge. The glancing blow felt like being hit by a medicine ball, blasting her off her feet, tumbling and rolling her to the very edge of the platform. There, on hands and knees, she shook her head.

But the heavy blow made everything, finally, real. Real, and solid, and something to fight back against. To pay back in kind.

She felt her lips peel back in a hungry smile, seeing a different face as she leaped up, spinning to once more face her opponent. Maneater clenched and unclenched her right fist in puzzlement, frowning from it to the small figure stalking back toward her. Looking a question at the mage who'd pronounced her opponent magic free.

"Have I been *very* bad? Do you want to punish me again?"

Something in the quiet words, or in the way she approached, made the larger woman step backward. Leeth halted, her smile an echo of the hunger inside, and turned in a casual, even balletically flowing movement, bending over as she did. She felt her black leather shorts stretch tight across her rump, the movement continuing smoothly until her hands rested flat on the ground, arms locking rigid.

Behind her, she could hear Maneater, still hesitating, perhaps confused.

And Leeth's leg lashed out and up, the meaty impact satisfying something deep inside as she slammed into the woman's sternum. With deceptive laziness she turned, rising to prowl toward the ogre-sized woman now teetering, dazed, on the edge of the dais.

Leeth stood in front of her, ready, just waiting. Letting the moments of vulnerability trickle away.

The only sound now was the steady roar of the bonfires.

Maneater drew a ragged breath, and brought her fists up warily, her face set in determined lines.

Leeth rocketed forward, focused, hammering the massive chest with a double palm strike. But she didn't stop: hands clenching instantly into fists, she smashed forward again, her whole body behind the doubled punch. So fast, the meaty impacts of the second attack sounded like an echo of the first strike. The silence deepened, as if she'd somehow shocked the crowd. No one breathed, the blows resounding over the soft snapping of the fires and a hundred in-drawn breaths.

For one second, two, the tableau held; and then the giantess toppled slowly backwards off the platform, crashing heavily to the ground. Rolling to her side, Maneater lay doubled up, struggling to rake in tiny, gasping breaths. Above, Leeth still stood, poised and alert, moving back to give the woman space to return to the arena.

A murmur of surprised approval rose from the crowd. She heard the words 'speed,' and 'breaking bounds,' as the *ringmaster* now stepped up onto the dais. Risking a quick glance at Maneater below, on her feet again, Leeth circled, shifting position so only one of them could come at her at a time.

The troll raised his misshapen leathery hands in a gesture of peace. "Ho. Chill, girl. Chill."

She watched him, alert for a trick, darting glances back at Maneater.

He shook his head. "You won."

"What? Won? How? Orange means knockout. We haven't finished!"

"She leave, she lose. Rules."

"You mean, because she fell off the platform, we have to *stop*?"

The troll looked at her strangely. "Next fight start soon. You won fight. Now go."

She took a step toward the edge, toward the fighter's walkway, then turned back. "But I waited *ages!*"

Robbie's expression of surprise was almost comical.

"Look, *I* don't mind. Just let Maneater back up, so we can finish it properly." Robbie growled, moving toward her and sweeping one arm around her back, scooting her into motion. "Okay, okay." *This was so unfair.* They'd promised it was going to be until one of them was knocked out. They'd *promised!* She stomped off the platform.

"What *other* dumb rules are there that no one's told me?" she asked, turning to look back and up at the ring-master as he continued herding her from the platform.

The troll shepherded her, still arguing, back toward the fighters' waiting area.

But minutes later, with a very few lucky gamblers counting their winnings, she reappeared, following the three figures descending the stairs from the fighters' balcony as they approached the dais; still arguing.

"But look, it's only fair that since my fight was cut short, you just *add* me and someone else to the next fight to even it up. That way we can have like two against two. It'd be great!" But she'd slowed down too long: another surge of electricity ran along her nerves, drawing her skin tight. She needed to scream. She *had* to fight... or fuck... do *something!* They continued ignoring her. She knew something was wrong with her, but she *couldn't* stop. She felt tears at her eyes. If she stood still, she'd *explode!* Couldn't they see that?

"Why not ask *them*," she shouted, in case they couldn't hear her. She gestured at the crowd, but the insistent music drowned out her words. Halfway to the platform, all three suddenly wheeled around to face her like they'd rehearsed it, and bellowed at her to leave.

Oh! I should attack them all, right here and now! I could kill them all! Her face lit up.

But at the last moment, she glanced across into the

area where Dad waited, and saw astonished delight on his face; saw him lean forward eagerly. *Eh?*

Kill Robbie? *What am I thinking? What's the matter with me?* With an effort that made her want to shriek, she straightened up, folding her arms.

Okay. Panting.

She'd just wait right here. She could persuade Robbie on the way back. She planted her feet. The others turned away, ignoring her, and continued to the fight area. Darting a glance to 'Dad,' his vanished smile told her she'd made the right choice.

Locked in her misery, she couldn't spare any attention for the stupid fight when it started, instead dancing and bouncing on the spot. They should've let her fight. It would've been twice as good with four fighters at the same time. When Robbie *finally* returned, the bout now well underway, he reached out as if to drag her along with him like she was a child. She struck his massive arm aside.

Instantly, the nearby crowd stilled, and Robbie froze.

"Don't frag wit me," he rumbled. "Frag wit ringmaster, make whole lotta people mad."

Mutterings from all about her made her look around, to the people now staring at her coldly. Disapproving. *Disappointed.* This time when his hand reached out to envelope her shoulder and haul her along, she just gritted her teeth and let him.

That didn't mean she had to go quietly, though.

CHAPTER 42

Normally she'd be happy to watch a sword fight. But she *couldn't* stand still, watching. The burning along her nerves wouldn't let her.

She'd talked Razors, one of the other fighters, into sparring with her. For a while, she lost herself in movement, enjoying the flow of attack and response. Sliding her body in and under the larger man's, heaving up and out-

Oops.

His mouth open in shock, Razors sailed over the balcony. A huge crash below brought sudden silence. She hunched her shoulders, then darted to the rail. All eyes stared up at her.

"Sorry! We were just practicing."

On the dais, Robbie glared up at her, veins bulging in his neck. "Fight down here!" he bellowed. "Not in fighter area!"

"But we were only practicing! Not fighting."

"Practice again, be your last!" the troll thundered.

She ducked back, her embarrassment deepening when she saw all the fighters staring at her, too. Below, she heard Robbie berating Razors.

I'd better do something to show I'm helpful, and sorry, before he comes back.

Ten minutes later, she dusted her hands. The area was now cleared of rubbish, including the furniture she and Razors had accidentally smashed. But as she paused, the internal itching returned. And it'd be gigayears yet before the match began.

Planting the punching ball to one side of the practice mats, she studied it, hands on hips. Why *have* stuff here if the fighters weren't supposed to practice, anyway?

The ball was mounted by a rod to a base-plate. Stepping onto it, she realized her weight would keep it upright.

Focusing past the ball, she struck.

The impact was like a small explosion, releasing a cloud of dust that made her blink and step away.

A fresh silence made her look around. Once more, all the fighters were watching her.

From below, Robbie's voice boomed up. "Twenny. Nightslice. Strong. Fast. Cy-blades."

At the solid cheers, Leeth ran over to watch. Nightslice

was a brown-haired, good-looking warrior.

Robbie announced his opponent. "Black Paul. Strong. Fast. Shocks. Hand to hand."

The massive troll drew a white cloth from his belt, dropping it as he left the dais.

"What does white mean?"

"Means gotta surrender," answered a dark-skinned man beside her at the rail. Leeth studied him, admiring the smooth geography of glistening muscle.

"That's it? Until one gives up?"

"Yeah. Till one *submits*, girl. An' it goes on till one does. You don't know 'Slice and Black. They got Rep. 'Bout the worst Robbie c'd do to 'em. Jagged."

"Jagged? What do you mean?"

He frowned. "Jagged. Ya know: rough. Cruel?"

She slid a hand over his chest, distracted by his muscles, tracing their outlines. He grinned, pointing to himself. "Name's Pump. Hey-"

A sudden noise from the crowd drew their attention back to the fight. Nightslice now sported a long set of narrow curved blades growing from his right hand. Retractable razor claws. *How cool was* that?

To her eyesight, the long parallel gashes through Black Paul's chest armor were clear. But instead of pressing his attack, Nightslice staggered back, having trouble breathing.

They circled, possibly resting, while the bonfires leapt and roared to the driving music of The Bitchlings. A beefy arm slid around her waist, drawing her close, as the song's lyrics came suddenly to mind.

> *I feel your body pumping*
>
> *As we're standing on the wire*
>
> *And the city's sinking deeper*
>
> *But its flames just raise us higher*

She needed to *dance* on that wire. Could you dance as you fought? Biting her lip, she watched the scene below. What was taking them so long? They were just circling and circling. Tugging herself from her companion's clasp she leaped up onto the railing, one touch on the concrete above to steady herself.

"No *juice*, guys?" she yelled down to the fighters. They turned to her. "Ringmaster should've picked *me!* I've got enough for *every*body. I'm *juicy!*"

Forty-five caliber stares from the two warriors, but the crowd laughed. Charged up by the approval, she felt like a battery about to start sparking.

She let the music move her body. Swaying, strutting along the railing like it was a narrow beam, she did a few dance steps. The charge rose higher.

Somersaulting in the air, her bare feet slapped down onto the metal railing as though magnetized.

The brown-haired warrior launched a lightning attack.

And now his blades gleamed black-on-silver in the fire-light. With infinite reluctance, Black Paul crashed to his knees.

"Come *on*," growled the other. "Say it!"

Black stared up at him, gasping, clutching his stomach. "Fuck. You."

And collapsed, unconscious from shock.

Cheers and catcalls erupted in equal proportions. The victor glared up at her before stalking from the dais, heading to the fighters' area.

She saw Dad watching, looking happier than he had for some time. He was grinning at her, super pleased. *He must've set up something nasty for me. I'd better be extra careful, from now on.*

Spinning around, she bounced down off the rail.

"Girl. *Sleena.*"

The man she'd been talking to before smiled down at her. "Sleek. Like the way you move, girl."

"Thanks," she said, heading back to her punching ball. Buzzing energy shivered through her. Even the light flared brighter. Ignoring the man, squinting against the glare, she snagged the springy pole, towing the equipment over toward the dead-end corridor, into the shadows.

The man followed after her, stumbling slightly. "Real graceful. Very smooth."

She looked up at him. "Thanks. But maybe later, okay? I'm too keyed up now. I might be next."

He blinked, slowly. "Sure, Sleena. Sum you later."

Rubbing at her upper arms, trying to flatten the buzzing in her skin, she considered. *I need a weight to hold the baseboard down.* A sagging couch leaned against the wall here, but it was too big.

Quiet footsteps approached from behind.

Turning, she saw Nightslice standing an arm's length away, glowering down at her. He was trembling, the tips of his implanted blades twitching in and out as if about to snap into combat position.

Chit! Couldn't she do *anything* without being interrupted? Heat flashed under her skin. She pushed the sensation aside.

"What?" she demanded.

He looked her up and down. "You hurt me out there."

"Oh. Well... thanks. But I wasn't really trying. Any idea how to stick this punching thing down so it won't fall over?"

Nightslice looked confused. "What?"

"I want to try some spinning kicks, but I don't want to have to keep stopping and-"

He stepped closer, reaching out to grip her shoulder, his angry face bending down. As if echoing down a long tunnel she heard the sound of his robospurs extending behind her. As multiple pins pricked under her shoulder blade, the energy flooded higher, surging under her skin.

"You hurt my Rep," he growled directly into her face. Like she was deaf, or stupid.

She exploded.

The cresting force swept her up and she *soared*, gyring, into the storm. Everything shattered into red and jagged motion, objects crashing and spinning together, falling. Then she was on his back, pinning him to the floor, one hand around his thighs while the other clutched his windpipe, bending his head back toward his spine. An echo of some girl's scream still rang in her ears.

But the tornado had passed. She leaped up, blinking, as the others approached the darkened alcove. Nightslice staggered to his feet, rolling his head.

I shouldn't have done that. Why did I do that? She shook herself. *Whatever. Time for some acting.*

"Gosh, sorry Nightslice. I didn't mean to go off like that. I'm a bit keyed up." *That was no lie!*

They offered him support, but Nightslice waved them away.

"I thought you looked really good out there in the arena," she added. The man shook his head, kneading his throat as he stared at her in disbelief. *Was that a good sign?* She took a step closer. *Keep talking.* "I didn't hurt you, did I?"

The others were looking uncertain now. Maybe *they* hadn't seen what she'd done, either?

"Nhh." He cleared his throat. "Ah. Took me by surprise. Still buzzed from Black's shocks. I'm steady." His razors flashed out.

"Shocks? Oh! Like a kind of built-in taser? And I, uh, jumped you while you were injured."

Ignoring his long blades, she went to him, laying both hands flat on his heavily muscled chest and snuggling her cheek against him. A healthy masculine smell filled her senses. She shut her eyes, breathing in the musk. "I'm sorry. That was *really* unfair."

The silence was broken by Maneater. "Break it, 'Slice. She's foggin' ya!"

Leeth felt Nightslice's head turn to face the voice.

"Jack out, 'Eater. You're just jealous."

Leeth stared up at him with wide eyes. "Come and lie down over here, 'Slice. Let me make it up to you."

She tugged him toward the couch. He let himself be maneuvered over, and the others shambled away.

Her skin still *buzzed,* but at least the light had returned to normal. She suddenly found she didn't want to take her hands from the chest of the man before her.

"Give me one reason I shouldn't frag you right now," he demanded.

She looked down, hiding a smile, the buzzing shifting to a more liquid heat. Her uncle was right, she had to admit – once someone accepted you into their personal body space, half the battle was won. So if she couldn't practice one thing.... Besides, he was tall, he was strong, he was healthy. And dangerous. *And I want him,* she suddenly realized.

"Do *you* think I've been bad?"

One large hand lashed out and grabbed her round the back of her neck. Blades *snicked* out, caging her throat.

"Don't shit me!"

She looked him straight in the eyes as her hands went to the ties holding her jacket closed.

"Why don't I prove to you I'm not?"

She couldn't read the emotions that flickered across his

face, but his razors retracted. She opened the jacket to his gaze. He didn't move, but his pupils dilated enormously. Knowing what that meant, she arched herself up to him. Maybe her lessons on body language hadn't been a complete waste of time? Maybe psychology *could* be a weapon.

"Not before a fight, girl."

She laughed. "Why? Afraid I'll tire you out? That I'll send you to sleep? *Drain* you? Come on – I'll charge you so high we'll *both* be sparking." She tried to keep the urgency from her voice, tried to seem cool. But she couldn't stay still any longer. Ants crawled along every nerve, tremors running through her muscles. "Come on, you're not so old you have to worry about *that*. Besides, exercise gets you over an electric shock faster." She had no idea if that was true. "It'll be *good* for you."

She pulled him with her as she backed into the darkened alcove, to its dusty couch. Drawing him down, she slid forward over him, rubbing her cheek against the tight muscles of his stomach, her skin dancing at the touch. A hot wet warmth flooded her, all pretense gone. It was no longer a game. Reaching for his belt, she let her eyes widen, now looking down into his. Parted her hungry lips.

"Hey! Not here!"

Leeth frowned in mild surprise, then smiled like the savage pixie whose name she'd borrowed.

She'd won.

She smiled fondly across at Nightslice, who lay back on a much cleaner sofa back out with the other fighters, looking smug and relaxed. It was kind of funny, the way he tried to catch their eyes even as he lazily followed her activities. It was even funnier how the other warriors pretended to ignore them both. *Jealous.* She and Nightslice shared a knowing look.

She slid one of the heavy practice mats over the baseboard of the punching ball she'd found earlier. Funny how it was the right height for her: she was by far the smallest person here. Nightslice smiled at her, shaking his head. No doubt admiring her energy.

Too much *energy.* She wished she *could* stop, but whatever was wrong with her, she knew the torment had hours yet to run. *Why'd it have to happen tonight, of all nights?* Feeling her nails dig into her palms again, she unclenched her fists. She began practicing her spin kicks, in time to the beat of the music pounding up from below.

Charged up, *too* alive, she surfed the crest of the wave of energy burning through her, prickling her skin. Feeling like she could do *anything*.

From the corner of her eye, she saw Nightslice shaking his head again. Why did everyone keep *doing* that?

She caught sight of Robbie standing over Nightslice, and cocked her head to one side to watch. The troll pointed to Nighstlice, then her.

"Eh? What's that mean?"

Nightslice answered for him, a crooked smile on his face. "It means we're fighting next."

"Yes!" She grinned in delight. "Who're we fighting?"

The smile didn't alter. "Each other, lover. Each other."

She looked, surprised, at the troll's retreating back. Wondering what she'd done to get such preferential treatment.

CHAPTER 43

Disten stood, watching. The girl was a good fighter, and unexpectedly strong for her size. The best tactic would be to grip her close and strike her head until she fell unconscious. She was not invulnerable, merely dangerous. She would damage this body, but that was of little importance. She was the key. The conduit. Through her, through connections from her to others, lay exponential growth.

Humanity itself would be Perfected.

Disten watched each of the girl's fights, her emotions a scour. So intense they hurt.

Yet Perfection would spread from her: ripples in a pond. A pattern waited, that linked her to this one – like a massive shadow, hovering at the edge of awareness. With her Perfected, new possibilities would align. Perfection would multiply.

She would not escape, tonight. If she lost, her broken body would be recovered. If she won, the girl would have impressed. The crowd would clamor for her. Disten looked around, constructing an insult to earn their anger, inflame a desire to see the foolish stranger punished by their new hero. Yes. That would provide the mechanism to challenge her directly.

Soon.

The girl's most recent bout had long ended, though her antics continued – throwing a fighter from a balcony, dancing on a rail. But travel through the crowd was more like burrowing through the packed mass of fevered humanity. It was impossible to fight the entire crowd, but with care and patience, it was possible to move through it, step by step. Using the smiling expression to show non-hostile intent.

And now, a clear path opened from left to right, ending in the set of stairs that led up to the fighters' private area. From above came the sound of a young woman enjoying vigorous sexual union. Each cry matched to clawing jab of senseless passion.

Disten stepped into the clear ground, moving toward the stairwell. A wild storm of hunger, lust, power and release, lashed the air. It had to be stopped.

One of several males clustered around the entranceway jumped up. "Yo. Blagg. Where toin'?"

Disten paused, as the sprawl of people shifted to a configuration that looked deliberate. Two drew guns. All were alert, watching.

"There is a girl," Disten began, but was instantly hooted down.

"Thass truth. 'N yo gonna grab sum bitch ass, eh? But, scan, only fighters 'llowed up there." The tone was almost genial, but there was no real humor. Just the feeling of a cat toying with a mouse.

"You misunderstand. The girl requires-"

The smaller of the two with guns approached. He thrust his face up at Disten's while stretching to jam his gun against the side of the larger man's head.

"No, you fugly piece 'a drek, *you* don' unnerstan. Shark jus tol you. Now you go, or I shoot yo fugly head off an' the Muties roun' here score a shitlo 'a meat."

Disten looked from them, to the nearby crowd watching in amusement, to the guns, then walked away. Meaningless hoots and jeers followed.

At least the girl, or the spirit, showed no sign of fleeing.

Disten worked back along the path to the dais, then stilled. Waiting. The girl would pass by here.

Watching, Disten saw the armed animals at the stairs take note of the new position, confer with one another, and felt fresh anger flare among them. As they approached along the path, Disten considered, then forced a way deeper into the crowd and away from their sight.

Why did they protect the girl?

CHAPTER 44

As she and Nightslice moved down the runway to the fighting platform, a murmur ran through the crowd as if something unusual was happening. Nightslice kept trying to tug his hand free from hers, like he was embarrassed or something, but she grinned to herself, refusing to let go as she bounced ahead, tugging him forward. She just had to keep moving. *I'm happy.* As long as she gritted her teeth, and ignored the itching under her skin.

Finally they all stood on the dais. She held on to 'Slice's hand until Robbie tugged hers free and sent them to their positions. Shivering, she pranced to her corner, then stood swaying, 'grooving' to the music, putting on a little show for the crowd. They seemed to enjoy it, and she started dancing on the spot. And the movement distracted her from the prickling along her nerves.

Robbie raised his arms. "'Fore we start, got something to share," he rumbled. "Some 'a the fists've let us grab a scan 'a their space." He placed a small trid projector on the center of the platform and looked down at it.

"Play."

Translucent three-dimensional images filled the air. On a shadowy broken-down couch hanging in space, a white-haired girl dressed just like her, wriggled her shorts down and pulled and guided... *Nightslice* atop her?

The crowd erupted into hoots and jeers.

"She's juicy, all right!"

"Save some for me!"

"Go 'Slice."

Her mouth dropped open. *That's* me!

She moved around to see how bad it was; how clearly she'd been recorded. She tried out her new swear word. "Funt-head!" *Pretty clearly.* She watched, carefully, no longer feeling like dancing. Pressure swelled from her nerves into tendons – her fingers snapped taut, and she felt her claws slice out. She forced them back inside, clenching her fists shut, and shook her muscles loose.

She noted the way the scene shifted, how fast the camera tracked, the occasional blink of darkness. *One of the fighters must've had cybereyes.* She watched, hungry for a clue as to which one, knowing she'd need the data cubes from his head, too.

She caught the flash of a dark arm as the 'camera' swung down for a moment, and swore again. "*Funt!*" It was the warrior she'd spoken to on the railing, who'd offered her sex! Why was he doing *this*? Had she annoyed him somehow?

Stepping up to the player she popped out the data cube, halting the projection. To an accompaniment of annoyed boos and catcalls, she dropped the chip on the ground, shattering it with a sharp blow from one heel and kicking the fragments off the mat.

She snatched up the projector and tossed it at the troll, hard, before turning to face the crowd.

"If you wanted to watch *trids*, why didn't you all stay *home*? How about some *real* action!"

Don't think about it, she told herself, ignoring the renewed booing that followed her back to her corner. *He's just trying to make you lose it. Forget about it.*

She turned and shut her eyes, letting the music wash it away, fighting the prickling under her skin. She didn't even pay attention as Robbie announced the bout. As he stepped off the dais, the rhythm took her, and the anger faded. She opened her eyes.

The music held her now and she danced, her back still to her opponent, as one by one she killed each sound in the tumult around her: her special trick. The crowd noises first. The rush and crackle of the bonfire, next to go. Then the music, forcing it down until it was just a pulse in her body. Finally, she found the sounds of her enemy – his breathing, the movements of his clothing – and locked her focus on them. She heard the soft click as his razors snapped into place, then heard him step to one side, heavily. Loudly, like he wanted her to know he was there.

He'd consider himself ready, now. Two meters behind her, a meter to her right. He'd placed himself exactly right for a high spinning kick to where he stood, just like she'd been practicing, before. In front of him.

So it was a trap.

His razors were the problem. Razors – she felt her hands *tingle* in reaction, felt her own hunger to *slice*, flood into her fingertips. She forced the feeling away; shook her head. Not tonight.

Seconds drained slowly away.

Now.

Jump back, pivot on left foot: his startled expression as she stood suddenly right before him, nose to his chest –

not what he'd expected. Her hands flashed forward and up, meeting his: left engaging right, right engaging left, keeping his razors away. She thrust out, throwing both his arms outwards, hard, then down. Again, saw his surprise at the force. But she was already leaning back, away, her left leg whipping around and up. *Fast.*

The impact with his head snapped him sideways as she twisted, somersaulting away to spring to her feet. He landed heavily, unmoving, his head at a sharp angle.

A murmur ran through the crowd.

"Nightslice? Are you okay?"

There was no answer. She took a step closer. She *had* struck hard. Very hard.

He didn't move.

"No! You *can't* be dead." She bent down. "Nightslice, no. Nightslice!" She hadn't had a proper *turn.* She'd been sure he was tougher than that. When they'd been making love, his muscles, his neck, had felt so-

The movement came then, just as she'd begun to doubt the ease of her victory. She barely got a hand up to block the slashing blades scything toward her neck.

The familiar tingle flared like fiery claws, unfolding before she could think to stop it, clashing slick and friction-less against his slicing blades to knock them aside. She clenched her fist, binding the razor force back in despite the anger of realizing he'd just tried to kill her. Jerking her head back from the deflected steel, she sprang clear as his other arm swung.

A burning line of pain blossomed along the side of her face and over one eyebrow. She touched it, her fingers coming away wet and darkly red.

He'd marked her.

Nightslice rolled to his side, then to his feet. Less than rock steady though, now.

She moved in quickly, angry now.

Again the razors flashed, but no longer blindingly fast, and this time she blocked forearm to forearm, slamming a knee into his belly with a grunt of exertion.

"Ah!"

Grabbing each of his wrists she snapped a second knee kick to his ribs, rocking him back. Then, balanced on one leg, braced by his body, she twisted in again with another brutal knee strike. And another, faster and harder.

His armored kevlar jacket – great for bullets, or knives – transmitted the force nicely. She heard ribs break. *That'll teach you to try to trick me!* She saw the pain rock him, and seized her chance, *finally*, to try the spinning kick she'd been practicing.

For a brief moment she stood, firelight limning the smooth muscles of her bare, dancer's legs, until the beat came in and she leapt and spun. Right on the downbeat, the ball of her foot crashed into his temple.

The ball, not the heel: she quite liked him. Even if he *had* tried to kill her.

This time, his collapse was no ruse.

Joy bubbled up, carrying her into a high, somersaulting leap in the air. She landed dead still in a fighter's crouch. "Yes!" Back-flipped. "Yes!" Dancing around the platform with high prancing bounds, she laughed and showed off for the crowd, who seemed to enjoy the simple delight she couldn't contain, the itching goad drowned out.

The troll's voice brought her down.

"Okay Sleena. We scan. You win. Now stop."

She looked around, and saw Dad scowling. Good. She must be doing something right. She resisted the impulse to wave to him.

But her joy had drained by the time she'd reached the stairs back to the fighters' area. She'd heard Nightslice complain she was either secretly cybered, or drugged up on Megapulse, and then had to pay *four hundred creds* to the shabby mage just to heal her cuts so they didn't scar her face. He'd even *increased* the price just because she'd dared to complain!

The crowd seemed grumpy, too. Behind her, some solid guy seemed to have annoyed the people around him. The tussle was being enthusiastically taken up, like a piece of inter-bout entertainment. Something about the guy tugged at her memory, though....

Growling, skin once again needling, she stomped up the stairs.

Back in the fighters' area, pacing by the balcony, she glanced out into the crowd. Up on the second floor, a girl in grungy clothes, with lots of piercings and wearing black and white makeup so heavy it could've been used for camo, was trying to jump up and down. The same girl who'd waved to her, before.

She was sandwiched so tightly in the crowd she had trouble just raising one arm clear. Then she began waving frantically, again, like she knew her, a crazy smile on her face. Behind her, a *big* guy stood, gold chains, studded collar, dressed in black Kevlar. One hand on the girl's shoulder. She didn't like the expression on his face.

Something about the girl seemed very familiar.

Leeth stiffened. It was Marcie.

Marcie? Here?

She felt her mouth fall open.

CHAPTER 45

"I don't have time for this! There's someone in the crowd I have to go and see!"

Robbie snorted. "Hah, so 'someone' fix you 'fore test. No. Lift. Now."

Leeth scowled at the people facing her as she stood before the barbell. From outside came the pumping rhythms of the fill-in event, a mock striptease-fight. "Why aren't you 'testing' anyone else?"

Robbie's breath gusted down over her, a sweet, organic, slightly moldy smell. "Know them. Know what they do. Now lift."

She looked down at the rusting black hundred-kilo weights with a doubtful air.

They'd cleared boxes and battered tables to make space. Surrounded by the fighters lounging on ripped and stained seating, she secretly savored the moment.

Robbie stood next to Deezer, the other troll, and Hag-jabber, making both look small. She only recognized a few of the faces from earlier bouts – the huge drug-boosted guy, Skulls, unconscious and breathing with difficulty, on the floor. Nightslice had made them test *her* for drugs, too. She scowled at her ex-lover, anger smoldering. He scowled back.

No one looked happy. Not Flick, the youth with the razorwhip; nor Maneater. Pump, the chit-head who'd filmed her earlier sexing Nighstlice. Razors. Or any of the others, who'd come later. She and Maneater were the only women, though. All the rest were men – scarred and hard.

A gust of wind whipped air heated by the phasion-battery furnace into the room, bringing smells of roast meat and onions. Outside, the strip-fight continued, to appreciative calls from the crowd.

The burn itched along her nerves, goading her. Bending to the bar, stretching her arms wide to grab it near the disks, she prepared to lift.

Robbie stopped her. "No: hold rough parts of bar."

Maneater snorted. Leeth nodded thanks, shifting her grip. Letting out her breath, she heaved the weights up while straightening her back, straining like it was an effort just holding the bar above her knees.

"Satisfied?"

"No. *Over* head."

Grimacing, she dipped as she swung the bar out, shifting her grip then struggling to drag and push the weight up to her collarbone, her face contorted like it'd been a real challenge.

The troll nodded.

"Uhh!" Grunting, she started the weights moving, straightening as she pushed. After a moment, every muscle taut, she jumped away, letting it crash down.

Appreciative murmurs greeted the effort. Someone whistled.

Robbie eyed the gray-haired mage, who appeared puzzled and annoyed. "No." He shook his head. "That was all an act – she was only worried about how she *looked*. Imaginally, she radiated confidence."

Oh, you horrible little spy! She glared at him, fighting the *need* to lash out. Her muscles actually trembled.

It was Robbie's turn to look surprised. He glanced to Nightslice who lifted his chin with an 'I told you so' expression. A growl rumbled the troll's chest, his tusks making his sudden grin look ferocious. "Okay. You try static our brains. So: private bout. Here, now. You gave cashstick. Said, bet half on you, each bout."

She nodded. Slowly.

"Next bout: you, Maneater. Winner lifts most. Parry, here, scan for acting," he said.

So that was the mage's name. She made a mental note of it.

Maneater stepped forward. "Now we see," she said, eyeing Leeth. "Lift'n not like fight'n. You goin' down, little bim. Need guns like dese," she said, slapping a bulging bicep. "You jus' skin 'n bone."

But Leeth thought she saw a trace of doubt behind the bluster. She also noticed several of the male fighters exchange glances at the comment, looking from her own curves – which she helpfully wriggled – to the amazon's slabs of muscle.

Robbie just stared at the big woman. "Start bout."

"Okay, okay. No hard feelings, eh, doll? I'll start on one sixty kilos. No sense straining myself, eh?"

Several of the others chuckled.

Hagjabber approached. Leeth let him grip her bicep, to squeeze it. He stepped away, looking doubtful. "Bet twenny on Maneater. Two to one."

Twenty? That's all?

Robbie took the bet on her behalf. Nightslice raised one hand lazily. "I'll take ya up on that bet, too, 'Jabber, you like."

Hagjabber hesitated, then nodded. Some of the others exchanged looks, but no one else bet, despite Maneater's pointed glares.

Leeth hid her own annoyance. Maybe she hadn't been as subtle as she'd thought.

Maneater bent and lifted. One grunt, two, then she stood, the bar bending slightly, supporting the weights over her head. Slamming it to the ground she smiled a predatory smile down at Leeth.

Something about the way the dark-skinned man, Pump, stood back, watching, suddenly made her turn away. "Can I ask a question?" She stopped in front of him. "Do your eyes have a built-in optic nerve monitor, to turn them off?"

He stared at her blankly.

"Oh, good." She punched hard into his stomach, and as he folded, met his descending chin with her knee. He crashed to the floor, unconscious.

"Hey-!"

"What-"

"Girl-" started Robbie.

"Sorry. But I *don't* like being recorded, and it was *rude* of him to spy on me and Nightslice before. He *deserved* that."

There was a mutter of agreement from the other fighters. Robbie shrugged. One huge hand gestured at the weights. "Lift."

She looked down, hiding her smile as she headed to the weights. Without an optic nerve monitor, by the time the sneak came round, his brainware copy of her fun with Nightslice should be cycled over by a recording of the backs of his eyelids.

Bending, she gripped the bar. This time, she kept her back straight.

By the fifth round, the room was silent, the raucous noise of the crowd outside an irreverent intrusion. Veins stood out on Maneater's red face, the bar sagging across her chest as she supported the new weight. Thrusting one leg behind for balance she forced the mass up and over her head. The floor shuddered from the impact after she released it.

"Two hunnerd, twenny," pronounced Robbie.

Ignoring the buzzing in her skin, Leeth bounced to the bars, weight-tool ready, and unscrewed the outer locking plate. Absorbed. *Should I try...?*

"Give me another twenty, Razors."

She heard several in-drawn breaths, saw looks exchanged. Maneater, hunched forward on a seat and breathing hard, stared angrily at her.

Two hundred forty kilograms. Over five hundred pounds. She crouched over the massive weights.

She grasped the bar firmly, breathing in and out and staring into the distance.

She lifted.

With a smooth economy of movement, the bar rose to her knees. She dipped her bottom down. With her back still straight, pushing with her thighs, she lifted the impossible-looking weight to her collarbone, to soft murmurs of surprise.

She felt tiny, dwarfed by the black disks. She was much less than half Maneater's size, with little muscle definition – until she actually used them.

She put the distracting thoughts aside. This was about her, not her opponent. She blew air out, in, out, gathering her reserves, ignoring the watchers. Then jerking a leg back, she thrust upward – but this time it genuinely *was* awkward. She'd pushed the weight too far back. It started to topple, and she staggered one step backwards under the massive load, knowing she'd screwed up, knowing she had to drop it and jump aside. And she had to do it *now*.

Time stilled. She felt poised at some crucial instant, as if this moment of decision would somehow define her forever.

Time restarted.

With a cry of determination, she lurched back, and down, correcting her stance even as the weight descended to crush her. She fought it back up a second time, silently screaming, *forcing* the bar on, and up, over her head. Stood under it, burning with rage at herself, at her stupid mistake, while the bar drooped under the weights.

Stood under it, as seconds ticked past.

Stood under it, until the anger passed, and she accepted that she'd actually done it.

And threw the weights down.

The room was silent but for her gasping breaths, the festive music lifting the moment into the surreal. She raised her head, glaring at the mage. Let Parry tell them she'd been faking that time!

No one spoke. Some shook their heads, or even rubbed their eyes.

A glow of satisfaction, of real achievement, warmed her, easing an ache she hadn't known was there. Maneater just stared at her.

Robbie spoke, sounding dazed. "Two hundred, forty." He, too, shook his head, his eyes distant. She wondered what it had looked like to them, that moment when she was sure she'd failed, but fought back. Even *she* wasn't sure how she'd done that.

The magician, blinking at her, finally pulled his gaze away to meet Robbie's eyes, his expression troubled. "That was... more than all-out. And yeah, there was something, I dunno, funny about it." He grimaced. "Maybe magic, maybe not. Not something I've ever seen before. Weird. Like she became *more there*, or something. Dunno. Weird."

Hmm. That was kind of interesting to know.

Maneater stood, and approached. Leeth looked up at her enormous opponent. But the woman just reached out to briefly clasp her shoulder, the meaty hand enveloping her still-heaving shoulder as she sat, panting. The look on Maneater's face held respect, sharing the moment – like she knew it had taken more than just strength to do that. For some reason, water suddenly brimmed in Leeth's eyes.

Maneater turned to face the bar, crouching. Concentrating. And then lifted. The same weight.

But... that meant she didn't think she could lift anything more!

With a grunting explosion of air, she hoisted the weights roughly to her solid chest. Stood, breathing hard, collecting her reserves for the next effort.

Leg back, powerful thighs bulging, she thrust up, and slowly, so slowly, struggling for every centimeter, fought the weight up into the air and over her head. For a moment she stood, trembling in every muscle, angry veins taut in her red flushed face.

Then with an expression of profound relief, dropped it to the floor. All were silent as Leeth moved forward, slowly, to the bar.

Her turn, again.

"Another ten," she quietly said.

Razors brought the weights. There was dead silence as she attached them. Bent to the bar. Lifted.

This time, she struggled to get the bar to her chest, and a moment of doubt shocked through her as she stood, staring into the distance, breathing hard.

You can do this!

Her leg went back, her arms up... but this time, though she managed to lock her arms rigid, the leg in front quivered under the strain of trying to straighten too. She tried again to bring forward the leg she'd thrust behind her. *Yes!* Two centimeters. Three. It started trembling. *You can* do *this!*

Snarling at herself, she fought to bring her leg forward just a hand span more. But it refused to move into position for the final thrust upward.

And then her arms started to fail her, too, the weight beginning to descend.

With a cry, she dropped it, spun away. *No! I failed!* She put her back to the room, shoulders shaking, shameful tears welling like she was some stupid baby, instead of a fighter.

Gulping air, she focused on her anger at herself and shook the tears away. Rubbing her eyes with the back of her hand, then, like she was just wiping sweat from her brow, she turned back around to face them.

Robbie looked an enquiry at Maneater. Who looked doubtful, very doubtful, but stepped up. No one spoke as the big woman *reduced* the weights by five kilos. Still five more than her own last successful lift. Maneater only had to beat that to win.

She fought the weights to her chest, then into the air, but instantly dropped it, shaking her head.

Robbie looked around the silent faces. "Sleena win."

Leeth felt her mouth fall in open in surprise. She'd *won?*

She dragged Robbie to the balcony. Spying Marcie still in the same spot, she waved. Marcie waved back, grinning.

"I need to talk to her. It's real important. Can I bring her up here? I think she may be in danger."

Robbie sighed. "Convince others, we fetch, you go down. Take time."

"How long?"

"Fi'teen mins."

Leeth grinned. "That's time enough for another bout. Since I passed your test, I wanna fight two people. Hagjabber and one other. Okay?"

Robbie looked thoughtful, then nodded agreement. She glared at Hagjabber.

Who looked back, worried. Until Robbie selected her second opponent.

CHAPTER 46

On the third floor balcony, Tash, one arm draped around the waist of her replacement prey, leaned out intently.

Below, Dad looked about ready to 'gasm. What the frag was the relationship between those two?

Frowning, Tash watched 'Sleena' face off against Hagjabber and Black Paul. She watched the bizarre contest Imaginally – from the girl's initial, faked fear, through her brutally swift disabling of the ogre, to her quite remarkable performance against the stunningly fast cyber warrior.

And then the astonishing finale.

Black Paul, ruthlessly pummeling the girl, who'd been tased into helplessness on the mat, her arms spread wide. Except, as he raised his fist for the final blow, Sleena *somehow* convulsed, bracing herself as one leg hammered him sideways, hurling him off the dais.

With the ogre out of action, his punctured lungs filling with blood, Black Paul out of bounds, and the girl unconscious, Robbie declared the match a draw.

But the troll looked furious. Leaving the ogre and the girl to be healed by the mage, he stormed up the stairs to the fighters' area, Black Paul beside him.

Looked like things were about to get interesting.

-

Hagjabber lumbered up the stairs, jerking to a halt at the top, facing a scowling ring of people. His hand went involuntarily to press against just-healed ribs and lungs. "Whoa, easy..."

Black Paul made a slicing motion with one hand. "Shut it, 'Jabber," he said, gesturing him to get out of the way. Robbie stared through him, down the stairs. Relief flooded through the ogre. They weren't waiting for *him*.

He gladly moved off to one side.

All the fighters stood gathered now around the ringmaster at the head of the stairs in the relatively lux fighters' area. Even Black Paul, who shouldn't really be there, not being an all-niter.

Hagjabber frowned, shuffling over to Maneater. "What's buzzin?"

"Robbie's been checkin' Sleena. What is she? Not norm: meb non-hume. Only bin roun' f'weeks. Some sayin' she sum'ting new, weird. Meb a supernat, disguised."

The troll's bass tones rumbled out. "What girl be?" he

demanded again, smashing one huge fist into his other hand. "Tik Tek spyborg? Why she here?" Abruptly his eyes narrowed as he glared down the shadowy stairwell. In the patterns of cool darkness a human figure appeared, and began ascending.

"I think she followed me," it said.

The man who emerged was known to them all. The troll ground his teeth. "Why girl follow *you*, dream dealer?"

Then Preacher's eyes widened.

"Robbie." From the empty room behind them all, a husky voice suddenly spoke. "Thought you *spun* fights, not nulled 'em?"

As one, the group swung round to face the tall, auburn-haired woman who leaped down off the balcony rail. Several of the older warriors took a step back as she approached.

"Tash-" began Preacher, then stopped.

"Dad," she sneered, then ignored him, facing Robbie. "*I'm* puzz, too. Bout your *tasty* little bit being healed out there nano."

Black Paul glared at Tash, looking as though he would've demanded her departure had his own position been less tenuous.

Robbie turned to Dad. "Tell this: what is girl? Who taught her fight?"

There was something unpleasant about the smile that came to Preacher's face. He shrugged. "You'd have to ask *her* that."

CHAPTER 47

She'd looked, but Marcie had gone, presumably being brought to the fighters' area. Hopefully, with people helping her squeeze through the packed crowds.

Leeth's head was buzzing as she climbed the steps, every nerve feeling like it was poking out into the air. She also thought she might be going to heave. *Plus* she was sure the other juiceless old wiz had left her with a cracked rib. *Some healer.* Maybe Parry could do some extra....

She was almost to the top of the stairs before realizing something was *off* up there. She emerged from the darkened stairwell alert and ready for attack.

Then saw Preacher.

She stopped, frowning. If he was here, something must've gone wrong. She looked around: every pair of eyes was focused on her; all the other fighters and the mage, too. And Tash: what was *she* doing here?

She stepped into the room, facing them, hands on hips. "What? What are you all looking at?"

"Why you come here?"

She turned to the troll, sparks once again pooling under her skin. She sashayed over to him with a smirk. "Maybe I came here for you, big boy."

The back-handed blow took her by surprise. Abrupt rage flowered, an impossible pressure in her head. She felt the tightening, the *sharpening*, as time slowed and she crouched to spring and kill.

But at the last instant, she glanced at Preacher. For a moment she thought she saw a look of anticipation before his expression shifted to disinterest. Meaning he wanted her to do what she was about to.

Namely, screw up monumentally.

They all expect me to attack, she realized, as the troll flinched back a half step. Somehow, his retreat made it possible to release the anger. A shudder ran through her, and time sped back up to normal.

Her chin came up, and she realized something else – *I did it*. In fact, she wasn't just holding her temper – she wasn't even angry any more. For a moment, she wondered if she was all right. But the flash of disbelief on Preacher's face told her she was doing just fine. *Funt, no one can say I'm hosing this up!* She smiled.

It seemed to worry the troll. Good. She made herself relax, and gestured casually at Preacher.

"I followed him – Dad – here," she replied at last. "So what?"

Robbie looked at Preacher. "You know she follow?"

"Suspected. Knew she wanted to come to the 'Fest. Her neck."

The troll turned his attention back to the girl. "Why you come?"

"Make money. Prove myself to people."

"To him? *Dad?*"

She shrugged. "Maybe. Maybe make him want me to join his gang." *Show him I'm worthwhile. Show everyone I'm worthwhile.*

Robbie frowned. "He say you can, if fight well?"

She opened her mouth to answer. Then closed it again. Wrinkled her brow. "Well, not exactly." A combination of hunger and nausea swept over her. "Not sure I really want to," she admitted, seeing the mage in the corner, eyes shut. Or was he secretly watching her? Suddenly she felt like krup, and swayed slightly. With an effort of will she pushed it away. A sharp pain stabbed her side, and she growled at it.

Robbie frowned at her, thinking. No one spoke. Finally he continued. "What you be?"

"What sort of stupid question is that? I'm a girl. Just a girl."

He shook his head, heavily. "No. Look like girl. Girl *form*. But inside... what?"

She gaped at him. "*Inside? Inside* I'm a girl! A *human* girl, all the way through."

He looked unconvinced. "Who teach you fight?"

"Father taught me heaps. He said a girl had to know how to fight, nowadays."

"What else father teach?"

She stared at him. "Stuff," she stated flatly.

Robbie stepped back to her, towering over her. "What you be? How you be strong like Maneater? How you fast, no cyber, no drugs?" Reaching out slowly, he took one of her hands, which she reluctantly allowed. He turned it over, feeling the soft skin.

She shivered, disturbed by the gentle touch of the huge, mutated fingers with their tough skin, then gritted her teeth at the pain the motion woke from her rib.

"Nightslice say you parry his blades. With bare hands.

Soft little hands. You fight much?"

"A bit."

"Practice?"

"Yeah."

"Why you hands no callus?"

Blinking, she pulled her hand from his grasp to examine it herself. The number of times Dojo had held her hand up, examining it just like the troll had: probing it, turning it over... but he'd never said anything. She looked up at Robbie.

"Why hands soft? Why strong? Why fast?"

She shook her head helplessly. "I don't know. Why *shouldn't* I be? I just am." Facing him defiantly.

Robbie held up one massive, horny hand.

"Hit."

She pouted. "You want me to break it?"

The troll opened his mouth to say 'yes,' then looked thoughtfully across at Hagjabber, like he was considering the lungs she'd ruptured. "No, not break. Hard like this," he said instead, slamming fist and hand together with a sound that made Hagjabber wince. Robbie held up his hand again. "Hit," he said.

And she did; judging it just right: the sound was the same. She smiled sweetly across at Hagjabber, despite the stab of pain from her side, pleased when he paled and looked suddenly ill. Like he'd finally realized that in fighting her out there, he'd been doing something truly dangerous, not just playing with a helpless girl.

It was nice to be appreciated.

Robbie frowned at the force of the blow. He took her hand again and she turned back to him, hiding the pain that even that small twisting movement woke. She could tell he noticed. "Hand not soft when hit. Hand soft now. Magic."

She pulled her hand back from Robbie's grip. Sharp pain flared in her ribs, but she steeled herself to ignore it. *Something else I'm good at.*

She pushed the self-pity aside. "I sort of tense it up when I hit." She didn't know how she did it. Didn't even feel comfortable thinking about it herself.

Tiredly lifting his head, Parry, the mage, shook his head. "Not magic. Least, nothin' I'd call magic." He slumped back, eyelids drooping shut.

So he had *been watching! These people are sneaky!*
She glared at the useless old healer.

"No. You wrong. Is magic," Robbie said.

Parry didn't even open his eyes. "Have it your way. But it's no form of magic I've ever seen."

"New magic, old magic." Robbie shrugged. "Magic be magic."

"Look, why all the questions? I haven't done anything wrong. I just want to fight. And where's my friend?" She ground her teeth as another surge of energy flared back and forth under her skin.

Robbie stared at her. Sighed. "Fren' be sent. You say, lev duo, so, dis crowd... meb 'nother five mins."

She poked him in the chest. "So how can I get healed up properly? That other withered excuse for a magician wimped out on me. Is Parry rested yet? Is there anyone else?"

They all looked at her, then at one another. This time, Parry didn't open his eyes. Maneater answered. "Nil. That's it, chickie. Now we be Red Zone: both healers're fragged. Parry and Shade. Maybe an hour, Parry'll be prep to try more. But chance is, you be standing in line. And others be bidding. If you smart, you stop now. What's axly wrong with ya, anyway? Ya look fine."

"I think I've got a cracked rib."

"Ouch. Yah. Pull out."

She wasn't going to give up just because of a cracked rib! Before she could answer, though, Robbie spoke again. "'Kay." He looked around, singling out Preacher and Tash. "This fighter area. Go, now."

Preacher lazily stood, and turned for the stairs. "Coming, Tash?"

"No. Meb it's time I enter ring again, myself."

"No one here fight *you*," asserted Robbie.

Tash smiled at the girl. "I think *someone* will. Yeah, Pretty?"

"Sure."

Preacher's mouth gaped open. "You don't know what you're letting yourself in for."

Leeth realized he wasn't talking to Tash, but to *her*. Warning her. So, he didn't want her to fight Tash?

Whose hungry gaze was almost physical. "Hey, I scan you like sweet. So I'll sweeten: I win, I slot you half my creds from the fight – but you gotta come with me. To my crash, for the rest of the night.”

Leeth looked at Preacher, who was scowling. That made up her mind. “Okay.”

Preacher swung to face Tash. “You *really* want to 'fresh everyone’s mem?”

The woman stretched lazily. “Too many forget too much. Time I unforget them. Hey, it’s not like I feed here, is it?”

Feed?

Preacher stared at Tash for a few seconds in silence, then turned to Leeth, looking like he’d swallowed something unpleasant, before stalking off.

“Hey, sweetling, come lie down.”

Leeth shrugged away, wincing.

“No. I don’t want to seize up. I’ll just walk around for a bit.” From the corner of her eye, she realized the troll was looking at her. She turned, her ribs stabbing her again, and opened her mouth to confront him.

But the suspicion she’d expected to face wasn’t there. The look was more like... pity? Dismissal?

A faint warning bell sounded, far in the distance.

Word of the bout spread quickly – the greeners saw to that. Especially with the odds Sleena was commanding after her last fight, against two opponents! What chance would this lone woman, this Tash, have?

The older greeners knew, and prepared to make a killing.

CHAPTER 48

"Twenny-do. Sleena. Strong. Trained. Hand to hand. Fast." He turned to Leeth's opponent. "Tash-"

The tall woman stood with hands on hips, smiling dangerously, one eyebrow raised, waiting to see what he'd say.

"Tash. Strong. Fast. Trained. Hand to hand. *Tough.* Heals."

Robbie looked across meaningfully at Leeth as he spoke. She frowned. What was 'tough' and 'heals' supposed to tell her? His expression was weird, too, like he wanted to say more.

She eyed the taller woman, trying to figure out why some of the older people seemed so scared of her. She'd secretly hoped to fight the biggest and baddest the Fest could throw at her, but instead she'd got this ordinary-looking woman, who didn't look particularly tough or dangerous. *But then, neither do I.*

Though Tash *had* said she'd fought alongside that old guy, Thor, years ago, even if she didn't look much older than Emma. Which was weird.

The biggest problem was going to be her cracked rib. She wasn't dancing, now.

Robbie was drawing out the orange cloth when the gray-haired mage wearily climbed up unto the fighting platform.

The ringmaster shook his massive head. "Parry, she choose. No stop."

Parry shrugged. "I've given up trying."

What's he going to do now *to try to mess things up for me?* She moved into a defensive posture as he approached, but he gestured wearily at her not to bother. "Just show me your ribs, girl." He glared at Tash. "This one's on the house."

Huh? It wasn't until she saw the look of hatred he turned on her opponent that she understood. Kind of. She didn't know why he didn't like Tash, but she did need the healing. She began untying the knots holding her grubby denim top together so he could get both hands on her easily. He swayed on his feet, looking like he might pass out any moment. Cursing the ties, she ripped the jacket open.

Her breasts stood proudly, bathed alternately red-gold and black by the caressing firelight.

Parry blinked, pausing like she'd surprised him somehow. The crowd reacted, too, appreciative calls bursting forth.

"Uh, that's not-. Never mind." For a second he still hesitated, before finally placing both hands over the injured area. She sighed as the magic flowed soothingly through her side and along her ribs. Even the pain as he gently manipulated the bones into proper alignment was bearable. She held still for him, looking out into the horde of people. She couldn't see anyone shepherding Marcie through the crowd. *Where was she?* But Barney looked excited, proud of her; though Teef, who caught her eye, frantically shook his head, mouthing words: '*No. Don't do it.*'

How could he still doubt her? She scowled. She'd show *him!*

Everyone waited, patiently, even though nothing visible was happening. In fact the crowd was quite still. Actually, that was a little strange, now she thought about it. Wasn't Parry changing the odds by healing her? But she didn't see any flurry of activity from the greeners, or anyone else trying to adjust their bet.

They must be really sure I'm going to win.

She looked at Parry. What was taking him so long? *Her uncle would've taken five seconds.* Hadn't he finished? It must have been two full minutes before he finally removed his hands.

"Hey, thanks, that's-" she started to say, then had to grab him as he collapsed. He'd- he'd drained himself completely, just to heal her? Closing her mouth she slid one arm around him, swinging him lightly up into her arms and carrying him over to the troll. Who accepted the burden with a funny expression.

"Hey, look after him. He's all right."

Robbie stared down at her sadly.

"Don't worry," she reassured him, "he's just exhausted. He'll be all right." It was weird that Robbie didn't know that.

She moved back to her corner, wanting to dance, wondering why the music had stopped.

Casually shifting the unconscious mage to the crook of one massive arm, Robbie's voice boomed out to the crowd as he awkwardly pulled out a pink ribbon from his belt, to add to the cloth he was still holding. "One more: girl bet more – girl bet self, to Tash, rest of night."

Whistles and catcalls greeted this announcement.

"Hey, scan, she's bare a'ready! Meb the plan's lezsex?" More laughter.

"Meb she *wants* ta lose!" someone called out in an urgent tone, waving a cashstick.

That remark got her attention, and she spun around, eyes stabbing into the crowd even as the effects of the suggestion rippled out like water over a fire, the air quietening dangerously.

"I came here to fight, sewer-mouth." She squinted into the crowd. "Stay right there," she pointed. "After I'm done with Tash, I'm gonna *talk* to you!"

Robbie stepped forward. "Fight be fair," he promised the crowd. "Parry scan. Nuff. Start." He lifted the cloth and the ribbon high, then dropped both as he left the platform, the overextended mage perched like a child in the crook of one arm.

Pink and orange cloth hit the ground.

Tash beckoned. "Come, sweetling. Don't make me wait."

Fine. Leeth moved in fast, dropping into a spin kick to Tash's side.

Which was caught in both hands, stopped dead, suspending her momentarily sideways in the air. Then Tash heaved her into the sky.

She tumbled, twisting and arcing in clear flight. Somehow, she oriented herself as she flew across the dais. Somehow, got her feet beneath her and soaked up the impact as she crashed down on the edge of the platform.

She felt like she'd just slipped inside an action trid. Like the laws of physics had just been turned off.

She moved forward, slowly. The force of Tash's grip on her ankles had been unbelievable. She knew *she* couldn't have done that.

I could be in trouble.

Tash smiled. "Nice landing," she said, awarding her three slow claps. "So: I scan you don't want Easy. Let's slot Hard."

Leeth considered. Tash was faster than her, and so much stronger it was a little frightening. And despite all Tash's sexual come-ons earlier, leaving her jacket open wasn't distracting her in the slightest.

She'd just have to move in close to null the speed and

reach advantage. From her lessons with Dojo, she knew you could still beat a stronger and faster opponent, if your technique was better.

She moved in.

For a moment they stood toe to toe. What happened then was too fast for untrained eyes to follow. Tash's right hand chopped down only to be knocked out of line. So too her left hand, striking up. But Leeth followed through, slipping around and striking past, her blow hammering into the larger woman's side even as Tash's elbow arced back at her own face.

Tash was no longer smiling.

From below, Leeth deflected the circular strike upward, smashing her own elbow into the woman's face, her left fist plowing into the woman's stomach as she pressed her moment of advantage.

It was a mistake.

Tash's hand clamped on her right shoulder with the force of a metal press, twisting and pressing down. Her teeth clenched against the agony, Leeth lashed out instinctively into the abdomen of the thing crushing her. Her tingling hand sliced deep into flesh, cleaving through organs.

Tash's arm jerked, and Leeth cried out as her collarbone snapped. Then a sledgehammer struck her head. As blackness fell, she saw the flesh of Tash's stomach flow back together, the wound vanishing.

She looked again for Marcie.

And then she was falling.

CHAPTER 49

Garland had had to release the city-watch drone kilometers back. Sara had indeed headed straight for the 'Fest. He worked his way into the crowds until he got a clear view of the chip-dealer, now looking settled in amongst others with the same gang markings – the Crazers. He clearly held a position of respect: probably their leader. Sara still hadn't spoken to the guy, though, and he checked his locator again. The signal was coming from somewhere across the way, lost in the crowd. Satisfied for now, he rolled his shoulders, loosening the tension as he scanned the scene.

The crowd stank; Dogmen – Homo Immutus Cani – mixed in with every other legal Altered variant, and some not so legal. People jostled and surged, laughing and shrieking. He growled at a young girl trying to pick his pocket, who just grinned and ducked away.

Eyes slitted, he moved deeper into the festive pandemonium, slowly working his way to a vantage point. Checking Sara's location, he noted her now moving *away* from the chip-dealer. Snagging some more food, carefully trying not to identify the roasted animal, he leaned up against a wall, relying on his height to keep an eye on things. Then stopped, his rat-on-a-stick halfway to his mouth as *Sara* jumped vertically down from one old planter box to the next before diving into the crowd. A brief struggle, then she was forcing her way amidst hooting jeers onto the fighting platform to start talking to the ringmaster. *What the fuck?*

But as he watched her appear, in fight after vicious fight, saw her strength and her ferocity, he grew more convinced she could indeed be Marta Sanchez's killer. And all those others.

She'd been trained, too, since she'd almost bested him and his entire team. He blinked. *Fuck. If she'd taken down the better part of my old paranormal SWAT team without formal training, no wonder she's been looking unstoppable tonight.*

Until Black Paul. Garland replayed that encounter, his combat comp analyzing the times and distances, and swore. *He's faster than I am – the scum's been boosted past milspec!* Yet that had been barely fast enough to lay a finger on Sara. 'Sleena.'

And then the whispers of the weightlifting contest had raced through the crowd. *Two hundred forty kilos.* Strong enough to do the things the survivors claimed The Breaker had done. Though they'd all provided a strangely uniform description of the perp: a large male, expressionless. He shook his head. Maybe a mask, and a bulky suit? Or some kind of spell? *Possibly provided by her smeg-head uncle.*

Garland stared down at the tiny package in his hand in distaste. So the Crazers sold NuLife. The best in town, too, he'd been promised. It must be, at a thousand creds for a single Scene. Even if addicts replayed it a dozen times before the kick got stale, driving them back for more, that was still ninety-nine percent pure profit for the seller.

The thought of an accidental discharge of the micro-probes made his skin crawl, even knowing it could do no harm there in his hand. It had to be applied to the back of the skull for the interfaces to form.

But who did the programming for the chip? That was where the value lay. How did a disreputable old ganger have access to that kind of tech? Could he have a link to someone in the Bureau itself, perhaps? The thought brought its own chill. What if this guy also worked for the Bureau, secretly? Could this smek in fact be sanctioned? Fund-raising for black ops, off the books? Would Eagle allow that sort of operation? Just how far had Eagle fallen?

Her final bout had been a surprise. He worked his way in closer after the woman, Tash, had revealed herself to be some kind of Unfolded creature and carried the girl off. He was glad he'd trusted his hunch and tuned his bug in when the main actors had disappeared before the fight. As they now headed into the quiet darkness of the fog and he trailed them, he considered again what he'd heard. Behind him, the desperate energy of the revels faded like a dying fire.

The older chip-dealer went by the name 'Dad,' and there'd been some story about Sara joining his gang. Which was obviously bullshit. The question was, why were Dad and the Crazers now following Tash as she carried off her spoils? Why would they care?

None of this added up.

Particularly galling had been that somehow, Sara had won over the locals. Watching Robbie pump up the crowd while Tash cradled the little murderess – the prize for *her* evening's work.... He'd felt like standing up and shouting out that their little heroine was the damned Breaker.

Tash reached a cramped and flame-lit 'parking lot' where a local ogre tribe waited, eager and wound up, ready to pound any thief entering the temporary neutral zone. The tiny lot held motorbikes, quad-treads, and even an ancient Boston Dynamics Walker; prestigious symbols which the ogres would guard until dawn. The vehicles laired like creatures from a dark techno-dream: a crazy contrast to the rubble and wreckage around them. He frowned. *How the* smeg *had anyone gotten bikes down* here?

Crouched behind a crumbling concrete pillar, he watched as impotently as Dad, while the creature mounted her big black Suzuki Panther, managing the dead weight of the girl in front of her with frightening ease.

She keyed the bulbous triple power cells, bringing the turbines to purring life, but before she could leave, some zoned-out blagg with smudged face-camo and a bandaged, bloody right hand suddenly appeared out of the fog and coldly demanded the girl. 'She is to be Perfected.'

Tash offered to shoot him instead.

The guy just stared at her, like he was considering the offer seriously. Completely deadpan, as if being shot would be a mere inconvenience.

But Tash simply hit the juice and the bike leaped forward, engines screaming, zagging up the twisted chute leading up and out of the broken grounds, leaving the guy standing there. Completely still. Something about him appeared to really twist the ogres: strangely, they backed away as he moved out. Dad and his crew, standing off to one side, also looked unsettled. Then, as one, they powered on and jolted up and away, apparently in pursuit of Tash and Sara.

That left the ogres – at the other side of the now empty bike area – and Garland alone with the zombie; who turned and strode away, his face expressionless as he approached Garland's hiding spot. But as he came alongside, the guy stopped, his head tracking slowly around until two dead eyes locked on Garland's own. And suddenly he felt what the others must have: something about the blagg got under your skin. Garland felt his augments trigger into combat mode, and he reached for the gun under his jacket, freezing at the last moment without drawing it, some sixth sense warning him to stop.

"She is connected with you now, too," the zombie said, tonelessly. Blank eyes looked down to his arm reaching under the jacket, then back into his face; then the man simply walked past.

Garland shuddered for reasons he couldn't explain, before returning to his real task: tracking Sara.

The arguments against using a mil-sat still applied, and it seemed like only a few of the older denizens here had ever heard of Tash – he was sure there'd be no point asking where she lived. All he had was the tracer on the girl.

It was better than nothing.

Fifteen minutes later, tired and scraped, he'd gained enough height to ping for one last fix before he lost the signal. It was heading north, to the Bay, but the roachbug only had a two kilometer range.

Staring out across the water he accessed a channel to his car and took direct control. He brought up a map of the area and ordered the car to meet him at the nearest edge of the Dumps – not far from the Lash Lighter cliff, as it turned out, where Sanchez and Henderson's bodies had been recovered.

Thinking about that, he composed and sent a message to Berlusconi, attaching the tip-off with the video. Just in case. 'May have a lead on The Breaker. Recognize the girl? Tracking her now. Find out what you can on 'Tash' – F, 185cm, 30s, para – things may be about to hit a new level. Meet @ StarJeans @ 8.'

Though there was a chance that by then, he might already have her in custody. Setting off at a jog, he decided he'd cast around across the Bay: patience, luck, and the bug's two kilometer range *might* still do the job. Then it'd be time for some serious questions. One on one.

He had gear in the trunk of the car that'd deal with things like Tash.

Or Sara, for that matter.

CHAPTER 50

Leeth woke to the brush of silk in a darkened room, the panoramic lights of New Francisco spread out in distant glitter like a fairy-tale city. She stretched, then stilled: someone had healed her collarbone. She kneaded the area thoughtfully, ready for pain that never came. She felt fresh, clean – her skin faintly damp, her hair smelling of flowers and fruit. Frowning, she stood up from the couch she'd been... placed on? – and felt silk whisper across her body. Her frown deepened. How had she gotten here?

Her stomach was a gnawing emptiness; aching. *I should have eaten more, at the Fest.* But the awful, twitching burn along her nerves was gone. Finally.

In the dark room, her grubby clothes lay piled together on a footstool. Eyes widening, she ran to it, frantically checking the waistband of the shorts until she felt Barney's device still there, in place. She tapped it, heard the whispered nonsense phrase that kept her free, and slumped in relief.

Standing, she cast her eyes across an echoing, empty space. A large empty studio, its polished wooden floor cool against her damp feet. The sofa she'd woken on, a double bed, unlit standard lamp, bookcase, and a few weird ornaments hanging on one long pale wall.

But the room was dominated by panoramic views from two adjoining plate glass walls. One overlooked a wooded hillside. She padded, silent on bare feet, to the other view. Touching her fingers to the glass, she looked out toward the far-off city. Staring out and down, rubbing her wrist absently, she suddenly realized her commlink was gone.

Where am I?

Behind her, the faintest whisper of motion, the sound of hair and silk brushing bare skin, whirled her around – bringing her face to face with Tash.

The taller woman wore a similar silk robe, untied, and a confident smile: proud of her own firm body. She sized Leeth up, admiring the healthy legs, taut stomach, and the swell of half-concealed breasts, before lingering on her neck; and then their eyes at last met.

It was very quiet in the large room.

With exaggerated caution, like Leeth was some wild thing that needed gentling, Tash reached out one hand to cup her face. Tash's mouth opened, the tip of her tongue sliding across her upper lip, admiring her prize.

With an effort, Leeth remained still: she *had* bet herself, and she'd honor that debt.

"I want you," Tash whispered. "But only if you want me." She moved closer, a possessive grin revealing unusually long teeth.

In the silence of the studio bedroom, Leeth realized something else as she stared up into the woman's face. "You're not breathing." Nor did Tash have a heartbeat.

Tash smiled down at her, one eyebrow quirking upward. "That's 'cause I'm dead."

CHAPTER 51

Father glared at Preacher. Mother merely stared at the agent coldly. Several cups of half-drunk coffee, now cold, stood on a table at the side of the briefing room. It was three hours before dawn.

"And you say you don't even know where this – this creature, lives?"

"Hell, Father, she's a *vampire*. They don't exactly spread that info around!"

"Don't raise your voice, Preacher," Mother warned. "You said you followed them, but lost them. How was that possible? Your bike has Stealth."

"Yeah, well, seems like Tash's does too. Once we got near Mount Diablo, off went her lights, and on went her cancelers. Even with light intensification I had to slow down because of the roads."

Father glanced at his watch. "The Doctor should be finishing his ritual in about ninety minutes. Hope that his Sending will not be too late, Preacher; and that he can locate her."

Mother's normally smooth brow creased. "I still have enormous difficulty in accepting the label 'vampire' for such creatures."

"Oh? How about the label 'dragon' for creatures like Lord Shen?"

"Don't bait me, Preacher. Portraying himself as a dragon is a mere tactic that's helped Shen rule China for the last twenty-six years. The use of these imprecise and archaic terms serves only to encourage error. They distort meaning. You may as well start talking of werewolves or ghosts."

Preacher shrugged. "Some of the Altered look pretty close to wolves or big cats. Ghosts? I guess not, or after '45 and that bitch d'Artelle, we'd all be drowning in 'em. But vampires – seems a pretty accurate label to me. *I've* met Tash. 'Sides, the Doctor sure didn't think it was crap – 'People or things that parasitically drain one kind of vitality or another make sense, from a theory of magic perspective'. So, yeah, as far I'm concerned she's a vampire."

Father spoke. "I hadn't realized the Doctor had studied the topic. Though his knowledge appears to be largely theoretical. You've met this 'Tash' creature. Are you sure you can't think of anything else?"

"Nah. I'd never heard of those weird kinds, that drain

youth or intellect. She's more in-your-face than that. The classic undead, suck your blood kind, I'd guess."

"Oh? The turns-into-bat, stake-through-the-heart, returns-to-coffin-before-sunrise type? Is that so, Preacher?" asked Mother.

Preacher flushed slightly. "No. Well, except meb the sunlight thing – I've never seen her in daylight. But she's sure as scheiss not alive like us. She doesn't eat, doesn't bleed...." He remembered Leeth's hand carving into Tash's stomach. "And you wouldn't *believe* how fast she heals. Er, mends."

"So she's a 'classic' vampire. She takes life. Does she kill her victims, or just drain them a little?"

Preacher shrugged at Mother's question. "She kills them. But my guess is she won't have killed Leeth. Yet. Tash likes to play – from what I've heard."

Mother continued to stare at him.

"Look, I can't be sure. She's *very* fastidious. I've never seen her with any of her victims."

"I am also having difficulty with your failure to report this 'unusual' inhabitant of the area until now."

"She's not an inhabitant. She hasn't been around for ten years."

Mother frowned. "All the same. She is a factor we should have known of."

"Why? It's not like you could've allowed for her intervention. You can't plan for interference by every possible player. You're always telling me the thing is to keep the plan simple but adaptable."

"Stop making excuses, Preacher! If somebody with the power to so easily outmatch an agent with Leeth's abilities is on the loose, we should have been informed!" Mother glared at Preacher. When he didn't challenge her, she continued more calmly. "She could also be a link to others like herself in New Francisco."

Preacher shook his head emphatically. "There ain't nobody like Tash. Even if there were other vamps, I reckon they'd avoid her like a sudden case of the Red Plague."

Mother shuddered. "Nevertheless. I suggest you consider how to present your information about this creature to Eagle. Perhaps it will compensate for the loss of the girl."

Preacher brightened at the idea. And maybe a vampire'd be easier for Eagle to control than Leeth.

Mother, Father and Eagle were all now linked in virtual conference.

"Why did the vampire choose this night to return?"

Father shook his head. "No information. As far as Preacher can tell us, it was simple chance."

Eagle was still for several seconds, thinking. "So Leeth may now be a vampire. Which would put her under the influence of the one who created her, according to the tales. Would the Doctor's prohibitions against speaking about us survive the Change?"

Father frowned. "He thinks so. For a time."

"He thinks so." Eagle's projection turned its back to the camera. "Very well. And the Doctor is performing a contact ritual, which may locate her, around dawn."

"How convenient," murmured Mother. "It should work now – even if Leeth is a vampire – yet wouldn't when she was merely 'too excited', before."

Eagle turned back to them. "Thank you, Mother.

"Father: you say agents James and Emma can be detached from their current assignments. The Doctor also believes the sensitivity to sunlight would take time to develop. If so, we can contain this within the Department. I cannot believe Leeth would squander her last chance to experience sunshine. And she can be quite persuasive. Have James and Emma on standby to collect her, if the Doctor can locate her. If she's with 'Tash,' have them bag the creature and bring her in too, if possible." He smiled. "I have a nicely-functioning Institute she could be sent to. Perhaps the Doctor might even be contracted out, temporarily, to assist with her. We may also need her if there is an option of reversing whatever effect she's had on Leeth."

"Capturing Leeth and Tash won't be easy," Father said. "We can issue James and Emma with web-guns to try the soft option first, sir, but Leeth has already demonstrated she can cut her way free of those. And we don't even know if bullets will stop them. I recommend flame-throwers too – as a last resort. Can the Doctor Heal her, if she's, er, somehow *dead?*"

"I hope we don't need to find out." Eagle's virtual figure looked around at them. "Is that all?"

"Yes, sir," Mother and Father answered.

"Then proceed. This is bitterly disappointing. I had in mind a wide range of operations for Leeth, thanks largely to her innocuous appearance under both technological and magical scans. Though you have been predicting an outcome like this for some time, have you not, Mother?"

Mother nodded.

"I believe she would have been aware of your opinion. Please include an assessment of *that* factor in your final analysis. Although I still hold hope that Agent Leeth may surprise us all, yet again. Out."

His image vanished from the digital meeting space, leaving Mother looking shaken, while Father moved to the virtual operations space and began issuing orders.

Flashing red alarms – both virtual and real – woke Nelson from sleep. Yawning and stretching, he called up a text window to read the urgent new orders. Then grinned, making a gun of one hand.

"Bzzt! Take that, bitch! You cannot oppose the mighty Nelson!"

Was this the right time to dump all the info he'd collected on her to Mother and Father? They'd spit chips when they learned how completely she'd disobeyed orders.

Nah. Probably best to wait for the truly perfect moment. Timing was everything.

It was kind of a shame she was gonna be brought in – or down? – by the agents. Though maybe, uploading a Traitor scenario to James and Emma, after a little tweak or two, might pay some dividends. "We'll see who wins *this* round, Leeth!"

CHAPTER 52

"That's because I'm dead," Tash said.

In the large, glass-walled room, the two women faced one another in the dark, Leeth with her back to the ceiling-to-floor window. "I only bet one night of my life: not all of it." She shook her head in violent denial. "No. I won't become like you."

"You don't wish to live forever? Never aging?"

"Who says *you* live forever? You'd need magic. And that's only been back for... since 2036. So how do you know you can live forever?"

"Verily; sooth." Tash smiled.

"Huh?"

"So you don't wish to join me in the night?"

"Well... *that'd* be okay. Whattya want to do? But I gotta leave in the morning. And I have to say, I'm *starving.*"

Tash threw back her head and laughed. "You are not a girl for poetry, I see."

"What?"

"You don't wish to join me in *eternal* night?"

"In...? Oh! No way. I mean... sorry, I'm sure it's fun and all being a vampire, but I love the sunlight."

She thinks it fun *to be a vampire?* "Yet you are happy to join me for one night?"

"Sure. I *did* promise. But just one night: don't try to turn me into a vampire, or we'll fight again. And this time, I know you heal real fast."

"Indeed." Tash looked her over carefully. "But nor are you the simple girl you pretend to be, Sweetling. You are more like me than you know. You will never fit in with *them.* The ordinary people."

Tash swayed closer. Leeth readied herself. "Stop. If you pin me, you've got me: we both know that."

Tash didn't slow.

"Stop! I mean it, Tash. If you come one inch closer I'll End you."

Tash stopped. And smiled. "You really would try, wouldn't you?"

Leeth nodded, once.

Tash read the honesty in that answer, and laughed. "Oh, Sweetling, I was right to bet you for a night of your life. I needed someone like you, tonight."

The sadness Leeth had seen in the older woman was

back. "Thor?" she asked, remembering the death of Tash's comrade in the arena.

"Aye."

Leeth's heart went out to the vampire. Stepping forward, she hugged her.

At first, Tash felt like a wooden statue in her arms. But then the statue thawed, arms wrapping close around her in turn.

Tash's body was cool.

"You burn, Sweetling. And so very, *very* sweet. I smell your blood beneath your skin. It would be... intoxicating. Are you not afraid I will take you, now that you have surrendered yourself into my arms?"

"Nah." Leeth eased back to look up into Tash's face in the bright-dark room. "'Cause you're not gonna. I can tell."

So innocent, Tash thought. *So trusting. But...* "No. No, I would not. We wagered for one night, and one night is all I will claim."

Leeth grinned up at her. "So, what do you wanna do? What do vampires do for fun?"

Tash's raised eyebrow suddenly reminded Leeth of Emma.

"Such an *open* question. Indeed." She traced a finger down the soft, pale skin... down Leeth's neck, lingering over the throbbing carotid artery as she held the girl's eyes.

Trailing her fingers lower, down her chest, she paused on the upper slope of a firm young breast.

The girl looked intrigued.

"You have been with a woman before?"

"Sure! I've been with lots. And girls, too. Oh... you mean sex, don't you? Why? Do you wanna have sex? I've seen that, on the net."

"You've *seen* it? Not done it? Nor with boys, perhaps, either?"

About to dispute that, Leeth paused. "Actually," she said, in a tone of surprise, only just realizing the truth, "I haven't sexed boys. Only men."

Curiouser and curiouser, thought Tash. "Yet you feel no reluctance to have sex with another woman?"

Leeth frowned, tilting her head. "Uh, no. Why do you think I might? I reckon it'd be interesting. On the net, it looked... nice. Loving."

Leeth thought Tash looked at her oddly, then. As if she'd said something strange.

"How very... modern of you, Sleena." She took Leeth's hands, examining the soft, slender fingers. Gently kneaded them, probing. Then stared at them with that slightly unfocused look that Leeth had become used to seeing from mages.

"What are you?" Tash's hands fell away to touch her own belly; remembering her entrails spilling out through her leathers; both flesh and clothing opened with silken ease. "You do have claws, don't you – and sharp enough to cut a shadow from its soul. How did you do that?"

"I don't know. I just can."

"Hmm." It had been a long, long time since Tash had seen anything the like. *Yet the girl was young, certes.* Stepping to her side, taking her hand, she led her back to the large picture windows. Together, they stood in the darkness, gazing out over the night-dark slopes of the mountain. It would be nice, not to be alone....

Tash frowned, again, watching the girl – her silk kimono open, yet apparently genuinely careless of that fact – as Sleena stared out, her eyes moving avidly over the nightscape. Tash, with her own uncanny vision, watched a Northern Saw-whet owl swoop down on noiseless wings to snatch up a field mouse – and saw the girl, too, had seen it, her eyes following the small predator with delight.

What was she?

She had a dancer's body, well-muscled but slim. Young, too. Tash estimated seventeen summers; eighteen at most. So frighteningly young. And burning hot; burning bright. She sensed fire, and passion, very near the surface.

Tash's fingers could no longer resist, and she began tracing the sweeping arcs of the girl's spine, curving in and down before arching out to the top of that firm, taut rear. And those legs....

The girl turned to her, smiling; willing.

Tash thought. "Wouldst thou come whilst I eat? Before...?" She let the invitation trail off.

Tash was unsurprised when her offer awoke an excited grin. "You mean, a Hunt? Ooh, yes, please!" Then the girl drew back, reconsidering. "Wait: you did say you protect the, the little people; the ones that people like Crack would slice. So, we'll be hunting bad guys." She watched Tash carefully. "Right?"

Tash blinked. She had expected the question '*what would they hunt*,' not '*who*'. She nodded.

"Can I visit the toilet first? Which way is it?"

The girl's excitement had returned. *Nor had she asked about her healing – taking that for granted, too.* "Down the hall, second door on the left." Almost, Tash added, 'there is a mechanical light switch on the right, as you enter,' but instead said nothing, watching the girl pad off, half-naked, in the dark.

The girl shut the door, but did not use the light; and in seconds Tash heard all the sounds demanded by the processes of living. She tried to recall what that had been like. The toilet flushed; water ran in the basin; and a little later the door opened and the girl returned. All in the dark.

"Uh – I really am starving, though. And *I* won't be able to eat what we hunt. Will you be drinking human blood? I couldn't do that."

Not: '*What do you hunt?*' but '*I'm hungry, but can't eat your food.*'

"Yes, I drink human blood."

She didn't need to ask if that was acceptable to the girl or not. How odd. "Are you sure you could not Drink, Sweetling?"

"No. That'd be like cannibals, and cannibals are bad. But a steak'd be nice."

Cannibals are bad. Why did it sound like she'd had to be taught that?

"I s'pose as a vampire, you don't get any choice, do you? So I guess that's a special case."

The girl appeared relieved by her own reasoning. As if she had been considering putting Tash in the category of 'bad.' Tash wondered what might have followed, if she had. "I think it probably best we feed you on the way."

"Great." Leeth padded unerringly to her clothes on the footstool, draping her silk gown on the couch and began dressing. "Hey! I just noticed: you're talking different – all proper."

Tash blinked.

"Oh. I get it: you blend in, don't you? You *are* real old, aren't you? But what did you do when the magic went away?"

Tash slipped back into Street while she selected her own clothes and emerged from her wardrobe. "'At's my seek." At the girl's confused look, she added, "Secret. Hurry up, Pet."

The girl stilled, somehow hearing the capitalization. "I'm not a pet. Don't ever call me that."

Tash Percepted her. "Are you not, Pet? I think 'meb you are. Yet I'll think on't. If you're good. Come."

"Where's my commlink?"

Tash shrugged. "I am no expert on the Bay's currents. Perhaps not far from Yuerba Buena Island."

Sleena scowled, but then gasped as she checked her cashstick. "Oh! Robbie must've paid me – but there's too much!"

She turned to Tash across the darkened room. "What happened after I fell unconscious? Did people... did they laugh, seeing me carried off? Seeing me lose? But why is there so much money – did *you* do that?"

So young. "No. No, I did not do that. And they did not laugh." Tash remembered the sea of silent faces as she had lifted the girl from the mat. One voice had started it, but it had quickly swelled, the chant of 'Sleena' taken up by the entire crowd.

Tash had paused, waiting to accept the girl's cashstick, as Robbie had started the bid for the award. 'One thou?'

The crowd had howled.

'Five thou?'

The crowd had only roared louder, incensed.

'Eight thou? Ten?'

'Todo,' they had cried. 'Todo credito.' *All the pool.*

A lot of money had changed hands that night. The girl had been lucky. And had also, somehow, won the crowd's heart.

'Girl win sissteen thou, tree hunnerd ten!' Robbie had shouted. 'New record!'

The crowd *exploded.*

Solemnly, Tash had held out the girl's cashstick, deluged by the tumult, which fell rapidly into silence after she tucked the stick into the girl's jacket pocket and turned to carry her away. Every eye had followed her, whispers growing as she moved off....

Sleena suddenly jerked upright, her aura flaring in a mix bright with shame and dread. "Tash, did, did a girl call out, after you knocked me out? Or come up while I was unconscious? Robbie had sent someone to fetch her." She described Marcie, in her disguise.

"No. No one like that. Fren' o' yours?"

Sleena nodded, hard. "She was on the floor below you. A *good* friend. She'd been there all evening, watching. But she wasn't from the Dumps: she'd snuck in. She shouldn't have been there. And there was this big guy with her.... But when you knocked me out, I looked, and she wasn't there. *They* weren't there." She shook her head. "But Marcie wouldn't have just *gone*. She wouldn't abandon me. Can I call her, check she's okay?"

"Not from here, Sleena. Not on my Link. Do it while you eat. Come!" Tash approached, with a velvet blindfold.

The girl rolled her eyes, but let Tash tie it.

Leeth had finished her first plate of warm bacon-wrapped yaki wings – she wasn't sure what a yaki was, but it tasted like chicken – in less time than it took to convince the street vendor to call Marcie for her.

"That's her, the second one," Leeth said, pointing with honey-glazed fingers to the thumbnail of her friend.

But there was no answer: the Link just went to message mode. Leeth and Tash exchanged looks. It was now three a.m.

"She's meb' asleep," Tash said. "But howz'about ya describe'm?"

Taking the last of the vendor's unsold food, the two retreated to sit on the edge of the gutter.

"You sure you don't want any?" Leeth asked, offering a wing, while the vendor finished closing and locking his stall, and walked off.

Tash just shook her head and sipped her coffee, her eyes slitting in pleasure. She sighed, and shifted to plain English. "*This* is the best thing to come out of the New World."

Leeth tilted her head. "What new world?"

Tash just smiled. "Well, coffee and chocolate."

Leeth thought of saying she was half right, but felt she'd wasted too much time already.

So while she ate, she described the big man. Glad of the training she'd had at the Department, she was able to estimate his height and weight, describe his face, hair, and clothes, the weapons she'd seen, even the jewelry he wore.

Tash stopped sipping her coffee.

"I think he also had a little tattoo, in the hollow of his neck."

Tash put her cup down. "Was it long and narrow? Perhaps, a surgeon's blade?"

"Yeah. Why? You know him?"

"And your friend, this Marcie, she is pretty? Young, like you?"

Leeth stopped chewing, and nodded.

"I think I know him. Marked him. Might be a snatcher for Club Juzz. Your friend could be in bad trouble. Get on the bike. We go, now."

While they rode, Tash explained how Club Juzz catered to a specific kind of clientele: violent bottom-feeders with money and drives that could never be satisfied legally. Behind her, she felt the girl go still.

More, Tash felt a peculiar pressure build, beating at her back.

"*Faster*," Sleena said at last. "Go *faster*."

"Tonight, we will rescue your friend and shut the hellish place down. Forever." Her voice fell. "I leave for just ten years, and foul fungus blossoms. Sometimes, I despair."

From that point, they rode in silence, all Tash's attention on the road. The girl made no complaint as they careered to their destination.

And when they stopped, all playfulness had fallen from Sleena. She asked questions: the club's layout, security, defenses, what kind of weapons their enemies would have. Strangely, though, she had asked for a gun only after some thought. Her movements had become brisk, abrupt. As though she barely held herself in check.

She had accepted the Sofplug eardrum protectors without question, though Tash noticed she'd not inserted them, despite careful consideration. When she thought Tash wasn't looking, she simply pocketed them.

Tash led the way, crouched in a splashing run through the dark storm-water tunnel. The din from the Club hammered through them, penetrating meters of solid earth. Tash steeled herself against the sonic assault. She'd sketched out their roles before they'd entered the tunnel.

Inside Club Juzz, no one spoke.

There was no point.

"You start from the third floor and work down; I'll start on the ground and work up," Tash had told Leeth. "Concentrate on freeing the young sex slaves. Send them down the back stairwell while I 'clean house.'"

"I've got a better plan: I'll kill all the rapists till I find Marcie, *then* collect them together and get them out."

Tash bared her teeth, grinning. "Works for me."

Tash carried two incendiary grenades. The girl had seemed to know what they were, and looked hopeful; but Tash would not trust a weapon so dangerous to herself, to someone who was still such an unknown quantity.

They emerged from the tunnel, Tash suffering despite the Sofplugs and their active cancellation. Yet the girl appeared not to notice the sound at all as she studied the Club's back wall. Puzzled, and standing behind her, Tash clapped her hands behind Sleena's head, as loudly as she could. She herself couldn't hear it over the ambient noise and the earplugs; and the girl could have been completely deaf for all that she reacted.

With a brief look back at Tash, Leeth nodded once, then ran forward and began climbing. Tash watched for a few seconds before sauntering around to the front, feeling a predatory grin stretching her lips.

Moving through an eerie silence, Leeth peeked in the window, touching the shaking glass, feeling her chest and flesh vibrating under the auditory assault. *Clever old magic ears*, she thought, fondly. Ripping the window open, she dropped inside. Tash had said there were no security cameras, and it looked like she was right.

She trod softly down the corridor, from force of habit. Only during the heavy assault weapons training with Father had she ever experienced such perfect silence.

This was a little unnerving. It was worse than working with her eyes shut. But she felt confident her hearing would return, like it always had with Father.

She paused at the first door, resting her fingertips on the surface, feeling them vibrate with the sound of the driving music. The walls, too.

The bedrooms were on the top floor, Tash had said. Leeth felt... not confused. Off-balance, mentally. Like the world she moved through had changed. It wasn't just Marcie they'd be saving. It'd be other people. Kids. *Sheep*. So why did it feel so important? *For the same reason killing Shepherd Fox had been.* Because the strong shouldn't prey on the weak. *But that's what animals do!* She came to the first door, frowning. *They prey on them to eat, though, to survive – not for pleasure. And I'm more than an animal.*

She was still wrapped in her own private cocoon of silence, even with her chest cavity vibrating from the massive sound waves. But a moment after throwing open the door, she knew why this was so important.

Two heavy-set men pounded away at each end of the child sandwiched between them – a girl young enough to be Marcie's little sister, Amanda. Leeth flew at the closest man, the tingle radiating from her fingertips like never before. The man farther away saw her first, his eyes widening in surprise.

The nearer man's head stayed on his body after she struck, diving over him. Still flying forward, she sliced upward through the second man's face. Her folded knees slammed into him, flinging him back from the girl pinned at his groin.

The girl heaved, collapsing as the male assault ended. Leeth landed as if dismounting from a vaulting horse. Spinning around, she saw the first man, still standing between the girl's splayed legs, tilt, beginning to topple. His head slid sideways, slices of neck following. The face stared in shock as it fell, blood pumping from the torso in powerful arcs.

The girl was a limp, heartbreaking doll's weight in her arms as she scooped her up from the bed. Weaving a path between sprays of arterial blood, she eased her down in the corridor.

Kneeling over her, she put one hand gently on the girl's shoulder – and the girl flinched, hunching into herself like an injured beetle.

And suddenly Leeth found *herself* racked by sobs, salty tears falling like raindrops from forest leaves. She found herself screaming noiselessly, hugging herself, before jumping to her feet, flooded with scorching rage.

The passage seemed to throb in and out of view. Then, as suddenly as it had come, the wave washed out of her, leaving her swaying on her feet.

Damn him!

Remembering Dojo's lessons, she forced herself to breathe, in and out, gradually returning to herself.

I have to save Marcie. She only came to the 'Fest to see me. I should have guessed, when she was asking me all those questions. This is all my fault! I'm always getting her in trouble.

She blinked down at the gun still in its holster at her hip. She hadn't even considered drawing it, shooting them. Despite the clear line of sight.

It wouldn't have been enough. Involuntarily, she flexed her fingers, feeling the *sharpness* slice the air.

Staring down at the girl curled into a fetal position, she frowned. *If they're all going to be like that, they'll* all *have to be carried out before we can burn the place down.*

She shook herself. *Stop wasting time! Find Marcie!* She scanned the corridor. There were a lot of doors.

She wondered if screams had started from below yet, as Tash wove her own deadly path through the scum who'd all die here tonight. *And if she hasn't, I will. After I've saved Marcie.*

Sparing one dismayed glance for the naked girl still futilely trying to disappear into the corner, she raced to the next door and slammed through.

This time, the sight before her drove her from herself completely.

A whirlwind of controlled fury scythed into the room.

By the fourth room, still without having found Marcie, she'd switched to using the gun, because it was faster.

On the second floor, she ran out of bullets.

Beheading was fastest, she found. She killed in a strange state of mind – retaining just enough control to take the time to fling the corpse across the room, so the victims were at least free of each body she left behind. Dimly, she knew she should pause, try to give comfort; but the hope and fear that Marcie might be in the *next* room drove her on.

Leeth skidded to a stop at the stairs, about to plunge down.

On the landing below, heading up, Tash jerked to a halt, her mouth falling open. Her eyes moved past Leeth, as if worried there might be enemies still standing.

'Where's Marcie' Leeth demanded in the unnerving silence, scarcely aware of Tash's damaged leathers, or the snub SMGs in each of the vampire's hands.

Tash nodded, giving a thumbs-up.

Leeth growled. *What did that mean? Is Marcie okay?*

Tash's lips moved. *Any more?* With a tilt of her head, she waved past Leeth with a weapon.

Leeth shook her head. 'Where. Is. Marcie.'

Tash seemed doubtful, but beckoned her down while she continued up, her eyes searching around, still wary. Leeth ignored her and flew down the stairs.

With her arms clamped around her shaking friend, who hugged her in quiet desperation, Leeth felt small warm splashes on her neck.

Sound returned mid-sentence. Marcie was saying "... you and Tash fighting. But everything went all swimmy, and the next thing, I was being shaken awake in a room here." She gripped Leeth tighter. "I've never been so scared. But I was certain you'd come. If you could. So when Tash stepped into the room, I knew straight away what it meant. Oh, Jane, they were about to- about to-"

"Shh. It's okay."

"She *killed* him, Jane," Marcie whispered, pulling back. "Cutter. Just snapped his neck!"

"Good. Saves me doing it."

Marcie gaped at her.

"What? He drugged you and kidnapped you! And who knows how many others?"

Marcie was dressed in a tiny black and white costume that left nothing to the imagination. No piercings, and her disguise makeup had been replaced with a look that Leeth had only seen on the net.

Marcie, following her eye movements, blushed.

Tash descended from above, moving past them and beginning to remove devices from her backpack. But her expression held something strange as she caught Leeth's eyes. A kind of quiet doubt? As if she'd seen something horrible upstairs.

Leeth frowned, even as she hugged Marcie, wondering what Tash might have seen, to disturb her.

Club Juzz was quiet. Her incendiaries planted, Tash returned to the foyer.

"Sleena: no time." Tash jerked her head toward the floors above. "Get others. More'n I expected, 'bove. You kill 'em all, or vics help?" Tash handed Marcie a bundle of clothes: what she'd been wearing at the Fest.

Leeth scowled. "Of course I didn't need help."

Tash got that weird expression again.

Leeth looked around. Bullet holes were stitched across the walls; along another, a liquor bar had a larger-than-man-sized section of glass shelving gone. She counted six male bodies sprawled around, in sight just from here. There were a *lot* of guns, chains, and other weapons scattered about as if flung or dropped. Several girls – maybe Leeth's age, or even Marcie's – sat in shock on a dark-stained red satin sofa. Two others were sidling out of the room, heading for the front exit.

"Stop!" Leeth called to them, seeing that they were all older than the victims she'd defended, upstairs. "We'll need everyone's help to get the kids out." She turned to Tash. "How long have we got?"

"I c'n choose. Say, five?"

A blonde girl, one of those who'd been sneaking out, stood wringing her hands. "Are they... upstairs... are they... how many could you save?"

She was crying, Leeth saw. She frowned. "All of them. That's why we need all of you to help."

The blonde gasped, stepping forward, then lurched to a stop. "Truly? *Truly?*"

Leeth nodded.

"Is it- safe to go up?"

Leeth took a moment to work out what she was asking. "Oh. Yeah. All the bad guys are dead." But taking in their expressions, and thinking about the amount of blood and bodies upstairs, she reconsidered. "But maybe you guys should just wait in the corridors, and we'll bring the kids out to you."

Tash was looking at her thoughtfully, but with approval. She nodded.

They started on the second floor, since some of the children had crept from their prison rooms, freezing in fear when Leeth and Tash stepped into the corridor. But at the appearance of the older girls behind them, they rushed forward in a desperate wave, clinging to legs and arms. Grimly, their two rescuers headed up to the third floor.

In the fourth room, after passing its sobbing victim out, Tash looked around the crimson-sprayed walls. "Damn, girl. I should'a given you more bullets."

But Tash's humor vanished in the room where Sleena had paid back the rapist of the most badly injured girl. Tash had nudged the abuser's body over on its back, seen what had been torn away, and her expression turned grim. "Breaker did that, too, once. Likes to play."

Leeth glared back at her. "I wasn't playing. Some people deserve it. Besides, I killed him before I did it."

Tash just stared at her.

They all watched as Club Juzz blazed in the night. All the victims had gathered, many holding one another. Others stood alone and rigid, still locked in misery. But all stood, staring, watching as flames engulfed the building. Even from this distance the heat was intense, but they seemed to relish it. As if that heat was cauterizing invisible wounds.

Tash had handed out the cashsticks she'd collected from the club to the victims, then left. She returned at the head of a trickle of locals that soon grew to a stream, bringing blankets, warm clothes, even, after several minutes, thermoses of soup and other hot drinks.

There was even one raw, heart-wrenching reunion when a mother found the son she'd been told had drowned, six months earlier. In the distance, an ambulance siren sounded; approaching.

The last thing Marcie remembered from the 'Fest was trying to stay awake, while J- *Sleena* and Tash fought. "Who won?" she asked.

Tash smirked. "You gon' intro me to your lover, Sleena? Marcie, yeah?" The older girl looked startled, Tash saw. Sleena, just puzzled. "Less you wanna join us?" Tash let the tip of her tongue dart across her own red-flushed lips. She was joking, but she let the girl feel the heat, pinning her with her gaze.

"Stop it, Tash!" Sleena thumped her on the upper arm, finally realizing Tash was teasing. "Marcie's my best friend."

Marcie looked from the auburn-haired vampire, who had curled her friend possessively in against her side, to Jane herself, nestled comfortably there. She blinked. "Oh. Oh! Your bet...." She felt her cheeks flush. "You two...?"

Leeth lifted her face. "That ambulance is real close. I guess you don't want your dad to know about tonight?"

Marcie's horrified look was answer enough.

"Tash, could you call for a car to take her home?"

Marcie looked around, then cringed as she recognized the skyline. "Please tell me we're not in the *West Oakland Dumps?*"

"Easy, girl. We walk you to Myrtle street. Not far. Car go there."

As the small vehicle whispered to the curb, Leeth gave Marcie a last hug. "I'll call you tomorrow, okay?"

She turned to Tash, her eyes alight. "Hey, let's do another!"

Tash and Marcie exchanged looks. Marcie shook her head. "I just wished I could've filmed you at the 'Fest. You were amazing!"

Another final hug, and then Marcie slid into the car and gave it her address.

"Destination understood. Distance: 6.83 kilometers. Estimated travel time: seven minutes."

Marcie craned around, waving goodbye, then watched Jane lift her head and say something to the vampire before sprinting off, Tash swiftly following.

She turned back around, smiling. *I reckon I know exactly how I'm going to play Stryker Zaxx in my audition, anyway!*

But at the very first intersection, a large man in a shabby, somehow-familiar suit stepped out in front of the car. It braked hard, slamming to a halt a bare inch from him, throwing her into the seat belt.

Marcie felt a peculiar chill.

The man moved to the front corner, and bent down.

And then the car was rolling onto its side.

CHAPTER 53

Garland cruised the SoMa area before crossing the Bay into Oakland. Four thirty a.m. It had taken *that* long to pick up the signal.

Now he crouched on the edge of a vast expanse of gently undulating asphalt, part of the no-man's borderland between the West Oakland Dumps and the sleazy parts of that city. To his right lay the dark and jumbled wreckage of a once-prosperous shopping area. To his left, dance music pounded from The Fryhouse, synchronized to flares of crimson, blue and yellow from inside. Gods knew how the bar's patrons could bear it: the resilience of youth?

In the distance, a kilometer away, at what had been a true viper's nest, the flames were dying down. He'd passed it an hour ago, when Club Juzz had still been a blazing inferno. Berlusconi used to say his ex-wife, Marta, and her partner Henderson, would joke about taking their refurbed Eco-war CrawlTank in there to level the place. It seemed like the locals had decided to take matters into their own hands at last.

Good.

In the security net, annotations from a drone's remote pilot said a 'refugee train' seemed to have been organized, an estimated thirty people taken to safety.

That local rescue effort meant they hadn't needed his help. But it had taken most of the hour since then, casting around the general area, before he'd gotten the ping from his locator that brought him here, outside the almost as notorious 'Fryhouse.'

"Dammit, Sara, where are you?" He pinged the locator again. When the violent trouble-spot had come in sight he'd been sure the signal would be coming from inside. But it hadn't.

He cautiously circled the semi-collapsed and now repurposed Fry's building. Pausing on the edge of the empty car park behind it, feeling exposed, he looked around. The locator's red dot moved in jerky hops across his eye-view map. Although weak, the signal strengthened when he stepped out onto the carpark. He looked around. *They're practically on top of me! Invisible?* Activating combat mode, he cursed the fact that with the noise of the Fryhouse, he had no chance of hearing them.

His gut was telling him they weren't here. He decided to take a risk. Cutting the signal from his flesh-and-blood ears, he fed the bug's input, and that alone, to his auditory nerves. Abruptly he was plunged into silence – which made sense, since he'd put the bug into passive mode hours ago, to save power.

With another quick look around, he crouched low, then shut his eyes. Trying to picture the device's location, he sent the signal that would activate its microphone and transmitter and make the bug live up to its name.

No sound at all. For perhaps thirty seconds he listened in puzzlement, before opening his eyes and broadcasting the signal to turn off the bug.

It didn't acknowledge the command.

He tried again, with the same result. *I'm missing something obvious.* A faint splash behind and to his right made him spin around, drawing his gun: but there was nothing there. Adrenaline scoured his nerves like acid.

Another splash sounded from right beside him in the bone-dry car park. *I'm hearing the bug! But why hadn't it turned off, on command?*

Still scanning the area, crouching low, he headed for the building, trotting across the asphalt wasteland's inter-secting troughs. Feeling like he was jogging over a frozen black sea.

He checked the locator again. Fifty meters ahead. Not far now from the Fryhouse itself. He sent the deactivate command again. This time the bug responded, plunging him into total silence. It must've been just far enough out of range for interference to screw the command channel. Relief swept through him as he turned his ears back on, the dance music once more pounding forth.

But how could she be here, yet in silence?

She's below *me, underground!* Probably some kind of storm-water tunnel. It explained why the signal had been cutting in and out, too

Activating his eyes' IR sensors, he moved cautiously forward. Going into the Hunter's Point Dumps during the truce of a 'Fest was one thing; going alone and lightly armed into the West Oakland Dumps was a whole other nest of bugs.

He assumed the Tash-thing was still carrying her. Dragging her through subterranean tunnels. To her lair? He shivered.

But the timing was wrong. If Tash had brought her

straight here, that left over two hours unaccounted for. The creature had to have been doing other things to the girl in the meantime.

Shit, this stank. Fucking Sara. He turned around, scanning the area, half expecting to see the glowing red eyes of a cyborg wardog as it paced toward him with weapons-lock on him. Again.

He wouldn't say no to some Bureau backup, but he still had nothing to justify actions which would probably piss off Eagle himself. Metrocop backup was even less plausible: no securicorp could turn a profit from an operation here, or would risk their personnel. A couple of months ago, he could have called on Berlusconi's ex-wife: Marta and her partner, Henderson. Not now, though. Not ever again, thanks to The Breaker. Sara.

He crept forward slowly, cursing the girl.

A minute later, Garland stopped, forty meters from the notorious bar. It'd be stupid to go any closer. Upping the sensitivity on his eyes, he crouched in the rubble of the nearest collapsed building to the merely *partly*-collapsed Fryhouse. From here he could see the cluster of bikes out front, but was still far enough away to remain undetected by the people entering and leaving.

He could also make out the gang colors on the bikes: PsychoBloods. *Shit a flaming brick, this was morphing into a nightmare.* He must be crazy to be here. As crazy as the girl herself!

He checked the locator again, its signal now coming from *inside,* and considered the course of wisdom – just getting the hell out of here. He wasn't paid enough for this. Spam it, he wasn't even supposed to *be* here!

But the locator's signal *strengthened,* suddenly tracking smoothly in his view. Moments later his head jerked up as a scream, then shots, interrupted the music. He stood rigid as more screams and shots broke out.

Snapping out of it, he triggered the bug, almost drowning in sound, plunged into an auditory madhouse of animal roaring, terrified screams, crashing objects and a hail of automatic weapons.

Someone dived out between the crazily-balanced beams of the entrance way in a rolling tumble that brought him up and running. Another emerged, then three together. They jumped on their bikes, burning off in shrapnel bursts of gravel from spinning wheels.

Then a bunch more ran out, not in gang colors, and the shots and cries died down. From the bug's audio channel, the animal snarling slowly warped, blending by stages into feeding sounds, and then – infinitely worse – into the sound of something chuckling with a mouth full of food. Something human. Something female.

That faded out, then in, and he heard the occasional crunch of something underfoot, and a groan that ended with a sudden wet meaty sound. Then more movement, until that too finally stopped. Considering how easily Tash had defeated Sara, he again considered calling for backup. Unlike Sara, though, he had heavy firepower. And the logic hadn't changed.

But why was the bug tracking the vampire? Had she taken Sara's jacket? Or...?

His eyes had shut involuntarily as he tried to picture the scene. Gradually he began piecing together a quieter organic sound that he couldn't define, but which made his stomach churn.

"Eww, that's gross!" a girl's voice said. "Wow, you must've been *starving!*" Sara's voice! Then came Tash's throat-filled reply, and abruptly his gut rebelled and he was violently sick. He savagely sent the signal to end the transmission, as his stomach went into fresh convulsions.

Jesus Christ! The two were working together!

A couple of minutes later, two female figures emerged into the darkness. Garland watched, absolutely still, as the smaller figure wiped at the wetly darkened face of the taller, who bent down in a hungry kiss.

Gradually the kiss changed into something else. He heard Tash, her tone teasing. "Come, Sweetling, taste them." He had to fight another surge of nausea as the tip of Sara's tongue flicked daintily, once, against Tash's lips.

The bitches were vampires! Almost, then, he called Berlusconi, before getting a grip on himself. *It'll be okay, if I pick my moment – and keep my distance.*

He drew a shaky breath. *Vampires. It explained so much.* With that understanding came the return of cool equilibrium. These two dirty sluks were going down. Especially Sara. The last thing he'd allow would be the Crazers gang to acquire a vampire. Or a vampire to team up with The Breaker. Had Sara been one all along, or had

Tash made her one, tonight? *Was* that *why Eagle had sent her to the 'Fest?* He groaned. *A vampire assassin working for the US government.*

The taller figure seemed a little sluggish, maybe drunk, but Sara seemed hyped. He watched as the girl tugged Tash back inside, presumably to return the same way they'd come.

He followed them, above-ground, still using the locator, wondering how much juice it had left.

Garland congratulated himself for placing the locator on the girl. Apart from a lengthy stop at one point – with sounds that all too soon made him realise the two were engaged in passionate sex, there in the dark in the underground tunnel. *I guess wholesale murder turns them on. Fucking perverts.*

But they'd moved fast, from then on. And after returning to Tash's bike, their lead had increased – until they'd reached the freeway. Then the greater power of his quad-engined Jaycar reeled in the distance.

Looking to the horizon through the city's jagged sky-line, he saw the first slight weakening of the night's solid black, and figured they were finally going to ground. While he'd been driving, he'd called up the metahuman statutes and done a search on vampires. There was nothing – apparently their existence was still rumor, not fact. *Good.* That meant he had free rein, could even call in backup. Here, he could expect a positive response from the city-cops. Too quickly for Eagle to intervene.

It was easier, this time, to co-opt a city traffic drone. He kept its viewpoint small so as not to interfere with his driving. He felt relief when it came on-line – each ping of his locator was now returning a low-battery bit for the roach's Phasion micro-cell. Not surprising, considering all the narrow-casting he'd had it doing.

The traffic drone's picture wasn't ideal – the sensor wasn't Bureau quality – but it'd do.

He crossed the Bay Bridge a safe half-klick behind them, only closing up when they left it to cut across onto the final spur of the old Embarcadero Freeway. They headed south then into Potrero, leaving the freeway at the last possible point before the final stretch where the road ended, jutting into empty space like an accusing finger pointing toward the shattered ruins of Hunter's Point.

When the locator showed they'd stopped, he pulled over, killed his car's lights, and zoomed up the picture from the traffic drone. The girl dismounted.

Dismounted?

It looked like they were saying goodbye! He'd felt sure they were heading for a shared lair. Now it looked like Tash was dropping the girl off! Burn it!

He signaled the locator to shift into bugging mode again.

"-Tash, I had a lash time- "

It died under the increased power drain.

He cursed. Now he had to make a choice. While the two creatures talked quietly, his thoughts churned.

He opened a link to the metro cops, shared the connection to the traffic drone, and arranged tracking of the bike and a backup unit. He'd follow, later.

Then, wincing, but knowing he couldn't let a support team walk into a paranormal situation unaware, he added that the target was a probable vampire. The reception-bot switched to prank-call-handling mode. He had to use an override code on it. Signing off, he hoped the stories about sunlight and vampires were true.

Still watching via the drone's view, now under metro-cop control, he grimaced at the oh-so-touching farewell. *Shit!* While they moved into a hug, he steered back out onto the deserted street, heading up the hill to the park or playground or whatever the place was. Stopping at the far end he jumped out, drawing his gun.

But how much use would it be if Sara now healed as fast as the Tash creature? Gods, she'd been bad enough back at the Institute for Paranormal Dysfunction, when she was just human – or whatever. Or had she been a vampire, even then?

Several head shots? Or to the heart? That was tradi-tional. But why take the chance? Getting out of the car he opened the trunk, thumb-scanned then flipped up the lid of the weapons locker, considering his options. The Nemesys Nova, he decided, and hefted out the small flamethrower. *If they can't stand the sun, they sure as hell won't like this.*

Pumped on adrenaline, the next minute seemed to take forever. Moving into the trees, he slowed as he caught sight of them in the distance. The two broke from their kiss, the girl waving as the bike powered off. He cut his link to the traffic drone as it followed the departing vampire.

Amid stark shades of light-intensified greens and blacks, he approached quietly through dew-softened grass. But fifty meters away the girl suddenly spun round.

She met his eyes.

Well, at least that answered the question of whether vampires could see in the dark. "Hold it right there," he called, continuing to close on her. He stopped when they were still four meters apart. He saw her eyes widen as she recognized him, saw her mouth open to speak-

Then she clamped it shut, her expression going from angry to cagey. As if she'd only just remembered she was in disguise, and hoped he hadn't recognized her. Inwardly, he smiled. *I can play along with that.*

"As a duly appointed officer of the law," he began, "I order you to stand where you are and put your hands on your head." Force of habit made him pull out his ID card and hold it up despite the darkness. Briefly, knowing Eagle would move to protect her if she was brought in, he considered just killing her here and now, claiming she'd attacked him.

For several seconds she did nothing, merely looked at the card, then at his face, then finally at his chunky flamethrower like she knew what it was. Slowly, she did as he'd ordered.

"I have reason to believe you were involved in a multiple homicide in the West Oakland Dumps at or about 5:35 this morning." He proceeded to tell her her rights, which she listened to with an odd smirk. Smug, like so many of these damned magical monsters. Especially the ones that looked human. "I have reason to believe you are a vampire," he added, wanting to wipe the smile off her face.

She looked surprised for a second, but then her expression blossomed into a full-fledged grin.

"Are you afraid of me?" she asked, sounding suddenly hungry.

He ignored the question, ordering her across the park. She didn't ask where he was taking her. That worried him.

He hadn't patted her down for weapons. But there was no way he was going to step within her reach. Ridiculous, perhaps, with his own augments powered up into full com-bat mode – neural reaction boosters, muscle amplifiers, not to mention being thirty centimeters taller and a hun-dred kilos heavier – but he'd seen her fight: months ago, when she'd almost taken down his team of five; and again, tonight.

He backed up another meter.

Someone had been training her. Was this just an acci-dent, or had Eagle sent his young assassin to be discovered by the Tash creature? To be *turned into* a vampire, if she hadn't been already? The idea of a *vampire* assassin was blood-chilling.

At the edge of the park, by his car, he ordered her to strip. He'd expected a protest – but she only smiled and seemed to relax. One by one her fingers worked at the ties on her jacket, then eased it off.

Against his will, his lips pursed in appreciation before he could school his expression. She smiled.

"The shorts too."

The smile became lazy as she slowly wriggled them down.

Nice, he had to admit, despite the shabby black panties.

"Where's your wristcomm?" It was inconceivable she wasn't Linked.

That brought a frown. "In the Bay."

O-kay.... "Now move back."

Her head tilted and she frowned. Suddenly she looked small, scared. "Please, I'm cold, couldn't you warm me up?"

Seriously? "Move back, miss." His finger tightened on the trigger.

Reluctantly she did so. "Further." When she was a safe distance away – he'd seen how fast she could move – he moved up to her meager clothing. Holstering his gun but keeping the Nova trained on her, he crouched and patted the things down, one-handed, sending a 'freeze' instruction to the roachbug as he checked the collar.

He searched it all. No gun, but there was a cashstick in one pocket – no ID, natch – and a small knife in the other. Stuck to the seam of her shorts he found a micro-speaker connected to what an image search revealed to be an acoustic transducer. He frowned at them for long seconds, but couldn't imagine their purpose. Some kind of audio recorder? Briefly, he considered crushing it, but decided against it. He took them all, then moved back.

"Okay, you can get dressed again."

She glared at him for long, long seconds before stalking back to the small pile of clothes. He could almost see steam coming from her ears. Not used to having her charms resisted, he guessed. How many men had she seduced and then killed?

Her eyes never left his as she dressed.

He drew out a nylon cuff-tie and tossed it at her feet. "Cuff yourself."

A strange look appeared on her face. "I don't know how to. I've never worn one."

She was lying, he could tell. Probably been in and out of cells before she hit puberty. He talked her through it anyway, watching carefully as she pulled the end of the tie taut with her teeth, locking her wrists together.

Something about the look in her eyes as she did so made him take another step back.

Then he opened the rear door of his car and moved away, gesturing her over, and had her buckle herself into the safety belt in the rear seat, passenger's side.

He tossed another cuff-tie into her lap. "Now the ankles."

She did that, too. He was getting worried by how calmly she was doing as she was told. Like she thought she could get out of the bonds any time she liked. He'd been planning to take her in himself, alone, but suddenly changed his mind. He imagined her getting free, tearing him apart from the back seat.

She stared at him, hostile but waiting. Not worried.

He could see her, slaughtering Sanchez and Henderson. The certainty flooded through him. He pictured Berlusconi's expression, in a few hours' time. Yeah, he'd take her in to the police, not to the Bureau.

Still she stared, and suddenly he needed to puncture that smug self-assuredness. He smiled at her. "You've been a busy girl recently, haven't you, Sara? How many people have you killed, the last few months?"

Her eyes widened in shock. With enormous pleasure he moved up, keeping the door between them, then slammed it shut and activated the locks. He checked the time. The metro police'd be here in just over forty minutes.

He could send the car off on its own, but his gut told him she wouldn't still be inside when it arrived.

In the car, Sara wriggled, looking uncomfortable. Voice muffled by the glass, she called out. "It's getting light. Unless you get me under cover you're going to have a burned corpse in custody."

He frowned, glancing at the dark sky, slightly graying. Clearly she was hoping for a chance to break free when he moved her. Instead he smiled, and ordered the car's windows to full opacity.

CHAPTER 54

Leeth blinked in surprise as darkness enveloped her. It wasn't what she'd hoped for, but it might be enough. Wasting no time, she unclipped the safety restraint, summoning the slicing sharpness into her hands, feeling the prickle as invisible claws unfurled. One quick movement parted the tough nylon ties round her ankles, but then she struggled, trying to twist her hands to angle the magical edge to sever the tie around her wrists.

She couldn't reach!

Gritting her teeth she tried again.

Nothing.

She brought the nylon bond to her mouth, and began desperately chewing at it. A minute later, teeth aching and wrists wet, she stopped. It wasn't going to work.

Panting, she pulled, the cords tightening, cutting into her flesh until they drew blood. He'd taken her knife, too.

A cool anger descended. Eyes shut, her breath started to come faster and faster, hissing through her nostrils.

'*You must control your anger.*' Dojo's words rose in her mind. This was just another kind of battle.

In the early morning stillness, locked in the car, hearing the tiny sounds of the man waiting quietly outside, she slowed her breathing.

Calm. She pictured her surroundings. The car. The man.

Opening her eyes, she studied the door on the side opposite him, picking out details in the gloom.

Gently, then, she stretched out full length against the back seat, her arms over her head, bracing her hands – still tied – against the door nearest her captor. Then slowly, mentally measuring, she drew up her feet to where the lock mechanism must be.

Garland saw the car suddenly lurch at some impossible impact from inside, and heard metal tearing. Jumping back, compact flamethrower up and trained on the car, reflexes boosted to max, he waited. Again the impact, but this time the sound of metal *snapping*. His eyes widened as he realized the thing had burst a door open.

Shit! Could he contain her on his own, or...? Fuck it! «Code Red»

The signal broadcast, he raced around the car and onto the quiet street, weapon tracking back and forth for a target. At the far side he stopped to take in the scene.

The door stood wrenched open, the car still shivering from the shock. Inside: emptiness. He dropped, scanning under the car to sight her: nothing.

Shit! Could she have crossed the street? Or had she circled back, into the cover of the park?

A whisper of sound from the road behind him brought him spinning up and around, but before he could bring the weapon to bear, a two-handed blow smashed into his wrists and sent the Nova flying.

He had the fleeting impression of a female face snarling into his as one slim leg deflected his own kick almost contemptuously. She somersaulted. *Something* slammed between his eyes, then doubled fists hammered his face, and a female fury rode him down into darkness.

Leeth stood over him, panting, wanting to rip him apart, hands burning with the urge to kill. Not sure why she even fought against it.

Three times! This was the *third time* he'd tried to capture her! *I should kill him, once and for all.*

And then she remembered Mother and Father's instructions: no killing, except nominated targets. Unless in emergencies.

Surely this was an emergency?

Decide later. Get us both out of sight, first. Hands still tied, she bent down, grabbing his coat front and dragging his body off the road and over to the bushes at the edge of the run-down, overgrown park. Had he called for back-up? She probably didn't have much time.

Moving straight back to the car, she hopped inside, and with a two-handed grip on the car mat, wiped down the places where she might have left prints. She wriggled back out, bumping the door as shut as it'd now go, and ran back into the undergrowth. Still dark; no one around; in the distance, the whisper of cars on the freeway.

What to do? The guy was still breathing. A bit unevenly, though.

With a practiced ease despite her bound hands, she hauled him deeper into the bushes, frantically searching his pockets till she found Barney's anti-Harmon device, with its double-bite-activated sound replay. A mountain of tension drained from her as she stuck it back into the waistband of her shorts.

She shook herself, then fished her cashstick and knife from his pockets. Crouching over the unconscious man in the undergrowth, she thought things through.

I should probably kill him. But suppose Mother and Father's instructions still apply, even though I don't report to them anymore? Eagle hadn't actually countermanded them. And it'd be pretty cool to have my own nemesis. Plus, if I don't kill him just because of their instructions, they'll have to admit it makes more sense to let me decide for myself.

She nodded. Besides, he was only doing his job. It wasn't like he was a bad guy. Just really annoying.

Then she paused. *So that means* not *killing him is the right thing to do?*

Feeling strangely troubled, she forced the philosophizing aside. With a smooth two-handed motion she reached into his jacket, where he'd gotten the ties to put on *her*. She pulled out a bunch, cheering up. It'd be kind of poetic, tying him up with his own cuffs.

A thought suddenly struck her then, and she slid both hands into the pocket where he'd put his ID card. The symbol on it had looked vaguely familiar.

Actually, very familiar, she saw. She read the card carefully, in the pre-dawn light: Bureau of Internal Development. And the Eagle symbol.

What was going on? That was *them.* Well, not 'them,' but the bigger organization the Accounts Department hid inside.

But then, why was he following me? Or... oh! He must've been following Tash. *That's why he thought I was a vampire.*

She tucked the ID back in his pocket then sat down cross-legged and thought, playing with her knife.

With a start she realized her hands were still tied. A little horrified that it hadn't seemed unusual. *Damn him!* Grinding her teeth, she worked the blade around, sawing at her bonds.

In one smooth movement she stood and stretched, both arms reaching out wide to the pre-dawn sky. She spun around, grinning. This had been the best night of her whole life – better, even, than killing the evil Shepherd Fox and escaping, with Faith! *I wonder what the scarier thing is, behind him?* She remembered the evil rising in his eyes. Something awful. Getting closer, reaching out for her. It felt real, again, as if her mere thought had woken it, like it was once again blindly stretching out-

No! Eagle said not to think about it.

She pushed the thoughts aside, and stared down at Agent Garland, frowning.

She should probably get back – they might've started to wonder where she'd gotten to.

Actually, I could race *back: see if I can beat my best time, in real life this time instead of a dumb VR run on the treadmill.* Her stomach growled as if in protest. "Oh, shut up, you," she told it. "If you're good, I'll hunt us some *chocolate!*" Spurred by the thought, she bent back down over the unconscious man to note the time, on his Link.

She heard the whine of electric motors and the sound of tires on the road beside the park, slowing. Stopping.

His backup!

A car door opened, the soft sound of a heavy tread, then the door closed. As she slithered from the bushes, the chill morning air seemed to wrap around her. But moments later, she was sprinting silently away, undetected.

Eight minutes later, steam puffing from her mouth in the light of the WalMech booth, she slammed to a stop in front of the vending mart and inserted her cashstick. "Chocolate. Dark," she panted. Four clearly numbered possibilities projected in front of her. She made her choice and slid the cashstick back into her pocket as the armored dispenser slid open. Ripping open the wrapper she crunched into the bar. "Mmm," she shut her eyes, savoring the chill still air and the deserted streets... but mostly just savoring the intense bitter sweetness melting slowly in her mouth. This had been the *best* night. Cramming the rest of the bar in, she jammed the empty wrapper into her pocket, then sprinted off again into the fading darkness, a foolish grin plastered over her face as the chocolate slowly dissolved.

CHAPTER 55

Marc Disten noted the damage to the inside of the empty car's door. His head panned across the scene, tracking the invisible resonance.

There: in the bushes. A groan followed by a wash of anger, of course. Disten walked over, staring down at a bound figure that rolled awkwardly to its side. Wrists and ankles had both been bound.

Another groan, then: "Shit." The man coughed, spat, then seemed to become aware of the presence. "Hey, give me a hand, would you? I'm- Holy fuck! You're the zombie from the 'Fest. Let me loose. I'm an agent of the-"

Ignoring the words, Disten drew on gloves, taking care with the injured hand, then clamped an iron grip on the man's shoulder. "You followed the girl here from the Dumps. How do you track her?"

Garland frowned, that same shudder of unease shocking through him, triggering his systems into combat mode. "I am an agent of the Bureau of Internal Development. You need to untie me."

The man continued searching through his pockets. "You will be released after you explain how you follow the girl." One hand clamped against his bicep, and squeezed. Immediately, diagnostic systems flared red warnings – *Excessive strain! Component failure!* – while flesh and bone sent their own, more urgent signals.

"What the fuck? Stop that!"

"You are augmented. You track her through implanted systems."

Jesus, what was this freak? He acted like a ro-

Holy fuck! 'A big man. Spoke like a robot.' The Breaker. That fucking idiot, Sara, had left him tied up for *The Breaker!*

He had to break free – now! Agony at his wrists as augmented muscles strained against nylon bonds. He ground his teeth as the ties cut through his flesh, right to the bone. Nylon *snapped.* But his arms remained bound. She'd used more than one set!

He triggered the distress call. But it wasn't enough. *I need to get word out, warn Berlusconi Sara isn't The Breaker.* That they'd been wrong all along.

Snap! But... Three *ties, Sara? You're fucking kidding me!*

"You are calling for assistance. That cannot be permitted."

His trenchcoat was flipped over his head, then hands clamped to the sides of his head, pressing inward with impossible force. Garland's vision went red as he heard his ex-partner's phone start ringing. Berlusconi answered. *Thank god!* «Sara-»

Red pain ended all thought.

The man's coat had prevented brain and other matter from marking Disten's own clothing. The ID card was studied while fluids from the crushed head leaked into the dry soil.

Disten read the card again. Apparently the Bureau of Internal Development was also following the girl. This man named Garland had been present – hiding – when the Tash creature had removed the unconscious girl from the fighting event.

Garland had been connected to the girl. Garland had a way of following her. Garland had been uncooperative.

But there had been no tracking equipment in any of the agent's pockets. The equipment was no doubt integrated. Which would likely make the death pointless.

Disten dropped the ID card and peeled the dampened coat back from the remains of the man's head, avoiding the clumps of brain matter that slid along it to the ground. The smell of blood and offal was strong in the still air.

Leaning forward, the brain was examined. Fishing around, threads could be felt. Glass-like fibers led from an optical implant behind the eyes to an unfamiliar device at the back of the skull. What remained of it. The device tugged free with only a little resistance. The only thing recognizable was a data cube.

Prised carefully free, it was wiped on the coat and pocketed. More delving revealed nothing further. Pushing out of the bush, then peeling off the rubber gloves, Disten carefully bagged then pocketed them.

The cube could contain interesting information.

CHAPTER 56

Beside the floating image of the state park, Father gestured another smaller holo into existence alongside, this one showing the Doctor seated in a comfortable lounge chair in the center of a ritual Circle. Abruptly he seemed to wake, and looked directly into the video pickup.

"Yes, Doctor?" asked Father, simultaneously patching sound into the link. "You have a result?"

"She's close, perhaps even outside! I'm going out." With one motion he broke the Circle and stretched out on the floor, his body slumping as if lifeless, while he astrally projected.

"Nelson, external scans!" Father transmitted. "I want her imaged, now." Another gesture and each external camera feed appeared, tiled as three rows of small images under the larger holo of the Mt Diablo park. He killed the main projection and zoomed up the smaller images.

"Got her," Nelson declared, linking in from his techlair, casually taking control of Father's display and zooming up one of the images above all the others.

On a view of one of the narrow streets above the Department's underground complex, deep gray in the early morning light, a lone girl was running – *sprinting* – down the street toward the camera. Leeth. Nelson blinked at the amount of blood on her clothes. She seemed to grin up at him as she flashed under the camera and out of view. "That's the entrance to the car park, Jessie St," he told them. He highlighted another of the floating rectangular images, this one a view in a stairwell. It only caught her for a second, as she jumped the entire flight of stairs, one hand on the railing to spin herself round the corner at the bottom. Nelson tracked her all the way to the final lock at the end of a long gray cement corridor, where she keyed for entry.

In the ritual magic room, Harmon stirred and sat up. His voice was hoarse. "I've just been Out. She's entering the complex." He took a breath, finally relaxing. "She will be coming in by entrance three right now. She should be on your security monitors already."

Father nodded, eyes still fastened to the camera viewing the street as he checked for any visible pursuit. "Thank you Doctor. Once again you tell us what we already know. Is she being followed?"

"Imaginally? No, nothing following her. Nor were

there any flares as she crossed the outer Barrier, so she's clean of spells and magical linkages."

A holo of Nelson winked into existence. He looked disappointed. "Preliminary physical security checks are clean, too. But there's still the bio and bug checks to come."

"And her state?" Father asked, turning back to Harmon's face.

"Imaginally, she seemed, ah, effervescent."

"Infected?"

"I don't... I don't think so."

"But possible?"

There was a silence. "Yes."

Mother responded. "Emma. James. Bring her here – but use caution. Doctor –" she spoke louder, to the mage in his rooms, "leave your body again. I want her watched Imaginally at all times. Return to warn us if you detect anything unusual."

"Certainly."

Mother turned to the two agents. "Well? Don't just stand there. Go, you two!"

She glared at Father. "This is ludicrous. Her second 'mission,' and she manages to go missing *again*, completely. Then, hours overdue, she fails to even make contact before returning. Clearly, her status as an operative should be revoked."

Father looked grim. "We should wait for the reports."

"Oh, boy! Has Preacher told you about it?" Leeth spoke in short breaths, panting. "It was boosty! I had a *savage* time." She grinned up at James. "Did you know you can fight in time to music?"

"Ah, no, I can't say that ever occurred to me."

"Yeah, it's like dancing, but you get to hit people! It feels *amazing* when it's all in time to the rhythm. You can even do it just to a tune in your head." She stomped and spun to an invisible beat.

James and Emma exchanged a look.

Leeth sighed exaggeratedly. "Ja-a-ames! I'm not *stupid*: I wouldn't do it if my opponent was really good. I *know* it'd make my attacks too predictable. But oh, it's so amazing, we should all try it next time we practice together." She came back and took his arm again. "Oh, oh, guess what else? I even had chocolate!"

Somewhere in the air near the three, the Doctor's astral form hovered, invisible. Imaginal. Pacing them, watching. Leeth's aura pulsed, coiling over her in excited waves, as healthy and energetic as Harmon had ever seen it – a marked contrast to those of the two cyberware-stunted agents alertly bracketing her. He watched her aura, suffused with affection for her colleagues. Affection that had once been there for him, too.

Leeth had one arm linked through James's, and walked pressed up against his side – somewhat to James's regret, when he noticed the fresh blood on her jacket. Emma, following behind, thought Leeth seemed a little... feverish.

She hadn't stopped talking since they'd stepped inside.

Leeth's panting had eased, though her cheeks were still flushed. Emma flipped her vision to infrared and saw the heat pouring from the girl. She was dripping with sweat, shaking it out of her hair – she'd said she'd run 'all the way home.'

"What happened after Tash took you away?" asked James. He didn't ask about the blood.

"Oh." For a moment Leeth quietened. "How did- Has Preacher already given his report?"

James nodded.

"I had to stay the night with her – I'd bet that."

"So Preacher said. But where did she take you, what did you do?"

Leeth fell silent, her shoulders hunching slightly.

The silence stretched as they walked the bare corridors leading into the Department proper, the whisper-soft echoes of their quiet footsteps a match to the still air and subdued lighting.

«What is your assessment?» Mother asked James and Emma over the Department's internal net, her voice digitally piped to the agents' auditory interfaces.

«Alive- very. Almost hyper,» he answered sub-vocally, along the same channel. «You heard me ask what she's been doing?»

«Yes. I'm patched in to you. I also heard her fail to answer.»

Emma, in the link-up, tried to think of something to say in Leeth's defense, but couldn't forget that the girl had shared *something* with a vampire, tonight. She too had nothing to offer.

Ahead, behind a stretch of unmarked wall, the final checkpoint waited. James and Emma's stomachs tightened with each step forward. Surely, she wouldn't have agreed to carry in any devices given to her by the vampire?

Leeth continued forward, moving past the scanner.

The alarm's buzz struck with the shock of an electric current. Emma chilled, smoothly stepping further back while drawing her weapon. James wheeled, holding up one hand to stop Leeth even as he moved out of her reach and drew his own gun.

Leeth looked from James, to Emma, to the two barrels trained on her; trying to understand.

A melodious synthetic female voice replaced the warning tone. "Unidentified radio antenna detected on operative Leeth. Probability 90%. Location: neck or collar." Leeth shook her head in denial, but the dispassionate voice continued. "Neural control circuitry detected. Probability: 98%. Location: neck or collar."

Emma saw horrified belief dawn on the girl's face, feeling the shame as if it were her own. The implacable voice continued. "Insect infestation detected. Quantity: one. Probability: 80%. Location: neck or collar. Family: roach.

"Analysis: Class A location or eavesdropping device. Probability: 95%. No transmissions currently detected. Electromagnetic shielding status: fully operational."

The voice fell silent.

CHAPTER 57

For Leeth, the shame of being bugged was nothing compared to learning that the two agents in the Department she'd thought liked her best were ready to kill her.

But how...? Had *Tash* put the bug there? She squeezed her eyes shut. *Another betrayal.*

She reached up to rip her jacket off.

James twitched his gun. "Stop."

Leeth froze, disbelieving. All this time, she'd thought they liked her. But one stupid alarm and they were treating her like an enemy. Her jaws clamped shut as her mind cooled to a chill clarity. Leeth remembered Tash's words. Was she right? Would she never fit in, even with people like James, and Emma? Had Tash bugged her just to make that point?

Had it been a mistake, coming back in the first place? Were Eagle's promises just more lies? *But Eagle's never lied to me. He's not like the Doctor.*

Or was this another stupid test? Did they want to see how she reacted? She wasn't far inside. If she took out James, used his body as a shield...

But from their expressions, if it *was* just a test, no one had told James or Emma. She'd have to hurt them. And she didn't want to hurt them.

She shook her head. When the words came, they sounded so worn down she hardly recognized her own voice. "What do you want me to do?"

Inwardly, James winced. "The checkpoint can burn the circuits, but that'd send the roach wild and it'd run. We want to capture it without damaging it. Wait. They're sending an aerosol."

Leeth grimaced. "I really have a *cockroach* in my clothes?"

Emma felt a surge of warmth and fought to keep the smile off her face. *Leeth was still herself.* Suddenly she was sure of it.

James simply nodded. "Just take off the jacket and roll it up, carefully and slowly. You've been bugged, literally. A neural implant to override the roach's own-"

"Brain functions. I know, I know, you don't have to lecture me! I *did* pay attention to my lessons." She sounded cross.

At that, Emma had to smile.

"I'm going to take out a knife now, James, to cut these

ties," Leeth said, gesturing to the knotted shreds of cloth tying the denim jacket closed. "I'm pretty dangerous, though, so you'd better watch carefully." She slid the knife slowly out of its wrist sheath.

With her back to the wall, she began undulating. "Look, I'm cutting the first tie, ever so carefully."

The two agents stilled as they realized she'd begun a striptease.

«Careful. This could be a trap,» warned Mother, observing through Emma's eyes.

Emma only snorted. Then together, she and James escorted Leeth to her meeting.

In the briefing room, Leeth examined their faces, not seeing understanding in any of them. Except the Doctor's. He smiled at her. Her eyes narrowed, and she turned away, to Father. "But I promised her I wouldn't tell. Not *anyone*."

Off to one side, Preacher slouched against the wall. He looked even smugger than usual.

Mother clicked her tongue in annoyance, looking away from the girl seated opposite her. "I think this shows more clearly than I can argue that the girl's first loyalty is not to the Department. I recommend-"

Harmon spoke quickly. "Excuse me, Mother, if I may interrupt for a moment. On the contrary, my young ward is demonstrating an *over*-developed sense of loyalty. So I'm sure that, given a moment to consider, her *first* loyalty will become clear to her."

Leeth bristled, annoyed that *he* was defending her. Probably just trying to worm his way back. She sighed. "Well. I had to at least *try*."

No one spoke.

"Oh, all right. She took me back to her place." Reluctantly, she described the location, not very well. "I was unconscious when she took me there, and she blindfolded me when we left."

"How convenient," murmured Mother.

Leeth glared. "Why are *you two* questioning me, anyway? I'm supposed to report directly to Eagle."

Father looked angry. "Eagle can not be at your beck and call. We will debrief you, and he will review our report. It's the same procedure for all our agents. Now, continue: Tash took you to her lair...."

Leeth scowled at him. "Yeah, real nice views for a 'lair', too." Father's expression hardened, and Leeth saw she wasn't doing herself any favors. She sighed. "I'd been healed, 'cause I was okay when I woke up. We, ah, went out for dinner, and, uh, *stuff*, then made love-"

Harmon's breath hissed out, and she stopped. His gaze was intense. "And did- was the experience, ah, unusually powerful?" he asked, face pale.

"Uh, yeah. It was pretty good."

"Exceptional?"

"Doctor, I really don't think this is the time for you to indulge your prurient-"

"Mother!" he snarled, "this is *not* for my amusement."

"It doesn't sound like it. You are already on thin ice and should consider yourself fortunate to be included in this debriefing," she warned him. "One more outburst and you can go back to your rooms."

Harmon calmed himself. "When a vampire drains its victim, Mother, they invariably describe an extraordinary bliss." He turned back to the girl. "Was it *exceptional?*"

She stared him in the eye. "Better even than *our* first time." She felt a curious pain as she saw her words strike home and his face freeze. She hardened her heart. Wishing she could stab him with more than just words.

But then she noticed all the others' expressions. "What? What's the matter?" she asked, trying to understand their reaction. Yearning to tell them *more*. But even those few words had pushed the limits of what she could say. "It wasn't *bliss*, though."

Emma touched her on the shoulder. "Maybe you should just go on, Leeth. What happened then?"

Then we rescued Marcie, and a bunch of kids. But if I say Marcie followed me, they might think she's been investigating the Department. Which would not be good.

"Well, Leeth? We're waiting," Mother said.

"Um, did I mention Marcie's got an audition for an action hero role? So I told her to disguise herself, get a bodyguard, and come along to watch the 'Fest."

Mother and Father looked at her in shock. Emma flinched, and James looked away. *Dammit!* But she had to protect Marcie. She let herself look embarrassed. "Yeah, pretty dumb, in hindsight. Unfortunately, the bodyguard was a scumbag. So the first thing me and Tash had to do was, um, rescue Marcie and a bunch of children from....” She stared grimly at the Doctor, before her expression went blank. After several seconds, she seemed to shake herself. “And then, we went Hunting PsychoBloods.”

The Doctor just sighed, then shut his eyes. Leeth looked around, seeing they were all watching her, again, like she’d said something strange. It was Mother who finally broke the silence.

“Leeth. Are you telling us you went out hunting this morning with a *vampire*?”

The girl cheered up, nodding vigorously. “Yeah. It was abz.”

“Abz?”

Preacher spoke up, automatically. “Absolute zero. Maximum chill.”

“Well, at least she seems to have picked up some of the street language,” offered Emma.

The look Mother turned on her was *not* one of amusement. “And where did you acquire the roachbug? This ‘Tash,’ I assume. Or did you provide other opportunities for people to try to penetrate our security?”

Leeth glared. “I haven’t been trained yet on how to stop people doing stuff when I’m unconscious.”

Mother glared back. “A good agent examines herself thoroughly after she has given hostiles an opportunity to compromise her equipment.”

Father interrupted the glaring contest. “Anything else?”

“Oh. Yeah. There is one other thing. That detective who keeps arresting me did it again a little while ago and I had to knock him out. Someone might want to check that out. I left him tied up in some bushes.” She scrunched up her face, trying to remember his name.

“You know, that big cybered guy, Garland. The one who brought the Doctor and me into the Department. I think he must’ve been following Tash. He thought *I* was a vampire, too.” She frowned. “I thought he was police, but his ID said he works for the *Bureau*. When did that happen?”

No one said anything. She looked around at them all, and it was like they’d all been turned into dummies. Again. She guessed that meant they wanted her to go on.

"I left him alive. He's dumb as a bag of rocks, but he was only doing his job. Maybe one of you could tell him to lay off me before he gets himself hurt?"

Still no one said anything.

"I knocked him out maybe... half an hour ago? How long does it take for someone to wake up after they're knocked unconscious?"

"That depends on how hard he was knocked out."

"Um. Pretty hard, axly. I didn't want him to wake up."

They all stared at her.

"'Axly' is just Street for 'actually'," she explained. Still they stared at her. *Unless...* "I don't mean I didn't want him to wake up *ever,* just not before I'd got away."

Mother took a breath. "Where exactly is the body, Leeth?"

"That old park on Potrero Hill. Where Emma took me for that first, test 'social interaction' exercise-"

Mother grimaced. "Yes. How could we forget."

"His car's parked at the south edge of the park. I, uh, may have broken its door. He's tied up in some bushes near it."

Mother massaged her forehead. "James, see to it. Don't take *your* car. Nelson, break into the city-sat systems for the time period shortly before dawn this morning. Edit Leeth from any recording at Potrero Hill. Ensure James is digitally masked while he cleans the site. Take copies of the original material for the Department first, of course."

She glared at the girl. "Any other 'minor details,' Leeth, you may have forgotten?"

All at once Leeth felt drained, exhausted. She didn't answer, just shook her head. A long time seemed to pass with no one speaking, and when she at last looked up, she wondered if she'd missed something, Mother looked so cross.

Opening her mouth for some other cutting remark, both Mother and Father jerked. And suddenly, Mother looked furious. *Now what've I done?*

But unknown to Leeth, Eagle's face had opened in a virtual window on the retinas of her two questioners, interrupting. «Further questioning at this time will be pointless. Allow her to rest.»

Mother's jaw worked for long seconds, before she focused back on the girl, snapping out words like they were bitter bullets. "Dismissed, then. Have your report ready by noon. And perhaps you might factor in Tash's bugging of you when you consider how much information on *her* to provide to us. It may help remind you where your inconstant loyalties *should* lie."

Leeth glared back – but nodded and left the room.

-

Mother pursed her lips. "You coddle that girl. Why did you terminate the questioning? At the end, she had finally reached a state of exhaustion. We would easily have had the truth from her."

Father looked away, wishing he could distance himself further as Eagle turned impassively to her. "Observe." A story-boarded transcription of the debriefing suddenly hung before Mother, bio-medical monitor tracings below each frame. "I draw your attention to her ATP levels, the lactic acid build up, the blood sugar level. She should not have been functioning. She was past the point of exhaustion by the time the de-briefing *started*."

He waited, silent, as Mother and Father examined the monitor traces carefully. Mother was frowning.

"It was clear to me she was concealing nothing. It's doubtful she was even aware of having done anything wrong."

Mother shrugged an ill-graced acceptance. "What about Garland?"

"You've seen his assignment schedule. He is currently on standby."

"Really. You hadn't assigned him to watch over Leeth?"

Eagle's eyes targeted Mother coldly. "You assume I am a fool, Mother? I have had Nelson access Agent Garland's virtspace. He recently began investigating violent deaths in and around the city, including the Hunters Point and West Oakland Dumps."

Mother frowned. "And you think Leeth may be involved?"

For the first time in Mother's memory, Eagle looked uncomfortable. "It is a possibility, yes."

Father spoke. "Nelson has just analyzed the roach: it was one of the Bureau's. Garland's?"

"Probable," Eagle agreed.

They absorbed that. No one, of course, suggested informing Leeth that Tash had *not* betrayed her.

Eagle updated them on Garland's movements and activities through the night, including a call for emergency backup shortly before Leeth's return. "That backup will arrive in approximately one minute. I have ordered James to hold back."

Mother shook her head. "This is a mess."

Father frowned. "Leeth does seem to have a talent for creating problems."

Eagle sighed. "Neither of you see it? It's not about controlling her. It's about unleashing her."

They both looked unconvinced.

Mother scrolled back to Garland's file. "I see he has video cyberware. You've sealed it?"

"That is not currently possible," Eagle said. "Garland is not responding to pings. I have given all accessible data related to his activities last night a level five clearance rating."

"Garland's not *Linked*? How hard did Leeth hit him?" Mother snarled.

"It's now 6:26. We'll find out shortly."

They did. Five minutes later, Nelson offered them a data feed with barely-repressed excitement.

Father watched the report from the scene with a heavy heart. The footage of Garland's remains was more than disturbing. His head had been crushed like a pumpkin. Indicating strength, probable martial skills, and a disrespect for human life bordering on sickness.

Leeth said she'd hit him hard.

Worse, though, was that she'd lied about it. She had been specifically instructed not to retire anyone unless warranted during her bouts at the FistFest, or in self-defense.

Of greatest concern, though, was that she'd been able to fool Eagle. Father had never heard of anyone doing that before. Perhaps Mother was right, and for some reason Eagle did indeed have a soft spot for the girl. A blind spot.

Which would make her incredibly dangerous to all of them. *Incredibly.*

CHAPTER 58

Her alarm dragged Leeth from sleep after four hours. She woke starving, buried deep in her bed. Struggling free, she almost tripped on the leather shorts she'd apparently fallen asleep removing.

She called Marcie, to make sure she wasn't in trouble with her dad, but there was no answer. *Probably hasn't replaced her Link, yet.* She sent a text, instead, asking her to call. And ordered *herself* a fresh Link to replace the one that Tash had thrown in the Bay.

Her denim jacket lay on the floor. Picking it up, she savored the smoky smells, surprised and impressed by the amount of dried blood on it.

The shower was bliss. She found herself daydreaming about the blood, imagining the Department analyzing it and discovering.... *Uh oh! Some of that'd be Tash's!* Scattering water, she raced back and grabbed up her jacket, darting back into the bathroom and throwing it under the spray. She stepped back in on top of it, where her massaging feet and the water beating down were soon washing ribbons of pink evidence into the drain. She sighed, just enjoying the beating spray... until she belatedly remembered the report she had to write. Wringing the jacket out, she jumped from the shower and tossed it in the dryer.

An hour later, tearing open another muesli bar and cramming half into her mouth, she reviewed her report.

Cross legged on her bath towel, naked on her bed, she frowned down at the display sheet, comparing what she'd written so far against Mother's long list of things 'essential' in a report.

Like who, and when. "Oops! Oh-" she clamped her mouth shut as those words popped onto the screen. She kept forgetting to hold the 'meta' key down on the stylus while editing. She pressed it now. "Undo." Nodding at the erasure, she focused on the top of the screen to re-position the cursor there, and released the key.

"Report by Agent Leeth on assignment of -" she held down the meta key and watched the words '2062/03/25' appear as she said, "yesterday."

She beamed, staring at the word 'Agent'. Then shook herself. *That should do.* It covered everything worth putting down. Was it too long, though? There were almost two whole pages just on the 'Fest. But then, Mother did always say completeness was important. She skimmed it one last time. Mission objective. Following 'Dad.' Meeting Crack; Tash. Hagjabber fight. Maneater. Distracting Nightslice, calming him down, the holo of them jamming – and erasing it, later. The Nightslice fight. Weight-lifting. Hagjabber and Black Paul; her broken ribs. The questioning about her fighting abilities; how Dad had helped; a bit. Then the final fight with Tash. The surprise healing, first. And that last combat: how strong Tash had been; how fast she'd healed.

Losing.

Leeth shut her eyes, fighting down the shame. At last, with an effort, she continued checking her report. Another whole page, covering Tash's place near Mount Diablo, biking back to West Oakland, the Club Juzz rescue, making love with Tash in the storm water tunnel, followed by the drug gangers hunt. Being dropped off a few klicks away by Tash. Garland capturing her, then turning the tables on him. She smiled. Finally, running back here, arriving before sunrise. And the bug. She still had trouble believing Tash had bugged her. She'd thought about suggesting other possibilities: like Preacher, or Nelson; or Nightslice. Or even some random person in the crowd. But she couldn't see a way to suggest that without making herself sound like someone easily tricked.

And her winnings: over sixteen thousand creds! Though she still owed Teef a thousand....

She'd even finished with a special 'Conclusion' section that read simply: *operation successful*. She stared at the words with pride.

Especially since she'd also avoided *actually* getting accepted into Preacher's gang. That would've sucked.

The report was now over three pages long, though. Maybe that *was* too much?

Well, too bad. It'd taken her ages to write it, so they could just wade through the whole thing. She held down the meta key. "Send a copy to Eagle. And Father. Oh. Better send a copy to Mother, too."

She checked the time and smiled – a minute before noon. She'd judged things just right, as usual!

Five minutes later, while finishing her interrupted shower, she got a call to come to briefing room two: *immediately*. Commanding the shower off, she hopped out of the stall, dripped across the floor again as she grabbed the fluffy towel from her bed and started flailing herself dry. At the wardrobe she gave her short hair one last violent scrub, dropping the towel and hopping into a pair of panties as she scanned the hangers. Nodding then, she grabbed a black leather microskirt to show off her legs properly, and jumped into it, wriggling it up over her hips.

Better check the jacket. She drew it, still warm, from the dryer. You couldn't see any blood, now. Holding the tough fabric to her breasts, she shut her eyes, remembering the night before: the heat of the fires, the cheers of the crowd, Barney bouncing with delight on Teef's shoulders. Lifting it to her nose, smoky aromas still clung faintly to the cloth, and she made her decision. Shrugging it on, she tied the front loosely closed, then just for fun pirouetted for the onlookers: the people in the poster images from *Dark Sorcery*; the singer, Jack Shadow; and the whole crew of the Phase Ship *Demons-bane*. And, in pride of place, the poster Marcie had given her, as a *gift*. The big red 'S' in its diamond-shaped frame.

Putting on the bot-delivered Link, she frowned when she saw Marcie hadn't called her back. *Probably hasn't replaced her Link. Should I call Amanda?*

But she knew she had no time. She paused, at a sudden thought. "Okay, Link: is Marcie Dunkirk still under observation? Is she at home?"

Her Link chimed. "Marcie Dunkirk is no longer under surveillance."

Rats! She grabbed up her last muesli bar – they sure disappeared quickly – and ran for the briefing room. She'd contact Marcie straight after her meeting, though.

She wondered why they'd wanted her to come to the briefing room *immediately*, though? *Had they been* waiting *for my report?*

She smiled. How good was that!

PART III

Foe

Father and Mother sat side by side behind the large black desk, looking unhappy enough for even Leeth to notice it, as she came to a stop facing them. She surreptitiously glanced down at herself. Had the jacket been a bad choice?

Even more puzzling, Dojo stood nearby, hands clasped behind his back. He nodded to her, but didn't smile. *What was sensei doing here?*

Mother spoke. "The woman- that is, the vampire, Tash – there was no trace of her at the dwelling you described."

Leeth tried to hide her relief.

"You don't appear surprised by that," accused Mother.

Leeth almost blurted out that she was *pleased*, but closed her mouth in time. As the information sank in though, her expression changed to one of genuine puzzlement. *How had Tash known to move?* Leeth's stomach felt hollow. *It* was *her: she* did *bug me.* She had trouble believing it, even now.

They were still waiting. "Uh... really?"

"Perhaps you described the wrong location. By *mistake*," Mother suggested.

Leeth bristled. "I did *not!*"

"Take a seat," Father gestured, waiting while she did so. He piped the real-time graphs of her biometric data into a small virtual window positioned just to the right of her face. For a moment, he felt nostalgia for the old retinal displays, but had to admit the visual cortex linkage was richer.

Interestingly, as the readings settled, it looked like she was feeling eagerness rather than worry. No fear, no remorse. No admission of her own wrong-doing. A compulsive liar? Mildly sociopathic, perhaps?

It also appeared she'd mostly recovered from her exhaustion after only a few hours of sleep. No surprises there. Dojo had described her recuperative powers at length.

"You have stayed in your room and made no outside net links."

Leeth wasn't sure if Father was asking her or telling her, but she answered anyway. "Sure."

"Did you warn her that people might come looking for you?"

"No!" At first indignant, her expression changed to one of consideration. She wrinkled her nose, uncertain.

"Maybe she's just very careful about that sort of thing. You wouldn't live to that age if you weren't, I guess."

Father's eyes narrowed. "What age, Leeth?"

She shrugged. "I dunno. A hundred, maybe? Two?"

"What leads you to believe that? Why wasn't it in your report?"

Leeth grimaced. "Uh, I didn't think about it till just now."

Father closed his eyes, gently massaging the bridge of his nose.

Mother looked at her with amusement. "Why do you think she was very old? Were her speech patterns particularly archaic?"

"Huh?"

Now Mother's eyes squeezed shut. With a very visible effort, she re-phrased her question. "Did she speak in an old-fashioned way?"

"Oh. Um, maybe? I'm not an expert. She used some words I didn't know. I picked up some extra street talk from her, axly."

Mother pursed her lips. "Wonderful. But since we are not especially interested in your wild guesses, I think it's just as well you chose to leave that out of your report."

Leeth bristled. "It's not a wild guess! It's intuition."

Mother stared at her a moment, teetering between anger and amusement. "You do realize magic only began working in '36?"

"Sure."

"Preacher reports that Tash appears about thirty-five."

The girl half shrugged, half nodded.

"Then *assuming* some creatures can magically avoid aging, and this woman became a vampire in her mid-thirties, growing no older from that point, she could be no more than sixty."

Leeth looked stubborn. "Sixty is old, sure, but she's wise, like someone'd be if they got *really* old. That's why I said a hundred. Oh: wait! She could speak like a pirate: that's old-fashioned!" Leeth sat back, triumphant.

Mother stared at her for long seconds with her lips parted, then closed them briefly before taking a breath. "Then you had better see if you can provide a concrete reason for that estimate. Since it will require the world's foremost theoretical mages to re-think their fundamental theories about the Unfolding, won't it?"

"Why? Lord Shen is thousands of years old."

Mother adopted an exaggerated expression of surprise. "Really? How do you happen to know the age of the Emperor of China?"

"I looked up dragons on the net. There was this old interview, before he took over China. Where he admitted he was thousands of years old."

Mother shook her head tiredly. "Leeth, you have depths of naivety we may never plumb. He was *lying*. Dragons are masters of the lie. That whole interview was simply an exercise in manipulating public opinion. Just one small move in the whole complex game Lao Pi Shen played to seize power at the end of '36."

"But there've been stories about dragons for thousands of years. Why couldn't some things, like dragons and vampires, have survived?"

"Leeth, those creatures only make sense, can only exist, through magic. And while magic may have operated in our distant past, there hasn't been any magic around to keep things like that alive- or, let's say 'functional' – until 2036 and the Week of Miracles."

"Well, I think he was telling the truth."

"Oh? Why?"

"I already told you: 'cause I have good intuition."

Mother raised her eyebrows in elegant disbelief.

Leeth scowled and hunched back in her seat.

"I'm sure your metaphysical speculations would be of great interest to scholars everywhere, but let's move on to the next point. Can you explain why, knowing you had been missing for half the night, you did not contact the Department before your return?"

"Why should I? Do the other agents call you if *they're* going to be late 'home?' Besides, I wasn't missing. I knew where I was. Pretty much. After the 'Fest I was mainly with Tash, and it would've been really out of character to buy a Link to make a call. She'd thrown mine in the Bay. I left her as soon as I could, though, after we'd, uh, finished. I got her to drop me off in Potrero. From there I knew I'd be back in twelve minutes or so."

Mother looked surprised for a moment, then smiled. "That's interesting. Where exactly in Potrero did this creature leave you?"

Father noticed the smile, knowing the trap was about to close. The shocking thing was that *Eagle* was unaware Leeth had to be working with an unknown party. They'd covered their tracks *almost* perfectly.

They might have gotten away with it, too, except he had checked the time recorded by the traffic drone before Nelson erased it. Between the time she'd left the park, to her return to the Department, she'd covered slightly over six kilometers – in 11 minutes 57 seconds. Absurd. A sustained average speed of over thirty kilometers per hour. *Another lie.* They'd even gone to the trouble of having her run the last distance to work up a sweat. The key thing now was to find out who she was working for; what group had transported her from the park.

What surprised him was how disappointed he himself felt. Had she gotten to him, too? He checked the bio-data from her chair. Strangely, it had not registered the lie. The evidence in favor of sociopathy was piling up. *Interesting that the Doctor had failed to notice that....*

"I already told you that, just a few hours ago. The park, remember? Where Emma had me do that social exercise."

Father barely heard her. Perhaps they could use the Doctor to uncover the truth: or to confirm that he too could not be trusted. Perhaps he was a part of it. He *had* helped her avoid them, at the Institute, scarcely a week ago. Had covered for her when she was 'on the run.' What had she really been doing in those four weeks? What secret help had she had, to evade capture? The more he and Mother had discussed it, the larger the ramifications had grown. The girl may even have been specifically designed to infiltrate the Department, trained to fool Eagle! Perhaps, even, by Godsson. And if Godsson and Harmon were both involved, it raised the possibility the Dragon Lord had also had a hand in Leeth's design.

He wondered if that was how she'd been able to retire Fox and smash his cult, where all their other efforts had failed. Perhaps that was why Eagle had recruited her? But the risks in such a game....

They really had to know. Eagle would not argue with that. Although perhaps interrogation under drugs would be a safer course. He glanced across at Dojo, then down at his own holster to check his gun was clear. When Leeth realized she'd been uncovered, things would undoubtedly get very bloody, very fast.

Mother nodded mildly. "Why did you happen to choose that location, Leeth? Are you sure it was that park?"

"Sure." Leeth shrugged. "I knew my way back from there, plus it was a safe distance away. You know, in case anyone tried to connect that location to here."

"You didn't meet anyone else?"

"Not after I got away from that guy, no." Leeth now looked puzzled.

Mother gently closed the trap. "That's a distance of six kilometers, Leeth. You ran all the way? Caught no other transport?"

"Nah. It was such a great night, dawn just breaking and I was still full of...." She shrugged. "I just felt like run-ning, hard. It was great, a really nice end to the evening."

"Six kilometers in twelve minutes." Mother's tone was suddenly sarcastic. "Thirty kilometers per hour."

Leeth frowned down at her hands. "Rats. If I hadn't stopped for chocolate I would have beaten my personal best." She looked up, with a shrug. "I stopped at a WalMech. They had Black Magic bars. *So-o* good."

«Apparently she does not realise we know she – or more likely, Nelson – tampered with the equipment during that 'Runner Grrl' nonsense,» Mother sent to Father.

«You *assume*, Mother,» Father responded. «Nelson swore he had nothing to do with it.»

«Nelson is a hormonal teenager, Father. With the right inducement from our uninhibited new agent, what would Nelson *not* do for her, and lie about afterward? Perhaps *Nelson* has been suborned?»

Mother's expression, which had been cold, had changed to glacial. Leeth sat back, confused. She looked at Father, whose expression was weird, too. It was hard to tell: but he seemed *nervous*. Something was definitely wrong. They both sat watching her, waiting for her to speak.

Mother thought she was lying? And from the look on Father's face, so did he.... They thought she was lying, and were trying to trap her!

With a shiver of excitement she realized she was in a kind of fight with Mother and Father – one of those ones where words and logic were the weapons. Like her uncle and the mean Dr Ahronian, back at the Institute. But now it was *her* turn. Savage! She leaned forward, looking down into her lap, thinking, trying to work out a 'knockout blow.'

The two inquisitors exchanged glances. Dojo's stance, too, shifted.

Abruptly Leeth's head lifted, eager. *First, though, let's soften them up a bit.* "Why am I here talking to you two? I've already been debriefed, even made a *written report*. Eagle promised me I'd be working directly for *him*. And why is sensei here?"

As she'd suspected, Mother and Father tensed, exchanging a knowing look, like they'd expected her to give up like that, and call for Eagle to save her.

She hid her smile, and began a mental count. *One.* From her jacket pocket she brought out the crumpled wrapper, tossing it onto the desk. "Have Nelson check the mech-mart I used. It was on Sixth Street. Near the Skyway."

She wondered: had they forgotten the 'Runner Grrl' VR incident? Or had they actually assumed she'd been *cheating*, back in the virtual marathon? No matter. *Two.* "Check my treadmill times. We could go down there now, if you like. I'll give you a demo."

She waited while they linked to her records; waited until she saw the dawning surprise on their faces. Then attacked again: *three.* "It's your *duty* to know the physical capabilities of your own agents, isn't it?"

Wow. They seemed to be reeling! She sat back in her chair.

Dojo spoke. "Maybe faster than exercise times." He turned to her. "Better in real life, hai?"

She looked up, and saw approval. *Dojo understood.*

Mother's nostrils flared, but she said nothing. Father... it was weird. He picked up the wrapper, his eyes went unfocused, like he was listening to something, and then gave her this kind of goofy grin, *visibly* relaxing.

"Very well, Leeth, that seems acceptable." Then he sighed, the smile vanishing as he moved on. "The next matter is your report itself, Leeth. After having to wait over five hours for it, I must admit I expected more meat. I take it you spent most of your time sleeping rather than working on this," he asked, tapping the side of his head.

Leeth looked mystified. "Working on... on your *head*,

Father? Oh! You can *see it* in your head? Can the others do that? James, and Emma, and Preacher?"

"Yes, Leeth. They can also do a lot more, thanks to Nelson's MetaLife chip. But we all have some augmentation, including access to the Department's net. All except you and the Doctor," Father said.

Leeth felt like smacking her forehead. "So of course they always know what time it is, too."

"Of course."

Rats. And she'd worked so hard to try to do the same thing. No wonder she was so bad at it compared to them!

"But let us return to the matter at hand. Do you think the vampire might have tampered with you while you were unconscious?"

"No-o. I felt okay when I came to at Tash's place. Pretty good, actually." She paused at some thought, then looked sour. "But I guess Tash might've done something to me when she put the bug on me, while I was knocked out." As her own embarrassment deepened, she didn't notice their expressions stiffen. "Uh... she *is* a mage. Did I mention that in my report?"

From Mother and Father's expressions, she hadn't.

"Wait! The Doctor checked me out when I got back this morning, remember?"

"Thank you for the reminder, Leeth." Mother leaned back in her chair. "Then you would attribute your reaction to the drugs you took last night?"

Leeth stared at her in disbelief, then at Father, but his expression was unreadable. She shook her head. "I didn't take any drugs!"

Both stared back at her.

"I didn't! I didn't have anything 'cept water after a sugarkaff with Crack."

Mother's eyes narrowed. *A deliberate ambiguity?* "Crack is an archaic term for a cocaine derivative. You had 'crack' in your drink?"

"No! No, Crack was the guy who bought me the sugarkaff. I had it with him."

"How do you know that's what it was?"

"Well. I do know what coffee tastes like, you know, I *have* had it a couple of times. And saccharin. Besides, I made him drink half of it, first!"

Leeth thought Father looked kind of disappointed.

Mother raised one eyebrow. "Really. How very thorough of you." Her tone of voice brought a flush to Leeth's cheeks.

She had the feeling Mother and Father were making some sort of mental black mark against her.

"Let's return to your report, Leeth," Mother said. "You concluded that the operation was 'successful'?"

"Yes." She lifted her chin. Knowing she'd nailed the Fest, at least!

"Agent Preacher's more detailed report gives a different impression."

Leeth rolled her eyes. "And that surprises you?" *So much for pretending to be my friend.*

"He said your behavior was..." Mother's eyes focused elsewhere, "erratic, jumpy and potentially harmful to the Department's interests." She looked back to Leeth. "He describes you acting as if you were high. Did you consume any prohibited substances, Leeth?"

"No! He's just mad because I beat him when he tried to capture me."

"'And yet Agent James described your behavior on the occasion of your first exercise at the Opera House restaurant in similar terms. Was he 'mad' at you too?"

Leeth looked puzzled.

"You *do* recall the evening? You convinced him to take you into the Tenderloin district, afterward, where you proceeded to kill someone."

"Did I?" She frowned in thought. "Oh. Yeah. The mugger. I remember." She chewed at her lip. She *had* felt kind of the same, that night. Though not quite as bad. *Maybe I should ask Eagle about it?*

Mother made a mental note, then smiled. "We may return to the FistFest at a later time. The next matter, however.... You will recall that before the operation, it was once again emphasized you were only to retire targets specifically nominated by the Department. Or in self-defense."

For the first time, Leeth looked worried.

"Although your report described it as a 'rescue', I believe the death counts across the Club Juzz and Fryhouse sites totaled thirty-eight." Mother raised a forestalling hand as Leeth bristled. "But we can ignore those egregious slaughters, given the nature of those you killed, and the metro police's disinterest in either incident."

She waited for Leeth to relax. "No, the next matter is more serious.

"Agent Leeth, we believe that at 5:53 a.m, in the Potrero Hill Playground, you retired Agent Adam Garland of the Bureau of Internal Development, the overarching agency this Department operates within. In addition, you falsified a report to your superiors."

Leeth gaped. "Did not! I *didn't* lie, and I didn't kill him! I could have, but I didn't!" She stopped, remembering how close she'd come to deciding the opposite.

"Really," Mother said, exchanging a look with Father. The stress monitors were clearly registering in the 'deception' range.

"Unlike the people you admitted killing at Club Juzz, and the Fryhouse later? Although your report estimated the number as 'a dozen or so'."

"Why are you pretending that's such a big deal? So I killed a bunch of people – they were *bad* guys. Look at all the kids we saved!"

Mother opened her mouth, but Leeth cut her off. "And don't give me that 'To avoid police questions,' or even 'It's important to follow orders' krek. I'm not stupid. There's some other reason, some *bigger* reason. And you all know what it is, but you're keeping it secret from me." She glared at them.

«Shall we tell her, Mother? That it's wrong to kill?»

«Surely you jest. A key value of Eagle's little Pet is that she is 'unburdened' with that knowledge.»

"There! *That* look! That's what I mean! You both know what it is, that there *is* something. I can tell. But you're not going to tell *me*, are you? You're just going to keep pretending I'm not allowed to kill *obvious* bad guys because it's 'orders.' Well, I want to know what the big secret is!"

For perhaps only the second time, Mother felt a twinge of sympathy for the girl: for the moral pit she'd been led into by her 'guardian.' Which they were helping to maintain. But who knew how she'd react if told that it was wrong to kill? The girl was clearly unstable. Once again, Mother wished she could punish Harmon for the evil he'd done. She considered asking Leeth how she determined who was good, and who bad, but decided not to open that can of worms.

"I thought so: you won't tell me. Well, *too bad*: I've worked it out myself."

For just a moment, Mother looked concerned, before leaning back. "I'm quite sure you're just imagining things, Leeth."

"Oh. Am I?" She shook her head. "Nuh-uh. There's a secret international competition." At their surprise, she allowed herself a moment of self-congratulation. "But, look, just tell me where I rank, even just what *grade* I am! It won't depress me, I promise; it'll just make me try harder!"

«Dear god,» sent Mother.

«*Thank* god, you mean.» Father responded. «Her willingness to kill is unchanged.» He blinked, thinking quickly. "Even if your wild idea held any truth, we would have to discuss the matter with Eagle."

Yes! But Leeth didn't let her glee show, simply inclined her head graciously. "Okay. But *soon*, right?"

"Let's set aside the matter of those killings for now," Mother said, "and focus on the murder of your colleague. You killed Garland, only mentioning him as an afterthought: barely in time for us to contain the scene. Suppose the Bureau people had not arrived first?"

"What is the *matter* with you two? I told you, *I didn't kill him!* Look, I came back here voluntarily, remember, to help you guys? *And* I'm s'posed to be reporting only to Eagle. But here you two are, telling me I'm lying, when I'm not!"

She glared at them. This was getting old. She considered storming out, but decided that'd only make things worse. She sighed. "Look, he was cybered, right? Probably with headware." She spread her hands. "So it's simple: he's probably got a recording of what killed him. No one healed him, I guess? So he was killed properly."

Mother looked at her a little strangely. "Yes. At least you remembered that part of your training. His body was beyond magical regeneration."

Leeth growled. "*I* didn't kill him. Somebody else did. Quit saying I killed him! Quit calling me a liar!" She slammed a fist down onto the desk, which *cracked* with a sound like a gunshot.

Mother flinched back, fear in her eyes before they narrowed, and went unfocused – another invisible black mark?

Dojo cleared his throat, and she saw him give a tiny shake of his head.

With a deep breath, she sat back in her chair. "Sorry." But she eyed the long split in the dense, composite material with secret pleasure. *That stuff was supposed to be really tough.* She stifled a giggle: *and expensive.*

"Really? Somebody else?" Mother rested her elbows on the desk and steepled her fingers. "Tell me, Leeth. What do you make of these facts: his skull was smashed open, and someone reached in and removed his headware."

Leeth thought about it. "Nothing springs to mind." She shrugged. "It's what anyone'd do, if they thought he was recording them."

Mother looked innocently surprised. "Oh? That's what you'd do, is it? If you thought the headware wasn't just recording on a continuous short loop?"

Leeth looked uncomfortable. "Well, yeah, I guess. Provided there was no one watching. But I didn't."

"So, what? You're asking us to believe that someone follows you around killing people *you've* been talking to, in the same manner *you* would choose?"

Leeth was about to answer when Father broke in coldly. "It was almost too late for us to put a security clamp on the findings from the scene. Only the fact that Nelson was accessing the traffic system computers alerted us to the arrival of a police team in the middle of your mess."

The words were harsh, but the way Father was looking at her was worse. Like she was dirt.

She didn't understand. Father *liked* her. Didn't he? She swallowed, suddenly having to blink back tears. How could he be accusing her like this?

Why didn't they believe her?

He hadn't finished, either. "And you lied about it to us. You *falsified your official report.* What were you thinking, girl? That we wouldn't check? That we'd assume some random street scum killed him? Your continued refusal to admit-"

She was on her feet, the shock of the unexpected attack cutting through her dismay and reigniting the anger. "I didn't kill him! Why aren't you listening to me? *I didn't kill him.* You're just upset 'cause you think I killed him against orders. That's what you're really angry about, isn't it? You miss being able to order me around, controlling me. Just like-"

Her uncle's face rose suddenly in Leeth's memory, eyes burning into her, forbidding her from speaking; and suddenly, sickeningly, the words drained from her mind. Like a nightmare, the confusion was back. *What was I saying? I'm furious at Father, and the Doctor – but... why?* She could barely think.

But it was desperately important to speak: urgent. Father. The Doctor. Controlling her – yes! Focus: her uncle. Tell them. *Break his control.*

Frantic, she pushed against the horrible piles of familiar mush, flailing for words. But the harder she grabbed at them, the faster the words splintered.

"You wan-, con-, c-. I won't, wo-, *w-! *Doc- *Doc-*"

Dojo tensed. Father and Mother froze at the girl's sudden incoherence, her stress indicators peaking and flattening like waves hammering rock. Father gave the command to arm the room's defensive security systems.

The girl was on her feet, leaning forwards, hands spread like claws against the slick black surface of the operations desk.

Then Dojo was there, beside her, one arm around her shoulder – but not attacking. Just holding her. She looked up, into eyes that radiated concern.

"Dojo! Stand back!" Father ordered.

It was the look in Sensei's eyes that cut through her confusion, not the ultrasonic whine of the weapon tracking systems. She stopped struggling. For long seconds she stood, panting, feeling Dojo's physical support, as she shook her head.

And at that precise moment a vidlink from Nelson appeared in Father and Mother's fields of view.

CHAPTER 60

«Is everything okay?» Nelson asked, by video. «Someone just activated the- Uh oh. Has Leeth gone crazy again?»

«What do you want, Nelson?» Mother snapped. «Now is not the time-»

«You're debriefing Leeth, right? And the defenses just activated? I have info you may need, since I've been investigating. It's just an idea, but I'm wondering if maybe Leeth doesn't always know when she kills? Like she's got a split personality, and it's the other personality doing all the murders?»

Father and Mother exchanged looks. «She's *supposed* to kill, Nelson,» Mother reminded him.

«Even without orders? I've got some data I think you'll be interested in.» Nelson paused then, as he saw that Leeth had finally rebooted her brain. It also looked like she hoped no one had noticed. *She really is nuts if she thinks that's possible*, he thought, not quite able to contain his snicker.

"You were asking about Garland's killing..." Leeth said.

To Nelson's eyes, she still looked pretty strung-out. Remembering her fingertips cutting into his chest like chisel blades, he shuddered, glad he wasn't physically in the briefing room.

"I didn't do it," she said, staring at Father.

Yeah, right, thought Nelson, but kept the expression off his face, pretending he hadn't heard. After all, he'd been specifically instructed to stop tapping into the Department's own secure data feeds – thanks to her.

Fortunately, Father seemed ready to hear his report. He held up one hand to Leeth, in the real world. "Wait. New information is coming in."

Leeth looked from one to the other, unimpressed.

Mother upped the bandwidth, opening full video links between the three of them to make a virtual conference. «Go ahead,» she practically purred. «What murders against Departmental orders?»

Nelson wondered what, specifically, Leeth'd done to get on Mother's bad side. Forking his attention, he hacked into the room's defense system. Just as he'd guessed: it already had lock on her. Would Mother object if it 'accidentally' fired? With Ghost, he could alter the targeting algorithm.

He considered it. But then pictured Eagle: those penetrating hazel eyes staring into his. Knowing about Ghost. Quietly, he slid out of the fire control system and brought his attention back to the dirt he'd dug up. It'd be enough, for Mother and Father. As for Eagle... well, he'd learned from the Doc that Eagle prided himself on hearing other opinions. Though the Doc'd be pissed by how he was about to apply that lesson.

«Well, as near as I can figure, basically *every* time Leeth has left here, somebody has been killed.»

«You mean, she killed them?» asked Father.

«Well, I wouldn't wanna say that exactly. I mean, sure, you could be right. It *could* be her. But it's probably just an odd series of coincidences, right? I wouldn't have mentioned it, but then I thought, what if she needs *help?* At first I just wanted to prove I was wrong. So I checked further back in her records... and found that, basically, every time she left the *mental institute* she grew up in, at least one person got killed. That is, after she turned fifteen or sixteen. But she was younger then, right? She might grow out of it, eventually.»

«Go on,» said Father.

«You remember the scare about the 'Golden Gate Park monster,' last year? The jogger who had his heart ripped out and the kid who had his head practically twisted off? That was her. And I helped cover it up,» he admitted. «I don't know if you know, but Eagle had me alter some DNA records in the police databases before she started here. Those kills were hers.»

«We know,» said Mother.

«Really?» Nelson pretended surprise. «But did you know she snuck out of the mental asylum a few months after, and killed three homeless youths? Slashed them up like she almost did to me, with her magic claws. It even made the news.

«There were some other murders, too, each time she went into the city, but I'm sure they couldn't have been her – I mean they were horrible, and just kept getting worse.» He didn't need to add that one or two had even been killed like Garland had: they'd see that for themselves.

«Then there was the Bureau crew that was sent into the asylum. She killed two of them – including Garland's partner at the time, Berlusconi, did you know? – though they all got healed up magically. But I guess you know about that, so let's ignore them. Besides, it was, like, special circumstances, yeah? She didn't wanna be captured, right? She probably didn't even mean to kill them – just did it by reflex, you know?

«So let's skip the ones I know you know about. Like the one she did right in front of James their first night out.

«As for Maria Lempriere, the opera singer? Leeth couldn't've killed her – James would've stopped her. And it's not like Leeth would've killed her just because she hated her voice, or James's choice of operas, right?»

Mother and Father looked at one another.

«I mean, she's there with James the whole time. It's not like she goes to the toilet, and climbs out the window to crush her head when she sees Maria taking a break outside.»

«Do you have any evidence of that?» asked Father. «Are you claiming there are cameras in the Ladies?»

«No, of course not. And I'm saying she *couldn't've* done it. I mean, I haven't checked the times and distances, but it stands to reason.»

Father called up a view of an inner courtyard of the Opera House, directly above where Lempriere's body had been found. «Nelson: superimpose the location of the female toilets on the image, and some measuring reticules.»

The requests were satisfied so fast it was as if Nelson had had them ready and waiting.

«Look, that's... three point two meters above the ground. She'd hardly have *jumped* down, right? And if she climbed back up via that down-pipe... then she'd have to jump sideways a meter and grab back onto the window ledge. Who'd do something stupid like that?»

Mother and Father highlighted portions of Preacher's report: jumping down the balconies; dancing on the rail....

Leeth watched the expressions moving beneath the poker faces of Father and Mother. *Funt! How much new info are they getting?* "Can you at least put this stuff up on a screen or something for me to see too?" Out of sight below the edge of the desk, she clenched her fists.

Father didn't even glance at her. "In due course, Leeth."

She threw herself back into her seat. *This sucked.* The ultrasonic chirp of the weapon system re-targeting only deepened her scowl. "I'm not even s'posed to be reporting to you two any more! Look, Eagle probably wouldn't be thrilled if you shot me, so how about you turn off the weapon system, at least? After all, you've still got Dojo here to protect you both." But the moment she said it, she stilled. *That* is *why Dojo's here!* She wasn't sure whether to be amused by their fear, or worried by the lack of trust.

She met Dojo's eyes, and thought she saw his lips twitch. But why wasn't Eagle intervening? Why was he letting Mother and Father question her?

She sighed. Knowing Eagle, it was probably yet another test. She rolled her eyes.

Nelson had silently continued. «Then after her schizoid episode as Jennifer Dei-»

«You yourself agreed the organic program had somehow collapsed. And the Doctor believes the persona overlay swelled into complete dominance and then burst. It is his opinion that Leeth did not have a 'schizoid episode'.»

«Yeah, well, he would say that, wouldn't he? But consider this: it *should* have worked. Maybe Leeth's unstable. Maybe she's got a whole deck of different personas that he didn't tell us about, and that's *why* it didn't work properly?»

«You're now accusing the Doctor of deceiving us? That's a serious charge.»

«Nah, I'm not accusing him. Anyone can make a mistake. I just thought I'd better mention the possibility. You two are the heads of Operations, so it's my duty to bring the possibility to your attention. But let me go on, there's more.»

Nelson continued at length in the same vein: murders each night Leeth went to the opera; the 'drama school' incident; until Father told him to stop.

«Oh! Can I just add one bit more? When Leeth was staying at Emma's apartment to attend the drama school. You remember that guy who fell down the stairs and broke his neck? Did you know the ETD was within a few minutes of Leeth entering the building? Probably just a coincidence.

«Oh, and you must've noticed that during the whole time Leeth was staying with Emma, *something* was stirring up trouble in the Hunter's Point Dumps. Stories of a thing hunting-» Nelson stopped himself, seeing Father raise a hand. And with perfect timing, Leeth chose that moment to interrupt again.

"Shall I come back later?" she demanded. "When you've finished your other meeting?"

Mother and Father both glared at her, and Leeth glared right back.

Nelson went on. «Finally, of course, Garland this morning. Just to cap off the night's slaughter. Even if we guess Leeth only killed half, that's twenty kills in one night. A personal best?» He shrugged. «But probably, after the 'Fest, she and Tash had to wind down, right? I gotta say, though, I know she's supposed to be our assassin, but I always thought assassins were supposed to work like surgical lasers, not fragmentation grenades!

«Anyway, I just thought you should know. I had to make a summary graphic, to understand it all.»

Alongside his own image he added a tilted 3D view of the city. Then one by one, like maps of sub-basement levels, a series of 2D grids appeared underneath the uppermost map, in a perspective view.

«Each of those lower layers is a projection of the city, on each of the dates Leeth visited it. The areas we know she went are shaded gray. Areas she *could have* reached on foot are a lighter gray. There was no need to show the areas she could've only reached by vehicle.»

A series of dots appeared on each layer. «These are all murders. The dots are color coded according to the level of violence. Heads ripped off, hearts ripped out – stuff like that – are coded red. Slashings are orange, shootings yellow. The dots outlined in black are where we know someone else did it. Domestics, hold-ups, and gang clashes mainly.»

Nelson stopped talking, but watched Father and Mother access the zoom and pan controls he'd provided. The correlation was impressive, he had to admit: all the killings happened inside the gray areas, within walking distance of Leeth's known movements. Only two grids had no violent death inside Leeth's range: the night of her schizoid episode, and her spanking, camera-spearing night. *The little bitch.*

Was it enough? He'd been reading some Tik Tek patent applications for brain interfaces, and had some ideas that'd even enable remote operation.

«Thank you, Nelson, that will be all.»

«Sure, Mother. Don't be too hard on her though, will you?»

Nelson probably thought he sounded sincere, as he signed off. There was a long silence before Mother finally spoke on the direct link to Father. «Well, it certainly shows she has an aptitude for killing. And clearly, Nelson still holds his grudge for her assault, so we should take this evidence with a grain of salt.» Mother knew perfectly well how Father would react to that apparent softening of her stance.

«It shows she hasn't followed orders, and has been falsifying her reports. The evidence looks solid.»

Mother found the whole thing more disturbing than she'd expected. Leeth was clearly effective – but not trustworthy. She herself had been surprised by Nelson's evidence, as deceived by Leeth as everyone else. «It appears she learned better than we knew, at the acting school. I doubt that Eagle is aware of this.» Mother, suspecting that Eagle was monitoring the entire interrogation, waited for him to interrupt. Concerned, even, by his silence. After a little, she added, «We will of course have to hear her side of the story.»

«She'll lie.»

Mother shrugged. «Then we'll expose them.»

Father nodded, troubled. «All right, Mother. It appears your reservations may have been justified after all. Let's confront her. Will you share the intel with Dojo? I have no idea how this will go.»

«She does have a knack for surprises,» Mother agreed, equally unsettled.

CHAPTER 61

Leeth sat up straighter when she saw they'd finally stopped ignoring her. Though the expression on both their faces was a bit worrying.

"Stand up, agent," Father said.

She looked from them to Dojo, who seemed lost in thought all of a sudden, and got to her feet, trying to think if she *had* done anything wrong.

"I have a graphic I want you to examine and comment on," he said, as a large hologram filled the air over the desk. Coldly, he began explaining it. "These show killings in the city and Dumps on each of the nights you left the Department, color-coded by the degree of violence."

Leeth frowned as he worked through the display.

"Well?" he asked, finally. "Do you have anything to say for yourself?"

It was weird. About half the kills were hers, half The Breaker's. Often, nearby. Was he following her around? She felt a chill, remembering Godsson's words. Robo was The Breaker, and he was seeking her: his 'mother.' The idea made her feel a little sick. But she'd already told them all that. So why were they showing her this?

"Is he in the competition, too? But his kills are cruel. *Sick.* Or was I supposed to be stopping him?"

Father looked confused. "Stopping who?"

"The Breaker." She gestured at the hologram. "Half those are *his* kills. Or isn't it allowed, to kill another competitor? Is that why you wouldn't give me permission to hunt him, when I asked?"

Mother and Father just looked at her, a funny expression on their faces. Almost sad.

"So you claim you *didn't* kill these people?" Mother asked.

"*Der.* I just said that." She was starting to get confused.

Mother ground her teeth, afraid that if she opened her mouth she'd scream in frustration. *Still the girl played her stupid games, wasting their time, exposing them all to risk. It was all just a joke to her.*

Holding her temper by the merest thread, she wet her lips, afraid she was letting Leeth draw her into her game. Or her fantasy world? Was the girl herself unaware of what she did? "You don't remember killing all those people?"

"No. Do *you?*"

Mother lost it. "That's it, you stupid little *funt*. This is not a joke! *Why did you kill those people?*"

Leeth looked at Father with an expression of 'what's frazzing her?' before answering Mother.

"Let me get this clear: you're saying The Breaker isn't in the competition? Good! But you also think *all* those kills were mine, and I 'forgot' some of them? Like, *I'm* The Breaker or something. Are you both *nuts?* Did you forget that Godsson said it's following me?"

Father drew Mother's attention to the bio-monitors. No one could be that good an actor, could they? Unless magic was involved. Or madness. Perhaps Nelson was right, and she really did have a split personality.

Leeth rubbed her fingers through her still-short hair. "Okay, look, these are the ones I *did* kill." She pointed them out. "The jogger in the park, a month or so before I came here – but just him." She frowned, remembering the way he'd looked at her. For some reason, the memory made her uncomfortable. Had that look been enough reason to kill him? She moved on. "I didn't do the other one, though. Um, the ogre and his friends when I was looking for the Red Fist Dojo – but *they* attacked *me*. The police, when they came for me at the Institute. Though they shouldn't really count, since they got healed. *One* of the muggers, the first opera night."

"No others?"

Leeth's brow creased as she tapped one finger against her upper lip, thinking. "I don't think so. Well, apart from the Club Juzz and Fryhouse funt-heads this morning."

"What about the man who somehow fell down the stairs at Emma's apartment, during your time at the drama school?"

"Oh!" She looked down. "Oh yeah."

"Why did you kill him, Leeth?" Father asked.

"Um." She screwed up her face as she struggled to remember. "Oh, yeah." She blushed. "He was rude."

"You killed him because he was rude?" Father did not sound happy.

Maybe that had been a bit... excessive. "Um, yeah. But I didn't mean to! He grabbed me, and I hit him, and broke his neck."

"And then covered up the evidence," said Mother.

"Yeah." They seemed to be waiting for more. "I used my lessons! I loosened his shoes to explain why he'd tripped – though he'd been all, wobbling like, anyway – and threw him down the stairs."

They didn't look any happier. "I *had* to! I didn't want to cause any trouble for the Department."

Those words registered clearly as a lie. Mother and Father took an iota of comfort from that: she could not *consciously* fool the sensors.

Mother shook her head. "No. You concealed your actions because you wanted to avoid another six months of training, didn't you? Because you'd been ordered to fit in. *And not kill anyone!*"

Leeth blushed. "Look, I know I wasn't supposed to, but that was while Tara was being a complete pickle with those AR penises, if you remember."

"I see: you were angry." Mother and Father exchanged a look. There was a short silence.

"And after you left us, to live in the Hunters Point Dumps. How many did you kill there, Leeth?" Mother wanted to know.

She thought. Hardly anybody, really: just the rape-gangers. "Three," she said, and explained.

But then blushed, remembering her first attempt to hunt the RedSkulls. And of course, Mother noticed, and wormed the story out of her. While Dojo, of all people, looked on.

She kept her eyes on the floor, and had to force the words out. "I only killed two of them, properly." She lifted her face for a moment. "But they *were* kind of ogres, at least."

She forced herself to go on; but couldn't meet their eyes. "They were members of the RedSkulls. Who are real bad, FYI – *everyone* in the Dumps wants them gone. But then they started hunting *me*. So I had to resort to just shooting some of them, instead." She shrugged. "Then they were all shooting, too."

She smiled, remembering. *That part had been so intense.* Quickly, though, the smile drained away. When she spoke, her voice was small. "But in the end, I ran away." Her chin dropped lower, remembering. She'd even paid for a magician she'd met, to heal her on the quiet, so no one would know.

Her face burned with the shame. She *couldn't* look at Dojo.

Mother's voice broke the silence. "How many did you kill on *that* occasion?"

"Three fully."

"A moment ago you said you killed two."

Leeth lifted her chin, briefly. "Sure. Only two, properly. By myself. I remember I got a head shot on another that would have made him impossible to heal. So that was three, fully.

"I might've killed maybe three others, since I wounded a few more. But they could've all been healed, I think. So I only killed two *properly*."

She glanced back up, but couldn't read the expressions flowing across Mother's face, they were so strange. She looked at Father, but his face showed nothing. He was just watching. Waiting?

"Leeth, what is the difference between a proper killing and a full one?" Mother asked at last.

Leeth looked puzzled. "A full killing is when the person's damaged so much they can't be healed up again. A proper one is where I do it by myself." *Obviously*, her tone of voice said.

"Are you saying you *didn't* kill these gang members?"

"Not *properly*. I shot more of them than I killed with my own hands."

Mother's expression kind of locked up, her mouth opening slowly. She shifted back in her chair, away from Leeth.

Father glanced across at Mother, raising an eyebrow. Dismissing her reaction, he turned back to Leeth. "This business of 'proper' killings – you're saying you find it unsatisfactory to kill people by any method except with your bare hands?"

Leeth wanted to agree, but sensed there was more to the question than she could see. She felt her way forward. "Um, basically, yeah. I mean, when I fight someone properly, then I'm proving myself, aren't I? Testing myself. Learning new stuff. But just shooting someone? Any null could do that."

Father looked suddenly tired. He began massaging his eyes and the bridge of his nose. "The reason the RedSkulls attacked you was because you let them, didn't you? You could have just avoided them if you'd wanted to, couldn't you?"

Her 'yes' was soft.

He stopped his massage and looked at her. "You have no objection to shooting people, do you?"

She looked resigned, and sighed. "No. I know it's more important to kill the targets than for me to learn something from it."

"And you ran away because...?"

"Because I would have lost if I didn't." Her voice sank toward inaudibility. "They beat me."

Father breathed out a long sigh. "You didn't run because you were scared? Because your nerve broke?" He watched the virtual readouts of the bio-monitors carefully.

She stood suddenly straighter. "No! Sure, I was scared, a bit. But mainly I didn't want to die. Someone'll kill me sooner or later, but it'd be awful to die stupidly like that, for something pointless. Probably I even did the right thing by running away. That doesn't mean I have to like it, though."

Father seemed to think for a long time. "You're quite correct, Miss Leeth. I'm just a little surprised to discover you know that. That's not to say I condone your actions. But let us return to this 'murder map'," he said, gesturing back to the large holo projection. "Would you like to reconsider what you have told us about the remaining deaths, now?"

She tilted her head, puzzling out what he meant. Oh. "No. I didn't kill any of the others."

"So what is your explanation? That The Breaker follows you around, killing one or two people nearby? But only on the rare occasions when you physically leave the Department, of course."

Leeth looked stubborn. "I guess. Pretty weird, hey? Unless Godsson's telling the truth, like none of you believe he ever does!"

The idea that David Benson knew something of The Breaker was *more* disturbing. Mother checked the bio-monitors again, hoping to see a lie. Hoping the girl did indeed have multiple personalities. Either way, they weren't going to wring any sort of admission from her. Mother thought for a little while. Then smiled.

"Well, in that case you're the ideal person to track

down this killer, aren't you? Because wherever you go, that's where the killings will happen." Mother leaned back.

Leeth's eyes lit up. "A hunt? Chill!"

Mother blinked, slowly. "I shall propose to Eagle that we give you forty-eight hours. Another mission, just for you. Find your mysterious 'shadow' hunter – bring him in, don't just kill him – and we will apologize."

"Gee, thanks. But if you'd let me hunt The Breaker when I'd *asked*, months ago, think how many people'd still be alive."

She hadn't expected them to be pleased by her response, but the looks they gave her communicated something more. "But if I fail, you'll try to retire me, won't you?"

"No," Father said. "No one is arguing you are incapable of doing what you have been trained for. No, if you fail you will return here, for treatment; perhaps some augmentation like the other agents, with a little more monitoring and control capabilities, however."

She gaped at him in horror. She hadn't agreed to return, just to have *that* done to her. "No," she vowed. Besides, Eagle would never allow that. *Would he?*

"Oh? You'll run away again, will you?" Mother asked.

Leeth's eyes narrowed. *Not until after I've come back and killed you, Father, Nelson, and the Doctor, Mother. Even if I have to go back to Godsson to get him to undo the Doctor's conditioning, first.*

Mother found something unnerving in Leeth's tiny smile.

"Well, no doubt Eagle wouldn't attempt to force you to stay in the Department if you felt conditions here had become intolerable."

Leeth said nothing. Just stared at her, remembering Dojo's advice: 'If you plan to kill someone, do not warn them.'

Mother repressed a shiver, relieved when Father changed the subject, though bristling at his first words.

"Ladies, I feel we all need to calm down. Leeth, we want to give you the benefit of the doubt." He opened his hands. "As you say, you chose to come back to us. You are an agent now, and that means something. We should operate under mutual trust and respect."

At some silent communication, Dojo bowed slightly to

Father and Mother – fractionally deeper to Leeth, who returned the bow – and then left the room.

"However," Father said, "the evidence against you is too strong to simply brush under the carpet. Our personal beliefs are irrelevant, and the Department is not all powerful. The law must be upheld. While we do operate with a reasonably free hand, even we have limits. We can't ignore serial killings. If the police got hold of this information they would demand your arrest and trial. Capturing this Breaker character will prove your innocence."

Leeth rolled her eyes, but stopped herself from saying '*der*' out loud, this time.

Father frowned. "But before discussing that with Eagle, there is one last thing we need to address. The matter of your drug habit."

Leeth gaped at them. "What? I don't. Use. Drugs."

Mother shrugged. "Then let's call it your mental stability. Your 'jumpiness.' You yourself admitted to that much."

"So what? I was just excited – I'd been looking forward to the 'Fest for months!"

Eagle's face appeared in a thin frame in the air before Mother, his image and words digitally transmitted directly to optic and auditory nerves. «Mother, Father.» Then his virtual face turned to Mother. «Thank you for your constructive suggestion regarding a forty-eight hour period for Leeth to find her 'shadow.' Let's proceed on that basis.» For some reason, the look he gave her made her want to draw back. «But for now, Little Brother is bringing the girl strong coffee. Have her drink it. Observe.»

Mother rigidly suppressed a snarl. *Finally* Eagle deigned to speak. At her nod, his virtual image vanished. Mother could no longer contain herself.

«He always does this! I'm tired of his spooky '*I have access to information you don't*' schtick. He and Abrams should share the information and plans they make!»

Like you do, Mother? Father thought to ask, but knew better. Instead, he allowed himself a grimace in response. Mother, fortunately, took it as agreement.

Glowering, she didn't answer. *One day I'll learn Eagle's and Abrams's plans.* She played Leeth's monologue back at triple speed, dismissing it as worthless.

Leeth spoke into a lengthening silence. "So, can I go?

Is that all?"

"No. Wait," Mother told her.

With a sullen expression, Leeth threw herself into the chair, daring them to order her to stand up again.

CHAPTER 62

The door chimed and the administrative assistant known as Little Brother entered. The aroma of real coffee preceded him across the room.

"Agent Leeth? Here's some coffee for you."

She frowned at him, then at the cup he held out to her. She looked across to Father and Mother. "I didn't ask for any coffee."

"Take the coffee and drink it," ordered Mother.

The young man smiled hopefully at her, but she wasn't looking at him. Slowly she reached for the cup. What was in it?

"No," she said at last. "I'm not drinking it. Not unless Eagle tells me to." She put the cup down on their desk and sat back, arms crossed.

Eagle's face appeared before her. "I was the one who ordered the coffee for you, Leeth," he said, mildly. "I assure you, it contains only coffee, and sugar. Not," he added pointedly "some drug that's undetectable by taste."

She pursed her lips.

But then his voice dropped to a level only she could hear. "I am making a small point to Mother and Father. And to you, too." His image shrank, and vanished.

Her jaw dropped at the implication: *Eagle knows about my super hearing!* Abruptly, tears welled, her fingers going to Barney's device at her waist. Always ready to play back the words to unlock the Doctor's cage. But maybe, with Eagle's help, she could find a better solution! *If* she dared trust him.

Mother and Father were watching her, looking mildly puzzled. Blinking away the tears, she picked up the coffee and sipped it. Nice and sweet, just how she liked it.

But *why* did Eagle want her to drink coffee?

Why did everyone make everything so complicated? She wanted to get along with Mother, and Father. Work for the Department; make a difference. Help rebuild America. Maybe the Dragon Lord *couldn't* be trusted – she knew, now, that people changed when they got too much power. And even *she* could see there was something wrong when a corporation like Newtopia held more power than most countries. Someone needed to stand up to them. And from her lessons here, she knew only America had ever done that.

Leeth didn't notice Little Brother's wistful departure,

his backward glance as he left the room. She drained the cup, wondering when she'd find out why Eagle wanted her to drink it.

"I gather you managed only a technical draw in your only fight against two opponents," Father said.

Leeth stared at him blankly, then put the empty cup down. "Uh. That's right. Sorry. The guy with shocks was *fast*; he managed to zap me pretty solidly. A draw was the best I could do. I don't actually remember it properly. I think the electric shock...." She shifted uneasily.

"Shockwires? Neither report mentioned them."

Under the guise of questioning some of the details of the 'Fest – uncovering that her opponent Black Paul had been augmented with finger-tasers, which *neither* report had mentioned; discussing the oddity of her deadly yet soft and uncallused hands; confirming that she had planned to hunt down and kill the entire RedSkulls gang in the guise of a supernatural 'slime monster' – Leeth had moved quickly from jittery to feverish to so hyper-active she was literally unable to stand still, even when ordered.

"You certainly seem well up to the mark in hand to hand combat," Father summed up. "I would say second only to Dojo, in the entire Bureau."

Second for now. But then the crawling of her skin distracted her.

Father had expected her to be overjoyed at such a glowing assessment, but after a brief flash of a smile, she stood shivering, hugging herself and bouncing up and down.

Mother stared at her, looked across at Father, and sighed. *Dammit.* She looked back to the clearly almost-feverish girl. «I've seen enough, Father. You?»

«I have merely been waiting for you to say the word, Mother.»

"Are you feeling well, Leeth?" Mother asked

Leeth quivered, unwrapping her arms from around herself reluctantly. For a moment she was still, then her hands began clenching and unclenching. "Sure. Fine. I'm fine."

"Really? You're not feeling a little 'jumpy'?"

The girl blinked, then stilled – a visible shiver running through her whole body. Nodded emphatically, once, then spoke, her words almost running together, now. "Chit, yes! I feel like I can't- like I gotta- I mean, if you're finished with me, now'd be a good time to get some gym practice in. Maybe Dojo'd like to spar? Some sparring'd be really good. It's good for me. Look, it's great chatting and that, but I've got stuff I've really gotta do!" *Like call Marcie, to check she's okay!* She jerked her wrist up, almost making the call then and there, before realizing that'd hardly be keeping Marcie off their radar!

She'd begun bouncing up and down on the balls of her feet again, looking ready to explode.

Mother sighed. "It seems," she said, sounding as if each word were being dragged from her, "you are hyper-sensitive to caffeine." She spoke to the concealed security camera mounted high in one side wall of the room.

"Caffeine?"

"We will note the fact in our files. Please remember it, on your upcoming mission. No coffee."

There was silence for a few seconds while Leeth vibrated on the spot. "Right. Find The Breaker. My next mission. Sleek!"

"We are certainly *not* happy at even those few unsanctioned killings you have admitted to."

For just a moment Leeth stilled. "Yeah, I guess I see your point." Then her eyes lit up again. "But hunting down The Breaker is another real mission. I'd better organize it with Eagle. Or maybe we could delegate it to you two: I'm told he's pretty busy. And when I bring in The Breaker, it might be best to send it away to the Institute. The Doctor could go and study it there."

Mother sighed again. "No doubt," she said, finally sending the signal to disarm the weapon system.

Leeth sprang across the desk, somersaulting to land right between her startled superiors and turning to engulf the seated woman in a sudden hug. "Chill! You won't regret it, I promise!" She whirled to Father and repeated the embrace more warmly, with a kiss as well, before leaping back across the desk with uncanny ease and darting to the door.

"Wait," Father called, recovering from the whirlwind assault while Mother still stared in dismay at the places where Leeth's disgusting jacket had pressed up against her own impeccable white suit.

One hand still visible on the door-frame, Leeth paused, vibrating.

"Present yourself at the infirmary. I will instruct the autodoc to be ready with a caffeine antagonist for you. Follow the on-screen instructions." The instant he'd finished speaking, her hand vanished, soft footfalls fading down the corridor.

Father looked at Mother in the sudden vacuum of her departure. "Burning forests! Imagine what she'd be like on *amphetamines!*"

Mother's only reply was a shudder.

Father continued. "All these other deaths were 'proper' ones, in her terms. Done in her rather bloody style, and with her considerable strength. But suppose Leeth *isn't* The Breaker, herself?"

"Oh? The Breaker selects its victims by their proximity to her? More likely, Leeth does it in some kind of fugue state. I have no idea how Eagle feels so confident he can use her, though. She causes chaos."

Father nodded. "Which may be precisely *why* he values her. He seems able to conceive ways of directing that chaos. Look how she dealt with Fox."

Mother's eyes narrowed.

CHAPTER 63

Harmon frowned when his door chimed – but felt his eyebrows twitch when his display revealed the visitor. "Enter," he ordered.

The door slid open, and Mr Abrams rolled in, in his silent wheelchair. Stopping in front of Harmon's desk, the man said nothing, merely studied him.

Harmon remained equally silent. Shifting his perception to the Imaginal, he once again tried to make sense of the man before him. The characteristic alignments of energy flows that marked someone as a mage *were* there, if you looked carefully enough. Those patterns spanned layers that grew progressively harder to see; deep within a well of strands that on the surface appeared open and fragile.

Abrams, in his turn, studied Harmon. At last, he shook his head. "Eagle tells me he's asked you to study the meta-spirits that troubled Godsson and Leeth at the Institute for Paranormal Dysfunction."

"Ah: 'Meta-spirits.' Am I supposed to assume that such labeling of them signifies familiarity?"

Abrams waved the remark aside, with a trembling hand. "He suggested I might work with you. But, Dr Harmon, I need to be convinced of the wisdom of doing so. Consider this a job interview."

Harmon bristled. "Why should I want to work with you? Who are you? Does Eagle assume I would share my research with you?"

Abrams began panting, which turned by degrees to coughs, finally revealing themselves as shallow chuckling. "I'm sorry, Doctor. Although you may have uncovered some fresh Truth, I do think the information flow is likely to be from me to you, not the other way around."

He made a placating gesture, before the smile fell from his face and his eyes bored into Harmon's. "Let me put my cards on the table. While you have been playing perverted games with your breakthrough, Eagle faces shadowy threats of the order of Melisande d'Artelle. And – perhaps in desperation, since I may not be able to assist him much longer – he seems willing to hope you might join our struggle. Eagle sees in you something more than a person who turned a deep discovery into a vehicle for his own pleasure. So tell me, Dr Alex Harmon, why does Eagle think you might be able to help us? What do you care about? What do you see as the purpose of your life?"

Those eyes stared deep – deep enough, perhaps, to see into his soul. Harmon, imagining the consequences if that were true, considered how his actions would appear, and felt a pain like something twisting his gut.

Harmon met the gaze. "Who *are* you?"

"Just a very old man who's been bitten once. Who doesn't want to see someone else make the same mistake he did."

Harmon refused to look away. "I turned eighteen in the Week of Miracles – when the magic returned. When Sondra Watanabe flew. When James Marsters rose from the dead. And my reaction was: 'why?' Not 'why them,' or 'why not me?' Just... *why?* I sensed, immediately, that this was not an event disconnected from myth and legend, but somehow bound up in it. I remember vowing, as I watched Sondra Watanabe escape the falling cable-car, her two children tucked under her arms, a third child hanging from her legs – that I would know *why*."

His gaze had turned inward, but now he once again focused on the compelling green eyes in that veined face. "Understanding why the magic returned; the how of it; that is the purpose of my life. And while I can offer no defense for much of what I have done in the pursuit of that knowledge, know this: it *has* made Leeth what she is today. An embodiment of the Huntress Archetype itself."

Abrams's next words yanked Harmon back to the present. "To what purpose, Doctor? For the 'greater good'?"

Harmon stared back. "No. For the knowledge itself. Only that."

"And what would you do with that knowledge?"

Harmon frowned, then sat back. "I don't know. I think that rather depends on what the answer is."

Abrams considered him. "I, like Eagle, see magic as a dangerously unbalancing element in a world already facing huge challenges. Magical power, like wealth, tends to collect in the hands of individuals. 'Ultimate power,' Doctor. You yourself have tasted that honeyed sweetness, yes?"

Abrams saw his words strike their target. Saw Harmon blink; saw his jaw firm, and his chin lift. For a long time, then, the two men simply stared at one another, assessing one another. Abrams saw no trace of awe, however, which pleased him.

Finally, Abrams nodded. "I believe we can work together, Doctor. Indeed, considering what you've already done, it's probably vital that we do. But you've done a very dangerous thing: activating Archetypes. *Mixing* them. So we have several areas to work on: the nature of these meta-spirits; how they are summoned, or perhaps created. What they are capable of.

"But there may also be one more, *key* question we need to ask: What did David Benson see, deep below the meta-planes that day in 2047, that sent him insane? What was so terrible that his mind had to wall itself off inside a belief that he was God's Son?"

"But let's start with a baby step. These meta-spirits. One of which, Godsson claims was created at the death of Melisande d'Artelle, far below Reality. Which Hunted him for fifteen years, until he and your ward together, killed it." He waited.

Harmon frowned. "Your point?"

"Think, man! No one can kill a spirit! With sufficient strength of will, a normal person can confront one – face it, even overcome it, damaging it so it dissolves back into the Imaginal. Or a mage, like you or I, can Banish them, with the same result. But in time the spirit re-forms, and can return.

"Yet this thing born from d'Artelle's murder, which Leeth and Godsson faced together, was much more than a mere spirit. And *Godsson* believes she truly slew it? Can your Huntress slay *spirits*, Doctor? Truly *end* them? Do you have any idea what that means, if it's true? Any idea what you've created?"

Harmon looked shocked.

"Good. You see a glimmer of how meta-magic works. Let us now turn our attention to this other meta-spirit Leeth spoke of. The one she named 'Robo.' The one she says Godsson told her that you and she created. And which he claims is part of this serial killer the media has named The Breaker. What can you tell me of *it?*"

CHAPTER 64

It was hard, just holding her arm still long enough for the autodoc to administer the drugs. It worked in seconds. At the relief of no longer feeling ants crawling over every nerve, she'd felt like hugging the robot arm.

But on the way back to her room, the corridor swooped in a big curl, almost tossing her to the ground. Then it swung the other way, and she had to put one hand on the wall.

Blinking, she realized it wasn't the corridor, it was her. From the drugs. Had they given her too much?

Minutes passed, and she realized she was standing still, propping herself up against the wall. This was worse than the buzzing of the caffeine. *I should get a small cup of coffee – just a little one – from the rec room, to counteract the other drugs.*

Her eyes widened as she realized what she'd just thought. *That must be how drug addicts start!* And she'd almost fallen into the trap herself. Gods, she was such a pickle, sometimes.

Drowning under a flood of tiredness, she wove an unsteady path to her room. Thinking about drugs, and death. And killing. Mother and Father's anger, at the thought she'd killed all those people. *Thinking* I *was The Breaker – that its victims were* my *work! Tortured, even worse than the Doctor did to me.* Didn't they know *she* only killed bad guys?

But that's not true, is it? a little voice demanded. *That guy in the park, or the one I pushed down the stairs: they'd been creepy, but was that enough reason to* kill *them?* She thought back to that day in the park. Her joy as she'd dropped the heart into her uncle's hand, and the expression on his face, those first few seconds. *Oh! He'd known it was wrong! So why tell me all that stuff about the sheep? Was that* all *lies?*

Maybe there weren't even any sheep? She thought of all the people she'd met: no one at the 'Fest had been a sheep. None of the people in the Dumps were. Look at Barney, working tech miracles with junk, knowing his fingers would grow too large for delicate work as he got older. Every one of them had their own hopes and dreams. Even the stupid boys at the drama school, or terrible Tara. And most of all, Marcie.

Marcie – I still haven't called her, or even Amanda!

I'm a terrible friend.

She fumbled at her door, the corridor really rocking now as she half fell inside. Blinking at the Link on her wrist, she tapped it awake and squinted into the projected screen, trying to get it in focus. "Call Marcie."

She was sitting on the floor, the echo of a negative tone in her ears. "Call. Marcie." There was text in red by the thumbnail of Marcie in the blurry scene when she peered into the virtual screen.

Another failure-tone. *Why am I sitting on the floor?* She gazed dully up at her desk. *Oh! I can use the built-in....*

She wasn't even aware of slipping sideways into sleep.

Her Link buzzed her awake, her mouth tasting awful and her bladder close to bursting. She keyed her new wrist-comm. "Urh." She swallowed. *Eww.* "Uh, Leeth here."

Mother answered, sounding pleased. "Leeth, do I take it you expect to find the killer in your rooms after all?"

"Huh?" She spun toward her bedside clock with the horrible feeling a lot of time had passed. Frick! Almost nine-thirty pm – she'd slept for nearly eight hours! And still hadn't called Marcie!

"Thirty-nine hours left, Leeth. Oh, and perhaps you might check this link for instructions, too, when you can find the time," Mother suggested sweetly before disconnecting.

The moment she finished on the toilet, Leeth called Marcie, sitting back down at her desk and picking up her carving of the dolphin. At the descending tone that indicated a failed call, she gripped it painfully tight, hunching in on herself. Looking into the privacy screen, unaware of the computing and optics required to track her eyes and focus the image, red text appeared beside Marcie's picture: 'Link offline.'

She stared at it in horror, fearing the worst. *Call Amanda.* If Marcie *was* okay, that way she wouldn't get in trouble with her dad. If she *wasn't* okay...

It didn't take long to look up Amanda Dunkirk and put the call through – after first setting her ID to Jane Baker.

It answered on the first ring, submerging her in a flood of words.

"Jane! Is Marcie with you? We're so worried! Where

are you? Is she all right? Are you all right? Dad's *spare!*"
Her voice faded slightly. "Dad! It's Jane Baker!-"

"Amanda, stop. Didn't Marcie- isn't she with-?"

The sound dropped, then a man's voice spoke: Graham Dunkirk, Marcie's father. "Jane bloody Baker. Where's my daughter?"

"She's not...?" Leeth's fingers slid over the dolphin's hard curves, her mouth working. She cringed, picturing Mr Dunkirk's reaction if she dared tell him the lie she'd given the Department, to protect Marcie. But she had to. It was better for Marcie's father to be furious with *her.* "Uh, I invited her to come and see me fight last night, in the Dumps."

The silence at the other end of the Link was glacial. Towering. "The *Hunters Point* Dumps, not the West Oakland one!"

The silence grew.

"Uh, she was-" *almost raped, but we got her out before anything worse than-* "she was, in a, a, sort of rescue. But," *me and this vampire* "I put her in a car, she was going straight home...."

She squeezed her eyes shut. *We should have gone with her. But she was okay! What could've happened?* "Are you sure she never got home?"

The silence grew to a mighty wave. Poised to crash down on her, its crest curled over....

Graham Dunkirk's voice was dangerously low as he asked "Rescue?"

The rest of the conversation went downhill rapidly. By the end of the call, Leeth was shaking, tears streaming down her face. She felt like he'd flayed her, yet wished he'd done worse.

Something terrible had happened to Marcie. And it was her fault.

And then something Mother had said returned to her, and her heart sank like a stone dropping into her stomach. 'Someone strong like you follows you around, killing one or two people nearby.'

The dolphin fell from her fingers. *The Breaker had taken Marcie.* Might be torturing her, even now. The tail of the wooden carving hit the hard tile, snapping off and floating through the air. Her mind went blank. Then began racing.

Seated at her desk, she called Eagle by vid. Explained about putting Marcie in a car, near the West Oakland Dumps. Myrtle Street. About four a.m. Asked if anyone – even Nelson, maybe – could find out what had happened to the car? Maybe check up on the victims they'd rescued from Club Juzz.

Eagle's eyes bored into hers. He nodded, and disconnected.

What else could she do? She should be out there, scouring the area! *At least it fits my current mission,* she thought, feeling like screaming. With that, though, she finally pointed to the icon representing the departmental communique, opening it. It was now a pulsing, angry red. Dated three hours earlier and obviously written by Mother, it outlined the equipment she should collect, and the time remaining: almost thirty-nine hours. She had to fight down hysterical laughter. If she couldn't find The Breaker before the next *dawn,* she doubted she'd see Marcie alive again. *If she's not dead already.*

On the floor, her small wooden dolphin looked up at her. She bent, scooping it up, and its tail. *I knew I'd carved that bit too thin. Sorry.* She felt her lower lip quiver. "You'll be okay, Toby," she whispered to him, kissing his tiny rounded snout. "A bit of glue and you'll be good as new. I *promise.*" She set both pieces back down on her desk, blinking rapidly.

And felt a slow anger rise. She needed to run, to be *doing;* but instead, she took deep breaths, remembering Dojo's words. *A clear mind wins battles.*

Grimly, she grabbed her cashstick and freshly-cleaned clothes, and dressed. Somehow, she'd finished her entire food stash. Flying from her rooms to the tiny and rarely-used cafeteria, she punched out six muesli bars from the food dispenser and tucked a couple of pouches of water into her jacket's pockets. Thinking.

How to find Marcie.

One muesli bar later she was at the office of the Department's admin assistant, fretting as she waited for his return while he fetched the tracer device she was supposed to wear.

Forcing herself to stay calm while he went off to get the equipment from stores, she thought about Mother's written instructions. *Should you remove the tracer once it has *been placed, the Department will understand you have chosen to retire. We will, of course, give you every assistance to ensure your decision is swiftly and thoroughly realized.*

Leeth snorted, rolling her eyes. The first step would be getting Godsson to undo the Doctor's conditioning. Scary, but necessary. Then, maybe give them a warning. It didn't have to be total war. Hopefully, she wouldn't have to kill any of them. Maybe just Mother. And Preacher. Maybe Nelson, too. Except he was apparently needed for the important work they were all doing: look how they'd over-reacted when she'd almost killed him.

What was taking 'Little Brother' so long? *Maybe he has to catch a cockroach?*

She shuddered, hoping it wasn't going to be *that* kind of bug this time. To distract herself she began prowling the room, devouring muesli bars.

The small office had a desk, a couple of plain chairs, and a taller chair at a workbench that stretched along the wall.

Scattered across it were grinding wheels, clamps, and all sorts of little machines she'd never seen before. Small steel gas cylinders, coils of soft thick wires and heavy flexible metal strips, pliers with pointy ends. Several different kinds of 3D printers. She crammed more food in her mouth while poking through the gear. Refilling a water pouch, she opened another muesli bar, still thinking about how to find Marcie.

And saw the solution, with a sinking feeling. The Doctor.

She slumped on the sofa by the other wall, eyeing the shelf beside it where packets of data cubes sat nicely arranged alongside a stimsense hairnet. She shuddered, remembering Nelson's attempt to trap her. Each cube was neatly-labeled – stuff on machining, electronics, 'Materials' – weird: did he make *dresses?*

But she was avoiding her problem, not facing it. She had to ask the Doctor for help.

Her Link chimed, caller ID Eagle. "Sir?"

"Only one vehicle was called between four a.m and four-thirty, in that area. Nelson interrogated it. Thirty seconds after the trip began, the car performed emergency braking to avoid a pedestrian collision. Five seconds later it rolled onto its side, *while stationary.* A door lock snapped. The seat belt was unlocked. The car was righted. Then the trip was aborted."

"The Breaker!"

Eagle nodded. "Mother notes that your alibi – Tash – is unavailable for questioning."

"That's ridic-"

But Eagle was shaking his head. "Quite. I look forward to seeing you correct her opinion." Eagle studied her intently, his lips pressed together. "Mother doubts your sanity. Imagines we need tighter control of you."

She clenched her jaw.

"I do not. I have faith in you. Don't let me down."

She blinked, her throat tightening.

"Do you need anything more?"

She was a little amazed by how quickly he and Nelson had worked to gather the information. "Uh... do I have permission to ask the Doctor to try to do a Sending to locate Marcie?"

Eagle raised an eyebrow. "Yes. But *you* fetch the necessary material from the Dunkirks. Some hair, perhaps?"

"Thank you, Sir!"

He nodded, still watching her with a somehow unsettling air of assessment.

She was about to leave when Little Brother *finally* returned, with a small lapel pin kind of thing and a hipbag.

She had a water pouch in one hand, about to take a drink, and her third muesli bar in the other. "You fix it on me, I'm in kind of a hurry." On her Link, she called a car to pick her up from the street, above.

Leeth saw his eyes catch on her barely-fastened denim jacket, and looked down at herself. After yesterday's activities, the cloth ties looked even worse for wear. If he did make dresses, maybe he wasn't too impressed with the outfit she'd put together? She straightened up a little. Strangely, he blushed. She wondered if he'd done something stupid.

She almost asked, but really didn't have time to be side-tracked. "Come on, come on."

Taking a swallow of water, she ripped open the wrapper on the third bar and bit into it, her hunger easing, while he very carefully pinned the tracer under her collar. As she finished the bar, a thought occurred to her. "It won't broadcast all the time, will it?"

"No, ma'am. Only when it's pinged."

"'Ma'am'?" she asked, disbelievingly. She looked at him properly for the first time. Older than her but a lot younger than James. A round and ordinary face, brown hair, big worried blue eyes. He was blushing again, not looking at her.

What is wrong *with him?* But she really didn't have time now to work it out. Draining the water sachet she rolled up its soft plastic, recapping it. "What's in the bag?"

"A gun. Some soybars-"

"I don't need a gun!"

His face creased into a worried frown that somehow made him look even younger. "It's Father's orders."

Rolling her eyes she stuck the last muesli bar, still in its wrapper, into her mouth. Grabbing the bag from him she unzipped it and took a small gun out, frowning. An HK Snub 7. Hooking the bag's strap over her arm she popped the little composite's clip, checking. Fully loaded with four rounds, the gun was smaller than her hand. She shook her head, slid the clip back home, then dumped gun, both full and empty water pouches, and the last muesli bar into the bag. She mentally shrugged as she slung the strap round her hip. She didn't need a weapon – which was just as well, since the Snub hardly counted as one.

"That it?"

He held his hands out, palms up. "Sorry."

Sorry? What was he sorry about? She stared at him for a full second before snapping out of it.

Next: the Doctor.

She wondered if Eagle had contacted him. Somehow, she suspected not.

At the door to his office, her hand dropped briefly to check Barney's micro-speaker at her belt, clicking her teeth twice to make sure it was still working. She tried, again, to memorize the string of nonsense syllables – and again failed. Scowling, she knocked.

The door whisked open.

"Ye-" His mouth sat open, then he collected himself. "Leeth. I've heard what happened, and I want to reassure you. Even if no one else does, *I* know the idea that you are responsible is ludicrous."

"But I *am* responsible. I shouldn't have left her."

At her words, he looked at first appalled; then, as she continued, confused. "Left who?"

"Marcie. The Breaker's got her. Eagle said he'll let you do a Sending to find her, if I can get some of her hair from her father." She swallowed. Again, she felt her throat constrict. "You *will* do a Sending," she told him, then found herself blinking rapidly. Wanting to *kill* him. Wanting to beg him to do his utmost to help her save Marcie. Like he'd once done, to heal Faith.

She spun away, so he wouldn't see her expression. "I'm going to get the, the hair."

She stormed from the room, furious at herself.

CHAPTER 65

In the auto-drive car, Leeth sat hunched forward, wishing it could go faster, yet dreading the arrival. Wondering what The Breaker might be like, in person. Wondering what she'd do if her uncle *couldn't* locate Marcie magically. Wondering how long it took to do a Sending. Frowning, she realized she had no idea. No idea, even, about most of the magic her uncle could do, or what was really possible.

Some searching on the net told her he'd need something called a 'ritual circle.' Assuming he already had one made – and surely he must, he'd tried finding *her* often enough while she'd been on the run – it should take him an hour.

And then the car was slowing down, and she was at Marcie's house.

Maybe she should have told them she was coming. She tapped her cashstick to the car's debit tab, told it to wait, and stepped out.

With a deep breath she strode up the path. Up the steps. Onto the porch. And pressed the bell.

Running footsteps approached from inside; Marcie's father called out for Amanda to stop. Heavy treads, then the door opened.

"Fook." Graham Dunkirk stared down at her like he wanted to wring her neck. Behind him, Amanda hovered, her eyes red, gazing at her like she was their Last Great Hope.

"Where's my daughter? What've you gotten her into *this* time?"

Leeth frowned, hearing two more people approaching from inside the house. One, *very* heavy, but both somehow stealthy...

Knocking Graham Dunkirk aside, she dived past Amanda, shouting back to them that there was someone else inside, and that they should *get out!*

Two men, one small, one *fat,* stepped into the corridor, half filling it. The Breaker was *two* people?

She leaped, ripping the gun from the smaller man's hand and somersaulting over him to the man behind, already casting some sort of spell.

He stiffened as she jammed the gun in his neck, then *she* stilled, recognizing him. Detective Berlusconi, or something. Garland's partner. A mage.

From back down the corridor, Amanda and her father

stared at her in shock.

"You fucker," the blobby man spat, then went on to accuse her of killing his wife, his partner, his *wife's* partner...

"Shut up, you idiot! Shut up! I didn't kill any of those people! I. Am not. The Breaker."

Lowering the gun she'd taken, she shoved past him, and the smaller man, who was now massaging his hand. She thrust the gun back at the little guy, but stayed close, ready to knock out him and the fat *mage*.

"You're cops! And *you're* Garland's partner!"

The fat cop pushed past his smaller, sandy-haired partner and bent down into her face. He stabbed a finger into the middle of her collarbone. "You sick, little- ah! *Holy fuck!*"

She trapped his pudgy hand in hers, then *trembled*, straining with the effort *not* to snap his fat finger off and shove it.... She let him go. "Don't. Ever. Poke me."

The detective spoke past her, to the Dunkirks. "Your daughter's friend here killed my ex-partner, the bravest man I ever knew, my *best fucking friend*, this morning at 5:53. Do not trust a *word* that comes out of this lying little bitch's mouth."

"I did not!"

He turned to her, fury blazing in his eyes. "Yeah? You're gonna lie to *me* now, bitch? Lie to my fucken face? Tell me he didn't arrest you this morning? Cuff you? Lock you in his car?"

Leeth opened her mouth to explain, then remembered Father saying Nelson had removed all traces of her from the scene. Which meant if she said she *was* there, she'd expose the cover-up....

She ground her teeth.

"Shall I go on? You smashed your way out of the car, took Adam down, cuffed *him*, then crushed his skull like it was a fucken eggshell! But only after you'd made him practically cut his own hands off, trying to snap the *three* nylon cuffs you needed...." He stuttered to a halt, swallowing. "Then you fished around in his brain and yanked out all his headware. And left him dead."

"I didn't kill him. I didn't."

The man was crying. For his friend. His friend, killed by The Breaker. *Because* I *tied him up*, she suddenly grasped. *Left him there, helpless. Unable to defend him-*

self.

"Yeah, you can't deny it, can you?"

She shook her head, stunned. *I gave him to The Breaker. Me.*

She knew Mother would be furious if she admitted to this guy that she'd been there. *But he's already guessed there was a cover-up.* "Okay, yeah, he arrested me this morning." Behind her, she heard Amanda gasp. "And I did get free, pretty much like you said, and tied him up. And I guess, in a way, I did kill him, because I left him there. But *I* didn't do it. The Breaker did."

The man stared at her in disbelief, then looked past her. "She fucken believes that. As far as she's concerned, she's telling the truth. And I've seen her do it before – fucken lied to my face, and told me she didn't kill a poor sodding jogger in Golden Gate Park, after she'd ripped his fucken heart out of his chest."

It was true. She remembered him asking her, kind of dimly. Her uncle had made her back into Sara, and Sara had answered him, told him *she* hadn't killed the man. He'd had a Truth spell running, her uncle had told her, later.

He had a Truth spell running now.

"Jane?" Amanda asked from behind her. "That's not true, is it? You- you didn't do that, did you?"

She was trapped. There was no answer she could give, no truth, no lie, that would fix this situation. She felt a terrifying sense of helplessness, like she was being boxed in so she wouldn't be able to help Marcie, and Marcie would die because of what she'd done in the past, everything *she'd* done.

She turned to Amanda, stricken. "I didn't kill Agent Garland. I'm not The Breaker. I came here to get some of Marcie's hair, from a hairbrush, so... someone I know can locate her, magically."

Amanda eyes were large, and round: wanting to believe, but suddenly uncertain. Half-hiding, now, behind her father. Hiding from *her*. Which hurt, more than Leeth had ever expected.

Why was this all going so wrong?

"Don't. Believe. A word. She says," the fat cop repeated. Then his eyes pinned her again. "I got some messages from Garland through the night, you know? 'Meet me for coffee.' 'Got news on The Breaker.' 'Following Sara, from the Park.' 'Sara's a vampire.'"

Another gasp from Amanda, behind her.

"And you know what his last message on this Earth was, 'Jane'? His very last word, while you were crushing the life from him? That one-" his voice faltered. "That one, was voice, not text. It was 5:53am. He called me. Just one word: your name, the name of his killer, while you murdered him, ending transmission."

Leeth reeled. Why would Agent Garland say *her* name? *Had* she killed him? She shook her head. *I didn't. I left him there. I ran back to the Department. I even had the wrapper from the chocolate.* Unless... had Nelson and her uncle programmed her to think that? Was everyone right, and she couldn't trust her own memories? Had Robo gotten inside *her*, so she didn't know what she was doing?

Was it possible?

No.

No, she was sure. And she was going to find Marcie, and save her.

They were all staring at her.

"Go up to your room, Amanda." Mr Dunkirk's words seemed to toll with the finality of a funeral bell. With a last, frightened look at her, Marcie's sister scampered back, and up the stairs. Though Leeth heard her footsteps stop above, on the landing.

"I came to get some hairs-"

"Liar," the fat cop spat at her. "Or if you did, it's part of some other plan. Because you know Marcie is already dead. Or dying."

But for the first time, the detective sounded less than a hundred percent certain of himself.

Leeth clutched at that. "Marcie's not dead. She can't be dead. You don't know that."

Graham Dunkirk answered. "Detective Berlusconi finished trying to locate my daughter thirty minutes ago, Jane Baker. *Sara*. And failed. All he saw was death."

She heard the heaviness in Marcie's father's voice, the angry grief, but she was watching Berlusconi's face. And she saw *something* there, some flicker of expression that gave her just a sliver of hope. "That's not exactly true, is it, Detective? There was something weird about it, wasn't there? You're not *certain* Marcie's dead!"

She read the accuracy of her guess from the way his eyes narrowed.

"What have you done to her?" he whispered, horrified.

"Nothing!   Nothing except leave her this morning, when Tash and I should have taken her home, after we...."

"After you what, Jane Baker?"

She wanted to turn, and face Marcie's father, but dared not take her eyes from the two cops. Both had tensed up. She sensed things coming to a head.

"I don't believe Marcie's dead," she told the fat cop. "I think you didn't try hard enough to find her. Or you got scared, or something. *Please*," she begged, wishing she dared turn around, "*please* give me some of Marcie's hairs so the man who healed Marcie can try to locate her; so *I* can save her. *Please*, Mr Dunkirk!"

Upstairs, she heard Amanda's quiet gasp of in-drawn breath.

"Don't trust her, Dunkirk. I don't know why she wants it, but *she* is The Breaker, and god alone knows what she plans to do with it if you give it to her."

"I'm *not* The Breaker. I'm Hunting it. I'm gonna save Marcie and *end* The Breaker, once and for all. Or die trying," she vowed.

"Fook," said Graham Dunkirk.

"You're not going anywhere, girl. You're under arrest on suspicion-"

Both cops reached for their guns, and Leeth swore as she flung herself first at the mage, then the sandy-haired man.

She smashed their weapons from their hands. Gut-punching the mage while kicking back into the thin one's belly, she brought both to their knees. She spun, a palm strike to Berlusconi and a knee to the other's head hammering them unconscious and to the floor. She straightened, feeling virtuous at how carefully she'd judged each blow.

Then looked up from their bodies to find Graham Dunkirk staring steadily at her.   He stood slightly crouched, well-balanced, and his eyes darted to one of the guns.

"No," she whispered, shaking her head. "Please don't."

From behind him, light footsteps came down the stairs, and Amanda crept around the corridor, her eyes wide.

"I trust Jane, Da."
In her hand, Leeth saw she held a hairbrush.

CHAPTER 66

Marcie came to, facing down a dark concrete stairwell, bouncing on someone's shoulder, the gray walls illuminated by flashlight. A brown painted handrail.

"You awaken."

Marcie stiffened, shock paralyzing her. Mark Dennis. Marc Disten.

No! Please, no, not again! I'm not strong enough to survive this again!

"You fear. This is good."

She grabbed for her Link – only to find a bare wrist. Her head was aching. She drew in a breath, and screamed.

"HELP! SOMEBODY HELP ME!"

He just kept walking up the stairs. She screamed until her throat hurt. When she paused, he spoke again. "No one can hear you."

He was only lightly holding her, and she twisted, pushing herself – and felt a hand clamp on her back, pressing her down against his shoulder so hard she gasped.

"Where are we?"

She shivered, and not just from the nightmare she'd woken to.

"You will recognize it soon."

For some reason, she felt she almost did. As he continued relentlessly up the stairs, she gradually noticed the whole stairwell was tilted.

A sick certainty flooded through her. She felt death, ghostly fingers, pressing all around her.

Candlestick Tower. She groaned, then started screaming again.

Before they reached the top, though, she'd stopped again. Regained control. Asking herself, 'Would Stryker Zaxx scream like this? Would *Jane*?'

Pretend it's just a movie, she told herself. *The tough-as-nails heroine's been abducted, but she's just biding her time.*

The stairs ended in a landing by a door. He calmly lifted her from his shoulder with one hand, gripping her with the shocking strength she'd felt once before, and set her on her feet. His hands blurred, and then he was pinning both her wrists in one of his large hands.

As she'd feared, she stared into Mark Dennis's eyes.

With an effort, she drew the Stryker Zaxx role around

her; pretended this was her audition. "So, we meet again, Mr Dennis. Or should I say, *Marc Disten*."

His head tilted, as if mildly intrigued. In one hand, he held a flashlight, which he slipped into a pocket, its lens facing up.

The light dropped, dark shadows pooling up from his features. She felt her nerve fade; then thought of Jane, and straightened her spine.

He seemed to focus on her with more interest.

"You control your fear."

She felt a thrill of horror shock through her, but quashed it. "Don't we all, Mr Disten?" She even managed a smile. As if she was used to getting kidnapped, and escaping. *Maybe I am.* A hysterical giggle swelled, but she fought that down, too. "You look... I won't say, 'well'. Perhaps 'recovered'." *You're Stryker Zaxx,* she told herself, and felt her lip curl confidently. She would have put her hands on her hips, if he hadn't been pinning them as tightly as steel bands.

"You had been paralyzed. Did Jane Baker heal you?"

About to say no, she changed her mind before the words left her mouth. "Yes. And she'll come for me, too. You have no idea of the spells she's mastered. The supernatural allies she can call. You'd be wise to let me go." She slipped deeper into her role. "If you release me, unharmed, I will try to convince her to take you in, instead of killing you."

But she saw that her words were having no impact on him. Reaching into his jacket, he pulled out nylon cuffs, threading them around her wrists and tightening them painfully. She tried to resist, but didn't think he even noticed.

She felt her nerve falter. "You don't need to do this. You'll gain nothing by hurting me. You'll only make her angrier. And I wouldn't want to be in your shoes, if Jane gets angry."

He watched her with interest. "You think she will come for you? You think she cares for you?"

Her chin came up. "I *know* she does."

"Good. This is good. You are probably unnecessary. But the wait has been long. And it is wise to have contingency plans."

He drew a wad of dirty cloth from his tattered jacket.

She began desperately struggling as he forced her jaws open, packing it inside.

She kicked futilely at him as he opened the door and dragged her, one handed, out into a circular hallway, then down a corridor radiating from it. Down toward a broken window that gaped onto empty space. Dawn was breaking.

But not for her.

He stopped, reaching up to a large stainless steel handle, pulling open a drawer. It slid out, and out, across the corridor, revealing a pallet contoured to accept a human body. She began screaming, begging against the gag, not to be put inside.

Effortlessly, he lifted her, slamming her down into the coffin-like pod despite her struggles.

"Do not panic and damage yourself. Food and drink will be provided, as long as you might be needed."

Sliding the drawer shut, he sealed her into claustrophobic blackness.

Packed in alongside all the other bodies.

CHAPTER 67

With the precious hairbrush delivered and the detective's worrying comments passed to her uncle, Leeth found herself at a loss.

She'd gone back to the place where they'd watched Club Juzz burn, looking for clues, but found none. Asking around, she'd gotten into several brief but satisfyingly brutal fights with locals who objected to her presence. But learned nothing.

And then she got the call from her uncle that sent her back toward Hunters Point.

"The Sending..." he'd started, then stopped. He must have heard her reaction, somehow, through the silence. "I understand why Detective Berlusconi said your friend is dead, Leeth. But, *you* were right, also. It was strange. The spell failed to... 'lock'. As it would if she were dead, or magically shielded. I sensed death, I'm sorry."

She'd heard the 'but', and waited till he continued, explaining more. And learned that, for no reason he could justify, he had found himself imagining the area he'd spent so many weeks searching recently, for her. The Hunters Point Dumps.

"Leeth," he'd continued, his tone softening, "we need to talk. About our relation-"

She ended the call. *How dare he!*

Paying off the car, she stepped out, breathing hard. *Don't think about him. He's just a distraction.* As the vehicle sped off behind her, she looked out and down into what had been, until 2044, Hunters Point.

It felt like coming home.

Why me? she wondered. *Is it really killing people near where I go?* That seemed a key question. 'It seeks you,' Godsson had said. But had he been telling the truth, or just making it up?

Standing there on the street, among people wandering the small night market on the edge of the Dumps, she felt the urge to just *run* grip her: south east and up, toward the Bay, to the highest point she could find. She imagined herself silhouetted against the night sky, gazing out over the sea of jagged-jutting slabs and concrete crevasses that fell away gradually to become the Hunters Point Dumps.

She shook the dream away. *Like I could magically pick out the right location just by staring at it?* She imagined Mother's sneer: 'I see. You spent *how* many hours in-

tuiting the location of your prey?'

But from what Godsson said, it was searching for her. *I wonder if he knows some way I could call it to me?* She didn't think she'd be able to convince anyone to let her go back so she could *ask* him, though. And she was pretty sure she didn't have the time to break in. Again.

Pulling herself together, she trotted south along the night-lit street, dodging through colorful crowds and stalls. *I'm a real agent, now. I have to do this like a real agent does. Marcie's depending on me.* She tried to remember what she'd been taught about tracking enemy agents.

A sudden aroma of toasted cheddar stopped her briefly at a food stall. The food smelled delicious, laid out in tasty strips, and she only had two of her dry, plastic-wrapped muesli bars left. She bought a hot cheese-filled cornmeal cake. Wolfing it down, she gulped some more water, then bought a sugary cone of *piloncillo* too, with a guilty air. Crunching off just one bite, she put it away, eyes closing in pleasure at the dark molasses flavor. But the thought of Marcie had her blushing in shame, and she swallowed with difficulty, and jogged on up the long steep hill toward the earthquake-thrust heights of Bayview.

Maybe all she had to do was just wander around and let The Breaker come to her? It sounded too easy. And suppose it *didn't* come to her? She'd been here for weeks, and it never had, so why should it suddenly come for her now? Besides, she was a Huntress, not bait!

No, she'd search around, talk to the inhabitants. See if they'd noticed anything strange. Any disappearances. Like a detective would.

She could call in on Barney and Teef, see if they knew any rumors. Pay Teef the rest of the money she owed him, too.

Frowning, she increased her pace, descending the first of the terraces leading into the Dumps.

Just for a moment a weird, depressing kind of cold shivered through her, like she'd felt sometimes back in the Forest, just before Mean Robo turned up. The feeling was so strong she paused, *not-looking* around, eyes unfocused, trying to sense an invisible creature. But 'seeing' Robo had always been harder than 'seeing' *Her*.

Robo....

Godsson and me killed Her. Is this all happening be-

cause Robo and me grew up together? Is it really looking for me, like Godsson said?

Pieces started falling together. She thought about her killing shadow – all those extra deaths, from the young guy in the Park, to Marie Lempriere, to the two detectives, to poor Agent Garland, this morning, who *she'd* tied up and left for his killer to find. Only the two detectives had been tortured, like The Breaker did. But could *all* of them have been kills by The Breaker?

She paused, blinking.

Godsson had *told* her: she and the Doctor had made Robo, and Robo had become The Breaker. It even thought of her as its mother, who'd abandoned it, he'd said. That idea stabbed right through her, the pain plunging so deep it made her sway on her feet.

Whoah. What was that all about? It required a conscious effort to unlock her muscles, and force her mind back on track. Robo was The Breaker, and it was following her: trying blindly to find her. Killing for no reason. Killing innocent people.

Tonight, she hunted Robo. A chill shivered down her spine.

Suddenly the hunt scared her. *Should I call the Department? Tell them what I've worked out?* But then she remembered Eagle warning her, with Mr Abrams nodding, that Godsson was called the Manipulator for good reason. That he told lies.

Gnawing her lip, she thought.... *But what* did *happen to Mean Robo? What would've happened if Mean Robo got inside someone, like She tried to do to me?*

The idea seemed really important. She imagined trying to explain it to Mother, or even Father, and rolled her eyes. She'd probably have a hard time convincing those two that water was wet.

She could call Eagle – he'd understand. He'd-

He'd call me back in. Re-plan. Involve the others. But no one – except me, and maybe Godsson – had ever been able to hurt Her. She remembered the FBI agents, and soldiers: vulnerable, helpless, while *She* coiled through them, invisible, whispering awful thoughts in their heads. What if *Robo* got inside the Department? Got inside James, or Emma? Or Eagle? Or the Doctor? *That* thought made her shudder.

And while they re-planned, Marcie might die. She re-fused to think Marcie might *already-*

Besides, she'd lived alone, in the Dumps, for four weeks, and it'd never searched her out. Had something happened to it? Maybe someone in the Dumps had already killed it? Or maybe she was wrong, and Robo wasn't The Breaker. Maybe Godsson had been lying, like everyone said.

She continued on. Alone. Uncertain.

"Hey, look, it's Sleena!"

Leeth turned, recognizing a tattered but vivid orange scarf; a splash of color in otherwise-drab clothing. She'd noticed it, briefly, in the crowd at the 'Fest the previous night.

The young girl, smiling, beckoned her over to what looked like a family group in the rusting minibus.

As she crossed the broken ground she noted the pleased faces, and a peculiar and much-needed feeling of warmth settled over her. That feeling strengthened when they asked her in to share their food. Especially consider-ing how little they had; and what she hunted.

Several people had called greetings earlier, too. As if they'd recognized her. Accepted her. It felt strange. Nice, but strange. She felt herself relax, just a little. It was weird how many of them now remembered her even here, deep in the Dumps, kilometers from where the 'Fest had been held. It must be really popular.

Looking around in the cozy warmth at the jumble of makeshift junk, neatly stored in carefully accessible order, she politely accepted a nibble of food and asked her ques-tions. Any disappearances? Unexplained deaths? Any-thing weird or strange at all?

They couldn't tell her much, but did want to know why she was asking. She said she'd heard rumors of something dangerous in the area, and had decided she wanted to Hunt it. They nodded to each other, pleased, which again made her feel strangely warm. She didn't want to say it was The Breaker – didn't want to start scaring people. She definitely didn't want to explain how it might be connected to her.

A few of the children wanted to come with her, but she explained that she hunted alone – to the parents' obvious relief. Could they think of anyone else who might know anything? Finally, with a shake of hands all round, she'd trotted off.

She also learned a little more about the places where some of the earlier disappearances had happened: that there had been some unexplained violent deaths nearby. Several of the people she'd spoken to reckoned some troll had gone mad.

It was almost midnight, now, and she must have talked to a couple of dozen different groups. The moon was half full and there was a chill in the air. Fog rolled in again from the Bay, glowing in the moonlight. In the distance a lone dog howled. She headed deeper into the Dumps, leaping from one concrete slab to another. Broken walls loomed up on either side, casting deep shadows as she moved on, considering what she'd learned.

All the water she'd drunk started to make itself felt. Scanning the area, she looked first for possible watchers, then for cover for herself. The wind was rising as she paused, listening. Concentrating, she *subtracted* the sound, remembering Dojo's words: 'Be wise like an animal: smell, look, listen. When you pee, you are prey.'

To her left the street tilted crazily, making a convenient gully of folded asphalt. Sheltered from the moonlight by the overhang of a broken wall, she entered the area slowly. As her eyes adjusted to the deeper darkness, she grew aware of the slow drift of pale moon shadows sliding across the empty night-scape.

Moving carefully over the broken ground, she reached a suitable point and stopped. Deciding it was safe, she squatted, panties pulled to one side as she relieved herself, staying alert.

It didn't look dark at all now. She had to tell herself she'd be invisible here except to other night hunters, or people with light intensifiers. She wondered... if The Breaker *had* been made by her and the Doctor, like Gods-son said, did that mean it could hear like she could, see in the dark like her? She didn't know how her senses worked so well. Eagle said he'd arrange some tests of her abilities, to compare her to the other agents. She looked forward to it – it should be fun!

She'd already decided, though, she'd keep her hearing secret. Even if the Doctor hadn't *conditioned* her to do that.

Her hearing went a long way beyond what even the agents could achieve. The agents could hear some of the high sounds she could, but not all the time – they seemed to have to specially activate it. And she was certain none of them could *tune out* sounds like she could, to hear the noises hidden beneath. They couldn't *hear past* louder stuff to quieter sounds underneath. That was her special ability. Her secret.

Hers. And the Doctor's. *And maybe Eagle's, too, now.* Who hadn't, it seemed, told anyone else. *How had he worked it out?* And if he had, how much else had he figured out? Was that part of why her uncle had seemed to be in trouble? *Though less than he deserved.* She fingered Barney's precious acoustic device, her Harmon neutralizer, its slim disk pressed flat against her stomach.

Finally, finishing, she dabbed with a tissue then tossed it aside and stood up. At her feet, the white paper glowed like a beacon. Wondering if it would later be collected by scavengers for some use, she smiled: then stilled. DNA traces could be used to track someone magically. With a grimace, she crouched back down and picked it daintily up.

A short distance away, scraping aside some rubble to bury it, she thought over everything she'd learned so far. The disappearances were usually humans; usually lovers, or family; usually two people at once. Which seemed pretty strange: two victims *had* to be riskier to capture than one. And mostly taken in the daytime, too, though always in the loneliest places. Rarely signs of a struggle: and even then, only brief.

Why did Robo-Breaker target couples so often? Was it jealous 'cause they were happy? Or because they were a family, and it was hunting for her, its 'mother'? The thought screwed a strange pain through her belly, again.

Brushing her hands clean she stood up and checked the time. Five minutes to midnight, and still nothing had shown up. She looked around, thinking. Was he out there, somewhere she hadn't seen? Killing people she talked to....

Her head came up. All those nice people she'd spoken to tonight! She spun around and raced off.

But as she accelerated, a rock shifted behind her, maybe a hundred meters back. Diving to the ground, she waited unmoving, just listening.

Whatever was behind her immediately stopped, too. Shutting her eyes, she concentrated, probing for the sound of breathing....

After a minute, though, she heard nothing further. Not a whisper of breath; not a brush of cloth against cloth; not a creak of leather.

I don't have time for this. She sprang up and sprinted away. *Those people might be in trouble!*

CHAPTER 68

Two hours later, Leeth leapt grumpily from one tumble of concrete to the next, once again on the edge of the Dumps. She hadn't been able to find everyone she'd spoken to earlier tonight, but all the ones she *had* found were still okay. Though the Blackberry tribe were worried about two of their teenagers, Billy and Anna, and had asked her to keep an eye out for the young lovers.

The one bright moment had been catching up with Teef, and Barney. Barney had been like a love-smitten puppy, though Teef had looked wary – if also impressed. And happy to be paid.

She'd also ordered and paid for a second, spare Harmon neutralizer. Just in case.

But she was still no closer to finding The Breaker. And time had to be running out for Marcie.

As she darted uphill she considered yet again what she'd learned. Something had been preying on the people here. For some reason it mainly took couples. *Like Billy and Anna?* She shivered.

She continued on.

But why take Marcie? Marcie, on her own?

She stopped, feeling a little sick. *Because it's connected to* me, *and it knows Marcie and I care about each other. It* is *coming for me!* But her delight changed to puzzlement. *But* how *does it know that? By watching us for a few minutes, last night?*

A lot of the people had disappeared from the fringes of the Dumps. There'd also been those violent deaths that no tribe or gang claimed, in the areas where people had disappeared. Had those people been killed because they'd seen something? Stumbled on the people being taken, and been killed for it?

But the other weird thing she should have seen ages ago, as a clue that it was Mean Robo: that boy who'd been turned into a 'zombie,' working like a robot to turn a patch of rubble into a garden field. Was that what happened if Robo got inside you? Could it somehow *infect* people?

Could Robo do that to *her?* But the boy had had a lover who'd disappeared at the same time he'd been zombied, they'd told her. Why would Robo-Breaker turn one boy into a zombie and kill the other? Was it some sort of magic ritual?

The idea felt right, somehow. She just wished she

could cut through the fog of possibilities. She felt again the urge to get up high, like she'd wanted to at the start, as if she could just look down over the jumbled land and pick the right spot by feel.

She faltered, struck by an idea.

If it *was* following her around, killing people near her, it had to have some way of knowing where she was.

Sure, *tonight* she wore a tracer, but normally she was clean. The Department made sure of that, electronically and digitally.

But not magically.

Her breath hissed out. Magically, as soon as she stepped out past their fixed magical Wards, she was on her own.

It was sensing her *magically*. Could she sense *it* magically, too, in that case?

But once again, it came back to those four weeks she'd been on her own, not behind any Wards. It hadn't come to her then. Even though Godsson said it was looking for her. Looking for its mother to hug it and heal it. He'd even 'blessed' her, to help her do that.

Why hadn't it come to her when she'd been living here, though? Practically sitting still, waiting.

Unless... had it been captured? Imprisoned, so it couldn't get to her? Straining to get to its mother, but failing?

Again, that strange pain twisted in her stomach, this time with a flush of fever that made her ears burn.

Captured, or... *injured*?

Her mouth dropped open in sudden realization. Who had once followed her, tracking her, making her feel strange, like Robo? Who had spoken like a robot, never showing any emotion? Who would have been incapacitated for at least four weeks, after she'd thrown him from the truck? By rights, Mark Dennis should have died, but what if he hadn't? His body had never been found. And *he* knew she and Marcie cared about one another!

Mark Dennis was The Breaker. She was sure of it.

Mark Dennis has captured Marcie! Again! No, no, no! But despite the horror of that, there was hope, too. The Breaker always tortured its victims in front of each other. *That's why he takes couples!* But it meant Marcie should still be alive – probably even, unharmed.

Mark Dennis wouldn't be, once she found him.

But why would he take Marcie, on her own? *Ohhh: because he knows Marcie's the person I care most about in the world. He wants to capture me too so he can torture us together, just like the others.* She felt her jaw clamp tight. *That's a bad plan, Mr Dennis. A bad plan.*

She shut her eyes, stilled her breathing, and listened. For long seconds, she just listened.

Nothing.

She took a deep breath and started walking again. She wondered what time it was. It felt like it was about 2am. She checked her wristcomm. Yeah, 1:53.

Her stomach felt tense. She broke into a jog. She needed *action*.

For a while, she thought she heard it, *him*, behind, following her. But each time she stopped to listen better, or even just slowed down, whatever faint sounds there were, simply stopped. Each time it happened, the thing was further away. Harder to hear.

She couldn't understand how it could tell when she was listening for it.

Surely, it had to be The Breaker – who else would be following her? Why didn't it come to her, though?

But when she revisited the first family she'd spoken to tonight, for a third time, a whole lot of things became clear. Horribly clear.

She still couldn't believe it, though.

"Hey! Sleena!"

The girl with the orange scarf had been delighted to see her again. "Are you and Tash hunting it together? Are you two a team?"

Leeth had just blinked at her, at first. "What do you mean?"

The girl fell silent; it was her father who answered, making an effort to speak carefully. "Tash wanted knowings: what you spoke us."

Leeth worked out what he meant, kind of wishing he'd let his better-spoken daughter answer. "And?"

He shrugged. "Told. You two: not paired?"

"Uh, no. We just... paired up for last night."

He nodded, his expression serious. "Heard. Club Juzz. You two: good pairin'. 'Spect."

She'd shrugged, feeling a bit embarrassed, but also troubled as she headed back into the rubble. *Tash* had the strength to kill in the way some of the victims had been. *And* she'd been nearby when Agent Garland had 'arrested' her. Had she circled back?

Leeth blushed, remembering her capture.

Had Robo got inside *Tash?* That was a horrible thought! But it couldn't be right: she knew Tash, and she was *nothing* like Robo. And The Breaker had been taking people for months.

Anyway, the victims were wrong. Tash only took bad guys.

That's what she told *you*, a voice whispered in her head. Mother's voice added: 'You have depths of naivety we may never plumb.'

If it *was* Tash, though...? *Her heart*, she decided. *Or maybe if I slice off her head....*

No. She shouldn't be thinking like that. Tash was nice. It wasn't her. Besides, Tash had been with *her* last night, when The Breaker had taken Marcie. No, probably Tash was hunting It, too.

And if Tash was the thing following her tonight, it'd explain why she couldn't hear it breathing. Tash was a mage, too, so if she watched her 'Imaginally,' she'd be able to sense when her attention shifted to what was following her.

But if Tash was following her, why not just come forward so they could team up and hunt it together?

Because I started first, and she knows I can handle it all by myself? She nodded: probably Tash was lurking, ready to spring out to protect her just in case she needed help. That sounded right. She smiled.

At least that was one weight off her mind!

Breath puffing in and out, Leeth climbed the last stretch of jumbled and eroded landfill. Smiling, she turned, looking east out over the vista below. It was just like she'd imagined it, earlier. The Hunters Point Dumps zone, a vast area of darkness, hard to distinguish from the waters of the Bay. Just here and there, slender bars of bluish light flickering from imperfectly blacked-out windows. She counted three others blazing a bright welcoming yellow: meeting places advertising their simple existence, for as long as their solar-pumped charge lasted. There were even occasional fire-lights burning deep within the twisted and crumpled terrain.

Farther east and a bit to the north, across the Bay, the lights of Oakland marked a more fortunate part of the sprawling city. *Well, most of it*, she thought, eyeing the dark patch that was the West Oakland Dumps.

She wiped an arm across her forehead, dust smearing into grime with the perspiration. Pulling out the water pouch she took a few mouthfuls, then clamped the lid back on and zipped it back into her hipbag.

She stood now on one of the highest points in the New Francisco landscape, catastrophically remodeled in a single night. Only the shattered finger of the old Skyway, far to the north, clawed higher into the night sky.

Slowly the grin faded, as her breathing settled back to normal and the sweat cooled on her skin. Why exactly had she come up here?

She checked her wristcomm. Then double-checked: 3:02am! It'd taken almost an hour to reach this height. Why had she come so far south?

She stared into the darkness below the crumbled roadway, where part of it had collapsed against its own supports. During the quake this whole area had been thrust up into the sky higher than Nob Hill. The massive old Skyway itself had snapped. She'd seen film of it: the ribbon of concrete twisting and re-twisting like a giant child's toy, until the massive thickness shattered. Blocks of cement exploded along stress lines, falling like a rain of slow meteors. Finally, the broken ends of the highway had snapped, descending with uncanny grace and unstoppable force. Tumbling amongst them, a single yellow bus and a cascade of cars, a splash of tragic color in the gray debris.

She shook herself. From this point, the series of broken terraces stretched like monstrous escarpments falling away through the jumbled chaos of the Dumps down to the waters of the Bay. A cold gust licked at her jacket, and she turned, facing into the wind. High overhead, across the night-dark sky, a massive cloud bank was rolling in, the storm front stretching as far as she could see.

Shivering, she turned around. Up here it was cold, and lonely. Depressing even. *Why* had she picked this spot?

She was supposed to be Hunting it. She imagined Father asking her what she was doing, asking if the idea that it could sense her magically scared her.

Had she in fact run away?

She shut her eyes, considering. Did she feel scared? *Yes*. Yes, she did. Had she run? *No*.

A sudden explosion of butterflies shuddered through her stomach and her hands tingled. It was close. She knew it.

There *was* a connection! She turned, slowly. But *this* time, she tried *not* to concentrate; *not* to think. Just *feel*. Not even imagining it captured. Just feeling.

And gradually, a strange kind of certainty grew. She turned, and started moving; slowly, at first, but growing more confident. North, and down, to where the roadway had collapsed. A kind of blind sureness took her, and she began picking her way faster; down into the deeper valley of the night below.

For just a moment, she heard a whisper of sound, from far behind. Tash. It had to be Tash.

Almost, then, she called for her to come out. She pushed the idea aside. *I can do this on my own. I don't need any help!*

CHAPTER 69

The large man with the dead eyes paused suddenly, and the boy slumped in relief as the pain lessened. Disten moved farther away, out from under this old, shattered part of the Bayshore Boulevard, and Billy and his girlfriend prayed with all their might for a rock to fall from the over-hang above and crush him. Something, *anything*, to stop the horror.

Both teenagers exchanged desperate looks, tied and bound to the steel reinforcing ribs jutting from the broken concrete. Those looks said that no matter what, they would never torture each other for him.

"She has returned to the area."

They both turned to him, then began looking wildly around in the dark, trying to see who he was talking about. They were in a kind of cave formed from a section of over-pass that had collapsed against the massive concrete sup-ports of its base. He'd captured them on their return from black-berrying.

He observed them. "You do not understand. Always, she comes, she is approached, she vanishes."

Billy and Anna tried to shrink away from him. Some-how, knowing he understood them enough to know he'd confused them made his dispassionate tortures even worse.

"Perhaps she feels the connection too. Perhaps she must be drawn in by her own actions." He nodded. "This time, waiting will be tried."

The man moved back to the boy, the large knife gleam-ing hypnotically in the moonlight. "Choose where your companion will be cut now. Or her hamstrings will be sev-ered next. Tell this one where to cut instead."

Practice was improving the teaching methodology, but these two were not co-operating. Disten considered ex-plaining the purpose behind the torture. Normally it was wiser to lead the recipients to the goal unknowing. But since this looked set to fail, it would be logical to vary the experiment.

"The mind clings tenaciously to habits of thought."

Both subjects looked toward him, startled.

"Reason and understanding is good, yes? But your ra-tional mind is enslaved to biology, brainwashed by hor-monal messengers. You find yourself goaded into actions by chemical drives that seize control of you. Over time, such actions set into patterns of behavior; patterns you tell yourself you have chosen, when the reverse is true."

The two were still listening, their faces showing, perhaps, dawning understanding. Or shock. It was hard to distinguish the two.

"Only when presented with life experiences irreconcilable with those habits can the mind reboot, freed from emotion. Life experiences such as co-operating in the harming of a loved one, and experiencing the same in return. Only when you confront the animal inside you, can you break the chains of your own habits and millennia of social conditioning. Rejecting that indoctrination frees you to adopt a superior mode of thinking. A perfect mode of operation of the brain that grants conscious control of all body functions, down to the autonomous level.

"This one is not torturing you: it is demonstrating a hidden truth. Bringing you both a great gift.

"Now, who will confront their inner monster? Which of you will tell this one where to cut your beloved, next?"

Later, Disten crouched to check the soaked bandages: the female had lost a lot of blood. The pulse was weak. This one would likely die before providing sufficient torment for its companion.

Suddenly, Disten's head came up. *She* neared. Jane Baker. Sleena.

Finally. All was ready. Her friend, Marcie Dunkirk, captured and stored: an ace in the hole if required. To be used if the existing methodology proved necessary even for Jane Baker to reach Perfection. If required. There was a belief, though, that the friend would not be necessary. There was something special about Baker. A magical connection. Mere contact might be sufficient.

But if not, Dunkirk would be conveniently at hand, in reserve. Even for the magically normal, either love or hope usually provided the key. The death of the loved one and the subsequent guilt and loss of hope was enough to break the emotional back. Or, equally powerful, the death of that love itself made the subject receptive. Without that death, hope hid, and clung. And while hope remained, perfection was unattainable.

Disten looked back down at the subjects collected today. It was good that Jane Baker came. These two resisted too well. The pair's youthful bodies were breaking faster than their consciousness could be Perfected, even with the emotional leverage the lover provided. Refusing to admit the monster inside, each stubbornly refusing every choice offered.

But the one approaching now was different. Her emotions would open all humanity to Perfection.

Hours later, Disten lifted his head, sensing the girl, again. Approaching; receding; approaching again.

For perhaps the tenth time, consideration was given to moving out toward the girl. She was so close now it was hard to wait. Yet the logic appeared correct. Now only a few hundred meters away, she drew steadily closer.

Her fighting last night at the pointless 'Fist Fest' had shown she had considerable combat skills. Tactics would be wise, even though special preparations had already been made. And failing that, her friend waited, to be used as a hostage for her co-operation.

Would she be drawn to the boy and the girl? Would she try to care for them?

The boy made a peculiar croaking sound, his body failing. Disten judged him unlikely to regain consciousness, though small sounds of pain still interrupted the labored breathing.

It was time now to move into concealment and wait.

Well back from the latest experiment, hidden amidst the rubble near the entrance, the special gun pointed toward the entrance, ready. It would be useful to observe her reaction to the dying children.

The better she was understood, the more surely she would be opened to Perfection.

CHAPTER 70

Her skin prickled. Robo – *The Breaker?* – was nearby, she could tell, and she moved cautiously, alert. Ahead, a strange, animal sound; a moan.

Treading carefully, she circled the huge slab of roadway collapsed at an angle against the vertical rise of massive support pillars. She sniffed: an awful smell here. Like poo.

She circled closer. As long as she watched where she put her feet, it was easy to move quietly from each piece of shattered concrete to the next. The smaller rubble had long since washed away.

Coming around the end of the huge tilted slab, she could just make out the empty space beneath it. The noise came from in there. Quiet, distressed breathing.

Vast shadows swept suddenly over the broken land, making her look up. The storm clouds she'd seen earlier now charged across the night sky, covering and uncovering the moon. And then it vanished for a final time, the night darkening. Dust and dirt flew, strong squalls of wind scouring the earth, dropping the temperature and ruffling even her short hair, flapping her denim jacket and tugging at its ties like a too-eager lover.

Stepping inside, it was quieter, a very dim light at this end of the urban cavern illuminating- *No!* Her muscles locked as her brain assembled the picture. Two small figures tied up, unconscious – or worse. Not Marcie though, she saw, relief flooding her. Then guilt, as if that thought had traded Marcie's safety for theirs.

She saw splashes of black. *Blood.* She was sure. Her heart ached.

But if it had taken fresh victims, it must be near. Robo, or The Breaker. She let her eyes go unfocused, *not-Looking* for It. Like she used to, back at the Institute.

Nothing.

Then from the closer body, breath juddered. Her eyes refocused and she took a step that way, before forcing herself to stop, and listen. With difficulty, against the background noise of the gale, she separated a sound somewhere between a moan and a whimper dribbling from... *his* throat. *A boy.* Was it someone she'd spoken to, tonight? Or one of the two missing young teens from the Blackberry tribe: Billy and Anna? The sound tugged her forward, even as she fought off visions of herself chained in her uncle's rooms. *The Doctor's* rooms.

She swayed, feeling cold, tired; squashed down. As if Mean Robo was here, right on top of her! She spun around, remembering the feeling of Robo chilling past her, there in Godsson's cell; more attracted to *Her*, the spirit that had come to destroy Godsson, than to herself. She felt again her own instinctive loathing, recalling her coward's jump away.

She shook her head, looking around, heart pounding, her eyes fully adjusted to the deeper dark, certain Robo was here. But not marching blindly up to her, like it used to in the Forest. She didn't understand. Something was different. Was it because it was inside somebody now? The Breaker? Marc Disten.

To her left, rubble and rubbish had piled up like ugly snowdrifts against the base of the roadway. To her right the roof angled down to meet the ground. Her nose wrinkled in disgust as the smell of raw sewage puffed past her in a sudden eddy of wind.

She was almost to the children now, and still no threat appeared. Adrenaline alertness drew her whole body taut, skin tingling, her heart hammering painfully in her chest. Where was it? Here? Or out, nearby, hunting?

Or *above* her, hiding?

Her head jerked up, and she braced for attack- but nothing happened. Scanning the darkness above, her skin prickled and crawled from the rush of adrenaline.

But at her feet the bubbling breath rasped and stopped, snatching her attention. A shudder ran through the body as his lungs clawed another breath from the air. With a last wary look around, she dropped to her haunches.

A normal boy, just a few years older than Barney; but he looked *broken*. That was her first impression. Hunks of hair torn away, swollen and ripped lips; blood smearing the mouth. The face bruised and bloody, an ugly tear down one cheek.

She knew how that felt.

His fingers had been broken, too, she saw, dismayed, and had to shut her eyes. At least her uncle had never done *that* to her....

Remembered images of herself, burned, or sliced, strobed across her vision. She had to open her eyes, breathing hard; though focusing on the reality before her was just as bad.

She reached out a hand, touching a cheek softly, but the pained quiver it evoked jerked her hand away in shame at causing more hurt.

He was human, and he was dying.

She had to force herself to look at the still, silent girl tied a short distance away, and when she did, her breath caught in her throat. She found herself panting as she cataloged the injuries, unexpected tears welling in her eyes, smearing her vision. She shook them away. A knife had been used, on her. A knife, and great force. The limbs were all wrong, like a broken doll's.

The girl was dead. So very dead.

The tears flooded back so she couldn't see properly. Again she shook her head to clear them away.

She had to force herself to go closer, to check for a pulse, or warmth. To try to guess how recently she'd been alive. Her teeth ached, clamped shut, but she couldn't seem to unclench her jaws. Her shoe came down in a wet, sticky puddle, and she stopped, staring, suddenly wishing she couldn't see so well in the dark, as she realized what had been done to the girl's legs. *Like a wishbone.* Somehow, she knew the knife had been used *after* that horror. She shuddered, her hands going to her own thighs for reassurance, feeling her own solid flesh, healthy and whole. *Healed.* But *this* girl's torment hadn't ended with a healing spell to undo the damage.

Her teeth were making protesting noises as muscles ground in her jaws; she had to force herself to reach out and feel the girl's throat. No pulse. Cool skin, but not yet cold: not long dead.

It must still be nearby. And James was right. No animal did this to its prey. And monsters didn't use knives. 'That kind of horror is something humans do.'

She stood up, fighting a storm of emotion. She wanted to scream and strike, to avenge the tied and helpless girl, kill the creature that had done this. *Now.*

But there was nothing here.

She moved back to the boy, forcing herself to calm down. To think. Outside, gusts of wind rushed and clawed at the earth.

Maybe the girl could be brought back to life; healed? No. She herself had taken almost an hour to get here, unencumbered. To do that again, only faster, *and* find a mage in time- it was impossible. The Doctor had told her, and Mother and Father had confirmed – a death was permanent after roughly sixty minutes. It was one of the things she'd been so carefully taught. How to make sure a kill stayed a kill, even with modern healing magic. There'd be no point calling for help from the Department, anyway: they wouldn't risk exposure by bringing a chopper here. And the girl was CID-less, so no ambulance would fly for her – even if some hospitals did keep a mage on staff, for those few patients who didn't believe that such healing made you a puppet for other spells.

No, that's *not how it's done.*

A bitter bark of laughter burst from her lips, and she found she could open her jaws again. She moved back to the boy, and crouched by him.

He'd stopped breathing.

No!

Then, a whisper of sound behind her, and Tash's furious voice.

"Step away from the boy!"

CHAPTER 71

Leeth jumped, spinning around and to her feet at the fury in those words.

Tash blocked the entrance-way, and began moving closer. "Further away." The voice was cold. Heavy with anger.

It *was* Tash, she saw, but the vampire neither spoke again, nor stopped moving. Intuition alone made Leeth throw herself backwards at the moment she came in reach, and the woman lashed out.

"Hey! What are you doing?"

Tash glanced down to the bodies at her feet, then back to Leeth.

"*Why?*"

"Eh? I didn't- it wasn't *me*! Why does everyone blame me? I came here to find the killer."

"Really. And have a few laughs?"

"What?"

"You like play-acting, don't you, *Sweetling*? And games," she sneered. "Like to get in close and personal, aye? Like to rutting *play with your food*, do you not? Like you did, Club Juzz."

Leeth shook her head in denial, barely registering the fury that stripped Tash's speech patterns back to an older style, even as it confirmed her certainty that Tash wasn't the killer.

"How'd you know to come here?"

"I just-" *How to explain it?*

"You felt drawn here, was that it?"

Leeth nodded. "I think we're connected, somehow-"

"Oh yes. Truly. Closely connected."

"No! I didn't do this! I don't know who did. I'm just-"

"I have no time for this. Mayhap I can save Billy." Tash bent down and with an effort snapped the ropes tying the boy, lifting the body with sudden tenderness.

"You can heal him!"

"Not I. Such insults are beyond my skills, now. Now I'm like *this*." Self-loathing roughened her voice. She was barely restraining herself, Leeth suddenly realized. "Upon my return, Anna's body had best not be mutilated any the worse. For your sake." Moving lightly back to the entrance, she turned.

"See you soon, *Sweetling*," she promised. Then was gone.

"No!" Leeth whispered to the empty air.

She felt simultaneously hot and cold. How could Tash think *she* was the monster? *What was the matter with everyone?*

She had to show them.

She'd bring the girl's body out of the Dumps. Call Eagle: make him send the Doctor; or call a car herself, on the way out.

But... Marcie.

She screwed her eyes shut. If she saved this girl, she might be dooming Marcie.

Might be.

She had to try. She still had no idea where Marcie was, or The Breaker.

She moved forward, hands tingling, slicing the girl's bonds and hauling the small body up. She considered the distance she'd have to run; the broken terrain; but her face set in determined lines. She'd bring her out, to her uncle, and *nothing* would stop her.

She was gathering speed, almost to the entrance, when something puffed from the rubble, stinging her in the abdomen – a silvery dart pinning the corner of her jacket to her bare stomach. She stared at it blankly.

Then dived sideways, curling protectively around the girl while plucking the dart free. But before she hit the ground, a second silver wasp appeared, quivering, in her side. Numbness spread. She hadn't even felt the impact.

That was bad.

She had little time, if it was that fast-acting. It had come from her right, and down low. That pile of rubble, there. Something poking out, in the darkness. She charged toward it, her legs feeling oddly distant; awkward. She stumbled, the barrel of the tranquilizer tracking her, and another dart puffed out. She twitched so it caught harmlessly in the folds of her jacket.

She reached the rubble at the same instant it exploded upwards and outwards, large arms reaching for her. She tried to change her motion, to twist aside. But the world kept spinning, and for the second time in twenty-four hours she felt a grip strong enough to crush bones clamp onto her, crushing her left bicep. A man, a large man, with camo-smeared face loomed over her.

Mark Dennis?

As her right arm flashed in to his side, she threw all her strength into wrenching her left arm from his grip – and felt her bones bend, start to break. The pain and the failed maneuver made the blow from her other hand merely slash his side instead of disemboweling him.

The grip on her arm tightened. Hauled up off the ground, his forehead smashed down into hers. His left hand clamped onto her other arm, swinging her upright. His face was a blur. Writhing in his grip, she swung a kick to his groin, but couldn't feel her legs, wasn't sure if she'd succeeded. Then his forehead smashed into hers a second time.

Lifting her to his eye level as if she were a rag doll, *Mark Dennis's* head crashed against hers a third time – and she slid, screaming silently, into a well of blackness.

-

Disten dropped her, blood leaking from the side she had struck. It was difficult to understand what had happened. Light was needed.

Moving back into the dwelling place, Disten picked up the lamp for a self-examination. Seams ripped as the blood-soaked jacket and shirt were pulled free. The wounds were probed, their surprising depth measured. The pain was sharp.

It appeared to be a series of gashes which a set of five razors might make; bone-deep.

Returning to the body of the long-awaited one, her hands were examined, the ground nearby searched.

Revealing nothing. No knives. Probing her hands, the fingertips, revealed no cyberware. Just flesh and bone. Strange.

But it confirmed that this one was special.

The medkit was taken from the supply bag; antiseptic, then liquid stitches applied, the edges of each wound pressed together in turn as the glue set. The body must be cared for.

Disten stared down at her, feeling the strange sense of connection stronger than ever. There was even the desire to perform the procedure here, now, lest she somehow escape during transportation. That reasoning, however, was faulty, coming from impatience and uncertainty. No, the Tash thing was dangerous and planned to return here. It would be best to bring this one to the place where Marcie

Dunkirk had been stored, ready to be used if this magical linkage proved insufficient.

The girl's wristcomm was removed and crushed underfoot, her cashstick taken. The bag she wore was ripped from her hips and searched. A water container. A toy gun? No: real, but very small.

The tiny gun was pocketed, the rest discarded. The medkit went back into the supply bag and the girl hoisted, one handed, over the other shoulder.

Ribs ground together, the pain a warning.

It would be sensible to carry her in a way that reduced the chance of further injury. There were several kilometers to travel.

She was lowered back down and lifted by the jacket, but spilled to the ground when the flimsy ties tore apart, gashing her cheek. The jacket was a hindrance. Disten ripped it free; briefly considered using it as a handle to carry her at his side. But the waistband of the leather skirt was stronger, and conveniently located at her center of balance.

One last look around, then the cave was abandoned, the prize at last claimed.

Perhaps this one could even be Perfected while unconscious.

CHAPTER 72

In a seen-better-times suburban street on the edge of the Dumps, in a boringly efficient airfoil-shaped rentacar, James stretched out, cat-napping. For hours now, in between short meditation sessions, the agent had followed Leeth's movements on a map projected directly into his sub-retinal implants. He'd also skimmed aerial footage of her travels so far tonight, courtesy of the neutral buoyancy stealth drone hovering one kilometer above. She'd covered a surprising amount of ground.

James dozed, unaware that back in the Department a timer now counted down. *Sixty seconds.*

When the tracer in Leeth's jacket detected its separation from her body, it transmitted one short packet into the net. A digital fuse had been lit.

Forty seconds.

She had, after all, been warned: leave the device on, or be hunted down herself.

Twenty seconds.

In its silent concrete cave, Leeth's discarded denim jacket lay limply, rag ties fluttering in the cold wind.

Zero.

With no countermanding signal from the tracer, no last minute 'abort,' its final packet was released and forwarded. Within moments the Department went to status yellow.

The security alert jolted James awake. Decrypted, it contained just a small systems patch from Nelson, and one terse directive from Father: "Leeth AWOL. Possible desertion. Locate urgently. Recover if possible. Retire *only* if she refuses to return."

"Damn." She *had* run. He really thought she'd had more spirit. He stared out at the lifeless street. He'd been sure she'd known nothing, consciously, of the killings; sure she'd do her utmost to uncover the truth. He'd even bet Preacher she wouldn't run, whether she found the killer or not.

Looked like he'd been wrong. *Shit.*

The car shuddered in a sudden blast of wind, and he saw that conditions had changed. Darker and colder, clouds now blanketed the sky. Strong winds tumbled wrappers and other rubbish down the deserted street.

A wash of mellow feelings told him his MetaLife had intervened, stimulating his hypothalamus. For a moment he considered countermanding it, but couldn't bring himself to sink back into the mental quagmire.

Instead he skimmed Nelson's note on the systems patch: an image-processing improvement to reduce noise in low-light vision enhancements. He okayed the upgrade, unaware that for this patch, his approval had been irrelevant.

Wind blasted the car again, rocking it, and he blinked at the realization of the force required to affect the stream-lined shape. Sitting up sharply, he tapped into the aerial drone's video, swearing as he compared its co-ordinates to Leeth's location of one minute earlier. The drone was kilo-meters off-station and moving farther away still, its small engines fighting hundred kilometer per hour winds. He jumped the video back two minutes earlier, hoping for a glimpse of Leeth, only to find the drone had been too far away even then, swept away in the first minutes of the weather change.

But while James used his MetaLife chip to call up maps of the area and calculate routes to her last known location, he was unaware of the contingency program included in Nelson's sensor patch. Hidden from his view of the chip's functions, it waited, already activated, invisibly monitoring his surface thoughts. Checking for the right conditions to be met, to splice in its payload – a visual AR filter of the sort fantasy gamers used to enhance live scenes. A secret from everyone, this was Nelson's little gift to help in Leeth's retirement.

Unsuspecting, James selected his route and started the car.

CHAPTER 73

Leeth clawed her way up from dreams of bondage on a cold stone altar. In the dream, wind gusted over her, spinning off into a darkened plain that stretched forever. At her side, her uncle stood, silent. Waiting for her to awaken, to taunt her for her weakness.

Nauseous, for several seconds she fought her churning stomach. Her cheek stung, and a place on her stomach too. Pain stabbed her head with each drum beat of blood. Some kind of ties pinned her wrists together, stretched out over her head. She kept her eyes shut as she searched her memories. The cave and its stench of excrement; the dying boy, the dead girl; *Tash*; and then the man who'd jumped her. *Mark Dennis: The Breaker!*

Smooth hard stone chilled her bare back and a knife-edged wind scoured her front. So she was naked from the waist up. Tied and bound. Cold. Light was shining down on her eyelids. A different smell, too. *Death.* She'd been moved.

"You awaken."

So much for that deception. She opened her eyes, blinking past a harsh white light that glared from a tiny LED lamp overhead. The room was large, crazily tilted; one wall completely missing. Strangely, the *angle* of tilt seemed familiar. Wind ripped past, gusting coldly inside. And it really was Mark Dennis. *Who'd tried to make Marcie a quadriplegic.*

"Where's Marcie?"

Partly blinded by the light, she peered into the darkness where he stood, trying to see Marcie. "Marcie! Are you okay? Where are you?"

It was hard to tell, but she sensed her question had pleased him. And also, that he knew where Marcie was. But he didn't answer, just watched her.

Twisting around, she scanned the room, but Marcie wasn't in sight. She eyed the bonds around her ankles, and wrists – cable ties exactly like Agent Garland had used on her, yesterday morning. *Exactly* like. Of course they were. *They were probably his.*

It was kind of ironic.

Tied up by Mark Dennis – again. *It was me he'd wanted, back then, too. My fault that Marcie had been paralyzed.* Dismay hammered through her.

'Bring him in alive,' Mother had ordered.

Screw that.

He moved closer. "It is time to begin."

But at his approach she tried to shrink away. Even with this amount of ventilation, he *stank*. He still wore the suit from her 'farewell party,' she saw, the jacket now ripped and torn, hanging from him in tatters. Like he'd been thrown from the back of a truck traveling at speed. And hadn't changed out of it, since.

Then something cold, and dull, settled over her, the feeling of Mean Robo, right on top of her. And she remembered that winter's night – her uncle's desperate summoning of Robo inside Godsson's cell, to attack 'Her' and save them both. Back then, briefly, she'd continued grappling Her while Robo enfolded them both; but she had cringed away, unable to bear its invading touch. She and Godsson had ended *Her*, later that same night.

Godsson *hadn't* lied. Mark Dennis – Marc Disten – was The Breaker. And she was supposed to *hug* him? *Mother* him? She found herself shaking her head, rejecting Godsson's advice. *Blessing or no blessing.* She didn't want to hug him, she wanted to kill him.

She looked quickly around. Everything was tilted fifteen degrees or more, the bottom of the room a jumbled tumble of smashed chairs and bronze-topped tables, broken pot plants and wind-blown rubbish. She lay on a cracked marble veneer surface, arms tied above her head. Cold. Everything was cold. To her right, empty shelves and cupboards with bronze colored doors hung from stainless steel hinges that seemed somehow familiar. Some kind of long-abandoned office cafeteria? But where? Not the Dumps, or it'd be stripped clean.

Like nothing she'd seen since *Her*, this man, who now had Robo inside him, scared her. She tried to keep that from her voice.

"It was me you wanted, all along, wasn't it? So why did you kidnap the whole school?" *And almost kill Marcie?*

She thought he wouldn't answer, as he stood looking down at her, his expression unchanging.

When he started speaking, it took her by surprise. "Sharing Perfection has proven elusive. Taking the school was convenient, to provide many test subjects." For long seconds he stared at her, unblinking. His eyes moved over her. Assessing? Finally, he nodded. "Others will not be required: you will suffice. You are the key. You... fit." And if not, Marcie Dunkirk would be brought down from the storage tray, and the usual techniques followed. It was clear that this one cared for the girl. Deeply.

"What have you done with Marcie?"

Again, he didn't answer, but if anything, she felt more certain that she'd pleased him. *Oh, no!* She shut her eyes in sudden dread. *You idiot! You've just made Marcie a target. Change the subject!*

He still watched her, she saw. "What do you mean, 'perfected?' Why do you even care about perfecting me?"

"When you are Perfect, others will be drawn to you. As they always are. They will seek the same Perfection."

He wasn't looking at her like men normally did. He looked at her like she was a piece of equipment he was preparing to install.

As he moved to her side, within striking distance, a sickeningly-familiar numbness spread like ice through her. Even as her hands tingled, her skin crawled. Adrenaline surging, her heartbeat accelerated so much it hurt.

At his touch, a dam of memories burst open. She remembered, then, another night, a night at the opera restaurant. She remembered touching his chest – then walls slamming down, separating her from herself.

She remembered a name: *Jennifer Dei.*

But this time, no walls fell. Because this time there was no false persona to trap her? But something still wasn't right: something had changed. She felt like some vast curtain had sealed this place off from the rest of the world, leaving only the two of them on the planet. Just herself, totally alone; and this empty Other, who watched.

He reached out to her forehead. All thoughts of calmly measuring the situation vanished as that chill hand descended, and she twisted, her legs swinging in a lightning kick to his side, lashing out with instinctive loathing.

But the angle was wrong, and she only succeeded in knocking him to the ground, and herself half off the bench-top. Her arms pulled at their sockets while her bound feet scrabbled to support her weight. She tried to cut the ropes binding her hands together, the *sharpness* in her fingertips throbbing so intensely it burned.

But she couldn't reach her wrists, instead slicing only the end that bound them to the long benchtop, making her slide abruptly to the ground.

The man lumbered to his feet as she slashed between her ankles, freeing her legs. Arms reached out toward her as the ropes fell away, large fingers clamping around her throat with such force that her vision darkened instantly. Her head slammed back down on the bench a moment later, furious darkness once more dragging her into its depths.

—

North of New Francisco, in his cell in the Institute for Paranormal Dysfunction, Godsson stirred. At long last: *contact;* a deep pulse resonating through the chaos below the Imaginal, rising like a tide under the magical walls of his small cell.

It had been such a long time. How strange that Sara had been able to avoid her complement for such a lengthy period.

Now it would begin.

For just a moment, perhaps a second, he felt a qualm. Then dived, dissolving, below the ooze of even primal consciousness.

CHAPTER 74

It took James an hour and a half to reach Leeth's last known location. There, tumbled in the entrance to the shelter, a girl's body showed faintly on his infrared. For a moment, he'd feared it was Leeth. Light intensification revealed the small corpse, and he'd had to activate nausea suppression to continue. The girl had been tortured to death.

Fighting to center himself, he sat back on his heels, breathing hard. There was no way Leeth would have done that, he was certain. Clean kills were her style. *At least, when she's in her normal frame of mind.*

Temperature readings indicated the girl had died two hours ago, which meant the torturer had been here. As had Leeth. But surely she had stumbled *over* it, not *done* it?

He checked the locators, quickly finding both her jacket – all its ties ripped, but the tracer still tucked under the collar – and her crushed wristcomm. But had *she* done that, or had she been attacked? He pulled out a plastic bag and tweezered the evidence inside, sealing it shut.

Checking the jacket, he found a paper-wrapped cone of something sugary in one pocket. He bagged that, too. Where was Leeth, though? Prowling the man and earthquake-generated cave, he noted the tins of food – about forty cans of condensed *beef 'n vegetable* soup, a few, emptied, nearby – along with water containers, and a small cesspit. Someone had been living rough here. For a day, perhaps two. So, not Leeth.

Which gave him a glimmer of hope.

By a slab of roadway with protruding rods of steel, he found ropes. All knotted, reasonably short lengths, but one set sliced cleanly as if by razors, the other set frayed or... snapped? He couldn't imagine the strength required to do that, thin as they were.

"Who in smekhell you?" a voice snarled from the entrance. Drawing his gun, he spun round to face a tall woman with auburn hair.

And no heat signature.

Uh oh. He'd read Leeth and Preacher's reports.

Her eyes were on his face, looking him up and down. She could obviously see in the dark as well as he could with his light intensifiers. She ignored his gun as she moved in with long, sure strides.

His mind raced. "You're a vampire, aren't you?" He was pleased by the cool, slightly amused tone he'd managed.

As hoped, it made her pause.

I could try a mixture of shots to the head and to the heart. One or the other should have *some* effect.

"Who you?"

"Connor. James Connor. I'm investigating some murders. And a disappearance." He fluttered the jacket he still held in his left hand.

The woman's eyes narrowed. "Sweetling's jacket. Why she strip?"

"The girl who wore this? I don't believe she *did* remove it. It appears to have been torn from her. I found her wristcomm as well, smashed. She was investigating the murders too, in her own way."

The tall woman stepped back suddenly, one hand over her mouth. "No!"

He looked at her, puzzled by her reaction. "Are you 'Tash'?" he asked, recognizing her from Preacher's visual download, but staying in character.

Suddenly-haunted eyes stared through him, the intense gaze fixed on some sight that seemed to pain her. At last, eyes focusing back on his, she nodded.

In uneasy truce, the two moved slowly through the debris and rubbish of the creature's lair.

'James Connor' explained he was a private investigator, and that the girl he knew only as Susan–

"Susan!" Tash snorted, then looked him up and down before shrugging. "Ya, meb for you, she give that name."

James Connor looked thoughtful, as if he might be counting, but then continued his explanation.

He'd noticed her living on the streets not far from his offices. She'd hung around them a lot, in fact, until the last few weeks. A few days ago, she'd told him of a series of murders in areas she knew – in the Dumps – and now they were both, independently, investigating.

He'd put a tracer on Susan. Just tonight, he'd added, seeing the vampire's eyes narrow dangerously.

Those eyes had stayed narrowed and watchful as Tash in turn told of returning to the Dumps a couple of months ago, after a request for help from an old friend. Something bad was being done to people in the area, her friend had said.

"Something bad? What does that mean?"

In response she'd pulled out a small data viewer and keyed a particular file, passing it across to him. He watched a short segment of an interview with a grubby human, the man responding in a flat monotone to a series of questions about a horrific murder.

It was chillingly similar to an interview he and Leeth had happened on one night, where a balding man had described torturing his wife and daughter, in tones of utter boredom.

"What does that have to do with these other murders? Are you saying this guy did them?" he asked, handing the screen back.

"Nah. He'uz forced ta kill's girlfriend. Broke him bad, but so'thing worse. So'thing drained his feelings dry's dust. Some new kind'a leech."

"A *leech*?"

"Vamp." She spat the word.

James frowned at her. *But you're a vampire*, he was tempted to say, to see what reaction it might provoke. Instead.... "You hunt vampires?"

A nod. "'Mong other things."

"And you think this was- is being done by a new kind of vampire?"

Another nod.

"One that drains feelings. Emotions?"

"Ya."

"Susan was hunting it, you know. I think it's taken her. Which is worrying." He stood there in the dark. It was troubling enough to think that whatever was behind the killings and torture had taken Leeth with no struggle. But a worse thought was what *she* would be capable of if stripped of all feelings. Gods knew she was ruthless and deadly enough already.

He shuddered, glancing at the vampire curiously, who was hugging herself in some sort of distress. "What's wrong?"

"I saw her here, hour 'n half 'go. Blamed her for the murders. Accused her. She denied, but I wouldn't listen!"

James raised an eyebrow at the change in speech pattern, then paused at a thought. He checked his chronometer. "Susan's tracer stopped transmitting exactly one hour thirty six minutes ago. Since you saw her about an hour and a half ago, it suggests the creature was very close at hand. Perhaps even here, waiting. I don't suppose you're any good at tracking?"

Tash seemed to recover. "Ya. Real good, acsh."

James's auto-translator provided: «*Yes, very good actually.*» "Susan's jacket was on the ground by the girl's body. So was her comm. I suggest you start there."

"What you do?"

"I'll make a call. I know a mage who cares about her. He may be able to locate her Imaginally."

Tash gave him a long look that seemed to say she wasn't all that surprised. When his eyes went distant and he stilled, obviously using some headware comm unit, she just nodded, then ignored him as she started casting around for tracks.

CHAPTER 75

By the hand still gripping her neck, Disten lifted the limp body, draping it back on the sloping food preparation surface. Releasing the bruised neck, the severed ropes at her feet were examined with interest; then the soft fingertips were probed and squeezed again, the small fingernails examined with puzzlement.

Disten stood, considering. Waiting. Again.

Unfortunately, even for this one, Perfection required consciousness.

-

The waking this time was worse. Something burned in her nose, her throat; made her eyes water. Abruptly her stomach heaved and she struggled against her bonds, barely managing to throw herself sideways as she was violently sick.

Doing great, Leeth. She panted. *Marcie'll be so pleased to know you have things under control. And you still don't even know where she is!* But she didn't dare risk asking Marc Disten.

Her head screaming in pain, arms still pulled upward, Leeth opened her eyes to the same sight as before. But this time the room swam blurrily, and she was cold all through. Cold forever.

Disten, screwing shut the smelling salts, watched her vomit, saw her eyes open, and knew that this time, it would work. Her mere presence reverberated into some dimly-sensed reservoir of deep Truth.

It was clear now why those earlier attempts had failed: the targets had been wrong. Even the two who had attained Perfection, and now lived on the edge of the Dumps, had not *resonated* as this one did. Clearly, magic had indeed been involved: both in that initial awakening into clarity, and in the ability to sense the Other's location. Together, they formed a whole: parts of a new mechanism, a transcendence of the animal nature that still plagued mankind after a million years of evolution.

The *next* evolution, in the end, would be easy. It was, after all, just a change in the mode of thinking, not in the animal itself. New software running on old hardware.

"It is time to begin."

She spat, trying to clear acid bile from her mouth. "I need water."

"Water is unnecessary." Disten moved closer, one hand reaching out to her forehead. She thrashed aside, trying to avoid it despite the agony that the movement woke: simply certain that it was better than being touched by him.

It was useless, though. He trapped her head in both hands, a grip like iron nailing her head in place. Her chilled flesh deadened at the touch, a half-remembered nightmare of falling and being trapped inside herself making her brace for that fall, that powerlessness.

But nothing happened. The wind howled. Her hands, stretched above her, still tingled with the familiar urgency.

They stared at one another, her eyes slightly unfocused but defiant, his as alien and dead as a shark's. Something numbing slid against her thoughts, shifting and prying at her, trying to find a way inside. Did that probe sense her uncle's magical controls? What would happen if it found a way to activate them? With a horrified shudder, she pushed the thought away; tried to hide it, forget it.

The man frowned, his hands squeezing harder, as if he sensed something important slipping from his grasp.

"What was that?"

In answer, she shut her eyes, and a second later, thrust her naked chest up against his arms, hoping to distract him. Perhaps fifteen seconds passed, the rushing wind tearing past the otherwise silent shell of the room.

"Some anger. Little fear. Is that all you feel?" Yet powerful depths of emotion stirred, just below. Hiding, somehow.

"Where is Marcie Dunkirk? What have you done with her?" She tried to sound casual, but the fear that rose just from asking the question had him leaning forward again. She tried to let the fear go; to have faith in Marcie.

He watched her carefully, comfortable that his next words would prove true. "Marcie Dunkirk is unnecessary."

You're dead, she vowed. "You killed her?" she whispered, trying not to believe him. The rage felt like magma, stirring somewhere deep, the pressure building.

He leaned forward again, and she hid it deeper inside. Feeling it burn all the hotter for that.

"You would feel pain, if the answer was Yes?"

When you decide to kill, give your target no warning, Dojo said. *Killing is not a game.* Eventually, she mastered herself. Tried for a dismissive laugh. "Hah! Don't tell me *that's* why you kidnapped her?"

He tilted his head to one side, studying her. "Marcie Dunkirk is... alive. She is ready to be used if you prove difficult."

"Oh!" The sound squeezed out before she could stop it, an awful constriction around her heart vanishing. She felt the *squirming* again, trying to get in, and again, unsure how she did it, she evaded; thought about something else. *Ah.* "You weren't always like this, were you? Something happened, didn't it? Something wanted to get inside you, and you let it in, didn't you?"

Marc Disten tilted his head. "Why do you say this?"

"When did it happen?" She started calculating. She'd stopped sensing Robo, when? It had disappeared years ago. Only returning, briefly, at her uncle's desperate summoning, to save her.

She swallowed. He'd cared about her *that* night. While she and Godsson battled *Her,* in his cell; losing. How had her uncle summoned it? It seemed suddenly important.

Marc Disten had gone still. "Four years ago."

But Robo had come, that winter solstice night, last year, and fought *Her.* Did that mean...? "What about last December, the twenty first?" She spoke carefully, fighting the simple physical pain in her head. "Did you change, that night? For a while? Did you feel, uh, like you used to? For a little while?"

He stared at her with a dead intensity. "That night, there was... a period of imperfection. What did you do, that night?"

"I was in a battle. And... there's something inside you. A kind of spirit. It's making you do bad things." She was about to say, 'You need to push it out,' but then wondered: *if he did, where would it go? How could I track a spirit? Right now, I know where Robo is: inside Marc Disten. But how do you kill a spirit?* If it was like *Her,* in any way... it had taken Godsson and her, together, to destroy that.

Together, as it had attacked them in the grounds of the Institute for Paranormal Dysfunction, where it had been trapped.

Her eyes widened. But *Robo* had come, and gone. Through the Barriers, since it had come *from* Marc Disten.

That seemed scary, somehow.

She didn't like the way Marc Disten, or Mark Dennis, was staring at her. Like she was feeding him useful information. *Maybe I should shut up? Or change the subject?*

And it was so hard to think against the pounding ache that made her voice slur. "You killed that boy and girl tonight, didn' you? Tortured them to death. Like you plan for me. Why?"

When no answer came, she opened her eyes. From his blank expression, she wasn't sure he'd even heard her. She had the sudden impression the face was false; a dummy's mask. Then the mask spoke.

"They did not achieve Perfection."

She exploded up against the hands pinning her head – only to find herself easily contained. Still she strained upwards, until agony blurred her vision and she had to cease, panting, her head still immobilized, uncertain whether it had cost him any effort. *Funt, he's strong!* An icy worm of doubt settled around her spine. *Tough*, she told herself, ignoring it. *What had he said – something about perfection?*

"Perfection: that's what you call death, is it?"

The mask spoke again. "No. Death is to be regretted. Sometimes, the death of one member of a pair awakens the truth in the other. On this occasion, the girl was weak and died, and the boy refused Perfection."

"So you tortured him to death as punishment."

"You do not understand. Perfection brings clarity and freedom, but pain is required to break the animal habits. Open yourself and understand."

"I don't think so."

He nodded. "All say that. It is time to begin."

He didn't move, but she felt something approach – something cold: Robo? – and instinctively, inwardly, moved back, *away*, stilling herself. Filling herself with silence.

He frowned. "Do not store your anger. Feel it."

She didn't know what he was doing, just knew she wasn't going to give him one single speck of help. She shut her eyes, shut him out, focused on all her simple physical pains.

"Do not hide."

Disten stared down at the girl. Eyes closed, she made

no response. Her emotions barely registered. Yet their potency could be felt: vast waters pressing behind a dam.

"Life is difficult. Often sad. Sadness hurts, impairs function, but can be removed. Remember something sad, and you will be helped. A loved pet, lost. A brother or sister who died. The pain of losing a parent or intimate friend. Yes? Such as your good friend, Marcie Dunkirk."

The girl's eyes opened, *burning*, and for a moment, despite the hunger to move forward, caution held him back. Then her expression cooled, and she studied him. "You're mad, aren't you?"

"Not mad. Rational. Man aspires to rationality. That is the ideal. But a rational creature would not engage in war, or destroy and foul its environment. There is a way to communicate rationality directly, as if it were a disease. Passed from one to another."

"You really are mad. I mean, *seriously* mad. I'm not kidding."

She rejected, as they all did. But the enduring pain would end as soon as she accepted Perfection. Pain belonged with the animal.

Reaching up the sloping bench to her bound hands, effort was applied, separating one finger from the clenched fist. Abruptly, her hand twisted, the finger itself stabbing through flesh. Jerking, she ripped it savagely across the left hand, slicing flesh and grating against bone.

Anger and exultation flared from her in skyrocket bursts. Ignoring the blood spurting from the wound, Disten moved the other hand back into contact. But the emotions had already dampened and vanished, dying and retreating before they could be gripped.

Nothing. But his senses, reaching out to the savage animal presence that fled like a shadow, touched something else. Something beyond the animal, beyond the focused female presence. Some kind of structure, or order, bound through it. Over it.

Blood flowed from the badly damaged hand, the gusting wind blowing it back against soiled trousers, flinging it against the side of the bench. The hand needed treatment.

With a thoughtful look at the girl, Disten moved away.

As calmly as the pain permitted, she watched while Mark Dennis stood, crossed the slanting floor of the room, and took a medkit from a canvas sack to apply a wound sealant.

She'd expected a beating for her retaliation, but instead he'd lunged at her with a kind of hunger, clasping her eagerly.   Something repellent but powerful had flooded around her, tried to reach *inside* her, as it brushed against her uncle's controls. She sensed it could break them, but instinctively, she'd retreated from it.

What was wrong with him? If Mean Robo *was* inside, had taken him over or something like that, what did that *mean*? She tried to work it out, scrunching her eyes against the pain in her head, trying to think.

Should she hug him, like Godsson said? Her spirit quailed at the thought.

He hadn't cried out when she'd ripped his hand. Hadn't even paid any attention to it until after giving up on... whatever he'd tried to do to her immediately after. Cold fingers had probed her mind; sliding in, around, searching. *Leeth, mode one.* She shivered, forcing the thought desperately away. He couldn't do that, only her uncle could do that. *Except now, I have a defense.* Or... should she hold those bonds out, let it shatter them?

But what if it took control *of them, instead?*

Should she risk it? After all, even if he did, she still had Barney's device tucked into her waistband. Just to check, she bit down, twice, sending the sound pulse through her body, triggering those precious five seconds of recording, played at a volume only she could hear. The confusing syllables once again whispered from the tiny speaker at her waist.

Concentrating on her arms stretched above her, she tried again to slice the physical bonds, but this time her aura grated against metal, sending a shock like nails on slate shuddering up her spine.

He abruptly crossed the room back to her, pulling her own Snub 7 from a pocket in his jacket. Pressing it to the side of her head, he flipped off the safety.

So this was it. Winter's chill gripped her bones and settled deeper in her flesh. She closed her eyes. Wished she could have had more time....

Long seconds passed.

"Do you not care for your own life?"

She opened her eyes, realizing it had been some kind of test.

The man frowned, clicked the safety on and pocketed the small gun again, staring at her.

"Remember entering the shelter tonight. You were disturbed when you examined the boy and the girl. Their 'torture' distressed you. Your hands clenched and you shook. You felt great anger. Now you are in the presence of the one who caused that suffering. Perhaps anger would give you strength to escape your bonds."

Despite the nausea and raw throbbing of her head, the words slowly made sense. Was he taunting her? She felt a little burn of anger start, and he leaned forward slightly.

She fought it away and he leaned back. *He can sense my emotions!*

"Your friend Marcie is in great distress. She is alive, but suffering."

She felt a surge of fury. Only the feeling of that fury being *touched, grasped,* let her drop it.

"What do you want from me?" she panted.

"Explaining the process interferes with the result." He was silent for a while, thinking. "An outline is possible. You will be Perfected; or killed in the process. Resisting the process makes death more likely. Do you understand?"

"What do you mean, 'perfected?' I'm pretty good as I am."

Again a long pause, while he apparently considered whether to answer or not.

"Actions to benefit the self impede the formation of efficient collectives. Distractions, errors in motivation, illogical reactions to stimuli, can all be removed: leaving actions pure, the self clarified and perfected. Perfection grants the ability to conquer the reptile brain hidden behind your actions. Perfection offers complete control of your body and your self."

She couldn't seem to focus on the words, and his lifeless monotone didn't help. Control of herself sounded good – but she just didn't trust him. *Look what happened last time I trusted someone to do weird magic on me.* "If you're the example of what that means, no thanks."

"Are you stupid? If you do as you are told, you will live. If you cannot achieve the goal, you will be killed. Now: feel anger." His fist smashed casually into her stomach, and she spasmed, bonds tearing into her wrists and ankles as she struggled for breath.

He lifted his arm again. And again. And again.

Disten considered. The beating had not worked. Instead of becoming trapped by the sensations, she had drifted further away. The reaction made no sense.

Rape? It was known to cause great trauma. Unfortunately, there was no interest in rape. No ability to perform. The girl had laughed at the effort. But not so heartily that the ripple of emotions had not faded before they could be drawn from her.

Her remaining clothes had been torn away, leaving her naked. The reaction had been unexpected: a feeling of pride, though with a strange flare of fear a moment later, her eyes following her skirt as it hit the fl4oor. But both faded as they were chased.

Perhaps, finally, it was time to bring Marcie Dunkirk into play? Yet the conviction that this one would be sufficient in herself was stronger, if anything. It was just that she dodged, and avoided.

No, all that was required was patience. She would make a misstep, sooner or later. She was a curious puzzle, simply requiring the right angle of approach. In a way, she was intriguing.

She held vast depths of emotion. The powerful animal patterns lay tantalizingly close. Tied to him, waiting for his control. Ready to be manipulated *through* her. She would become a tool to bind to, stimulate, and replace those animal patterns with more rational constructs. Together they would become a machine Perfecting and connecting others; each in turn Perfecting still others, spreading in a great web to reshape all humanity. At that certainty, his breathing had accelerated, skin flushing with an almost-forgotten sensation. Clarity had dimmed.

The girl watched, calmly.

Blood rose in Disten's face. The girl lay naked, her expression insolent. Mocking him.

"That is enough. You will feel anger. Now. Or your leg will be broken."

She did not react, other than a kind of contraction. Was that a breath of fear? Perhaps the pain had not been enough, the beating had not been enough. Perhaps for this one, there would be no reaction until she was at the point of death.

But that was not normally required except for the final step, to remove the most stubbornly held animal emotion. A moment of doubt passed through him. If she died, what would be left? Bringing these animals awake one by one, over years, decades? Fortunately, it should be unlikely. And Marcie Dunkirk would be brought into play before exploring that option.

Disten measured the small but healthy body, and made the decision. She was far from death, yet. "You have not felt enough pain. Not enough fear. You do not believe you have to choose."

She shook her head. "Wrong. I've felt more pain than you can cause me. And I've already chosen."

Goaded, he moved to her body, grasping one shin in both hands, bending-

Pain exploded in his injured hand – which *she* had wounded – as glued flesh tore again, bones rasping together and blood once more pumping free.

The girl laughed.

Laughed!

He leaned in to grab the emotion, but again she snatched it away, moments before he had it.

Through a red haze, he hefted a stainless steel bar from the floor, smashing it down. She swung her tethered legs aside so the blow missed; and a second time. But the third time he grabbed the leg with the injured hand, ignoring the pain as flesh tore further. The heavy bar was smashed down on her left shin, splintering bone. And smashed down again while she thrashed in pain. But she writhed in silence, her screams contained. It seemed strange. Even disturbing.

Bloody weapon in hand, he spun to her face. "Is that enough pain?" he shouted, excitement burning through him.

She gasped and writhed, and finally he sensed fear. But not enough: not as much as there should be. And if he took the fear now, she would be impossible to deal with.

Then, incredibly, her fear faded. "No," she whispered. "I know this place too well."

Then she was gone. For a moment he didn't understand, then saw she had fallen unconscious.

Breathing hard, he stared at her body, at the splintered bones protruding from torn and bleeding flesh, feeling the terrible pain in his own hand, the blood running from it and realized the clarity was gone.

The anger and fear were back, weeds returned to a garden. And *she* had done this. Had re-birthed these feelings in him.

With an effort, he *reached*, and *twisted*: raising the empty winter within to wash over the emotions. Felt them caught by it, gripped; struggling vainly before flickering out.

Breathing calmed. Perspective returned. Clarity.

Much pain from the left hand. It looked very bad: split down the middle, halfway to the wrist, two fingers to each side. Ligaments could be seen through the blood.

An unusual sight.

The blood loss could not be ignored. Back to the med-kit. Disinfect, then seal the torn blood vessels: patiently, one by one, until the bleeding stopped. Then glue the halves of the palm together.

Disten considered the repair. The hand still looked very bad. A surgeon would be required. The tube of flesh-sealant was considered: very little remained now. As much had been used today as had been required in the previous months in this area.

It was too easy to forget injuries when pain was so distant. Turning back to the girl, it could be seen that her own injury still bled.

Should the sealant also be used on her? Another journey into the city would be required, to restock. And passing without detection was becoming more and more difficult. But the girl was the key needed to form the web. Letting her bleed to death would be wasteful.

Glue the bleeding vessels shut, then.

CHAPTER 76

"I can't believe she's causing the same kind of trouble a second night running. The girl is an impossible drain on our resources."

"Well, you know what they say, Mother: the teenage years are always the most difficult," Emma said.

The look Mother turned on her made her wipe the smile from her face. Quickly. Before Mother could respond in more detail, a movement in the hovering trid image drew everyone's attention. Harmon sat up inside his ritual circle.

He looked calmly up at the camera. "It is there, whatever it is." He sounded bored, distant. "I believe I have damaged myself, in entering and exiting the area. The Imaginal there is Patterned in Death. Penetrating the structure was difficult in the extreme. Probably unwise. But I can report that Leeth has found the entity that has been killing things. It is currently torturing her. I have seen it before, too." For a few seconds he sat nodding, as if lost in thought. They looked at him strangely.

Abruptly a shudder ripped through him, the blood draining from his face. "My god! It's got Leeth! She's injured, in shock, and the thing is *right there with her-*"

"Doctor! Calm yourself! *What* is with her?" Mother fought to keep her own voice calm. Seeing the normally cool Doctor flip from unnaturally detached to visibly distressed was... disturbing.

"I don't know." His voice was husky, raw. "Imaginally, it's an icy waste, black, complex. Numbing. I remember it from a time before. Leeth had sneaked out of the Institute and into the city, gotten into a fight, and been shot. She did in fact die just after I located her Imaginally. And then this... *thing* approached. It had a kind of freezing gravity to it. It pulled at you."

"What happened? Why did you never report it?"

"It was before we came here. And nothing happened. I located her body, arriving just in time to restart her heart and heal her, repair the damage of oxygen depletion. By that time there was nothing around. I thought the thing had just been my imagination. A stress reaction."

There was a small silence, then Father spoke. "That's significant information. But did you achieve your objective tonight: can you tell us where she is?"

Harmon looked stricken. "No. Distance and direction

in the Imaginal is... irrational. And I don't know the area well enough. She's south of here, somewhere near the Hunters Point Dumps. In a seven-story building that's canted over like the Leaning Tower of Pisa, but thick with death. South of the Hunters Point Dumps."

"'Thick with death?' How far south?"

"I don't know! A few moments' thought away. Not too far. One kilometer? Forty?"

"Can't you be more precise?"

"Distance in the Imaginal-"

Eagle interrupted. "Candlestick Tower."

Father didn't hesitate. Didn't question. "I'm relaying that to James."

"I want to go too," Emma suddenly said.

"Don't be ridiculous: it will be over before you could get there," Mother told her. "Has this whole Department gone mad?"

"Authorize a chopper, then! I can be on the pad at the Westin St. Francis in... seven point six minutes. You sent her out there, not believing her when she said she wasn't behind the killings. Now she's found the creature and it's killing *her*. She's my friend. I want to help her!"

"What next? Will Preacher ask to be sent, too?"

They all looked at the frozen avatar projected in the corner. Preacher himself was with his gang in the slums, far from the Dumps. Asleep by the look of it.

"Well, I'm glad someone at least is behaving normally."

"Would you be equally glad if it was me, or James, or Preacher, Mother? The Department isn't exactly rich in human resources."

Nelson smiled, saying nothing as Eagle's information was passed on to James. Not long, now: provided the *thing* didn't kill her, first. Assuming she survived till James and Tash arrived. He hoped she would: that way he'd even get to watch, through James's eyes.

Eagle cleared his throat. "This thing that has captured Leeth, Doctor. Could it be The Breaker?"

Everyone stilled. Then looked to Harmon's avatar, its face registering shock. A shock that continued to grow, and deepen. "Sweet buttered- It could, yes. And it came –
the thing Leeth calls *Robo* – to Godsson, when we needed it. *Dear god*. It really was real. All those years...

"And I had her *hunting* it. A mere child. Dear god

almighty...."

He slumped back in his chair, in horror. Gazing into space.

They all stared at him; all but one of them unsure what he meant, but shaken nonetheless by his reaction.

Eagle looked grim. "Agent Emma: you will have your chopper. Leave now. It will be cleared and at the Westin pad in twelve minutes."

CHAPTER 77

Leeth's captor was so focused on applying the wound sealant that this time she managed to regain consciousness without him realizing it. Her leg still screamed in pain, though: almost drowning out the pounding in her head. She wondered if she had a concussion.

Leeth watched his hands as he patched her up. So she'd last longer. *Just like the Doctor*, she thought.

He seemed calm again now, but he'd lost it before, just a little bit. At least now she knew their link really did work both ways.

Which gave her an idea.

She concentrated on his hands. Watched the care he used. He'd hurt her, but now he was tending to her, caring for her.

Such a familiar situation.

She relaxed, opening herself slightly, working on feeling grateful.

He looked up from her injured leg, into her face.

She made a small smile of gratitude. "That's a much better way to make me feel, instead of using pain. If you want me to feel, make me feel nice."

Disten finished tending the wound, thinking. Considering the girl's words. Certainly it was best to use animalistic bonds with others, to draw out the emotions for removal. Bonds of caring could be used to create intolerable pressure, impossible choices that could not be faced.

Unlike those taken in recent months though, and despite taking Marcie Dunkirk to supply emotional leverage if needed, there had been confidence that Dunkirk, in her storage tray on a floor above, would not be required. That the bond between this one and the girl would be more than enough. There was the strong sense that she was a tool, waiting only to be properly gripped to be wielded.

Perhaps the suggested approach made sense. She had not reacted normally to the simple pain stimuli, nor to the degradation. Perhaps to complete the linkage, she should be made to form an emotional bond with the one present, her complement? To the self? *Him*self?

Such a reaction would not be normal. But many of her reactions were abnormal. There was remembered knowledge of some kind of 'captive syndrome,' too: where victims transferred their attachments to their captor.

"Mmm," she murmured.

The tone was soft. Some emotion there, too. Warmth. Directed toward the one present.

"I've known too much pain. I need comfort. Touch. Won't you give me that? Make me feel that? Hold me?"

The girl's eyes focused on the one who watched her. On Disten. On himself. Despite an underlying weaving of fear, a gentle feeling of caring – tentative, fragile – began to unfold around her. One of the good emotions. One that was reluctantly removed, and only because leaving even a single emotion opened the way for re-infection by all the others.

Still. If it would open her.... Her face was symmetrical, the body firm and healthy.

The sense of connection swelled. Her scent reached out, tugging forth warm memories. That warmth would lure her to her Perfection.

Getting up on the sloping bench next to her was awkward. The bandages wrapped around the injured hand reminded him not to stress it. Clumsily, he grasped her, recalling how to hold a woman. She was stretched tight by her bonds. Gentleness was required. Curling, curving together.

"I think you need to untie me," she murmured gently into his ear.

He drew back. "No. You are dangerous. You injured the hand. This one's hand. This is a trick."

Her face was pale, but she spoke calmly. "We were fighting then. You were causing this one pain. Now you are caring for this one. Let this one hold you, as a mother would."

Beneath the words, the fear pulsed. He hesitated. "There is loneliness," he offered, feeling curiously light.

Holding her, touching the soft skin, the impression of some rigid structure overlaying her fluidity suddenly returned. Curious, he took hold of it.

Leeth shuddered at the invisible thing snaking coldly around her thoughts, seeking entry. The pretense of calm was strangely easy; his own calm, his certainty, called to her, promising an end to all the confusions: her uncle, Emma, Tash, James, Marcie, Mother; even Preacher. All so confusing. Especially her uncle. *The Doctor*. And it wasn't like Mark Dennis was a trap, waiting to spring shut on her.

Besides, Godsson had promised this was the right thing to do. Had even 'blessed' her, so she could do this. It made sense: she had to use their connection, despite the fear that he could somehow feel the Doctor's magical controls, that he might somehow activate them. But that was silly: only the Doctor could do that.

Don't be such a coward, she told herself. *Besides, hadn't the Doctor taught her, all unknowing, how to defend her thoughts? How to hide her true self away?* She forced the doubts away and nestled her head against his shoulder. "Yes. There is great loneliness."

As she rested against him, she did feel calmer, too. Felt the burden shift. A loosening, deep inside. She wondered again if Mr Dennis could somehow sense the Doctor's controls. If so, maybe he *could* break them, setting her free. And Perfect. Maybe his way *would* be easier. Maybe she *could* be Perfect. Wasn't that what every adult seemed to want from her, after all? Weren't they always making fun of her feelings and intuitions?

She'd be a better agent if she was Perfect. How much more could she do, and how easily, if she was Perfect? No doubts to hold her back.

Mr Dennis wasn't so bad. Just different. Different wasn't always bad. They could be together. She sensed it: so close together. Together, they'd form two halves to a strange new whole. And she wouldn't be lonely, not ever again. It felt like he'd been made for her; and her for him....

Disten sensed the sympathy for the loneliness; sensed her own loneliness. Should he take that, now? Would doing so now, weaken the nascent bond, perhaps break it? Or bind them, finally, together?

He got up from her. Her feet were tied together at the ankles. Another rope looped around that, tying them to the lower end of the benchtop. Loosening the second rope only, he waited. Felt more warmth radiate from her. She did not lash out. Very rational, considering the injury to her leg.

He moved to the other end of the bench, reaching across to the wire that stretched her arms above her. He began cautiously unwinding the wire from the nylon ties binding her wrists. It was only her fingertips that cut, he knew now. He kept a careful grip on the ties between her wrists, remembering the damage as her fingers had stabbed into his other hand.

Warm breath whispered in his ear. "Come. Hold this one. This one is chilled, and would share warmth."

Her words... appealed. And in her eyes... he could see it: a yearning. He saw that she too sensed the completion awaiting them both. Saw her fear at the possibility; saw her realize she stood at the very brink.

"Feel the loneliness. Let this one take it from you."

Outside, the wind still rushed, gusting and swirling into the empty cafeteria.

And as he clasped her, she felt cold tendrils slide suddenly inside, and align. *Mode one.*

Dismay shocked through her, before vanishing in a vast echoing stillness. No gray confusion, no storm of conflicting emotions. Cool, crystal clarity reigned. Below lay anger, fear, love, hate, pride, shame. All visible, separate; ready to be awoken and harnessed: all the engines of desire, ready at their command.

Briefly, she considered the child's protective device, in the discarded skirt. No longer relevant. This was different. There was no confusion of motivations, no struggle for control. Just clarity. Perfection.

Together, they sat up.

CHAPTER 78

James and Tash crept up the tilted stairwell, pausing at the top.

"*Come. Hold this one. This one is chilled, and would share warmth.*"

They exchanged a look. That was her voice, both knew. It sounded odd, though. Uninflected.

Then a man's voice. "There is loneliness."

"Yes. There is great loneliness," Leeth, toneless, agreed.

"Feel the loneliness. Let this one take it from you."

Separating left and right, James and Tash entered the room. They were greeted by the sight of the naked girl cuddling into a large man's body. Both lay on a sloping bench top. Above his head he held her outstretched arms by ropes binding her wrists. His right hand appeared to be injured. Her left leg appeared to be very badly broken, *bending* unnaturally at the shin. Blood covered it.

Abruptly, both spoke, the male and female voices in perfect synchronization. "The bodies should first be healed."

Tash raised her perception to the Imaginal, and black coldness smashed into her mind, shocking her into a hissing in-drawn breath.

The girl shifted at the sound, and the man swung around.

For a moment, James hesitated, recognizing the poorly camo-ed face. *Good Lord: Marc Disten.*

James brought his gun up.

The other seemed to recognize him, somehow, and flipped Leeth's arms over his head to drape her naked body against his as a shield, like the figurehead of an old sailing ship. His freed hand flashed down to draw a gun while he effortlessly jumped the bench. James dived desperately to one side, seeking cover.

Leeth stared at him with a calm expression, using her still-bound arms to twist herself round to shield her captor.

He looked back at the expressionless man. *My god, it's him. He did it. She's been Drained.*

And with that thought, Nelson's modified Traitor program activated.

James watched in horror as the flesh of Leeth's face rippled. Skin melted into strings, dripping to form long tendrils. Her nose lengthened, curving, sharpening and darkening into a burnished black parrot-like beak. Her cheeks *pulsed* as her mouth puckered open, lips and teeth vanishing into a sucking hole. Hair twining into snakes, her eyes enlarged hypnotically as lids and eyebrows retracted.

Stunned, he watched blisters bud on the fleshy fronds fringing the maw of her face; then erupt into suckers as squid-like tentacles extruded, waving, from the octopus thing on the naked female body below it.

"My god, her head!"

Strangely numbed, Tash shifted her perception from the Imaginal to stare in confusion from the girl's pretty face to her companion.

Their enemy fired, and Tash ducked to one side. James didn't flinch: Leeth had to be destroyed. Raising his own gun calmly, he shot to kill.

As he squeezed the trigger, Leeth tried to twist aside, jerking the larger man off balance even as the bullet struck home under her breast. Beside him, James heard an animal snarl. Then an iron vise fastened over his gun hand. Bones cracked with crippling pain as a pale hand crushed his fingers against the steel of his gun. Swung like a doll to face an enraged Tash, he barely saw the other arm smash into his chest with the force of a sledgehammer, snapping ribs and exploding the breath from his chest. Time froze on Tash's outraged expression as he sailed across the room, crashing amongst the rubble as the vampire blurred into motion.

Tash skidded to a halt in front of an almost-religious tableau: the naked girl now laid out on the cracked stone surface as if on an altar, her bound hands pressed against the arterial blood bubbling past them. The large man stood behind, paying Tash no attention, gazing expressionlessly down at the girl's life bleeding away.

Cold.

"Don't worry, Sweetling, I can heal you if you just hold on."

The man's head lifted then, watching her, and for a moment she considered dealing with him first.

He stepped back. "Heal her."

Time was fleeing. Sweetling was dying, and although Tash had some magic, she could no longer bring someone back from death: not since her own. *Why had that idiot shot the child?* She wanted to scream, but forced it away, searching instead for the kinder warmth needed for healing. Able at least to heal a simple gunshot.

But as her anger died, arctic winter flooded in behind it. She stumbled, pressing down on the girl's still-bound wrists and forcing a cry from the small form. Sleena's eyes looked up into hers calmly; trusting.

With an effort, Tash brought leaden limbs back under control and slipped one hand gently under her recent lover's head, cradling it. "Shh, it's all right." She reached for the love to trigger the spell, reached for the healing pattern... and instead found herself noting with clinical precision how slowly the blood now pumped beneath the young girl's hands. She timed the struggling pulse. Dazed, she found herself calculating that less than thirty seconds remained before the heart would stop.

She felt stupid, sluggish. She was supposed to be healing the girl, not letting her die. But the fire was gone. She reached again for the magic – and found nothing. The girl's eyes drooped. "It's okay, Tash. At least I'm me again." Her eyes widened, and her hand tightened slightly on Tash's wrist. "Marcie: you have to save Marcie! He has her here, somewhere." Her hand relaxed, and her voice fell to a whisper. "I think I'll sleep now. I'm tired."

"Sweetling, no, hold on." Again she reached. But there was only the void. Only the cold. *What's wrong with me? I'm letting the child die,* she realized numbly, but not quite sure why that mattered. Struggling to care, but unsure why she should. Caring was illogical.

"It's okay, Tash. You tried. Never expected..." The eyes shut. The chest rose, slowly. Then fell heavily. The lips parted in a whisper. "...to grow old."

And stilled.

With a superhuman effort, Tash lifted her head to face the man across the wintry bier. "It's you. You somehow block magic. You blocked the healing. She dies. She needs my love, she needs someone to care!"

The man took a step backward, shook his head. "No. That is not possible. You must heal her. You said you could heal her."

A lick of anger curled. "I could have. But *you* took the magic away. You sucked it away into your frozen heart."

"No! She is the key. She must live!"

"Then you shouldn't have used her as a shield for your worthless body, you worm!"

She leaped the bar, lashing a backhand into his face, only to find it caught in a grip that matched her own, their eyes inches apart. Something – doubt? – seemed to stir in those shark-like depths, and his grip faltered. "She offered companionship." He stepped back.

Tash burned in anger; felt it burn away the cold. *You fool,* she thought, raising fire to blast him, the magic once more eager to her fingertips. *It was back!* Shoving him further from her, she spun back to the girl, sliding both hands under the small ones over the bullet wound, and quickly, desperately, *reached* for the healing magic. It flooded through her like long-forgotten sunlight, a storm of love pouring out as the energy rushed in. "Live, damn you!"

For seconds, long seconds, nothing happened, but Tash refused to consider defeat; remembering the girl's silly smile, her childish delight at the distant lights of New Francisco through the windows of a night-dark room. She felt a flutter under her hands, and against all sanity, slammed her hands down, hammering the heart into motion. She swallowed a gulp of unfamiliar air, bending to blow it tenderly into small lungs; felt the sudden butterfly pulse; and rejoiced as the girl's eyes cracked open in surprise.

Warm lips twitched against her own cool ones, the tongue flicking once, teasing, before the eyes shut again, in ease. The heart pounding bravely beneath her cold hands, she poured healing down into her like a torrent, careless of the drain.

Across the room, she heard the idiot who had fired the killing shot coughing and scrabbling awkwardly amongst the rubble where she'd flung him. Lifting her head from her young friend as she felt the wound seal, she saw him staggering around, apparently trying to find his gun. Fool!

The girl stirred, eyes opening fully.

"*Tash!*"

"Careful, Sweetling. Be at ease. You've lost much blood."

Behind her, a voice spoke, the magic slipping suddenly from her hands, doused like a flame in a waterfall.

"The girl cares for you, yes?"

Tash spun into a defensive crouch as winter touched her and the large man stepped forward. She snarled happily, driving a fist into his heart, staggering him even as her other fist smashed at the side of his head. Then hands clamped over hers, and she found herself trapped, straining against a strength greater even than her own; drawing her hands inexorably together; feeling her strength ebb. Then the left hand suddenly shifted inhumanly, enveloping both her wrists, and she looked down to see it split in half, raw flesh and bone draping her wrists. *What?*

Leeth cried out a warning as the man's other fist crashed into the side of Tash's head with the sound of a pumpkin smashing. Bone and brain sprayed out.

"*No-o!*" Leeth stared in disbelief. *Remove the vampire's heart, or head,* the legends said.

Tash crumpled; collapsed.

Lightless eyes met hers as the man stepped forward, treading Tash's body into the ground like so much rubbish as he bent toward her. Leeth had scarcely a moment to think before being lifted from the bench, her bound arms draped over his head once again. As if nothing had happened.

As if he hadn't just killed her friend.

"Come. Hold this one. This one would share warmth."

Even as she heard James scrabbling through rubble somewhere behind her in the darkened room, she felt cold tendrils sliding back inside her, aligning.

The warmth of Tash's healing vanished. In moments he'd have her again; she had to do something, *say* something.

The link! She had to make it work *for* her, make him angry.

"You don't really want to Perfect me at all, do you?" *He was just like the Doctor.* The oily mental slithering paused. "What you really want is me with all my emotions alive, to enjoy me more when you control me, don't you?" She let herself remember the helplessness, the torture. Touched the molten core of rage inside.

The cold tendrils withdrew, but she sensed them massing even as they pulled back. In a flash of insight, she knew he'd sensed it all – was simply afraid she would snatch it away again. He was trying to lure her anger out.

Instead, she had to draw out *his*.

"You say you're rational. Logical. That you'll Perfect me. Strange how that meant you had to beat me, torture me, strip me naked. Funt, you even tried to rape me, earlier." She rubbed her bloody, naked body against his smelly clothes. Pain flared in her smashed leg, but she used it to feed her anger. "Only that didn't work so well, did it? You couldn't get it up, could you?"

"That is not-"

"And your sick little game didn't get the reaction you wanted, did it? You pretend to be strong, to be rational; but you're just bent, and weak, and a liar. You're even lying to yourself."

"This one-"

"Say 'I,' dammit! It's always 'this one doesn't,' or 'this one would,' or 'this one seeks.' Just say 'I' and cut the lying crap. You're *always* talking about yourself. You only sound like a big jerk when you pretend you're not!"

She felt her words strike home; and acted. With all her strength, she clamped her arms hard around his neck, flinging herself twisting up and across in a vicious somersault.

It would have broken a troll's neck. But though the force sent the two of them spinning apart, the man's neck hardly flexed. Twisting away through the air, her hands sliced between her feet before she crashed to the ground, pain exploding from her broken leg in sheets of red lightning.

She rolled, rising on her right leg, balancing; the left touching the angled floor, *dangling* at the shin.

A white agony of pain blanked the room from her sight. But over that, towering over it, was fury – at her uncle who tortured her for her own good; at this monster who tortured innocent children to 'perfect' them. Who'd abducted Marcie, and killed Tash.

The man rose to his feet. For once, his face showed expression: hunger.

"Yes! Give me your anger!" With one step he was on her, clasping her.

In reach.

Got you! Releasing her anger she struck coolly upwards with all her strength, both wrists still bound together, reinforcing each other, slicing and thrusting under his rib cage, arms plunging in as far as her elbows. Gripping her target, she smiled up into eyes already glazing in shocked dismay.

"Gee. Did I *distract* you?"

Her fingers closed, *sliced*, and with a sucking, tearing sound she wrenched her arms down, hopping backwards a step. In her still-bound hands she held a pumping red muscle.

The man collapsed like a mined office block.

-

James stared at the octopus-headed girl, painted in gore now from feet to elbows. Leeth was gone, he knew. Changed. This female monster had to be stopped before she escaped.

Endorphins flooded his body, canceling the pain from his broken ribs and right hand. Carefully, he bent and picked up the gun with his left, turning back to the thing that had been Leeth.

The tentacled head. The blood-drenched breasts, nipples standing out in the cool air – it was obscene, yet fascinating. A surreal contrast -

"I did it, James! Just like Dojo said! I let the anger go. And I beat him, all by myself!"

He hesitated. Strangely, she didn't *sound* any different. Shouldn't her voice sound different coming from that mouth-hole? "What happened to your face?" he asked.

"Nothing, compared to my leg. It really hurts, too. He smashed it up pretty badly."

Still balancing on one leg, she dropped the heart. "He sure smelled. I hope he didn't have any bad germs infecting his blood," she muttered, flicking her hands to try to shake some of the gore from her arms, not very successfully. She brushed both hands through her hair, wincing at the mess she was making of her neatly-trimmed cut.

Hair? puzzled James, as Nelson's program struggled to integrate the octopus overlay with Leeth's unexpected actions. But the sound of something scrabbling behind the bench paralyzed them both. Trying not to move his upper body, holding his broken ribs, he circled around to cover the Leeth-thing and whatever was behind the bench; starting to wonder whether he might be just a touch out of his depth. Sending his GPS location and a request for assistance to the Department, he trained the gun left-handedly on the pale form that seemed to be gathering itself together.

Emma responded. «I'm in a chopper. ETA four minutes.»

«Make it sooner.»

On the floor, two hands worked their way up a neck, onto a head, and *twisted*, and suddenly Tash's face was visible. James's mouth fell open as a large piece of skull slid back into place and flesh started flowing back over it. One eye socket gaped blackly empty and Tash, now-sitting, reached out surely behind her, without looking, lifting a small, pale, limp sac. This she popped into her mouth, her tongue moving over it; and with something tucked into a cheek, spat dirt onto the ground, then calmly transferred the pallid sac into her empty eye socket where it inflated back into an eyeball.

"By all the prophets, that hurt."

James stared, open-mouthed. He'd read Leeth's report from the night before while waiting in the car at the edge of the dumps. But he'd felt she'd exaggerated – first, the extent of the damage she'd inflicted on Tash, and second, how quickly the vampire had regenerated.

"See, James, I said Tash heals well, didn't I?"

His head swiveled slowly round to Leeth. She was grinning. Grinning? How could he know the octopus head was grinning? *Something was wrong here.* As Tash got to her feet, shaking her head, he risked shutting his eyes briefly, and reset his visual processing system.

When he opened them again Leeth's head and face were her own once more.

"You're back to normal!"

Tash looked at the girl's swollen, bruised and bloodied face, at her balancing unsteadily on one leg, naked and bloody, starting to shake – then back to the man. "You one sick pup, you think that *normal.*"

James just grinned.

Moving forward, Tash gently scooped the girl up to lie her back down on the only available surface, then carefully snapped the ropes at her wrists.

But Leeth clung to her as the woman started to straighten, tugging at her and pulling her back down into an awkward embrace. James heard softly murmured words, saw Leeth's fingers clench tightly around the vampire's arm. *So she did have her limits, after all.* He looked away.

At last, Leeth relaxed, and let Tash ease her back down. The taller woman bent tenderly over the girl, gently holding the shattered leg. The soft rhythm of her words and the intentness of her stance told James she was, indeed, casting a healing spell.

Leeth tried to stop her, tried to get her, or James, to go searching for Marcie.

"Shh, Sweetling, be easy. 'Twon't take long. We all three can search for her; and much faster, with your help."

He shook himself; he even composed, then encrypted a brief status report and sent it back to the Department, and Emma: *situation under control, assistance recommended but no longer code thirteen, killer not L. Killer was Marc Disten. The Breaker.*

As he settled gingerly back against an angled support pillar, for a moment he considered asking Tash for healing from the injuries she'd inflicted after he'd shot Leeth – but on second thought decided not to push his luck. Best not to remind either of them of that.

Strange that Tash hadn't seemed able to see Leeth's... he reached for the memory. But even as he tried, it slipped further away, like a fading dream. She'd been... monstrously hostile...? Well, hostile, anyway. He played the scene back, growing progressively more unsettled. She looked more worried than hostile. But hadn't she... no, it was gone. Had something been interfering with his systems? The visual system reboot had fixed it, however.

He let out a long breath, wincing. He'd get Nelson to look into it when he get back. *Nelson will sort it out. I can trust Nelson.* Yeah. He felt a wave of calm. Everything was going to be all right. On the ground, even Marc Disten's body looked somehow more relaxed in death.

Well, he'd wanted to feel nothing. Now he did.

James frowned as a kind of smoke began streaming off the body, coiling up and around the two women, darkening the scene. Automatically, he increased the light amplification from his optics, but the tableau continued to darken even as the rest of the room brightened into glare.

The blackness condensed, suddenly solidifying into a ball that swallowed Leeth even as Tash collapsed, as suddenly and gracelessly as a robot with its power-pack snatched away.

"Leeth?"

She didn't answer.

He sat up, raising his gun. "Leeth?"

CHAPTER 79

It washed in, an arctic wave once again extinguishing the warmth of the healing, submerging her back in the grating agony of her shattered leg. Tash's gentle touch fell away in a chill black gulf and all light vanished.

Robo!

Her eyes flew open into the kind of pitch darkness she remembered from her childhood. Numbing cold settled like silent snowflakes.

On the edge of audibility a voice, remote and neutral, chanted repetitively. There was something repellently insistent about it. What was it saying? She strained to hear.

Sa... ra... ?

Was it repeating her old name? She shook her head. That wasn't her name anymore. She tried to shut the whispering out.

Blindness. She held her hands up before her, but there was nothing to see. She felt her face in the darkness: her eyes *weren't* covered. *What was happening?* Glacial cold settled deeper, easing the terrible pain in her leg. She felt tired.

The darkness was a tunnel trying to work its way inside, bringing calm. Like Robo, only bigger. Vastly bigger. Like he'd unfolded, filling all of space. So easy to fall into it, endlessly. Rest.

Disappear.

Sara... Sara... Sara...

The voice rose and fell with hypnotic regularity. She blinked, slower and slower, feeling her eyes shutting. The cold was easing, slipping by degrees into a sleepy warmth. Mental processes slowed.

She could sense changes. Rivers of thoughts shifting from their accustomed channels; new patterns forming.

She started sliding deeper into the dark. Familiar thought drifted away as something larger rose *above* her, even as the dissolving darkness drew her down.

Memories floated past. Running, with Faith, through the Jungle. A woman bending over her, her hair a silken black waterfall. She grabbed for it, but it spun away, out of reach.

Another memory floated past: *Jennifer Dei.*

A feeling: *trapped.*

Trapped!

Nightmarish familiarity shocked through her even as

the vast, chill leviathan continued ascending from below, towering over her. Pain and terror flailed at her – but she clasped the emotions like a barbed wire lifeline in boiling black seas.

She felt cold tendrils wrap around the image of a woman's face smiling down into hers, holding tiny fingers; and felt them *tug* at the memory.

Anger sparked; and burned; and grew. She began hauling herself stubbornly from the depths. Up *into* the thing above her.

It enveloped her, engulfing her in arctic cold – and she exploded, ripping into it hungrily with the bared teeth of her soul, feeling it shredding, retreating, collapsing back down into the depths.

But instead of fleeing, and letting it get away, with a howl, she turned in pursuit, flinging herself back down, into its heart.

-

"Leeth?" James asked, as a wave of cold washed across the room, the air *crackling* as a dust of white began to fall in a freezing mist, a sphere of absolute blackness stretching to the ceiling, centered on the place where Leeth had vanished.

He took a step forward, but sensors red-lined, indicating the temperature had dropped to minus twenty. "Leeth?"

CHAPTER 80

Instinctively, she knew there would be no returning from this battle: that it would be a life for a life.

But she also knew that no one else would be able to destroy Robo. Maybe they *had* been made for each other, somehow: except she'd been made to *destroy* it, to keep everyone safe.

It was a giant, dark shadow. Cold, and black.

But strangely bad at defending itself, she discovered when she threw herself into the attack. She didn't even understand half the ideas it was trying to force into her head. Rejecting its stupid thoughts, the lies that made no sense to her, she slashed and burned as she tunneled her way to its heart.

But as she cut, and stabbed, and raged, she felt herself grow colder. At every step of the way as she fought onward, cutting a path ever deeper, life and heat leached from her.

Robo opposed her every step of the way, plucking at her, trying to rip parts of her away. It telescoped distances; forked paths to mislead her; and all the time, pressed cold into her.

She didn't let it slow her as she focused, eyes burning, on the beating center somewhere ahead. Hidden in the darkness, yet connected to her somehow. Even as it struggled to escape her, a part of it still called to her.

She heard Godsson's words in her head, tearing at her heart – '*You are its mother.*' That thought burrowed deep, softening her resolve. But this thing had taken Marcie, and tortured and destroyed others. It was time for it to die.

She was its death. None of its distractions or deceptions would turn her from her path.

But each step came slower as life ebbed and an insidious cold seeped inside her, spreading through her.

She stoked her anger higher, each tread now falling more heavily, with more effort. But like a deep bell tolling, each footfall reverberated through the whole structure, shaking its foundation as she stalked ever closer to the core; with limbs like lead, yet hoarding a tiny warmth deep inside herself.

Ideas, concepts, patterns of logic, flailed at her, but she ignored them all, refused to hear them.

An eternity later, shivering, she reached the center. She stood inside a mechanism like reflecting mirrors, complexity multiplying from simplicity. A stunning, beautiful elegance to the design. Turning, she lost herself in awe. Robo was magnificent.

She reached out... plunged a hand into the icy engine... and tore it down.

Destruction echoed outward, magnifying in a chaotic crescendo that radiated away at the speed of thought. Leaving in its place a ringing silence that echoed into infinity.

As the last shards splintered and vanished, she stood alone on a strange plain. It curved around her in all directions, seen but not seen. She felt her legs, but couldn't feel the ground.

She walked, feeling her legs move, but not sensing any change in location.

James? she said, but didn't hear the word. She touched herself, but wasn't sure she was even really there.

Tash? she called. *Marcie? MARCIE!*

She'd killed Robo, cut him into a thousand pieces.

But now she was lost.

And she never *had* found Marcie, and rescued her. The whole point had been to save Marcie, and she'd failed. She'd defeated The Breaker, and killed Robo. But she hadn't been able to save her friend.

She kept walking. Kept calling.

Lost.

CHAPTER 81

Marcie Dunkirk was naked from the waist down, blind. The madman had casually stripped her of her soiled clothing when he'd given her desperately-needed water and food, at midday. He'd kept her wrists secured by the police issue cable ties. The only words he'd spoken, the whole time, were 'Eat. Drink.'

When she tried to delay, he'd simply taken away the food and water and re-packed her mouth with the gag. He'd lifted her from her messed techno-coffin and placed her back into a clean one. Then slid it back into darkness, ignoring her stifled begging, closing her in with an ominous *click*.

She'd pushed, to no avail.

For hours then, in the pitch dark confines of the pod, she rasped the cable ties back and forth against a jagged spike of metal in the mess of wires and tubing inches above her head. She rested when her arms grew too tired, but always continued. And *finally,* felt her bonds part.

She cried out, in relief, the sound muffled by the rags she tore from her mouth, gasping and swallowing.

It took her a heart-breaking hour of tears, fumbling in the blackness above her face, before she found a recessed lever. Pulling it sent a familiar loud *click* resonating through her coffin-pod. And then, with a desperate grip on the complex mechanisms pressing just above her in the dark, she shoved with all her might and felt the slab roll out on its sturdy runners.

She swallowed a shout of joy as solid black eased to murky darkness, in a blissfully larger space. Half-crawling, half levering herself up and off the slab, she dropped the short distance to the floor, and saw she was in a moonlit, empty corridor.

A few minutes later, she was ready to move. Wrinkling her nose, shivering at the sight of the rows of stainless steel handles, she pulled her skirt, at least, back on. She looked around, nervous, listening.

Where was he?

Keeping an eye open for anything she could use as a weapon, she crept along the dark and moldy corridor, looking a way out.

-

James heard a soft sound, followed by a stealthy tread. His eyes tracked across the room to a stairwell door now swinging open in the dark. Infrared imaging revealed-

"Miss Dunkirk! My name's James, James Connor. I'm a friend of Jane's."

He watched her step cautiously into the tilted room, one hand waving before her in the darkness.

"I knew she'd come for me!" she said. "Where is she? We need to get out of here – Mark Dennis is around, and he's crazy!"

"Sorry, let me give you some light," he said, activating the torch from his gun-sight. "Are you all right?" he asked, standing and moving toward her, noting the blood on her wrists, and her face.

"I'm fine. Considering. But we've got to get away from- *aaiee yah!*" She jumped, staring at Marc Disten's bloody corpse. "Holy fuck! Did *Jane* do that? Where is she?"

She looked around. "Oh Em Gee: what's *that?*" she said, pointing past him to the slowly-collapsing bubble of blackness. Moving forward, she circled it. "What *is it*? And why's it so cold in here? And where's Jane?"

In the distance, a chopper sounded.

"Ah, I don't know. But I think... inside that."

The sphere was perhaps two meters across, visibly shrinking.

"Then we'd better go and get her!"

"Stop! Don't! It's some kind of magical-"

Marcie disappeared from view.

"Oh, shit!" Her voice came from the blackness. "It's f-freezing in here!"

James moved up. "Are you- can you come out?"

"Not until I find Jane! J- Jane! Jane? It's black as ink in here, I c- can't see a thing! Jane?"

James could hear her, moving. Stepping up, he first waved the barrel of his gun through – the beam swallowed utterly as soon as it crossed the surface – but reappeared, apparently unharmed. He then waved his hand through, and apart from the cold freezing the hairs on his arm, it too emerged unscathed.

Outside, the chopper sounded closer.

James stepped into the still-shrinking sphere. "Miss Dunkirk? Oh! Sorry!"

"Ow! Watch it, mister!"

He heard her voice sink to the floor, and he joined her,

on the ground, searching, bumping heads as they met in the middle.

She touched his arm. "I've checked everywhere, I c- can't f- find her. Are you sure she's here?"

James stood, confused, his head emerging into the merely-dark room. "I don't understand. She went in there." He took a step back. Already, the temperature was rising again.

"Miss Dunkirk," he said. "Perhaps you should step out, before the, whatever that is, vanishes? It might take you with it."

It was perhaps only a meter across, now. He could see one of Marcie Dunkirk's knees poking from it.

"You s- said Jane went in here? In that c- case, I'm staying! Jane! *Jane – can you hear me?*"

On the empty gray infinite plain, Leeth plodded doggedly on. Wondering where Marcie was; what Marc Disten had meant by her being 'in distress.' Just wishing she could go to her. That she hadn't failed her.

That she'd been a better friend.

She even imagined Marcie, calling to her. She remembered the first time they'd ever spoken, and it was like they were together again, in the cafeteria, and she was hearing Marcie telling her, 'Hope is indestructible.' Like Marcie was there beside her, trying to light her way home, willing her not to give up.

For some reason, then, she looked 'up,' and saw a golden ray, almost like a rope.

She imagined Marcie calling to her. "Jane! Jane, can you hear me? I'm here, take my hand!"

On a hunch, suddenly certain, she threw herself *forward, up,* and grabbed the rope.

And began climbing. "I'm coming, Marcie!"

From below, something *other* heard the cry, and began twisting and curving, coiling darkly around her. Hunger engulfed her. She felt strong fingers close around hers, and clasped them in turn. They pulled her up, and away, freeing her from the maelstrom.

James heard a wailing cry from far *below,* the sound eerily distant. It was the only warning before *something* exploded toward him from the sphere, throwing Marcie backward.

Reflexively, he fired, jerking aside as the magical construct broke into a rapidly-shredding vortex, then into shattered tatters of black smoke that faded to nothingness.

Leeth.

He stood, statue still.

But apparently his shot had missed. He caught just a glimpse of water streaking her cheeks as Leeth, naked and dirty, in pain and bleeding, flung herself back on top of her friend, the two hugging fiercely in a torrent of tears and laughter.

It's a good thing the Shutz unit hadn't been programmed to throw angry wildcats at us!

On the ground, over her friend's shoulder, Leeth's face shone up at him like dawn.

Emma's voice came to him as the chopper began its descent. «Sitrep, James?»

«Ah. Good, I think. I have no idea what the hell just happened. But good, definitely.»

«We'll be with you, one minute.»

-

James saw that Leeth was in shock, shivering, her leg bleeding badly again, her friend holding her, the two of them crying happy tears. Leeth's jaws were clenched against the pain, he saw, fighting to halt the shuddering that made her leg a torture.

"Sweetling?"

The three of them stared in surprise at the voice from across the room. Tash had been lifeless, dead, but now rose to her feet as if nothing had happened. She looked confused, puzzled.

"What happened? Why do I feel so fine? I do recall a midnight wave crashing upon me, thinking the leech had taken me – yet now I feel quite the thing. Was it not a leech, then? Where is't?"

A small smile flared against the pain in her face as Leeth, in Marcie's arms, turned to James. "See? I *said* Tash was old."

Tash seemed to shake herself, her shoulders moving lazily back. "Who you, to say Tash old, sweet?"

CHAPTER 82

Tash left before the helicopter landed. Now she just observed, from a hundred meters distance, hiding in the stormwater drain. She ducked down briefly as James Connor once again scanned the area, as if he suspected she lingered.

She watched as the cold man with hooded eyes performed his healing: with shocking speed, for such terrible injuries. Molding the girl's bones and flesh like putty. Had *she* dared stay to heal her, she would yet be at work on the girl. Was he some godling?

But Sleena's lightly injured friend, Marcie Dunkirk, who Sleena had insisted he treat first, had been healed with unremarkable speed.

Tash shifted her perception to the Imaginal, assessing the mage: strong, but not inhumanly so. And with genuine concern for the girl.

Who for her part, seemed barely able to tolerate his touch, her aura churning with hatred.

The girl bounced to her feet and away from him the moment he finished healing her. So perfectly. So quickly. Tash felt her cold flesh stiffen. Did the girl's friend, James Connor, not know what that meant: how many times the other must have healed her? From what injuries?

Watching James Connor, and the other two Imaginally – the smartly dressed and alert woman, and the even more alert Asian man who moved with deadly grace – she saw that none of them understood the implications. The mage did, though: she recognized that possessive certainty of touch. That air of ownership. Although also, with a core of gladness to it, too.

Tash watched, knowing she observed something very wrong. Turning away, she found herself thinking of awakenings. Of her own beginning. So often, magic was born from suffering and need.

From pain.

Her eyes were drawn back. The Asian man, who Sleena had called 'Dojo', and hugged, moved with a familiar sure grace. Sleena's instructor, she was sure, even before the girl named him 'sensei.' He helped the girl's friend, Marcie, into the chopper. Tash noted he did not offer to assist Sleena, who leaped nimbly inside. The mage, in turn, watched the girl, smugly appreciating his own handiwork. Tash felt suddenly certain that he too knew of the forging fire.

And that the girl was his sword.

She watched, and as she did, she grew more certain. Did he tell himself he did it for her own good?

She remembered the girl's pleasure at the cessation of pain; saw in hindsight that she had expected such healing.

How often had that pattern repeated?

Almost, then, Tash moved from her hiding spot, determined to remove the girl from them. Almost. But the long habit of self-preservation froze her limbs as dawn's first tinge dusted the horizon, and instead she simply watched as the stylish young woman settled into the pilot's seat, and the mage clambered aboard.

She wondered who they were. Who Sleena was, really. Who was 'Garland,' whose ID they'd been so pleased to find on the monster's body, which the two men had already loaded, bagged, under the aircraft, by the time the healings had finished? What was on the data chips they'd found with that ID?

Instinct warned her against trying to find out.

The girl turned, looking back into the night, and from a hundred meters away, despite her concealment, her gaze found Tash. Sleena winked.

Two things Tash was sure of: that the girl had potential; and that these younglings had no idea what they nurtured.

What desperate need in the world had demanded her creation?

EPILOGUE

Not too many kilometers north, but at an impossible depth below human consciousness, the web of identity that was Godsson watched the pattern he'd created envelop the tiny, intense flame; only to recoil, then shred and shrink, spinning off in chaotic whorls.

Splintered.

But not destroyed. Merely divided and weakened. It would be interesting to see what new forms it took.

Later, fully en-fleshed, his reaction would be one of dismay and surprise. But now, even in this bodiless state and *directly* perceiving the confrontation, it made no sense.

Sara should have been swallowed whole. Should have formed the seed.

What was she?

AFTERWORD

And there we'll once more leave our characters until next time.

I hope you've enjoyed this third episode of Leeth's story. If so, you may be pleased to know I'll now be returning to work on book four, *Violent Causes*, which I completed in the 1st half of 2019.

If you did enjoy this, there is something you can do that makes a real difference to authors like me, and other readers, like you. Please see the next page if you'd like to know more.

PUBLISHING, 2017

I still feel the publishing world is about midway through a seismic change, where the power of publication is shifting from the giant traditional publishing companies to authors and readers.

I think it's a healthy change, too, allowing readers and authors to connect more directly, supporting each other. The old publishing model assumed an economy of scarcity, but the truth is that it should be based on abundance.

The key issue is how to find books you'll enjoy reading. For that, readers using their social media to let other readers know of books they like, is enough. Even, occasionally, writing a review. I think each book can then earn the degree of success it deserves.

To the first 50 people who publish a substantive (say, 50 words or more) and honest review of *Shadow Hunt* – good or bad, I read them all – and the first 20 people to find a previously-undetected error in this book: email me at my address below to receive a free electronic copy of either the sequel when it's ready, or any of the earlier books, at your choice. As ever, though, I reserve the right to decide if something is a genuine error or my peculiar style. I keep email addresses strictly private, and only use them to send the free ebook.

https://www.goodreads.com/review/edit/34823396 is the link you'd use to review on Goodreads.

If you have questions or suggestions, check out my web site www.AToeInTheOceanOfBooks.com, where I discuss this series, writing, and self-publishing.

Finally, if you'd like a sneak peek of what's in store for Leeth, I've included part of an early chapter of Vol. 4 of The Leeth Dossier.

luke.kendall@gmail.com, Apr 2017. @LukeJKendall

VIOLENT CAUSES, (SAMPLE)

Mother led the way for the review of Leeth's performance in the special exercise that morning, only to stop one step inside the large briefing room. Sniffing disapprovingly, she did an abrupt about face, Father almost walking into her.

"It stinks in there." She strode back past Father, Emma, James, and Preacher. "Either Nelson has been playing games with the maidbots or Leeth is exploring new ways to annoy." Dojo stepped to the doorway and smelled for himself, his nose wrinkling. Frowning, he followed the others, letting the door whisk shut behind him.

They reconvened in the smaller briefing room, its space reduced by cupboards that stored a ludicrous selection of out of date electronic interface devices and data converters.

With ill grace Mother seated herself and dimmed the lights.

Earlier that morning, all lights throughout a whole level of the Department had been turned off. James and Emma, between missions, had been paired up against Leeth in a laser tag challenge.

"She is good at hunting," the Doctor had explained to them beforehand. "Indeed, she considers it an area in which she excels. After the stress of her recent mission, it will help settle her, re-engage her. If she loses to Emma and James, it will spur her to improve her skills. If she wins...." He'd chuckled. "Then it will lift her spirits."

Mother and Father had approved, confident that James and Emma – fully-trained agents with augmented reaction speed, low light and infrared vision, linked in wireless communication – would teach Leeth a valuable lesson.

A simple test, inside the Department itself, but in pitch darkness. They had even had Little Brother disable the emergency exit lights. Each participant had been armed only with an electronic paint gun.

The computer-generated reconstruction began, thermal images overlaid on a suitably darkened 3D model of the complex. But as the group sat in the dim light, the certainty grew that they watched something uncanny. Reminiscent, even, of a horror film.

A peculiar tension gripped them as they saw how Leeth evaded James and Emma's first coordinated sweep of the level. Hushed, they watched her 'chimney climb' a service corridor's walls while her two hunters closed in. They met

directly below her.

Emma, seeing it now, audibly drew breath. In best Hollywood drama style, the computer zoomed-in on Leeth's face. But lacking adequate sensory data, it left her face empty, inhumanly expressionless.

For perhaps thirty seconds Leeth hung at full stretch above Emma and James, a silent predator lurking directly over their heads while they conferred electronically below.

"That's not possible," Emma whispered. Beside her in the darkened room, James reached out and took her hand. Their eyes met in shared disbelief.

Long seconds later, after the two left the corridor, Leeth dropped, her landing equally skin-crawling in its utter soundlessness. Crouched in pitch darkness she waited a full count of ten before finally prowling off, following James.

No one spoke as James hunkered down behind the Rec room counter, in darkness too complete even for low-light enhancements. Waiting, gun trained on the open doorway for his infrared imaging to reveal Leeth.

The virtual camera shifted, showing her creeping down the lightless corridor. At the doorway she paused, then lowered herself to the floor. They saw her choose the *only* angle of approach that gave her the cover of the couches and chairs. Wriggling serpent-like in the dark, she weaved her way in perfect silence toward James, closer and closer.

In the computer-generated image she circled behind him with painstaking care, outside his field of view. Inexorable. Something about that stalking sent goosebumps prickling up every spine.

Leeth rose behind him: silent, graceful. Deadly.

In fairness, they hadn't said each participant had to take out their targets using *only* the electronic guns.

James's strangled cry, Emma's broadcast queries – «James? *James!*» – then Leeth's silent, deadly stalking of Emma herself....

Both Leeth's opponents had required the Doctor's healing.

The view split, the right half showing Father seated in his well-lit office, monitoring; answering Emma's not-quite-panicked message that something had gone wrong, that somehow Leeth had taken James out too literally.

"Continue," Father had coolly responded, before the view returned to showing just the action in the darkened corridors.

Watching the reconstruction now, neither agent spoke, but Father noted all three looking sideways at him. "I *did* assess James's bio-telemetery. He was only unconscious a few dozen seconds. And his broken collarbone demonstrates the need to upgrade from the old carbon fiber."

The scene continued, gripping them as surely as a movie drama. It soon became clear, watching the constructed visuals, that despite James and Emma's optical augments, Leeth somehow functioned better in the dark than either of them. Seeing her prowl implacably and unerringly from the unconscious James to the now tense and mobile Emma, who had intuited that Leeth was stalking her, raised hairs on the backs of several necks. Dojo's skin prickled. For several seconds his eyes searched the darkened conference room before returning to the projected view.

Emma took her final stand, her back to the dead-end wall of the long corridor. Her finger rested tense on the trigger, her gun raised to give an unbeatable 'kill' zone, she waited for Leeth's thermal image to appear....

In the reconstruction, Leeth approached the junction, then stopped and knelt. The virtual camera zoomed in, clearly showing her very deliberately scratching the polished concrete floor – her fingertips an inch *above* its surface. Even now, the drawn-out sound scraped down spines like nails on a blackboard, inhuman and horrible in the pitch dark.

Emma's vital signs spiked, and Leeth, once again silent, retreated, leaving Emma standing alone in the dark, her heart pounding in her chest....

Leeth's final approach was through the ceiling spaces. Father had been able to track the whole business, but Emma had not been privy to those same security systems. Leeth closed the final distance with a strange assurance, like she'd done it all before. Once again, her movements were those of a predator, nerve-wracking in their certainty.

In the last seconds, Emma's heart had practically fibrillated, as if subconsciously sensing the approach of her invisible stalker, moments before Leeth plunged down on her from the ceiling.

Just reviewing it, every watcher's pulse rate soared.

Of course it raised the question of just *how* Leeth had done it; but all she could offer, immediately afterward, was that she could somehow sense the others even in the dark. The Doctor had confirmed she spoke the truth. "I saw signs of it even when she was young. She often prowled the grounds of the Institute for Paranormal Dysfunction at night."

At the time, Harmon had seen her frown, confused by his support of her deception. But that turned into a sneer, as she of course misinterpreted it as a desire to use it against her. He let her see the hurt that caused, and looked down, sensing her frown return.

As for Leeth's earlier 'explorations' of the ceiling spaces, both Mother and Father had been aware of it, merely noting and reporting it on each occasion – perhaps waiting for her to try to use the route to access a secured area. But as time passed, it seemed she did so merely because she could. Father had opined that she simply enjoyed exploring.

«You know,» James messaged Emma, «in her first month here she scared the juice out of me, watching *Alien Infiltration*. But that wasn't the most frightening part: it was that she found the ending sad because the hero died.»

«The *hero* died?» Emma asked. «No he didn't. In the end they kill the creature and return to Earth.»

«Exactly,» replied James.

Their eyes met again. This time, Emma visibly shuddered.